Beyond the Cobbled Road: Fading Light

STACEY BUREKER

STACEY BUREKER

*To my husband, my first reader, editor and biggest fan.
Without your support, this would have never been possible.
Thank you for helping make my dream come true.*

There was never meant to be, a cobbled road for me,
A straight and even path to wander by.
The path I take I forged my own, through brambles, thickets overgrown,
On a trek that few would take, but I.
And though I stumble, though I fall, every scrape that I recall,
Reminds me of this tangled trail I roam.
There was never meant to be, a cobbled road for me,
But this barely beaten path will lead me home.

Contents

1. The Maister's Manor — 1
2. A Secret Study — 27
3. A Peculiar Proposal — 47
4. An Atypical Acolyte — 63
5. The Call of the Council — 84
6. The Horrible Human Mage — 113
7. Comprehension of the Craft — 136
8. An Aggressive Altercation — 152
9. A Talented Traveler — 164
10. An Atrocious Act — 178
11. A Ruthless Rival — 195
12. A Secluded Solstice — 214
13. The Domain of the Dwarves — 244
14. A Hellish Horde — 266
15. An Execrate Encounter — 275
16. The Shadows of Shades — 300
17. A Daemon of Death — 313
18. Last Light Before the Night — 320

Acknowledgments — 333

CHAPTER 1
The Maister's Manor

The sun hadn't yet streaked past the horizon when the roosters awoke Kye from his listless slumber. He slowly opened his dark blue eyes and rolled off the pallet he slept on. Still groggy, he reached for the threadbare sweater draped over the window sill. Kye took a moment to stretch out his sore muscles and brush back his black, mid length hair before rising fully. Searching around in partial darkness, he located his shoes stuck in the corner of the room and exited the woodshed. Creeping through the manor as quietly as possible, Kye grabbed the water pails from the kitchen and headed out of the servants entrance toward the well. The early morning air was cool, signaling to Kye that summer was departing and fall was fast approaching.

Attaching a pail to the well rope, Kye used the first pail of water he pulled to wash his face and hands. The splash of frigid water to the face instantly abolished any reminiscence of sleep that had remained. After washing up, Kye filled both pails with fresh water and headed back into the kitchen and set about pulling wood and starting the stove. The sun had fully risen when Kye looked out the window in the kitchen to see a horse and cart slowly making its way up the long carriageway. Kye smiled and cleaned off his hands before going out to greet the cart.

"Jitar," Kye stated with a wave. An older human male with stringy brown hair and kindly green eyes, wearing peasant clothes, smiled and waved back. Jitar came from the neighboring human settlement of Camris, a town of freed human slaves and the elderly. Most humans were enlisted into service over all of the Six Realms and were not welcome anywhere else. Camris was one of the few places freed slaves could set up something of a life for themselves. It was rather successful, too. Camris had managed to achieve abundant commerce, selling food and goods to all those around Helia. Jitar slowed the cart to a stop as he hopped down and grabbed Kye's hand in a hearty shake.

"Kye, good to see you!" he exclaimed with a grin.

"Same here. How's your family?"

"Good, good," Jitar replied. "Kids are active as ever. Wife threw in an extra loaf of bread for you."

Kye smiled. "Please give her my thanks. Here, I'll help you unload." Kye headed to the back of the cart to grab the goods that had been ordered for the manor. Jitar held the back of the cart before Kye could open it and hesitated. "Uh...Look, Kye, the order is in there but...we still don't have any sage."

Kye raised an eyebrow. "Still?"

Jitar nodded. "Sandstorm took out a good portion of our crop, and what we had left was quickly snatched up by other essential buyers to the town. I know Umbree has been trying to order some for a while..."

Jitar's voice dropped a bit as he looked around. When he spoke this time, he did so in Effali, the language of the slaves. It was a dialect humans often used for conversations that they did not want overheard by others. Kye remembered the basics from his childhood and from conversations from time to time with Jitar.

"*And I know he won't be happy,*" Jitar muttered.

"*Well, he isn't happy about much, so what's new?*" Kye replied.

Jitar got a serious look on his face before he asked, "*I mean, will this make trouble for you?*"

Kye paused for a moment. Probably? Umbree stubbed his toe; it seemed to be Kye's fault. But what was Jitar going to do about it? No use in him worrying about something he had no control over.

"It will be fine, Jitar. Don't worry about it," Kye stated in Common. Jitar sighed and nodded slightly as he opened the back of the cart. Kye helped him unload the supplies into the pantry before wishing him well and waving him off. He then focused on preparing Umbree's breakfast. Kye pulled fresh fruit from the pantry and a few eggs from the basket hanging above the door. Next, he set the kettle on the stove and started cutting fruit and frying the eggs. He tried adding a few of the new spices to the yolks. Kye had to admit, out of all the jobs he was tasked with, cooking was one he actually enjoyed. He liked creating new dishes, even if his efforts were never appreciated. Kye scooped the eggs and fruit onto a plate and poured a cup of tea. Placing both onto a wooden tray, Kye carried it through the foyer and up the staircase toward the second floor, where his master's room was.

The manor was a sprawling structure that towered three stories tall, with an elaborate garden, a grand dining room, parlor, large master bedroom, and five guest bedrooms. There was also a library, study, and conservatory. In Kye's mind, far too many rooms all in all. Especially since it was his job to clean them. Kye often wondered why Umbree went to the trouble of having such a large manor when he hosted very few guests. He supposed it was Umbree's way of trying to give the illusion of wealth and show off to what few friends he had.

Kye's favorite room in the manor was the library. Often, after Umbree had retired to his room for the evening, he would sneak off there to read by candlelight about the wonders of the world he was not able to see. Books about the Six Realms, politics, history. Umbree probably wasn't even aware that Kye could read, seeing as most slaves couldn't. But his mother had taught him young, and Kye had been engrossed in the written word ever since. The books in the library were all non-fiction, though, as Umbree didn't seem to enjoy flights of fancy or fun in any form. None of the books within the library contained anything on magic either. Umbree was sure to keep all those books stored away in his private study. The study was hidden behind a false wall, off the library, behind a painting of a gray-scaled dragon breathing fire. By holding a candle's flame against the dragon's fire in the painting, the false wall would instantly slide to the right and allow access to the study behind it. Umbree thought no one was aware of this trick, but Kye had seen Umbree perform the task on a number of occasions from the hallway while he was dusting. Besides spell books, Kye wasn't aware of what else Umbree kept in his study for safekeeping. Kye often theorized it was the small amount of gold Umbree still held to his name, for besides the sprawling manor, Umbree seemed to be broke — or extraordinarily cheap. The roof of the manor leaked in places, and it was Kye's job to fetch buckets for the cracks whenever it rained. The gardens were overgrown and badly in need of maintenance, and the fountain in the front entryway was clogged and filled with algae. If Umbree had bothered to keep the place in good condition, it would've been a truly beautiful house.

The main reason that Umbree could afford such a lavish home in the first place was because his house was on Helia, the human realm. Considered by other races to be little more than a slave world, this was the place where humans were bought and sold as servants for mages and the wealthy of all the Six Realms. The world was mostly desert, with long hot days and very little greenery except in tended gardens. As such, other races thought the realm a wasteland and would only grace it when they needed to buy a servant, such as Kye. Still, since humans had become used to growing food in such a harsh landscape, they had managed to become experts in agriculture, which was the most common job slaves were enlisted for throughout the realms. That had, in fact, been his and his mother's job, before Umbree.

They had lived in a small shack at the end of a large farm on Helia. His mother had been in service to an Orc landowner named Belthier, growing crops to be sold all over the realms. That was before Umbree met Belthier. The two soon became friends, as they were both underhanded businessmen. Umbree had convinced Belthier Kye was too small for field work and offered to buy him at a fair price, as he was in need of a house servant. Belthier jumped at the chance to turn a buck and sold Kye to Umbree when he was eight. Kye still cursed the day he met Umbree. Kye had been making structures in the sand while his mother hung laundry outside their shack. He had been so focused on his task he hadn't seen Umbree's approach until a shadow fell over him. As Kye looked up, he saw a goblin standing in front of him. Even though Umbree was a good foot shorter than Kye now, he remembered him looking so tall staring down at him, almost like a giant. Umbree didn't so much as utter a hello. He simply sneered at Kye and grabbed him by the arm, dragging him off to a carriage without a single explanation. Kye was screaming and reaching back with all his might for his mother, who was being held back by Belthier. He remembered her tears, pleading and shouting after Kye until the carriage drove out of sight. The sounds of her cries still echoed in his ears.

When Kye first came to the manor, he tried everything he could think of to escape and get back to his mother. But every time he thought he'd gotten away, Umbree would appear out of nowhere, like he was all-seeing. He would drag him back to the manor and lock him up or give him a lashing for his efforts. This continued for years. Things changed when Kye turned thirteen. Belthier came over for dinner one night. While handing Kye his cloak in the entryway, he casually mentioned to him his mother had died from an illness. Then he continued inside to greet Umbree as calmly as if he had remarked on the weather. Kye stood in shock in the entryway, holding Belthier's cloak, for a long time, his breath choking him as it stilled in his throat, his eyes wide in disbelief. He felt the world slowly crumble around him, along with all hope he had left. The realization gradually dawned on him that he had no one to get back to anymore. He was alone now. He stopped trying to escape for a long time after that.

Upon reaching the second floor, Kye entered through the large double doors at the end of the hall. As soon as he stepped inside the master bedroom, he carefully set the tray of food down on the armoire close to the door. Walking over to the window, Kye pulled back the huge dark blue drapes to allow the morning sun to stream into the room. His master sat on the floor in a meditative trace that replenished his energy and refreshed his mind. Humans were the only creatures that actually slept, each and every night. The elder goblin cursed at being disturbed by the sudden flash of bright light as he became aware of Kye entering the room.

"Good morning, Lord Umbree," Kye said as he picked up the tray of food off the armoire and placed it on the floor in front of his master. Umbree leaned over the tray and inspected his morning meal. Kye went about the room, picking up stray clothes as Umbree stared at his breakfast.

"What the hell is this, boy?" Umbree hissed regarding the plate with disgust.

"Eggs and fruit, my lord," Kye replied as he laid his master's robe on a high-backed chair in the corner of the room.

Umbree snorted. "Tastes like shit. You still can't prepare a decent meal!" Despite Umbree's complaints, he started eating the food and drinking the tea Kye had prepared.

"Apologies, my lord," Kye responded. "I can fix you something else if you would prefer."

Umbree sneered as he dug into another piece of fruit. "What use would that be? The next meal you prepare would be just as abysmal. I swear, you are a useless human. It is only by my good graces you're allowed to continue existing."

Kye continued his morning routine, not even breaking stride. This was nothing he hadn't heard before. Umbree's favorite name for him was useless, favorite compliment an insult, and Kye honestly couldn't recall anything he had done which had ever pleased his master. If Umbree was dissatisfied with Kye's service, Kye was far more unhappy with the arrangement. He slept on a pallet, with a blanket as thin as a sheet. He ate scraps and worked from dawn 'til dusk. But that was his place in the world, for he was human. The lowest creature on the magical totem pole, with short lives and weak bodies. Not worthy of learning the magical arts—not worthy of much of anything really. Humans were seen as nothing more than a resource to the more powerful, beings that existed only to do their bidding. And that resource was sent via portals to all the Six Realms where their services were required. They were tasked with the jobs those higher in society thought beneath them—farming, cleaning, building and such. Kye had read in Umbree's library that over the centuries, humans had tried to fight back against their station more than once. Only for any rebellion to be squashed by the mages and the rich and powerful as quickly as it had begun. There were a few places where humans could find some measure of freedom, like Camris, for slaves freed from their service or unable to work. It was Kye's hope to end up in such a place one day. Maybe after Umbree died...a hopefully miserable death.

Kye placed Umbree's slippers at his feet and took the tray as he finished scraping the breakfast plate of its contents. Umbree drained the last bit of the tea and handed the cup to Kye. The goblin then slowly stood up, as Kye helped put on his slippers and slid on his robe. Umbree shuffled to the armoire, looking at himself in the small tabletop mirror. He observed his deep green complexion and silver-colored eyes in the looking glass, searching for any new wrinkles before attending to his bright white hair. Along with being a spiteful old bastard, Kye also knew Umbree to be incredibly vain, taking great pride in his appearance. He was also particularly sensitive about his age, overly anxious for any new wrinkle or crease that might appear in his already leathered skin. Kye had never heard Umbree's age, nor did he care enough to ask. But from what he knew of goblins, he was guessing his master was somewhere around five hundred years old. A long life for a goblin, certainly longer than any human would ever have. But clearly too short a time in Umbree's eyes. Umbree began searching through his armoire drawers, pulling out one of his potions and taking a long swig from it.

Kye stood in the center of the room, awaiting any final instructions from his master. Umbree started digging through his drawers for some trinket or another, completely oblivious to the fact Kye was still standing there.

"Is there anything else you will be requiring, my lord?" Kye inquired. Umbree grunted dismissively and shooed Kye away.

Kye gave a slight bow and was leaving the room when Umbree replied, "Oh, some guests will be joining me for dinner tonight. You will make sure APPETIZING food is served."

Kye replied with a "Yes, my lord," as he closed the door behind him, but inwardly he was swearing. Umbree had entertained guests at the manor before. The event usually consisted of Kye spending the entire day cooking and the entire night cleaning up the drunken havoc that they wrought.

The rest of the day was spent weaving in and out of rooms, setting placemats and sweeping the floors here and there. Kye pulled the fine dinnerware down from the buffet cabinet and put out the best brandy in the parlor. He had decided since Umbree requested "edible food," he would make a hen, with roasted chestnuts. Kye took an ax out to the chicken pen and slaughtered the fattest hen he could find. It was always a task he hated, no matter how old he got. He didn't enjoy killing things. The first time Umbree had made him kill a chicken, he had been eight. He had cried through the entire process. Granted, he was used to it now, but Kye still found himself muttering an apology to the animal before he did the deed. Carrying the bird inside, he set to plucking it, removing the giblets, and buttering it. Deciding that Umbree would undoubtedly be drinking tonight, Kye decided it was best to collect a few bottles of wine from the cellar.

Kye lit a small candle from a table in the entryway and grabbed a basket from the kitchen. He passed through the main hall, into the kitchen, and took the stairs in the butler's pantry to the basement. Six cedar rows of expensive wines that Umbree most likely couldn't afford filled the length of the damp and dreary cellar. Kye skimmed along the bottles until he found suitable vintages that he thought Umbree wouldn't complain about. He had to be sure the wines were properly aged, or Umbree would complain about the taste. But not too old that Umbree would chastise Kye for wasting his best wine. Picking out six bottles that Kye deemed acceptable, he turned and started heading back toward the stairs. Kye stopped in front of the stone statue of a gryphon in the corner. He always took the time to admire it when he was in the cellar. Because, known to him, and no one else, there was a passageway behind that statue. Kye had discovered it when he was fourteen. Umbree had locked him in the cellar for a couple days for ruining one of his favorite robes while washing it. It was obvious that this manor was used for smuggling of some sort before Umbree had become the owner, for the passageway went under the manor into spillway tunnels below. It was dark and treacherous. Only a tiny walkway led along the rushing water. On top of that, it was a maze. Kye had tried to explore it more than once, thinking it might finally be a way to slip out from under Umbree's watchful eye. But every turn he had taken had led to a dead end. Besides, even if he was able to escape, where would he go? There was nowhere on Helia he could find freedom as long as he was still indentured to Umbree. And a slave caught running from his master's service was punished most severely. Still...he often imagined where he would go if he could escape. He would spend his life touring the Six Realms. See the great forests of Isalia, the impressive dwarven structures of Brooma, the luxurious markets of Proxa, the dense jungles of Daiga, and count the stars shining under the eternal night on Savena. But he also knew...he would never see any of those things. Books were the closest he would ever come. Deciding he had wasted enough time daydreaming, Key picked up the basket full of wine and proceeded upstairs to finish preparing dinner.

It was mid-afternoon when the first of Umbree's guests arrived —Torha, a goblin mage Kye had met before. Once an acolyte of the Magi High Council, he had long since put the days of duty and honor behind him, considering it to be more profitable to invest in shady dealing and practices. He was, by far, Umbree's most consistent partner in crime, with less of a conscience and more of a temper. As soon as Torha appeared in the manor courtyard, Kye gave a slight bow to him (an action that made his skin crawl) and held out an arm to collect Torha's cloak. Torha didn't even acknowledge Kye's presence, shrugging off the cloak and walking over to give Umbree a hug.

"It has been far too long!" Torha announced.

"Or not nearly long enough," Kye mumbled, taking the cloak inside to deposit it in the hall closet.

The next guest to arrive was Belthier, much to Kye's distaste but not surprise. He was also a frequent dinner guest at the manor. Belthier greeted the other two with the same enthusiasm Torha had shown and dropped his cloak for Kye to catch, which he barely managed to do before it hit the ground.

"So, has the honored guest arrived yet?" Belthier inquired of Torha and Umbree.

"Not yet," Umbree responded. "But I am assured he will be arriving this evening. We must make sure he is greeted with the utmost enthusiasm."

Kye continued inside to deposit Belthier's cloak. He wasn't sure who the final guest was supposed to be. Kye had expected only Torha and Belthier for dinner. But considering Umbree had referred to the final mystery guest as "honored," surely he would be just as intolerable as the other three.

Kye had already served before-dinner drinks and appetizers

to the guests as they sat in the parlor. He then went outside to grab a few fresh apples, since Umbree loudly demanded "a fresh fruit platter" and insisted that any idiot would have known to prepare one. Kye figured he would play it safe and grab some blackberries and blueberries as well, or else Umbree would most likely complain about the lack of selection. He was placing the last of the fruits in the basket when a bright blue light appeared behind him. As Kye turned, he could see a swirling vortex in the middle of the courtyard. A portal. He had heard Umbree speak of them before. Rather than simply teleporting, portals were used by mages to cross great distances, mostly in between realms. That meant that the final dinner guest must not be from Helia. The swirling light began dying down, and at the final flicker before it disappeared entirely, a figure emerged from within. Kye was surprised to see an elf standing before him. He was dressed in deep green robes and had his long brown hair tied back. His eyes were a chestnut color, and he had a lean but tall stature. Kye would have guessed him around thirty if he were human. But considering elves lived exceptionally long lives, who knew what his true age was. Elves were not common around Helia, and this was the first one Kye had ever seen. The elf slowly looked around, his sharp features furrowed as he observed his surroundings. His gaze then fell on Kye, when he finally noticed him standing off to the right, staring at him in surprise. Kye quickly snapped out of his daze and bowed to the elf.

"Good evening, my lord."

The elf opened his mouth to respond when the front door suddenly burst open.

"Lord Arden!" Umbree proclaimed. "We have been awaiting your arrival. These are my guests for dinner this evening, Torha and Belthier."

Both of Umbree's cohorts bowed slightly as their names were mentioned. The elf eyed them cautiously.

"Please, come inside!" Umbree continued with the widest smile he could manage. The unnatural contortion of his mouth gave away that smiling was not second nature to him.

"We have prepared a lovely, glazed hen with roast chestnuts."

We? Who was we? Kye thought while glaring at Umbree. "And currently we are partaking in pre-dinner drinks and appetizers in the parl—"

"Not looking to be wined and dined by you, Umbree. This isn't a date," Arden proclaimed.

The silence was deafening. Kye was shooting glances between Arden and Umbree. To his utter delight, Umbree seemed to be a cross between baffled and blatantly pissed.

"W-well, no, of course not," Umbree continued through partially clenched teeth. "But surely you wouldn't deny me the chance to entertain a fellow comrade."

"I wasn't aware you considered us comrades," Arden continued. "It is certainly a kinder term than I would have chosen."

Kye coughed slightly to try and cover a laugh that threatened to escape his throat. He noticed a particular vein throbbing on Umbree's forehead. Kye had not seen him this furious since he had accidentally knocked an ember out of the fireplace while stoking it and caught the hall rug ablaze.

"I am certain dinner to discuss current affairs is not an outlandish request. Wouldn't you agree?" Umbree asked in a rather sharp tone.

Arden seemed conflicted, as though he had much more he wished to say to Umbree. But finally, he seemed to relent. "If you are that eager to hear council affairs, I can speak briefly to the matter."

Umbree bowed slightly as he uttered, "It would be an honor to host you for dinner, Lord Arden."

Arden barely inclined his head in Umbree's direction and strode past Torha and Belthier as though they weren't even there. Umbree glared after him as he walked into the manor. He then turned his frustrations toward Kye.

"Boy!" Umbree growled. "What are you doing just standing there! Get inside now!"

Not a problem, Kye thought as he hurried past Umbree. If this show was a prelude to dinner, he wouldn't miss it for the world.

You could practically cut the tension in the air with a knife. Arden sat in the farthest corner of the parlor, away from Umbree, Torha and Belthier, eating blackberries out of the fruit plate Kye had placed out. Umbree had a fixed smile plastered on his face, but his eyes told another story all together. Kye was the first to break the silence as he approached Arden carrying a drink tray.

"Can I get you a drink, my lord?"

Arden turned to meet Kye's gaze. It was honestly the first time since his arrival Arden didn't look irritated.

"No thanks, kid," he replied, pulling a silver flask from his robes. "I brought my own."

Kye nodded in response and moved over to refill Belthier's drink.

"W-Well, Maister Arden," Torha spoke apprehensively, "to what do we owe the honor of this visit?"

"I was sent on official business by the council," Arden replied. "I'm sure Umbree knows why. If he didn't feel the need to share that with you, I see no reason to argue with his judgment."

Now it was Torha who looked irked, as he quickly chugged the contents of his glass to keep his words in check. Kye went over to refill the glass when Umbree snapped his attention toward him.

"When is dinner, boy?"

Kye finished pouring Torha's drink before turning to Umbree. "The hen was done some time ago. I just basted it and was about to go check on it."

Umbree pointed a finger toward the door and sneered, "Then go check on it."

Kye set the brandy down on the bar and bowed his head slightly to Umbree before exiting the room. Arden eyed the exchange through a piercing gaze. He landed on Umbree with a disapproving expression as soon as Kye left, one which Umbree seemed entirely unfazed by.

"What news of the council these days?" Belthier chimed in.

"Answering calls of the Six Realms, maintaining order, keeping the peace, things of that nature," Arden responded. "Are you digging for any specifics or just shooting the shit?"

"How is Valor doing?" Umbree replied.

Arden gave a snide smile in response. "Your protege is still alive and kicking. He's seated himself at the head of the council. He sends his regards."

"How nice." Umbree smirked back. "I was curious why the council decided to send you instead of him?"

Arden swirled his flask and stared back at Umbree unflinchingly. "He did not agree with the other council members' decision. Argued against it, in fact. I volunteered to come collect on the council's behalf."

"So it seems he still has faith in his old master, huh?" Umbree replied.

"It would appear so," Arden responded plainly.

"How nice. I always knew that he would go far. Best decision I ever made, making him my apprentice. I hear that you still haven't chosen an apprentice yet. Is that right, Arden?"

Arden took another swig from his flask. "You have heard correctly."

"How odd," Umbree continued. "I mean, as a maister of the magical arts, I would think you would want to pass on your knowledge. Not to mention someone to take your place at the council once you see fit to retire. Yet, to have still not chosen an acolyte, after all these years. I'm surprised the council has not brought up these concerns to you."

"They have mentioned it more than once," Arden replied.

"Well, there are many talented successors out there. If you are having trouble finding an appropriate replacement, then clearly your standards are too high. A great many affluent elves that come from long lines of magical lineage would jump at the chance. Valor, for example, came from such a background. And as you can see, he is doing quite well."

"Well, what can I say, Umbree," said Arden. "I guess we all can't find such a very talented candidate with so very deep pockets."

Umbree turned a flash of red at Arden's obvious accusation, while Arden didn't even bat an eye. He took another drink from his flask and stared out the window. A heavy silence settled on the group yet again. Kye entered the room to the tense exchange and cleared his throat slightly, which cast all eyes toward him. He placed a hand on his chest and gave a small bow to the group.

"Apologies for interrupting, my lords, but dinner is served."

Kye was standing in the corner of the dining room, holding a bottle of wine and observing the dinner guests digging into the main course. He had laid out a fresh salad, a fresh loaf of bread, buttered corn, roasted red potatoes, yams browned in honey, along with glazed hen with roast chestnuts.

Umbree snorted slightly as he started scooping a second helping of the hen.

"This meal is barely passable, boy!" Umbree scolded Kye. "It's dry and tasteless. I thought I told you to prepare a decent meal."

Kye concealed an eye roll as he bowed slightly to Umbree. "Apologies, my lord."

"I didn't know goblins had such discerning tastes, Umbree," Arden interjected while scooping up more red potatoes. "Your kind always struck me as the 'gnaw on it raw' type."

Umbree shot daggers to Arden as Kye turned toward the buffet table to hide a smile. Umbree quickly chugged his glass of wine, then snapped his fingers to Kye to refill it. Belthier cleared his throat and tried once again to engage Arden in conversation.

"After dinner, I hope you will join us for a round of cards in the parlor, Lord Arden," Belthier added.

Arden took another sip from his flask. "I will be departing after dinner," he replied, "after I collect a specific item from Umbree's care, that is."

Umbree once again plastered on his widest, accommodating grin. "Oh no, Maister Arden, the sun has almost set. It would be ill-mannered to cast you off in the middle of night."

"Since when are you so concerned with manners, Umbree?"

Umbree's smile didn't waver as he disregarded Arden's statement.

"Please," Umbree continued, "enjoy accommodations here for the evening. We can send you off at first light with the article you have come for. Let it not be said I was inhospitable to a mage of the High Council."

Kye was as equally baffled by the situation as Arden appeared to be. It was blatantly clear Arden and Umbree could not stand each other. Yet despite butting heads, Umbree seemed damned and determined to keep Arden at manor since the moment of his arrival. Kye decided it must be Umbree's way of gaining more favor within the council. He was trying his best to make a good impression on Arden, in hopes of gaining Arden as his ally. But to what end, Kye wasn't sure.

"Well, seeing as you are unwilling to hand over the item I have come for until tomorrow, I see that I don't have much of a choice other than to take you up on your 'gracious' offer," Arden replied. "But I WILL depart at first light, WITH the item I came for." It was not a question, and Arden's gaze said as much.

Umbree held two fingers up and whispered, "*Bòid fala*." His fingers began to glow as he drew a sigil in light across his heart. He then smiled at Arden. "You have my word, on pain of death," Umbree promised, as the sigil of light slowly faded.

"Well, that's good to know," Arden replied. "Either way, I'll have something to look forward to come sunrise." Umbree's face fell as Arden stood up from his seat. "Excuse me, gentlemen, I believe I am in need of some air." Arden turned and left the dining room without so much as a glance back. Kye couldn't help but feel if Umbree was trying to gain favor with Arden, he had miles and miles to go.

Arden did not return for the remainder of dinner, and the three at the table seemed much happier for it. Umbree, Torha, and Belthier started exchanging jokes and relaxed conversation while draining several bottles of elven wine. There was a direct correlation, Kye noticed, between how much they drank and how loud they got. Kye was refilling their glasses for about the fourth time when Umbree laughed out loud at a joke that Torha made and hit the table with his hand causing the dining surface to move. As it shuddered, the glass Kye had been pouring wine into shifted as well, causing a fair amount to splash onto Umbree's sleeve. Umbree stopped laughing instantly and held his right arm to eye level, examining the fresh wine stain upon it. He then turned to Kye with a contemptuous glare. Umbree held the sleeve of his robes so that Kye could clearly see the stain.

"What the hell is this, boy?" he growled to Kye.

Kye bowed his head in response. "The table shook. I'm sorry, master."

"Yes...you are," Umbree hissed in response. "Sorry is the perfect description of you."

Kye remained silent and picked up Umbrees's wine glass to wipe the spill underneath. As he held the glass in his hand, Umbree uttered, "*Crith.*"

The wine glass instantly shattered, spraying Kye with wine and cutting his hand with the jagged shards. Torha and Belthier started cracking up laughing as Kye quickly grabbed a napkin from the table and wrapped it around his now-bleeding right hand. Turning back to his guests, Umbree gave Kye a nonchalant glance before commanding, "Now clean it up and fetch the cake."

It took some time to mop up the wine and glass splattered all over the dining room floor. Kye was moving slower than usual, considering his right hand was throbbing. He kept silent, though, for any excuse would only incite further retribution. Umbree had proven that before. Kye then moved around the table and cleared the dinner plates to make room for dessert. It was due to many years of practice that Kye could carry the platters and cups balanced on his arms through the long trek down the hall, past the foyer, and into the kitchen.

Kye pushed open the kitchen doors with his foot, careful not to tip the massive stack of leftover dinner dishes before depositing them in the sink. He could hear Umbree, Torha, and Belthier laughing and talking from the dining room as he took down the dessert dishes and started stacking slices of chocolate cake on the serving tray. As Kye was about to add the last slice, his thoughts momentarily flashed back to his master shattering the wine glass and ordering him to clean it up for the amusement of his friends. A small flame of fury began to grow as Kye held the slice of cake in his hand. If he were able to utter a word and cause mayhem as easily as Umbree, he would have brought the dining room chandelier down upon the miserable goblin's head. In a quieter act of rebellion, though, Kye held his arm out, stiff as a board, tilted the saucer of cake, and watched in satisfaction as the slice fell to the floor with a small *"thwat."* Kye then bent down and placed the saucer on the floor beside the mildly mangled desert and proceeded to nudge the slice of cake back onto the saucer with his foot. He retrieved the saucer from the floor and put the cake back onto the tray as though nothing had ever happened. His master was so drunk, Kye was convinced he would never even notice the difference. Panic spread through his veins like ice water as he heard a small chuckle from behind him.

"Well, certainly glad I passed on dessert."

Kye felt his heart beating against his chest with the ferocity of a bird trying to escape a cage as he slowly turned. There, sitting in the corner of the kitchen on a stool, was Lord Arden. The high elf was drinking the contents of his silver flask and looking at Kye with a mixture of curiosity and amusement. Kye knew that if Lord Arden reported his little act of rebellion to Lord Umbree, he would undoubtedly receive a few lashes and more than a few days without a meal. Kye gave a small bow to Lord Arden, his mind racing for a way to salvage the situation.

"My apologies, my lord," Kye began. "My hand slipped

while holding the cake. Of course, I would not have served this to—"

Lord Arden held up his hand and cut Kye off.

"Relax, kid," Arden replied. "I don't give a rat's ass hair what you feed that prick. Go ahead and spit on it for good measure, as far as I'm concerned."

Kye eyed Arden cautiously. He was trying to decide if the elf spoke the truth, or whether he was trying to trap him into admitting wrongdoing.

"I get the impression you are not a fan of Master Umbree?" Kye asked.

Arden chuckled again. "If by 'not a fan,' you mean I retreated to the furthest corners of the kitchen and proceeded to drink myself stupid so as to stand another moment of his presence, then yeah, I'd say 'not a fan' about sums it up."

Arden took another swig of the flask and pointed to Kye. "Which seems to be a sentiment we share."

Kye knew this subject treaded on dangerous territory, one which he was wary to walk.

"I would not speak ill of my master's care, he has been…"

Arden shook his head. "Already ate dinner, so don't try to feed me bullshit. What's your name?"

"Kye."

"Well, Kye, how long have you been in service to your master?"

"Nine years."

Arden raised an eyebrow in surprise. "Then you have my sympathies, for I have spent less than three hours around Umbree, and I already want to kick his ass. And I'm fairly certain, given your indentured servitude, it is a familiar feeling. So let's cut right through the false fealty, shall we?"

Kye paused. Lord Arden certainly didn't mince words. He carefully considered the proposal as he wasn't really sure what to make of the elven mage yet. But deciding that they both had similar opinions on the matter, Kye cautiously nodded in agreement to the terms. Arden took another swig from his flask as Kye noticed the design upon it. It was pure silver and ornately decorated with an oak tree, whose branches wrapped around the flask's base. Kye wasn't aware what liquid could be inside, but Arden certainly seemed to be a fan of whatever it was. When Arden caught Kye eyeing the flask, he extended it out towards him.

"Care for a drink?" he inquired.

"You're offering some to me?" Kye asked, nonplussed. No non-human had ever offered him anything.

"If you're quick about it," Arden replied. "Otherwise, I'll drain the whole damn thing myself."

Kye gave a slight nod of thanks as he collected the flask from Arden and took a very large swig. It was an action he immediately regretted. It felt as though he had swallowed a lump of hot coal that was determined to scorch him from the inside out. Kye doubled over and started coughing, gasping for air to diminish the flames as Arden gave a small chuckle.

"It takes a bit of getting used to, but it's good stuff."

"Wh-what is it?" Kye sputtered between coughs.

"Dwarven fire whiskey," Arden replied with a grin. "And if there is one thing dwarves know, it's their whiskey."

Kye began to pass the flask back as Arden's eyes drifted to the napkin wrapped around Kye's right hand. His expression switched from cavalier to serious in a second as he inquired, "What happened there?"

Kye merely shrugged in response. "Careless with the kitchen knives."

It wasn't as though Kye was trying to cover for Umbree, far from it. But he also didn't much feel like relaying the truth of the injury to someone he had just met. What would it solve even if he did? Arden's gaze told Kye he didn't quite accept the explanation, but he seemed to capitulate on pushing the subject any further. Instead, he held out his left hand over Kye's injured right and muttered, "*sylven tela.*"

Kye felt the throbbing in his hand instantly cease. As he pulled back the napkin, he saw that the cut had completely vanished. Kye gawked at his hand, thunderstruck. He didn't quite know what was more surprising, that the wound was now gone or that a mage had been the one to heal it.

"You can heal?" he asked in awe.

"All mages can, to various degrees," Arden replied. "Cuts and scrapes are a simple matter, but the more severe the wound, the more power it takes to mend it. There are some mages that specialize in the art of healing and can bring someone back from the brink of death."

"Brink of death?" Kye clarified. "Can you not bring back the dead?" He had always thought if mages were powerful enough, not even death could stand in their way.

"Mages are not gods, no matter what Umbree may want you to believe," Arden replied. "We may bend the laws of nature, but we cannot break them. Life flows in one direction."

Kye's experience with mages had been limited to Umbree and his horrible friends. As such, it had taught him that mages were selfish, inconsiderate, arrogant, and callous. Mages from the High Council were a special case of incorrigible. Arden, however, was an enigma. He was the first mage Kye had met that seemed to actually possess consideration and a semblance of a conscience. The fact that he was a member of the High Council made it all the more surprising.

"What?" Arden inquired to Kye's puzzled expression.

"Nothing...I'm just...are you sure you are a mage of the High Council?"

Arden grinned. "Questioning my abilities, kid?"

"No, just your demeanor. You are not like the other mages I have met."

"Well, given the current company, I take that as a compliment."

"That's good," replied Kye with a small smile. "For it was meant to be."

A loud, raucous laugh emitted from the dining room, as the drunken shouts and slurs could be heard from Umbree and his other guests. Kye found a good bit of pleasure that Arden's immediate reaction was a sheer look of disgust.

"BOY!" Umbree boomed. "BOY, WHERE THE HELL IS OUR DESSERT!!"

The whiskey had made Kye feel a bit braver than before, and for a split second, he thought of telling Umbree exactly where he could find it. But he knew that his moment of defiance, no matter how satisfying it might be, would not be worth the fury Umbree would rain down in response. Kye gave a slight bow to Maister Arden. "I should return to my duties, Lord Arden, but I thank you for the drink."

Arden nodded as he replied, "Anytime."

Kye collected silverware from the cabinet, before grabbing the dessert tray and heading toward the kitchen door.

"Hey, Kye!"

Kye looked back as Arden motioned toward the dessert tray.

"You're not REALLY going to serve your master his cake in that condition, are you?"

Kye's brow furrowed; he had thought Arden had stated his feelings about the condition of the cake quite clearly. But as a smile began to spread over Arden's face, Kye began to grasp his understanding. With a grin himself, he leaned over the dessert tray, inhaled deep, and spit right on top of Umbree's piece. Arden laughed out loud, clapped his hands together, and proclaimed, "Now that's the cherry on top!" Kye smiled back at Arden, pleased as punch, as he exited the kitchen.

It would take two days of scrubbing pots to clean up after the grand meal Kye had prepared. Umbree and his guests had retreated to the parlor, all except Arden, that was. He had only talked to Umbree and the other guests shortly after dinner before retreating upstairs, stating he would retire for the remainder of the evening. Umbree didn't try to stop him or convince him to join the others in the parlor, which only further begged the question as to why he had insisted Arden stay in the first place. Whatever the reason, Umbree showed Arden to a guest room on the second floor and wished him a pleasant evening before returning to the parlor. Kye was carrying out remnants of leftover food to the compost bin, soaking plates and cookware and carefully washing wine glasses. Kye noticed that only two bottles of elven wine had remained untouched from the six that he had carried up from the wine cellar. And for how intolerable the food supposedly was, there were basically no leftovers in sight. He had been hoping some of the hen would be left for him to eat, but sadly, only the bones remained. Kye would have made extra for himself if Umbree didn't keep such a stranglehold on ordering supplies for the manor. He was quite thankful for the extra loaf of bread Jitar had brought. He tore off a piece and ate it while completing his chores. Kye was seated at the small dining table in the kitchen, cleaning the silver piece by piece. He wasn't sure if it was the monotony of the task, the busyness of the day, or the result of the fire whiskey, but he found it difficult to keep his eyes open. It was a fight Kye eventually lost, as he laid his head down on the table for just a moment.

The sound of the hall clock chiming midnight awoke Kye from his slumber. Looking around, he realized he had fallen asleep halfway through his cleanup duties. Considering that Umbree never set foot in the kitchen, Kye decided he would finish collecting the dinnerware from the dining room and complete his cleaning in the morning. Umbree would never know the difference. Kye rubbed his eyes wearily as he made his way back down the hall to the dining room. The lamp from the parlor was still on, which told Kye that Umbree and his friends were still in the midst of their card game (and a bottle of brandy, no doubt). Kye snuck past the door so as not to alert the voices within to his presence. As he passed the crack of light streaming on the floor, the raised voice of Torha met his ears.

"So, Orin is coming tonight?!"

Kye halted right outside the door. Who was Orin? He was pretty sure Umbree didn't have any more friends. It was a miracle he had found the two. Kye leaned in to better hear the conversation.

"Yes, he will arrive as soon as we give him the signal that all is clear. Then we will hand him the stone," replied Umbree.

"So he doesn't intend to help us then?" Belthier asked.

"Of course not!" Umbree hissed back. "This is a test of our allegiance. Besides, we do not need his help with this matter!"

"But Arden is a powerful mage," Torha responded.

Umbree snorted in response. "Powerful indeed! His power cannot match my own. You needn't worry about Arden. I have a plan. He will not live past tonight. I shall see to it."

CHAPTER 2
A Secret Study

It was almost as though time itself had stopped. Kye was frozen to the spot. His chest constricted, his lungs unable to take in air. His mind was stuck on repeat, replaying the words over and over in his head.

"You needn't worry about Arden. He will not live past tonight."

A wave of panic hit Kye like a punch, but his feet still refused to move. They were going to kill him. They were going to kill Lord Arden. Kye shut his eyes and took a deep breath. As a thousand thoughts raced through his head, one stood out amongst the noise.

What do I do?

What could he do? If he warned Arden about what his master had said, Umbree would kill him. If he tried to persuade his master against attacking Arden, he would kill him. If Umbree got even a suspicion that Kye had overheard the conversation, he would kill him. Three different scenarios, all ending the same way. After all, if they were plotting to kill a maister of the Magi High Council, a mere slave's life would be of no consequence. What options did that leave? Finish cleaning up? Go to bed? Try to pretend a cold-blooded murder wasn't occurring on the floor above him? Kye could hear footsteps approaching the parlor door as he quickly and quietly bolted down the hall and rushed into the dining room. Kye crouched down and slid underneath the dining table to hide from view. Umbree, Torha, and Belthier filed out of the study and proceeded to the back door. As they walked away, Kye could hear Umbree say, "We shall place talismans around the grounds to dampen his magical ability and prevent him from teleporting. Then he will be no match for us." Those were the last words Umbree whispered as all three of them headed out the back door onto the manor grounds. Kye remained crouched underneath the table for a long while, trying to figure out what his course of action should be. He was human, and this was a fight between mages. It should be no concern of Kye's. And involving himself in the matter could definitely spell his end. But...if Umbree was successful, if Arden was killed, would Kye be able to live with himself, knowing he did nothing to try and stop it? Ignoring Umbree's actions made him complicit. And Kye knew his survival at the expense of a good man wasn't an even trade and one that would no doubt haunt him. No matter the risk, he had to get Arden out of the manor before Umbree got to him, and he had an idea for doing just that. Kye snuck out from under the dining table and pressed his face against the corner of the window in the dining room. The view out on the grounds was pitch black, and there was no way to know for sure where Umbree and the others were in the darkness.

Kye had no idea how long it would take for Umbree to place the talismans. He would have to be quick or risk both Arden and himself being caught. It was now or never.

Kye snuck up to the guest room on the second floor, quiet as a mouse. He kept his eyes peeled on every window that he crossed to keep a line of sight on Umbree and his cohorts returning to the manor. Standing outside the guest room door, Kye began to knock, loud enough in hopes of gaining Arden's attention, but quietly enough so as not to draw Umbree's. To his relief, Arden opened the door and stood before Kye with an expression of bewilderment that was clear even in the dim light.

"Kye?" Arden questioned. "Are you aware of the hour?"

Kye nodded. "Yes, and I'm sorry, my lord, but I had to—"

Kye stopped short when a noise down the hall caused him to snap his attention away. He was still as a statue for a moment, making sure the sound was not a person coming up the stairs. Arden could see Kye was noticeably on edge and stepped aside to open his door in response.

"Come in, kid," he said, to which Kye instantly darted inside, free from the observance of any evil in the shadows. Kye brushed past Arden as he closed the door behind him. He immediately glued his face to the window. Since Kye was human, his eyesight in the dark was not great, but he wanted to see if he could at least detect Umbree and his guests' figures in the blackness from the second-story vantage point. Unfortunately, the only thing he could see was shadows and a pathetic sliver of a moon. What he wouldn't give for a full moon tonight.

"Kye? What's wrong?" Arden inquired.

"I had to warn you," Kye whispered in response as he gave the grounds one last look.

"Warn me? Warn me about what?"

"They are going to kill you," Kye stated, turning back to Arden.

"Who?" Arden replied in confusion.

"Umbree and the others. I heard them discussing it in the parlor."

Arden sighed and walked over to sit on a leather chair in the corner of the room. "Your concern is touching, but no one is going to kill me," he replied. "Now, I doubt they will be crying over my grave when my time does come, but trust me, that feeling is mutual."

"This wasn't idle talk," Kye insisted. "I know what I heard!"

"Kid, I'm here on official business from the council," Arden continued. "So what's Umbree's plan— bury me in the garden and hope the council doesn't ask questions?"

"I-I don't know," Kye replied. "Maybe he hasn't thought that far ahead?"

Even in the darkness, Kye could see the skepticism on Arden's face, and it fueled his frustration. He didn't have time to try and convince him; Umbree would be back any minute!

"Or maybe he is getting help from Orin?"

Arden's head snapped to attention. "Who did you say?"

"Orin. I heard Umbree mention him in the parlor. He said he was coming tonight and that they are giving him a stone."

"You heard Umbree say that Orin was coming here tonight?" Arden asked as he rose once again. "You heard him mention giving Orin a stone?"

Kye nodded in response. "Umbree said that he would arrive once he gave the signal, after he finished you off."

Arden was silent for a long while, staring at the floor deep in thought. He finally chuckled, stating, "Well hell, I didn't know Umbree was that desperate or stupid."

"His stupidity, at least, I can attest to," Kye responded.

Outside the window, Kye noticed a sudden flash of red, as though someone had set off a firework. The red light shot toward the heavens and burst. Sprinkles of crimson rained down and hit the manor and grounds, causing the room to illuminate in an ominous blood-red glow. The red light lasted for only a moment before dissipating. Arden stared at it knowingly. "A barrier?"

"Umbree said he was going to place amulets on the

grounds," Kye responded, "to dampen your abilities and keep you from teleporting."

"Cowardly bastard!" Arden growled. "Afraid to face me at full power, huh? He should be!"

"I can get you out of the manor," Kye said. "But we have to move fast before Umbree and the others return."

Arden turned to Kye and smiled slightly. "I appreciate the offer, but I can't leave yet."

Kye was flabbergasted. "What? Why?!"

"The stone," Arden replied. "The one that Umbree mentioned. It's my whole reason for coming here."

"Is a trinket really worth your life!?"

"This trinket is. Especially if Umbree really is planning on handing it over to Orin. In his hands, people could die. I can't leave without it."

Arden walked over to his cloak hanging on the wall next to the wardrobe and pulled a golden amulet from his pocket. He whispered to it, and the amulet glowed for a moment, then dimmed as Arden put the chain around his neck.

"Listen, kid," Arden stated as he turned back to Kye. "Things are going to get messy. I want you to go somewhere, far from the manor, and hide. And no matter what you hear, don't come out. You got it?"

But Kye didn't answer. If Arden was willing to put his life on the line for that stone, it had to be important. Kye wasn't going to just hide, not after he had already made the decision to help. He knew Umbree to be a cold-blooded bastard, and if the stone could hurt people, Kye didn't want Umbree anywhere near it either. Besides, helping Arden had already guaranteed Kye a short life of misery if he were caught. In for a penny, in for a pound.

"Kye?" Arden inquired. "Did you hear what I—"

"What does it look like?" Kye interjected.

"What?"

"The stone," Kye clarified. "What does it look like?"

Arden hesitated for a moment before replying, "About the size of a fist, citrine yellow, glows slightly." Kye's eyes drifted to the floor as he quickly ran through every gem he could think of in the manor. There was the jewel in the suit of armor by the landing, but no, that was red. Or the display case in the living room, the jewel in the crown on the top shelf, that was yellow...but no, it didn't glow and wasn't the size of a fist. There was also a gem in the scepter adorning the wall in the conservatory. But no, that was an emerald.

"Have you seen it?" Arden inquired.

Kye shook his head in response. "No..." he replied. Just then, Kye was struck with a sudden thought. "...but I think I know where he would keep it."

Kye didn't give Arden time to inquire as he rushed to the bedroom door and peered out into the hall. No Umbree, Torha, or Belthier.

"Come on." Kye motioned to Arden. "We will have to be quick if we are going to retrieve it before they return."

Arden seemed as though he would argue, but the look on Kye's face must have told him it would be futile. Arden grabbed his cloak and followed Kye out onto the hall landing. Kye's eyes darted around nervously as he led the way, looking for any sight or sound that Umbree had returned. The lighting in the manor was dim; only the soft moonlight through the windows and the sporadic lamps still lit from the day illuminated the space. But that didn't matter to Kye. He had walked the halls so many times he could do it blindfolded. Kye followed the hall up the stairs until he reached the library on the third floor. He pushed open the double doors and proceeded past the high-backed chairs in the middle of the grand two-story room. He immediately headed over to the painting of the dragon hanging over the fireplace mantel in the center of the room. Kye grabbed the candelabra off the coffee table and searched for something to light it.

"What are you looking for?" Arden inquired.

"A light," Kye whispered back. As he searched for matches on the mantle used to light the fireplace, the wicks of the candles instantly ignited as Arden held his hand out. Kye had forgotten he had a mage in tow. He gave a nod of thanks to Arden. He held the flames up to the dragon's fire in the painting and watched as the flames in the picture began to glow and dance just like the flames on the candle. There was a click, and a door formed around the fireplace and then slid back to reveal a room behind it. Kye and Arden stood at the entrance of Umbree's study as a lamp within instantly ignited, illuminating the hidden room. This was the first time Kye had actually seen inside it. It looked like a fairly large but rather ordinary study. There was an ornate writing desk in front of a huge window in the center of the room. The walls were lined with books that appeared to be on a variety of magical subjects. There were some sort of beast-remnants in jars on shelves above the bookcase, a morbid collection of magical creatures. As Kye entered, he could see there didn't seem to be gold hidden anywhere, save for an ostentatious letter opener on the writing desk. It alone was coated in gold, with rubies inlaid in the hilt.

"You think the stone will be here?" Arden inquired.

"If it would be anywhere, it would be here. Umbree never let me enter this room. It's where he stores everything he wishes to keep hidden."

Arden accepted Kye's explanation and started scanning the drawers of the bookshelves for the item he was looking for. Kye dove in to help, searching bookcases and boxes as quickly as he could. He ran his hand along the volumes, looking for anything that could be out of place or tampered with. By the dust coating their spines, the books on the shelf hadn't been touched lately. Kye turned to inspect the room in its entirety once more. Arden was busy searching the desk, looking through the drawers, under papers, and inside the cigar box on Umbree's table. But as he scanned the room, the one thing that caught Kye's eye was a small clock on the shelf near the window, amongst the dusty volumes. What was strange is that the clock displayed midnight when Kye knew the hour had come and passed long ago. Not only that, but the clock was not coated in a layer of dust, unlike many of the other trinkets within the study. It seemed to be the only thing on the shelf that did not show signs of neglect. Kye approached it for a closer look. The face of the clock was onyx, with gold numbering carved into it. The minute and the hour hand were made of ivory and intricately designed. Kye noticed the hands were not set behind a glass casing but could be moved and manipulated at will, without the use of a dial. Kye tilted the clock face and held it up to the light. Clearly illuminated against the pure black back, Kye could see fingerprints at only four of the numbers. The eleven, nine, six, and five had previously been tampered with. Kye poured over the clock, desperately trying to think of what the numbers could mean in relation to Umbree. When Arden saw Kye intently observing it, he came up beside him to inspect it as well.

"I think this could be a trick, like a code or something," Kye said. "Only these four numbers seem to have been touched, but I can't think of what they could relate to."

Arden stared at the face for a long while before muttering, "You've got to be kidding me."

He then took the clock from Kye's hands and pointed the hour hand toward the five, the minute hand toward the nine, then the hour hand toward the six, and the minute hand toward the eleven. A tile in the center of the room gave way, as a pedestal slowly rose from under it. Kye stared at Arden in bewilderment. Arden said, "It wasn't numbers. They were letters. V-IX-VI-XI. *Vix vixi* means barely alive in the old tongue. No doubt Umbree's way of bitching about his less than extravagant lifestyle." Kye raised an eyebrow in response. If Umbree felt the manor was not extravagant enough for his tastes, he should try sleeping in the woodshed.

It was not a natural gem. That was the first thought that crossed Kye's mind when he saw the yellow stone floating mere inches above the pedestal in the center of the study. It had a strange aura to it, one that even a non-magic-wielding human such as him could feel. As Kye stepped toward it, Arden's arm shot out to stop him as he shook his head, a warning Kye took to heart. Arden then began to approach the stone as though it were an explosive, set to go off at a moment's notice. Kye saw a sudden flash pulse throughout the ground. When Arden noticed it, he closed his eyes and began to chant under his breath, words that Kye couldn't quite make out. The whole room began to glow and tremble as though it were alive, a fading heartbeat almost. With one last gasp, the light dissipated, and the room stilled. Arden opened his eyes, reached out, and grabbed the floating stone. He then nodded to Kye and said, "There we go, easy."

"I think we have different definitions of the word," Kye replied. "I suggest we hurry, though. I doubt that Umbree—"

Kye stilled, suddenly silent. Arden shot him a quizzical look in response. "Kid?"

Kye didn't have time to blink before an unknown force sent him hurtling across the room, pinning him to the south wall of the study. Arden cursed and spun around to see Umbree standing in the doorway.

"Good evening, Arden," Umbree said with a sly smile. "I see you have made yourself at home."

Kye couldn't move a muscle as an invisible force held him fast to the wall. Arden kept his hands at his side. They twitched slightly, preparing to attack if Umbree so much as flinched. Umbree looked from Arden to Kye and then to the stone Arden held in his hand.

"I see you have helped yourself to the trinket that you have come for," Umbree stated with noticeable disdain. "Though I fail to see the cause for this invasion, considering I would have handed the stone to you willingly. Is this to be the thanks for my hospitality?"

Arden chuckled slightly. "You seemed less than willing to hand over the stone. And as for your hospitality, as gracious as it was, I think we both know it was nothing more than the means to an end."

"What end?" Umbree snapped.

"Mine," Arden replied. "Which is no doubt your intent when you hand the stone and me over to Orin."

Umbree's left eye twitched for just a moment as he held his calm demeanor.

"Wherever did you hear such a tale?" Umbree asked. His gaze drifted to Kye, anger burning within his eyes. "Don't tell me you heard it from this boy? I must warn you, Arden, he is a most gifted liar."

"A trait, no doubt, he has learned from you," Arden rebutted. Umbree's attention snapped back to Arden.

"You would trust this boy's word over mine?"

"I would trust a lowbrow pickpocket's word over yours, Umbree," Arden bit back. "But yeah, I trust the kid speaks the truth."

Umbree sighed and shook his head. "Well, I suppose the game is up, then."

Umbree took a few steps closer to Arden and held out his hand. "Now I have someone who will be arriving very soon expecting that stone. So if you would be so kind as to return it to me."

"Or what?" Arden scoffed. "You'll fight me for it?"

"Good gracious, no," Umbree replied with a sinister smile. "I see no need for things to get drastic. After all, there are other means of persuasion."

Umbree held up his left hand and pulled it into a fist while shouting, "*OBSTRINGA!*"

Kye gasped as an invisible cord wrapped itself around his neck, cutting off almost all his air supply. He tried to free one of his hands to claw at the force that was choking him, but his limbs were still pressed firmly to the wall. Kye's wheezing breaths caused Arden to summon a bolt of lightning within his hand in retaliation. He pointed it straight toward Umbree.

"Uh-uh-ah," Umbree responded, shaking his finger toward Arden in a mocking manner. "An attack on me would not be quick enough to spare his life, Arden. For I assure you, I can kill him in the time it would take you to finish the incantation. And whilst I have no qualms about snapping this pathetic human's neck, something tells me that you might."

Arden's eyes narrowed in contempt.

"Umbree..." he growled.

Umbree merely smiled in response, extending his right hand toward Arden. "Give me the stone, Arden."

Arden hesitated, the stone held fast within his hand. Umbree didn't give him time to think; he tightened his fist again. This time, as Kye gasped for air, none came. The world around him was starting to blur, and he could hear his heartbeat pounding in his ears.

"Alright, you son of a bitch!" Arden shouted as he held out his hand with the stone. Kye couldn't comprehend what Lord Arden was doing. He wanted to shout, "Don't!" but no sound came out, and his vision was getting darker. Umbree grinned and reached out his hand for the stone. Arden muttered something under his breath, and as soon as Umbree's hand made contact with the stone, a brilliant, blinding light emitted from it, filling the room. Umbree stumbled back with the stone in hand, shielding his eyes as Arden shouted, "*FERRIM METAIUM!*"

A force like a hammer hit Umbree square in the chest, causing him to stagger and release his hold on Kye. Kye hit the floor hard, coughing and gasping to reclaim the air that had been denied him as the world blurred back into focus. Umbree was quick to recover, shouting, "*FLAMENIA*!" at Arden. An intense wind hit Arden and sent the desk and books flying across the room. Kye covered his head with his arms as he too was pushed back across the floor. Arden stood his ground, shouting, "*RADACIA SUBSTANA*!" The wind could no longer move him as his legs seemed rooted to the floor.

The mages continued exchanging spells as Kye crawled out from the clutter of books that were strewn atop and around him. He could see Umbree, eyes wide, desperately trying to advance on Arden. Arden stood his ground, warding off the spells that Umbree flung at him. A soft yellow glow could be seen from the left pocket of Umbree's robe. An idea formed in Kye's mind as, off to his right, hidden partly by loose books, Kye caught sight of a ruby hilt lined in gold.

"*VINCULA LICIO*!" Umbree shouted as the same invisible ropes that had held Kye tried to entwine themselves around Arden. Arden attempted to raise his hand to shoot a ball of fire at Umbree, but the spell worked faster than expected, locking Arden's arms to his side. Umbree smiled as Arden started chanting, trying to break the invisible binds. Umbree summoned an astral weapon that resembled an ax. It hovered, mimicking the movements of Umbree's hand. The ax was mostly transparent, save for the bit, which looked very real and very sharp. As Umbree raised his hand, the astral weapon hovered high above Arden. With a sinister grin,

Umbree stared back at Arden as his hand twitched, ready to bring the weapon down on Arden's head in one swift motion.

A sudden scream echoed through the study. The ax instantly disappeared as Umbree flailed backward in agony. There, standing behind Umbree, was Kye. He had taken the ruby-hilted letter opener from the floor and driven it into Umbree's back, beneath his right shoulder blade. Umbree staggered away and immediately wrenched the blade from his flesh, a stream of green blood now staining his robes. He spun around to meet Kye's face, utter fury glowing in his eyes. Unflinching determination glaring back in Kye's.

"*GLACIA ASTA USAT*!" Umbree roared, holding out his left hand. A ball of ice formed within his palm.

"KYE!!!" Arden shouted in warning, but the words barely left his mouth. The ice ball that Umbree held shattered, sending ice shards hurtling at Kye like daggers and propelling him backward. There was a spatter of red as Kye hit the wall behind him and fell silent. The lapse in concentration on Umbree's part was long enough for Arden to free himself from the invisible bonds.

"*PYRAELA SPAHARA*!!" Arden yelled, his voice shaking in anger as a giant flame within his hand hit Umbree square in the chest. Umbree was knocked to the ground. Arden towered toward him.

"*Dimmora*," Umbree whispered and disappeared from the room in a flash. Arden gritted his teeth at the coward fleeing. He immediately rushed over to where Kye sat slumped against the wall, muttering a healing spell as he went. His powers were diminished due to Umbree's talismans, but it was possible he could repair some of the damage.

"Kid?" Arden asked. Upon closer inspection, Arden could see how badly Kye was injured. Deep gashes covered his right side and his right shoulder, along with a long cut on his head.

Multiple other cuts of varying depths marked his arms and legs, and his clothes were soaked with blood from his wounds.

"Can you hear me?" Arden asked again, hoping for a response. "Kid, say something if you can hear me."

"...ouch..." Kye mumbled barely above a whisper. Arden breathed a slight sigh of relief.

"Yeah, no shit," Arden replied. "That's what you get for picking a fight with a mage. What the hell were you thinking, stabbing Umbree like that? You know that a tiny little dagger isn't enough to do him in."

"...distraction..." Kye whispered back. Speaking was difficult for him, and his breathing was labored.

With great effort, Kye pushed his left hand forward toward Arden. Upon opening his closed fist, Arden was astonished to see a familiar yellow glow. Kye held the stone Umbree had taken from him. Arden realized that Kye's attack on Umbree had not only saved him from the astral weapon. It had also distracted Umbree so that Kye could lift the stone from his pocket without him noticing.

Kye opened his eyes and lifted his head, so his gaze met Arden's. "Said it was...important," Kye continued, "...people die...if he had it... right?"

Arden nodded. "That's right."

Kye lifted a shaky hand and gave the stone to Arden.

"Then you can't...let him have it."

"I won't, kid," Arden answered sincerely. "Just try not to talk, ok?"

Umbree appeared on the ground at Torha and Belthier's feet outside the manor. He was gasping in extraordinary pain and trying to focus on healing the knife wound in his back. Torha regarded him with skepticism.

"I see that Arden wasn't quite the easy task you made him out to be," he commented. Umbree snarled at him in response.

"Arden is of no consequence!" Umbree snapped back. "I have reclaimed the most important piece. He won't be able to escape the barrier. And it will be easy to hunt him down. As long as we..." Umbree reached into the pocket of his robe to show the stone to his other two comrades. As soon as his hand brushed the fabric, though, Umbree's face turned white, and he looked noticeably ill.

"What is it?" Belthier inquired.

"That...worthless...traitorous...fucking...HUMAN!!" Umbree's voice was shaking with rage. His fury bypassed all pain he felt from his wound as he shot to his feet and summoned two magic weapons into his hands, a crossbow and a battle ax. He handed the bow to Torha and the ax to Belthier.

"We are going back inside to reclaim the stone and Arden's head!" Umbree commanded. It wasn't a question, and Torha and Belthier seemed to pick up on that.

"Arden may not be at full strength, but he has enough power to prove troublesome. We should confront him together," Belthier stated.

"He will no doubt try to leave the manor," Torha replied, "in order to escape the confines of the barrier."

"He cannot escape," Umbree seethed. Instantly, he summoned a fire that surrounded him and the outside of the manor in an impassable blaze. The fire quickly licked up the manor walls, as though the whole building was coated in oil. "If I have to burn this manor to ashes, I will pull Arden's corpse from within it." Umbree swore as he watched the flames grow higher. "As for the boy...he best pray death finds him before I do."

A loud ruckus could be heard outside, and Arden could now see flames rushing up the exterior walls just outside the window. Umbree was either trying to force them out or burn them alive. And if they took too long to decide on which they preferred, he would most assuredly come in to get them. Kye looked toward the billowing smoke cloud enveloping the window.

"They are...blocking...escape," Kye stated. "They will... come in."

"Don't worry about it. I'll handle them when they do," Arden said as he went back to chanting the healing spell. Kye took a deep breath, drawing the last of his energy.

"Past the kitchen...in the cellar..." he began, "there is...a gryphon...statue."

"What did I tell you about talking?"

"Statue...leads to...spillway...under the manor," Kye continued. "Umbree...doesn't know. You can...get out...that way..."

"First step is patching you up."

Kye looked back to the windows, noticing the flames growing higher. He felt a rush of frustration and fear coming to terms with his situation. No matter how much he wanted to leave, he could barely move. And Lord Arden staying here any longer was just ensuring he didn't get out either. As such, Kye slowly shook his head.

"There is...no time!" Kye stated as sternly as he could. "They will...kill you. You...have to go...now!"

Kye's breath shuddered, and his focus blurred. His eyes rolled back into his head as he fell silent once again. Arden checked to make sure he was still breathing. He had a pulse, but not a strong one.

Arden stood up and looked around, taking stock of his

surroundings. Kye was right. It was only a matter of time before they stormed inside the manor. And once they were inside, Arden wasn't sure he could hold all three of them off, thanks to the barrier. And definitely not if he was trying to keep Kye alive. The healing spell had cost Arden a great deal of energy, and it had only slowed the bleeding, not stopped it. Kye was fading fast; he wouldn't last long without help. And the only way to achieve that was getting the hell out of Umbree's manor. Deciding on a course of action, Arden bent down and lifted Kye into his arms.

"Statue in the cellar, huh, kid?" he muttered. "Alright, we are getting out of here then."

Arden was moving as quickly as possible through the flames that were enveloping the manor. Smoke was now filling the interior and Arden's lungs as he ran through the thick, eye-watering smog. The fire was growing, licking toward the roof, breaking windows with blasts of heat as Arden ran past them. Arden headed down the hall, descending the staircase down the three flights, toward the kitchen. As soon as he passed the main entrance, the front doors blasted inward. Amongst the splintered wood stood Umbree, Torha, and Belthier, shoulder to shoulder, armed and obviously angry. Umbree locked eyes with Arden for just a moment before shooting a fireball at him and Kye. Arden bolted past it, singeing the hem of his robes in the process. He propelled into the kitchen, slamming the door behind him.

"*Motia imparia!*" Arden said with a wave of his hand at the buffet cabinet. The large structure glided across the floor and planted itself in front of the door. A moment later, a loud bang hit the door and began to break it. Arden did not stick around to watch his pursuers bust through. He swiftly opened the door to the cellar and raced down the stairs. As soon as his feet hit earth, Arden shouted, "*LIQUIA!*" as the staircase he had just descended melted into a puddle on the ground.

Arden locked eyes with the gryphon statue in the corner of the room just as the cellar door shot open.

"*LIBERIA*!" he shouted at the statue. The statue began to contort as if it were alive and stepped aside, bowing to Arden and allowing him access to the tunnel behind it. "*SAPARIA MATIRA*!" Arden directed to the statue as soon as he entered the tunnel. The gryphon placed its stone body directly in front of the tunnel entrance and once again became inanimate.

Arden's elven eyes allowed him to see perfectly in the darkness. All he could hope was that the lack of light would slow Umbree down. Arden barreled down the narrow stone walkway as a swift river of water rushed by at his feet. The path ahead broke off to the right and left. Arden took a hard right as he heard voices enter the tunnel behind him. The only option at the moment was to flee. But if he could follow the tunnels beyond the confines of the barrier, he could make a stand and summon a portal to get the hell out of here. Another dead end, with the path splitting off to the left. Arden noticed the river rushing by him had started to retreat, leaving nothing but the dry stone underbed.

"Shit!" Arden cursed.

The sudden disappearance of water told Arden he better quicken his pace. Racing on ahead, the tunnel twisted to another right, then a left. The further in he went, the more Arden felt the effects of the barrier lessen. Another left turn, and the amulet around Arden's neck began to glow, telling him the barrier was weak enough that he could call out. Arden focused his thoughts and reached out.

"Valor! Valor!"

"Arden?" a voice responded in his head. *"Do you know the time?"*

"I need a portal! And have Mireen standing by."

"A portal? At this hour? What the blazes are you—"

"I haven't time for twenty fucking questions, Valor! Just summon the damn portal, now!!"

Arden's concentration was broken by the intense sound of rumbling as the ground beneath him trembled ferociously. Arden didn't have to guess the source of the vibrations. He bolted forward as fast as his feet could carry him. Arden followed the twists and turns of the tunnel, indiscriminately taking a left or right at every fork. The rumbling was approaching, and from the sound of things, it was catching up. Arden looked over his shoulder for just an instant to see a wall of water charging toward him, chasing after every twist or turn he made, as though it possessed autonomy. Arden pulled a hard right at the next divide and then stopped in his tracks as he was met by a dead end. He quickly turned back to try and correct his mistake, but the water was already upon him.

"*VENTIA MURIO!*" Arden shouted as he grasped the stone within his pocket and held it toward the oncoming wave. A wall of wind hit the water, halting its procession. Arden was supporting an unconscious Kye with his left arm and holding back a tidal wave with his right. The wind was blasting against the water, but Arden could tell he was losing the fight, being pushed closer to the wall behind him as the water inched forward. It was taking every last ounce of energy he possessed to keep the water at bay. Behind the wall of water, Arden could make out the form of three figures approaching him.

Arden's arm was shaking, and his strength was all but spent. Torha took aim with his bow, and Umbree continued to advance toward Arden. Belthier held his place at the rear, blocking a sudden exit with his stance and a very sharp ax. Whether death came by water, arrow, or ax, there was nowhere left for Arden to run. Torha shot the first bolt. Arden was able to divert a gust of wind to reflect it. But his momentary lapse in concentration cost him as a surge of water slammed him back against the wall. Arden quickly redirected the wind back toward the water, but he was now pressed firmly against the wall behind him. Umbree smiled as Torha knotted another bolt. Umbree continued advancing as Torha once again took aim. Arden was bracing for the inevitable impact when, out of the corner of his eye, a familiar and welcome swirling blue light appeared. Arden was certain he had never been so happy to see such a sight in his entire life. From that moment, time seemed to slow. Torha's last shot whizzed harmlessly past Arden's shoulder, disappearing into a vortex of blue. Umbree could be heard shouting, "NOOO!!!" as Arden stepped back into the portal behind him and disappeared with the stone and Kye.

CHAPTER 3
A Peculiar Proposal

Mireen rushed down the white marble hallway, flying through doors as she passed. Upon entering the great hall, she was greeted by several familiar faces, all transfixed by a great, blue swirling portal of light, which filled the center of the room. The other mages in attendance had no doubt heard the same news she had. Maister Arden had run into trouble during his visit to Helia. The message they had received had been brief; they were unaware of how much danger he was in. Only that he had requested the immediate creation of a portal for his departure and to have a healer standing by. Mireen fiddled with the emerald necklace she always wore and silently prayed to the spirits that her healing powers would be enough to mend any injury he might have sustained. She turned anxiously to Maister Valor, who stared unblinkingly at the portal, waiting for Arden to emerge.

"Has there been any more news?" Mireen inquired.

Valor shook his head. "Only the message that we have given to you, Lady Mireen. We are unaware of how bad his injuries might be. We can only wait."

Mireen clasped her hands tighter together in anxiety. Maister Luell caught her eyes. She gave a soft smile to Mireen.

"Do not fret, my dear," she said. "I have known Arden for far too many years. He has proven himself very adept at dueling. I doubt he has sustained more than a mere scratch."

Mireen grinned slightly at her and nodded in response. She hoped it was nothing more than a scratch. Though she doubted Arden would have asked for a healer to be standing by if it was. Suddenly, the portal before them began to ripple, ever-expanding from its center like pebbles falling into a pond. The audience looked on in anticipation, awaiting the mage emerging from the other side. The portal began to flash, deteriorating and shrinking into itself. At the last flash before it disappeared, an arrow shot through the ripples, hitting the double doors to the great hall, causing all present to jump aside in surprise. An elf stumbled in after it, landing on the ground hard as a wave of water coated the great hall's floor. Arden was disheveled, wet, and covered in blotches of blood. As he crouched on the floor, the group noticed he carried an unconscious young man in his arms. Stunned silence fell over the room as the portal vanished from sight, shrinking back into the glowing orb it had been produced from. Maister Valor was the first to speak.

"Maister Arden! N-now, see here...What is the meaning of this!?"

Arden completely disregarded Valor. He turned his attention to only one in the room who mattered.

"Mireen?"

Mireen was instantly snapped out of her shock and rushed toward the young man Arden was holding. The boy was unmistakably human. No human had set foot within Caelum Vallis in over five hundred years. The boy looked young to the elves that surrounded him, but she guessed by human standards, he was close to the age of adulthood. His complexion, normally tan, looked extremely pale due to the injuries he had sustained. There was a deep wound on the boy's right side that was bleeding profusely, not to mention various other slashes that covered his skin. His clothing was stained in red, and a deep cut across his head coated most of his face in blood.

"What happened?" Mireen asked in astonishment.

"He was hit by an ice incantation," Arden replied. "Can you heal him?"

Mireen placed a hand on the boy's chest. She could still detect a heartbeat, but it was erratic, and his breaths were very shallow. She furrowed her brow in response.

"I cannot say for certain. I have no expertise in healing humans. Their forms are more fragile than our own, and the wounds he has sustained are severe."

Arden's eyes darkened from the news. Mireen touched a comforting hand to his shoulder.

"I can promise you, though, that I will do all within my power to save him."

Arden's eyes lightened a bit as he replied, "I know that you will."

Mireen gave him a reassuring smile as Arden passed the young man to her. Mireen teleported away with him in her arms. As Arden rose, Valor stepped forward.

"Arden! I demand an answer!" he shouted, obviously angry that Arden continued to ignore him.

Arden slowly turned, acknowledging his existence.

"What is the meaning of this!?" Valor continued. "Who is that human!?"

"He is Umbree's servant and the main reason I made it off Helia alive," Arden replied.

Valor was taken aback by Arden's words. "I-I do not understand. Maister Umbree..."

"Is no longer an ally or friend to us. He's aligned himself

with Orin and sought to offer the stone and my head as fidelity. That human is the reason he was able to offer neither."

Valor was visibly shaken by the news. Umbree had been his teacher during the time he had served on the council. And it was clear that his protege was unnerved by his former master's betrayal.

"So you brought the boy back here to heal him?" Luell piped up. "Honestly, I don't know why you wasted your energy, Arden. It's just a human. They have short lives anyway."

"I wasn't aware that our oath to protect all within the Six Realms came with caveats, Luell," Arden bit back, noticeably angered by her comment. Luell made a face as though she swallowed a lemon as she turned away from Arden's gaze.

"Calm yourself, Arden," Valor replied. "We can understand why you brought the human here, considering the assistance he offered. But I doubt it can be counted as a kindness. Even if he survives his injuries, I doubt he will be met with mercy when he is sent back to Helia. They do not take kindly to slaves who betray their master."

"Which is why I have no intention of returning him to Helia," Arden responded.

"What, are you planning on making him your servant?" Luell inquired.

"Actually, I was planning on making him my acolyte."

Both elves wore an expression as though Arden had slapped them, staring on in stupefied shock.

"...Ludicrous..." Luell whispered as Arden turned to her.

"The choosing of an acolyte is my choice, and mine alone. So states the Code of the Magi. Since I have so far not chosen an apprentice, a fact pointed out on numerous occasions, I would think members of the council would be overjoyed I had finally found a worthy successor."

"Worthy indeed!" Valor hissed. "You know full well the

weight of selecting a human as your protege! Your decision will not sit well with the council!"

Arden sighed. "Then might I suggest the council take the time to put pen to parchment and write down in great detail their grievances with my choice…"

He then scooped up his singed cloak, covered in blood, and began exiting the great hall, pushing open the double doors before adding to the two standing behind him. "…So I can tell them precisely where they can shove it."

Kye was floating in an ocean, weightless, slowly drifting along with the gentle waves that carried him. It was peaceful. As he stared up at the night sky, his vision was filled with thousands of stars, littering the black backdrop with diamonds. As Kye looked around, he saw an island off to the west. It was still a fair distance away, but Kye could make out a willow tree wafting in the breeze. The island itself was lit up with glowing balls of light that hovered just above the tree line. Kye wasn't sure what the balls of light were, but they made the island shine in the dead of night. Kye noticed a figure walking along the shore of the island. As he drifted closer, Kye could see the figure was a woman, decked out in a long, flowing white dress. The breeze caught the fabric, making it dance as yards of lace and silk streamed behind her with each step. Kye wanted to call out and ask who she was, but he found that no matter how many times he opened his mouth to speak, no words came out. He tried to turn, to swim toward the island, but his limbs were not listening to commands either. The woman, however, seemed to sense Kye floating off in the distance. She stopped in her path along the shore and turned to face him. One of the floating balls of light broke off from its place along the island and headed toward Kye. The closer it got, the more

Kye's vision was enveloped by the bright white light. When it finally stopped to hover above him, Kye had shut his eyes tight to prevent it from blinding him. The immense light was breaking through his eyelids as the silence was slowly replaced by the gentle songs of birds. As his senses slowly returned, Kye began to realize he wasn't floating in water but lying in a bed. As he gradually opened his eyes, he could see the room in which he lay was surrounded by white. It was fairly obvious to him that he must be dead. After all, bright white lights are often said to be what is seen when crossing over. Kye once again tried to move and sit up, surprised that, this time, his limbs actually responded to his command. But as he moved, it became apparent that everything hurt. A lightning bolt of pain shot down his right side, causing Kye to hiss through clenched teeth and immediately lay back down.

"Ah, he awakens," a voice stated. "I was beginning to wonder when that might happen."

Kye turned to see a woman standing in the white room with him. She was stationed in front of a tall shelf full of apothecary bottles in the corner. It was not the same woman he had seen walking along the shore of the island, Kye was certain of that. This woman looked to be in her early thirties and very pretty. She had ebony skin and deep fiery red hair that fell down her back in a spiral of curls. Her eyes were a vermillion shade, and she had an almost ethereal appearance, which further proved Kye's assumption that he was dead.

"Hello, Kye," she said warmly.

"Who...are you?" Kye questioned. His voice sounded hoarse, and his throat felt like sandpaper. The woman immediately walked over and collected a glass of water from a pitcher on a table in the corner. She deposited the water glass on Kye's bedside table before continuing.

"My name is Mireen. I am a healer for the High Council."

"High Council?" Kye questioned. Now that she was

closer, Kye noted her stature and the tell-tale point to her ears. "You're an elf."

"And you are a human," Mireen stated with a smile. "First I have ever treated, in fact. Although I think I did a pretty good job, if I do say so myself."

Kye tried once again to sit up and was finally able to push himself into an upright position with some effort. Mireen placed a pillow behind his back as he did so. Kye collected the glass of water, as the cooling liquid instantly quenched his thirst and soothed his throat. Looking around the room, Kye could see he was surrounded by marble and silver, with a decadence of silk and other fine goods strewn about. A floor-to-ceiling window was cracked open to allow a breeze as the finely stitched lace curtains swayed periodically.

"Where am I?" Kye questioned.

"The castle of Caelum Vallis," Mireen responded, "just outside the Silver City of Isalia."

"The land of the elves?" Kye asked in shock as Mireen nodded in response. The information slowly sunk in that he was no longer in Helia. "How did I get here?"

"Arden," Mireen replied. "He brought you here when you were injured in Helia."

Suddenly it all came rushing back. Umbree's manor, Lord Arden's visit, and then Kye was hit with a spell, and it all went black from there.

"Did Lord Arden make it out of the manor alright?" Kye inquired.

Mireen gave a smile and a nod. "Without a scratch, which I am told is no small thanks to you. You were the one we were worried about. You were in bad shape when you first arrived four days ago. I wasn't certain you would survive. But it seems like you are on the mend now. A few more days of rest should find you right as rain."

Four days? Kye looked down. His body, which had been

cut to ribbons by Umbree's ice spell, now only carried scratches. His right side was bandaged, and he was sore, but alive. He wasn't sure how that was possible, but Lady Mireen was apparently the cause. The fact that Lord Arden had brought him here was hard to fathom. Kye was bewildered that any mage would go to so much effort to save the life of a human.

"Speaking of Arden, he wished to know when you awoke," Mireen stated. "I shall go inform him."

Kye didn't get a chance to utter a response before Mireen headed for the infirmary door and stepped outside, leaving him in the opulent white room by himself. Kye's mind was playing through everything that had happened, while at the same time trying to grasp the fact he was in Isalia, the land of the elves. He had spent so much time reading about the Six Realms, but he never thought he would be able to visit another one. From everything he read about, Isalia was a lush landscape and temperate climate with greenery and rain. No harsh winds or sandstorms. Kye's eyes drifted to the window at the opposite end of the room. He lifted the covers off and threw his legs over the side of the bed. Every muscle in his body protested, but he was driven by determination. He had longed to see the other realms his entire life; he wouldn't miss the opportunity to see one now. Kye pushed himself into a standing position and leaned against the bedpost as he regained his composure. His legs were shaky, and the wound on his side clearly hadn't healed completely, given the spasms of pain that were periodically radiating from it. Kye pushed the pain aside as he stood up and started limping toward the open window. The twenty feet he walked felt like several miles. When Kye finally reached his destination, he held the wall by the window and caught his breath. As he pulled the curtain aside, he realized all the effort had been more than worth it.

Kye froze in stunned disbelief, looking out on a world of

green. Towering trees with drooping branches surrounded the grand building in which he resided. Emerald green grass stretched as far as the eye could see. Flowers every color of a desert sunset could be seen sprouting up all around him. The river running alongside the castle wall caught the afternoon sun and shimmered like sapphires. The air smelled fresh as the first rain after a drought. The spring breeze was soft and cool, unlike the harsh winds of Helia. Kye marveled at the sight around him, mesmerized by the breathtaking beauty everywhere he looked. The landscape was so stunning, it didn't look real. Like a dream brought to life. Kye had trouble believing what he was seeing. The books he had read didn't do it justice.

"It's quite a sight, isn't it?"

Kye turned around to see Arden standing by the door to the infirmary.

"Isalia, land of the elves and the eternal forest," Arden continued as he approached the window where Kye stood. "And my entitled brethren aside, one can't deny the view."

After looking out at the brightly painted landscape for a while, Arden leaned against the window sill and turned to Kye.

"How are you feeling?" he inquired.

"I'm fine, and I have you and Lady Mireen to thank for that," Kye replied earnestly, then hesitated for a moment before also adding, "but also...confused."

Arden chuckled. "Well, I'd say that's understandable given the sequence of events."

Arden left the window and walked over to a table in the corner of the room, pulling a wooden chair out from the small sitting area. He sat down and pulled a pipe out of his pocket. Arden loaded the end of it with some type of herb Kye had never seen before. He then muttered a word as the end of the pipe ignited. The smoke that filled the air reminded Kye of sandalwood and thyme. After several pulls of the pipe, Arden gestured toward Kye's sickbed.

"Have a seat," he stated. "Mireen will pitch a fit if she sees you up and about already."

Kye nodded in compliance, not wishing to anger the woman who had helped save his life. He walked back to his bed as effortlessly as he was able, biting back the desire to wince with each step he took. Once he was seated on his mattress again, Arden reached into his robes and pulled a familiar sight from his pocket. The yellow stone, the one that had been in Umbree's manor, glowed in the afternoon sun that streamed through the window. Arden held the stone up for Kye to see.

"Do you know what this is?" Arden inquired. Kye shook his head. Umbree had shared no knowledge of the stone with him; he had shared no knowledge about magic in general.

"This," Arden continued, "is called a creation stone. It is one of the first elemental stones created by our mage ancestors several thousand years ago, when we first learned to tame and control the elements. This one is Ventia, the wind stone. Now, these stones have been spoken of in tales but never found, until this one was located about fifty years ago by Umbree. The locations of the other four—Ignala the fire stone, Aquillia the water stone, Terrilla the earth stone, and Fulmenia the thunder stone—are still a mystery."

Kye inspected the gem of obvious value, curious how his previous goblin master had come to acquire it. "How did Umbree get it?"

"By sheer dumb luck," Arden replied. "He found it in a tomb, during a mission on Brooma when he was still a well-respected member of the council. Back then, Umbree seemed to possess some semblance of honor, and was—and still is—a powerful mage. The Council seemed confident to leave the gem in his care for safekeeping. However, as time went on,

Umbree became less preoccupied with duty and honor, and his character leaned more avaricious in nature. It wasn't long before the Council wondered whether the priceless heirloom they wished to protect would still be seen as priceless in Umbree's eyes."

"They thought he would hawk it?" Kye questioned, amused.

"It had crossed their mind," Arden agreed. "But Valor is the current leader of the Council, and Umbree's protege. He feverishly argued his former master could be trusted with the stone in his care. The other members were not so certain. They wished to bring the stone to Caelum Vallis for safekeeping but were concerned about angering Valor. I, however, held no such concern. So I volunteered to go retrieve it. I never thought for a second Umbree would be foolish enough to try to kill a maister over the coin he could make by selling it, but it seems as though Orin offered him something worth the effort."

Kye looked at the ancient artifact far older than much of magic itself. It appeared in perfect condition despite its age.

"What can it do?" Kye inquired. Arden shrugged slightly in response.

"It gives a boost of wind magic to any mage holding it," Arden replied. "It can help calm winds, summon tornados, basically anything that a maister worth their salt can do. It is considered more of a relic amongst mages nowadays."

Kye's eyes narrowed in response. "So it was just a trinket."

"To us, yes," Arden replied. "Not to Orin."

"How can you be sure?"

"Well, I can't say for certain, but let's say I prefer to err on the side of caution. Orin practices dark magic. He is one of the most powerful and dangerous mages of our time. He has no use for a wind chime like this unless he can use it to cause damage. While this may be a relic to us, I'm betting Orin's interest in it is far more sinister. And whatever reason that may be, I am damn well determined to keep it far away from him."

Kye stared at the stone for a while, absorbing the information Lord Arden had just given him. He had never heard of Orin, nor had he heard Umbree ever mention him before that night. But if he was as bad as Arden described, then he could understand his desire to keep any possible weapon out of his hands.

"So, what now?" Kye questioned.

"The first step is to research more about the creation stones, to try and understand why Orin would want them. I have been digging through texts as far back as I could to try and decipher just that."

"And...what will be done with me?" Kye inquired.

Arden paused for a moment before responding. "Well, we can't send you back to Helia—that much is certain." He stated finally, "Slaves who betray their masters are met with a short life of misery. And that will be paradise compared to what Umbree will do if he finds you."

Kye had guessed as much. As such, he wondered why Arden had bothered to save him in the first place.

"One option is, you could remain here," Arden continued.

"In Isalia?" Kye asked.

"In Caelum Vallis, to be more precise," Arden clarified.

"Does the High Council allow slaves within the castle?"

"They haven't," Arden answered. "Only maisters and acolytes are allowed within the castle walls. Which is why I was thinking of you remaining here not as a servant, but as my apprentice."

Kye chuckled slightly as he grabbed the glass of water to once again soothe his parched throat. As he set the glass back down, his eyes drifted back toward Arden, who was staring deadpan at Kye as if waiting for an answer. The realization slowly dawned on Kye that Arden's statement wasn't meant to be funny.

"You're...serious?" Kye inquired.

"Completely," stated Arden. Kye was thunderstruck. He gawked at Arden, mouth open and mind blank. This must be a joke, but Arden wasn't laughing.

"Are you...mad?" Kye uttered in disbelief.

Arden chuckled as he took another pull from his pipe. "Depends on who you ask. I've heard arguments on both sides."

"And yet I feel they'd be united in this matter!" Kye retorted.

"And why is that?"

"Humans cannot be mages."

"Now that's not technically true," argued Arden. "Humans have never been allowed to become mages, but there is actually nothing suggesting that humans aren't just as capable of learning the craft as any other race."

"A slave would not be welcome here," Kye clarified. "The Council wouldn't stand for it."

"The Council can sit, stand, or roll the fuck over, for all I care," retorted Arden. "They have no say. It is the right of a maister to choose his own apprentice. So selecting you as an acolyte is my choice, not theirs."

"You would incite their wrath!"

"Hell, kid, that's a weekly occurrence," Arden muttered dismissively as he blew out a puff of smoke.

Kye was silent for a long while. He was trying to discover Arden's true purpose. For as much as he wanted to believe his offer was in good faith, he was a mage. And Kye's experience with them had told him they were not to be trusted.

"Why?" he finally inquired. "Why me?"

Arden leaned forward in his chair.

"I could ask you the same question," he replied. "Why did you help me?"

"I told you. I overheard Umbree. He intended to kill you."

"Right, but that doesn't answer my question." Arden clarified, "You knew me for less than a day, Kye. You didn't owe me anything. Yet you damn near died trying to get me and the stone out of Umbree's manor. Why?"

"What should I have done?" asked Kye. "Ignore what I heard? Gone to sleep? Let Umbree kill you if he wanted to?"

"Why not?" Arden shrugged as Kye stared back incredulously.

"It wasn't your fight," Arden continued. "It was a battle between mages. If he wished to kill me, you had no reason to get involved. No use risking yourself. After all, Umbree was the cowardly bastard with the plan."

"And to know of it but do nothing, just what would that make me?" Kye shot back.

Arden flashed a knowing smile as he replied, "Exactly."

Kye was now thoroughly confused. He couldn't tell if Arden was appreciative of his assistance or chastising his choice to get involved. He seemed to be teetering between the two.

"Do you know what the Magi High Council is?" Arden inquired.

"Arrogant omnipotence," Kye muttered as Arden laughed out in response.

"Well, that may be what they have become now," Arden chuckled. "But it's not what they started out to be. The forming of the High Council is as old as the creation stones themselves. It was a coalition of the strongest magic wielders with just one purpose: protection of all within the Six Realms. The oath a maister of the High Council takes is to use their power, and even their lives, in service of every living being. But over time, that oath has become less and less important.

Serving on the council has become less about duty and honor and more about status and money. Many sneer at the other races they swore to protect, and benevolence is a dying trait."

Arden pointed at Kye. "And then, there is you. Indentured into servitude simply because of your race. You would be well within your right to feel not a drop of sympathy for another non-human, given the station that was forced on you. Yet as soon as you heard my life was on the line—or the lives of countless others—you sprang to help. You displayed a compassion that was never shown to you. And without magical assistance at your disposal, you stood your ground against a goblin maister, armed with nothing more than a letter opener. Now if that's not brave, I don't know what the hell is. So if you're asking me why...I guess the short answer would be, I think you could be the best of us."

Kye was speechless. He had never heard himself spoken of in such a favorable light, and certainly not from a mage. He didn't know what to say. Arden was being far too generous; Kye was neither brave nor noble. His desire to help had been driven by fear and without a drop of forethought. And he was honored that Arden thought him worthy, but a small thread of doubt was also pulling in the back of his mind.

"If I refuse...I will be sent back to Helia?" Kye clarified.

Arden raised an eyebrow in response. "Gods, kid, if I wanted you dead, I would've left you on the floor of Umbree's study."

Arden sighed and clasped his hands together, being careful with his words to help Kye understand his intention. "If you refuse, you will be able to remain in Isalia if you wish. I will make sure you are given some land. If you want nothing more than a life of quiet, you can have it. This offer I'm making isn't meant to be an ultimatum. It's just the one thing you've been denied your entire life."

Kye cocked his head slightly in confusion as Arden clarified, "A choice. And it's not an easy one at that. So, think carefully before you make your decision."

Kye pondered Arden's words. It was true—he had never been given a choice; no human ever had. Until now, he had not thought it possible he ever would. He assumed he would be in service to Umbree the entirety of his life, no matter how long or short that may be. Arden rose from his seat at the table and placed his pipe back into his pocket. He pushed the chair back into place before heading toward the door.

"I'll come back to check on you later," stated Arden as he opened the infirmary door. "In the meantime...get some rest, kid." He gave Kye a reassuring glance before closing the door behind him.

Alone in the silence of the room, Kye leaned back against the pillow and closed his eyes. He listened to the branches swaying in the wind while he tried to organize his thoughts. His body was tired, but his mind was wide awake. For the first time in his life...he was free. His future was in his own hands, to shape as he saw fit. So the question that remained: what did he want it to be?

CHAPTER 4
An Atypical Acolyte

Kye didn't sleep a wink, lying in the infirmary staring at the ceiling all night. He was replaying over and over in his head the words Arden had said and the choice he had laid before him. Kye had thought of rejecting it outright, simply taking a life of quiet, away from crowds. It wouldn't be so bad. He'd be alone, but he'd have books, and he wouldn't be in service to anyone. And the prospect of becoming one of the mages he had resented for so long seemed abhorrent. But mulling it over, he was reminded that while Arden may be a mage, he was nothing like Umbree. He genuinely seemed to care about others beyond his own interests. And an acolyte wasn't the same as a servant. Not to mention, he had gone to such an extent to save Kye's life. While he had often thought of mages with disdain, he could not discount that Arden seemed different, honorable. If his offer was in earnest, would it be so bad to become a mage like him?

"Good morning," Mireen sang brightly as she entered the infirmary. "I trust you slept well?"

Kye slowly sat up to greet her, wincing once again from the wound on his side. Mireen noticed his discomfort.

"Your injuries are still mending, I'm afraid. But this—" Mireen placed a bottle on the side table next to Kye's bed. "—should help with that."

Kye picked up the bottle and inspected the swirling orange liquid within as Mireen went about refilling the water basin and pulling out fresh bandages.

"What is it?" Kye inquired.

"A healing potion. It contains certain magical plants and herbs, collected from Isalia and other realms, that have been proven to help treat wounds and lessen pain. It will help speed your recovery."

Kye opened the bottle and took a deep breath. He couldn't pinpoint any spice within that was familiar to him. If he had to pick something close, he would say the potion smelled like mint, garlic, and juniper. It had a very strong, bitter scent to it, one that made Kye instantly retract the bottle from his nose.

"It does not smell the best," Mireen noted his reaction. "But it works far better than it tastes, I can assure you."

Kye eyed the bottle carefully, taking a deep breath, and quickly chugged the entire contents, trying his best not to gag. Once the bottle was empty, he set it back down on the table. As Kye tried to clear the last remaining taste of the potion from his mouth, he noticed that Mireen had been right. Almost immediately, he felt less sore, and sitting up felt easier. She smiled in acknowledgment.

"Better?" she asked.

"Much," Kye replied. Mireen grinned brightly, adding "Good" as she went back to setting up vials on the table. Kye realized that he had never gotten a chance to properly thank her for saving his life.

"Thank you, Lady Mireen," Kye stated sincerely, "for all you've done."

"Your thanks is appreciated but completely unnecessary, Kye," Mireen replied, collecting the empty potion bottle. "I am happy to help."

Mireen, like Arden, did not seem bothered by the fact that Kye was human. She did not speak down to him or look at him with disgust. It was a reaction he was unfamiliar with after his life on Helia. But one he was grateful for, nonetheless.

"Are healing potions like that rare?" Kye asked, gesturing toward the empty bottle in Mireen's hand.

"Not necessarily rare. But the strength and effectiveness depends on the one who produced it. Potions made by healers such as myself are far more powerful than ones whipped up by a mage who does not possess the talent, such as Arden."

Kye remembered Arden stating that all mages could heal to various degrees. He then thought of the spell Arden had recited after Umbree attacked him but could not think of the words.

"When I was injured on Helia, I remember Lord Arden chanted a spell..."

"*Sylven tela,*" Mireen instantly replied. "In Ancient, it literally means 'stitch skin.' It's a basic healing spell mages will use in the field to mend superfluous wounds or stop bleeding. But for more serious injuries, the assistance of a healer and potions, such as the one you just drank, is often required."

It was strange to Kye that Mireen answered his questions without hesitation. All the time in Umbree's service, he had not learned even a sliver of the information Mireen was relaying to him freely.

"You are very open with your knowledge of magic," Kye noted with an air of bewilderment.

Mireen looked confused. "Is that unusual?"

"Magic is forbidden to humans on Helia," Kye explained,

"and the punishment for trying to learn is severe. Even outside of Helia, I doubt many would be happy to know of a human learning the craft."

"Ah," Mireen stated in understanding. "Well, since you have not been outside Helia until now, I feel the need to share a secret with you that is well-known throughout the Six Realms..."

Mireen leaned slightly closer as Kye waited with rapt attention. In one exaggerated breath, she whispered, "Idiots are everywhere."

Kye chuckled as Mireen added with a grin, "I find it best to pay them no mind or risk becoming one of them yourself. Besides, if you do decide to take Arden's offer, you will be learning far more intricate spells than just basic healing magic."

"You would have no objection then?" Kye asked. "To a human learning the craft?"

Mireen crossed her arms and pondered for a second. "Well, I suppose that depends on the human. If you are asking if I would have an issue with a thief, or a ruffian, or some brute becoming a mage, then I would have to say most definitely that I do."

She smiled at Kye. "But if you are asking me if I would have an issue with YOU becoming a mage, then I would have to say most certainly not. I rather think it would be a welcome addition, in fact."

Kye fell silent to her praise, uncertain of how to respond.

"Your race is not important, Kye," Mireen continued. "Despite what others may say to the contrary. Arden asked you to be his acolyte because he sees in you the same thing I do. You are courageous, intelligent, and kind. And those are qualities that I am sorry to say are in rather short supply nowadays. Especially amongst mages."

Kye shifted slightly, uncomfortable with the description she had given of his character. Mireen noticed his unease.

"What?" she inquired.

"I believe you and Lord Arden think too much of me," Kye stated honestly.

"Hmm," Mireen mumbled in acknowledgment, thinking over his interpretations. "Or," she finally stated, "could it be that you think too little of yourself?"

Kye met her gaze as she beamed back at him. He could tell she was being earnest. In truth, he wasn't sure what he was capable of. But it was apparent Mireen and Arden saw promise in him. Could they both be wrong?

"Now," Mireen stated, grabbing strips of white cloth from the armoire, "let us address those bandages, shall we?"

Arden steered clear of Kye for the next few days, checking in with Mireen on his condition instead. He wanted to not only give him time to recuperate but a chance to thoroughly think over his decision, without pressure. If Kye chose to learn the craft, he would be the first human mage in history—a decision that could very well paint a target on his back for those who thought humans were unfit. Of course, should he wish to leave Caelum Vallis and never deal with another mage as long as he lived, Arden couldn't really blame him. He had never agreed with the servitude forced on humans by some of his mage peers. The belief that mages were above any race was the opposite of everything they were supposed to stand for.

A few days later, Mireen told Arden that Kye was completely healed and ready to leave the infirmary at any time. Arden thought it as good a time as any to see if he had arrived at a decision. Opening the door to the infirmary, Arden was met by a familiar sight. Kye was once again positioned in front of the two-story window, seated in one of the chairs he pulled from the table in the corner. He held a book about Isalia in his lap and was exchanging glances between the pages and the view. A spring storm raged outside, with blasts of cool air rushing in through the open window. The sky was steel gray as rain hammered against the roof outside, interspersed with the booming sounds of thunder in the distance. Honestly, Arden considered it to be abysmal weather, but Kye seemed transfixed by it, nonetheless.

"I see you haven't tired of the view," Arden commented. Kye's head spun around hearing Arden's voice before nodding in agreement.

"I honestly don't see myself ever getting tired of this view," he replied, closing the book and putting his full attention on Arden. Arden approached his seat and cast another glance out the window.

"I'm not sure what there is to look at today," Arden commented. "It's not really sightseeing weather."

Kye was silent for a moment before replying. "Well, I guess that's a matter of perspective. When you grow up in a world scorched by sun, rain is a welcome occurrence."

"Valid point," Arden conceded. Kye turned his attention back to the storm outside.

"I suppose...the same could be said for me," Kye began. "I have spent my whole life hating mages, but then again, the only mages I have ever known were Umbree and his friends. To judge an entire group on the actions of a few... That, too, is a matter of perspective."

"I take it that means you now see mages in a more favorable light?" Arden inquired.

"Well, a select few at least," Kye responded earnestly. "But if I could become a mage like those few, then maybe even I could make a difference. At the very least, I'd get to see with my own eyes the realms I have only read about."

"Would it be worth it?" Arden questioned. "It will not be an easy path, especially for a human like you."

"Never meant to be a cobbled road," Kye muttered almost under his breath. Arden caught him with a questioning gaze as Kye clarified, "The things most worthwhile are often the most difficult."

"And the most dangerous," Arden stated. "I'm not going to sugarcoat it—the dangers we face could very easily kill you."

Kye paused for a moment, reminded of his rather recent brush with death. "Humans are well acquainted with death, since it visits us more often than other races. I don't wish for it, but neither will I run from it," he stated firmly.

Kye's expression was unwavering, and Arden could see he had clearly made up his mind. He set the book down and rose to face Arden. Placing a hand over his chest, Kye gave a deep bow, stating, "I would be honored to be your acolyte, Lord Arden."

Arden chuckled and shook his head in response. "Well, in that case, stop calling me lord. It's just Arden."

Kye lifted his head and smiled back, nodding in acknowledgment.

Arden had honestly never thought of taking on an apprentice before he had met Kye. He had spent enough time at Caelum Vallis, watching the chosen, spoiled, little rich brats flaunt the title "acolyte" without ever understanding its meaning. From the time of his own acolyte days, Arden had thought being on the council was essentially pledging your life to helping others. It seemed as though many others saw it as a status symbol—a title to impress with, nothing more. But Kye was different. Humans had long been considered fragile, pitiful, incapable. They could break easily, die easily, and were only useful as servants. Kye, however, had demonstrated more courage in the past few days than some mages had their entire life. As such, Arden was certain he would demonstrate to all who doubted it that humans were not the weak creatures they were thought to be.

"Well, I'm fairly certain by this point you have memorized every inch of the infirmary," Arden stated. "Are you feeling well enough for a walk?"

When Kye nodded, Arden added, "Then follow me, kid."

Kye trailed behind Arden as he led them out of the infirmary and to a flight of stairs leading down to the main floor below them. As soon as they stepped off the bottom stair, Kye gaped at the sight before him. The passage opened up to an enormous atrium. Spires of silver jutted out along the walls of the huge castle. White marble covered the floor; every door leading off the main hall had a unique ornate design cast in silver and jewels. Kye's eyes drifted upward. The ceiling was made entirely of glass, some fifty feet above his head. He could see the rain pounding down upon it. Watching the storm from such a vantage point was mesmerizing.

The great hall was bustling with a variety of mages from all races. Kye could see orcs, goblins, elves, and dwarves standing together in different clusters about the main floor. They were all decked out in fitted robes made of silk and other fine cloth. Kye was wearing a white tunic and pants given to him by Mireen. He imagined it was because his previous outfit had been coated in blood and cut to shreds. These garments were by far the finest cloth he had ever worn, yet they paled in comparison to the clothing around him. Kye noticed that everyone he passed stopped their conversation to turn to look at him. And he knew all too well it had nothing to do with his attire. As Kye weaved through the great hall, it was apparent humans were not a common occurrence here.

Arden was completely unfazed by the onlookers, continuing to lead Kye through one door and then the next.

"I'll point out a few important places you'll want to know about," Arden stated while leading Kye around another bend. "You'll get more accustomed to where things are in time."

A variety of twists and turns later, he stopped in front of a pair of double doors at least ten feet tall. They had the same kind of oak tree carved on the front that Kye had seen engraved on Arden's flask. In this case, however, the base of the tree bridged the two doors, its branches stretching out to the edges of the entryway.

"I have seen this symbol before," Kye stated, looking over the grand tree.

Arden gestured to the sigil on the front of the doors. "That is Yggdrasil, the tree of wisdom and knowledge. A sacred deity to elf kind. We elves value knowledge and wisdom." He then noted dryly, "It's compassion and understanding we often lack."

Arden pushed open the double doors and entered. As Kye followed, he was met with an inspiring sight. Light streamed in from a giant stained-glass image of Yggdrasil on the north wall, front and center of a grand library. Looking upward, Kye could see rows and rows of bookshelves that seemed to never end. The stairs spiraled upward, each level opening up to a brand-new row of books. Kye guessed the library must be four stories tall. He was captivated looking up to the seemingly endless rows. Umbree's library had been a pebble in the ocean by comparison. Arden strode ahead, and Kye had to snap back to attention to keep from losing sight of him.

"Most of the books in here are beyond your capabilities as of now," Arden stated as he led Kye through row after row of wooden shelves. "Not to mention the majority are written entirely in Ancient, the language of the magi, as old as the creation stones themselves. So don't be pulling random volumes off the shelves and practicing incantations when you have no idea what they do. There have been many acolytes greeted by an early grave attempting magic beyond their abilities. Nonetheless, knowledge is power, and this is where you will gain it. A majority of your time will probably be spent here delving into one of these dusty old books."

"I would gladly spend a lifetime here." Arden looked back to see Kye, gawking at the dizzying rows of bookcases in amazement. Arden smiled in response.

"A fan of the written word, I take it?"

"I read every book I could in Umbree's library," said Kye, closely inspecting a book whose cover seemed to be made of some type of skin. Kye was certain he didn't want to know what creature had donated it. "But this collection puts his to shame."

"Indeed," Arden responded. "These volumes come from several millennia of collecting knowledge from mages and philosophers all over the Six Realms. Even if you had the lifespan of an elf, you could never hope to read them all. So we will focus on the knowledge that can be obtained within a human's lifetime. But first things first. Knowing the language of the magi is essential to reading almost all of these books."

Kye nodded in determination. Arden continued his tour through the library, pointing out different sections and areas of study. Kye had never known there were different proficiencies of magic, but listening to Arden, he learned there were nine schools of study. Alchemy was focused on brewing potions and elixirs. Evocation was offensive magic. Conjuration had to do with summoning of spirits, and teleportation was travel magic, including the creation of portals between worlds. Enchantment focused on manipulation of the mind and senses. Divination was reading the signs of nature to foretell fate. Remedium magic was the mending of wounds and the curing of sickness. Transmutation was transforming a body or object from one thing to another. The one area considered off limits to all mages was necromancy, dark magic and manipulation of the dead. As Arden continued, Kye couldn't help but feel overwhelmed and anxious. It was an honor Arden thought him capable of being his acolyte, but it did fill him with apprehension about disappointing him. He couldn't understand how he could perform the feats Arden had listed so nonchalantly. He was human. He had never spoken to the spirits, brewed a potion, or enchanted anyone in the slightest. He felt as though there was a canyon, long and vast, between where he was and where Arden thought he could be. And standing on the precipice looking out, he hadn't the slightest clue of how he was ever going to jump it.

Arden gave Kye a cursory tour of the library before guiding Kye back out to the castle's main atrium toward their next destination. Kye followed closely behind Arden, convinced that if he lost sight of him, he would be lost forever. The sheer size of the castle was intimidating—twisting hallways leading off in all directions, and towers with winding staircases that led up and up, far past Kye's line of sight. As Arden led him through the maze of marble and silver, he thought the first thing he would need would be a compass. Arden stopped outside two wooden doors, with grapes and fruit etched into the oak.

"This is the dining hall," he declared upon pushing the doors open. Kye could see long tables spread out across the width of the giant room, with seating for a few hundred people. At the head of the room were several large fires, with pots boiling over and the smell of a stew wafting through the air. A short, stocky, round dwarven woman with blond frizzy hair stood over a very large pot, cutting vegetables and humming to herself. As Arden walked toward her, she glanced up at him.

"Ain't seen the likes of you in here in a while, Ard." She smiled. "Usually be requestin' meals brought to yer tower."

"I'm not much for communal dining," Arden replied. "But I wished to introduce my apprentice to you. Kye, this is Celeste, the chef for all of Caelum Vallis. Celeste, this is my acolyte, Kye."

Kye bowed respectfully. "It is a pleasure to meet you, Lady Celeste."

Celeste turned her gaze from Arden to Kye. A sudden shout caused Kye to snap his head up. Celeste came rushing out from behind the counters toward him. There was concern clearly written on her face, and Kye's first thought was it must be because he was human. It would be in line with all the other looks he had received walking the halls. Celeste grabbed Kye's hand and held out his arm, shaking her head from side to side.

"Would ya look at him, ain't nothing but skin and bones. Don't ya eat, boy?"

"Uh...y-yes," Kye stuttered, caught off guard by Celeste's reaction.

"Well, not nearly enough, by the looks of it. It's no doubt dis one's doing," Celeste commented, shooting an accusatory glare at Arden. She then leaned in to Kye and muttered, "Don't you be takin to an elf's diet, lad, munchin' on plants like yer grazin'. Else you be lookin like this scrawny spindle."

"I heard that," grunted Arden. Celeste spun around with hands on her hips.

"Aye and you was meant to!"

Celeste turned back and patted Kye's hand comfortingly. "Don't ya worry, I'll see ya get a proper meal brought to ya. Something that'll put some meat on yer bones!"

"Thank you, Lady Celeste." Kye smiled back.

"An' you can stop that 'Lady' nonsense. No one to stand on ceremony here. Celeste is fine."

Kye bowed his head slightly and replied, "As you wish, Celeste."

Celeste nodded at Kye and grinned. "Got manners, this one," she stated before looking to Arden, "Obviously not somethin' he learned from you."

"I'm suddenly reminded why I don't frequent the kitchen that often," Arden muttered.

Celeste laughed out loud. "He's a stodger, this one. Ayes convinced he would never find himself an acolyte. It's a pleasure to have ya, Kye."

Kye was genuinely grateful. Celeste was the first person he had run into today who was welcoming to him. And Arden seemed to respect her, despite their verbal sparring.

"Well, will you lot be sticking around for dinner? Fixin' a stew, should be ready soon."

"A kind offer, Celeste, but we still have other places to see," Arden noted. "If you could, bring up a few bowls..."

"To yur tower," Celeste added with an eye roll. "Aye, aye, I know, ya antisocial bugger. I'll be bringing your plates up in a bit."

"Thank you, Celeste. Your disposition, as usual, is a breath of fresh air," Arden added with a grin as Celeste grunted in response. Arden gave her a slight bow before starting to head toward the kitchen exit.

Seeing his master leaving, Kye bowed to Celeste as well, stating, "It was a pleasure to meet you, Celeste."

Celeste smiled back at Kye and said, "Aye, same to you, Kye. Don't ya be stranger now, ya hear?" Kye nodded in agreement and followed Arden back out to the castle's main hall.

They made several other stops outside the castle once the storm had passed. Arden showed Kye the location of the castle greenhouse, the sparring grounds, the pond, the stables, and meeting hall for the maisters of the High Council. The meeting hall was a grand building, separate from the castle. It was at least three stories with the same marble design as the main building, but it also hosted a number of guest quarters apart from the main hall. Arden told him that the purpose of the meeting hall was to host guests from all over the Six Realms who came to plead their case while the council was in session. After the cases were stated, the council would then decide if the assistance of a mage was in order, or if they would merely act as diplomats to settle the dispute. Kye was surprised by the explanation. He had always gotten the impression that mages had no limits in using their magic to tip the scales of power in any way they saw fit. But according to Arden, their goal was to maintain balance and order, and any mage taking it upon themselves to disrupt that would be punished severely.

As the sun began to once again dip back to the horizon, Arden led Kye back through the halls to the far east wing of the palace. He opened a solid wooden door leading to a twisting set of stairs that seemed to reach to the heavens. As they began to scale the stairs, Kye could see out of the tiny portholes in the staircase, watching the landscape shrink the higher and higher they climbed. Kye had plenty of practice running up and down flights of stairs in Umbree's manor, but even he could feel himself getting winded as they continued to scale upward. After what seemed like an eternity, Arden finally stopped at a landing and opened yet another wooden door.

"And this is where you'll spend most of your time," he added, stepping inside the room.

Kye entered a two-story, circular room. Most of Caelum Vallis was ostentatiously decorated in white, silver, and silk. This room, however, was eclectic and homey with wooden rafters and gray stone. The floor was made of well-fitted wide walnut boards. It reminded Kye of a cottage set atop a mountain. Within the tower was a seating area in front of a fireplace. A high-backed chair and a sofa, both upholstered in a deep brown leather, were positioned in front of it. On the far side of the room was a small wooden dining table next to a bar. There were double doors leading out to a large veranda that gave an amazing view of the landscape. Past the fireplace was another small staircase leading up to a loft on the second story, with some sort of potion bench tucked beneath them.

"This is the common area," Arden explained. "My quarters are up the stairs there. And yours are over here."

Arden opened a room to the right of the entryway. Kye entered a moderately sized bedroom. A smaller fireplace off to the left hosted a side table and plush armchair. There was a tall bookcase filled with a variety of volumes off to the right. The center wall of the room framed a large bay window that let in an immense quantity of light and whose sill was cluttered with several different types of herbs in porcelain pots. A thick mattress rested on a platform in the far-left corner of the room, right next to a full-size wardrobe.

"Your washroom is through there." Arden pointed to the door to the right of his bed. Kye peeked his head inside to see a full bathroom complete with a claw-foot bathtub, sink, and indoor running water. Indoor water had been considered a rare luxury in Helia. Even Umbree's manor didn't possess it. Kye remembered many cold wash bucket baths in the dead of winter. Not to mention the arduous task of carrying buckets of hot water upstairs to the second floor whenever Umbree wished to bathe. Kye walked over to marvel at the bed, placing a hand upon it. It had a warm quilt and a feather pillow. He had never had his own bed, unless you counted his pallet in the wood shed, which he really didn't. In the shack with his mother, they had just slept on mats on the ground.

"It's not much," Arden commented as Kye's eyes darted around the room that now belonged to him. "But I value solitude above all else. Far away from distraction. And you can't get much further away than this."

Kye wasn't sure how much more lavish you could get.

This was already a far finer room than you could have found in Umbree's manor. No cracked windows, leaky roofs, or furniture splintering from age. It was all well-crafted, well kept, and certainly leaps and bounds above what he was accustomed to. Arden walked over and opened the wardrobe in the room. "You'll find your robes in here," he said, showing Kye some that already hung in his closet. "They are required dress for all mages of the High Council. The cloth is enchanted and serves as light protection from offensive spells."

Kye pulled out one of the robes to get a better look at it. The first of several was deep blue. The fabric seemed a mixture of cotton and silk, with a light sheen to it. The top portion resembled a fitted tunic with a collar. The bottom half was a much looser fit, with a hem extended down to the ankles. There was a silver design around the sleeves and buttons in the center. A thick leather belt looped around the middle. It closely resembled the robes Arden wore, although it was far less detailed.

"You'll also need this," Arden added, handing Kye a golden amulet. There was a star sigil in the center of the medallion, but Kye had no idea what it meant. "Later, you'll learn to focus your thoughts to communicate with it. But for now, it will help center your magic when you cast. Keep it on always. It is the sign of a mage of the High Council."

Kye put the golden chain around his neck, the sigil coming to rest across his heart. He inspected the amulet in his hand, turning it over in the light. A question nagged at him, and it was one he felt compelled to have answered.

"Not many within the Six Realms can wield magic," Kye began carefully. "In fact, there are few by comparison that can."

Arden nodded in acknowledgment. "True."

"Then are you sure that I am one of them?" Kye inquired.

"Absolutely," Arden replied without hesitation. Kye was stunned by his rapid-fire response.

"How can you be sure?"

"Because of the creation stone," Arden continued. "Magic recognizes magic. If a non-magic wielder tried to grab a magical item such as that, the item would react and protect itself, almost always resulting in injury to the user trying to wield it. But you were able to swipe that stone from Umbree as easily as if you were lifting a pocket watch. And the stone had no issue with you holding it."

Kye thought back. Now that Arden mentioned it, Kye had felt an aura emanating from the stone, though he hadn't thought it was unusual at the time. He remembered Arden warning him not to touch the stone. And he had seemed surprised when he had seen Kye holding it. Kye had assumed that was relief that he had been able to retrieve it from Umbree.

"Trust me, kid, you got the gift." Arden added, "The only thing you're missing is instruction. Which is what I am here for. So, I suggest you get settled in." Arden headed toward the door of Kye's room. "Your lessons begin tomorrow."

Kye felt a renewed sense of encouragement as Arden left. Knowing that he had the gift meant learning the craft was an attainable goal. To be able to control fire within his palm, summon wind, and bend the elements to his whim had always been nothing more than a dream. Kye was slowly realizing that the dream could come true. Granted, it was still a long road to reach that destination. But right now, that deep canyon he stood before felt just a little bit smaller.

Umbree was pacing back and forth in a small forest clearing. It was the dead of night, with the light of a full moon shining through the trees. They were currently hidden in a camp in Proxa, far away from any villages. Umbree had cast a blood circle around their camp, masking their presence from anyone attempting to scry for them. Belthier and Torha stood off to the side, crouched on rocks and noticeably on edge. It had taken several days for them to cover their tracks from the Council and reach out to Orin. Wishing to speak in person, Umbree had suggested this destination for a meeting. Umbree still wasn't certain how to tell him that he had failed, not only at killing Arden but at keeping the stone in his possession. Orin would undoubtedly be upset. Which could very well mean death for Umbree. But not even death would be an escape if Orin wished it so. Umbree wracked his brain to try and think of an explanation that would placate him. And hopefully preserve Orin's goodwill and their bargain. He was so deep in thought, he did not notice the figure appearing in the brush behind him. Nor the one walking toward him through the trees. Their shadows were silent, every step light and swift.

"Umbree."

The figure from the tree spoke, and Umbree, Torha and Belthier all jumped in response. A white-haired male elf stood before the group, his pale skin practically glowing in the moonlight. His crimson eyes were clearly visible, even in the darkness. He wore a smile from ear to ear that was no doubt meant to be welcoming but instead unsettled anyone who looked upon it.

"Apologies, my friends," Orin started in a raspy and quiet voice, for he did not need to shout. When he spoke, all listened. "I didn't mean to frighten you."

"O-of course not, Lord Orin," Umbree replied with a deep bow. "We are thankful you could meet us here."

"Certainly," Orin replied. "I heard about your troubles,

Umbree. I am glad you were able to find a safe location, free from the prying eyes of the Council."

"Thank you for your concern, my lord," Umbree replied.

"I also heard that you lost your house to a fire," Orin continued. "Pity, it was quite beautiful. You have my condolences, my friend."

"Y-yes, thank you, my lord."

Umbree was unsettled; why wasn't Orin mentioning the stone? Or Arden? Surely, if he knew all that, he must know what happened—Umbree's failure.

"My lord, if I may," Umbree started, "I would like a chance to explain—"

Orin looked toward him, still wearing an eerie smile. "Explain?"

"Y-yes, about what happened with Arden? H-how I lost the stone?"

Orin waved a hand dismissively. "You needn't worry about such trifles now, my friend. Not when you have the Council after you. You must worry about yourself first."

A second figure stepped out from the brush, causing the group to spin around in surprise. It was clearly a shifter by his reptilian eyes. His large form was formidable, and he had long black hair that blended in with the darkness around him. He gazed down at the group as though they were prey.

"No need to be alarmed," Orin stated. "This is Amon, my right hand. He will be continuing the search for the creation stone."

Umbree's head snapped around in shock.

"B-but the deal we struck!?" Umbree asked, his voice sounding desperate.

"You did not hold up your end of it, my friend," Orin replied. "Surely you don't expect me to hold up mine."

"Wait...My lord, please," Umbree begged. "I-I can get the

stone back. I know where it is, where it must be. It is at Caelum Vallis."

"The fortress of the High Council, in the heart of Isalia," Orin added. "It is no simple task, strolling in there."

"But I can get in—there are ways to get in. I was a member of the High Council for many years. I know that land and the castle like the back of my hand. I will be more prepared this time. There will be no mistakes. Please, my lord, I am still your best bet at getting you what you wish."

Orin sighed and set down on a nearby log. He was silent for some time as the group looked on with bated breath.

"Very well," Orin replied. "I think you will find that I am a firm believer in second chances. Not only that, but I will assist you, Umbree."

Umbree was gracious but cautious as he asked, "Y-you will, my lord?"

"Of course," Orin answered with that unsettling smile. "After all, helping you helps both of us."

Umbree bowed deeply. "You are too kind, my lord. Rest assured, I will not fail you again."

"Certainly not," Orin agreed. "After all, no one who serves me makes that same mistake twice."

Umbree shivered slightly at the veiled threat as Orin and Amon turned to leave the camp. Umbree felt it urgent to convey to Orin that this would not be a quick endeavor.

"It will take time, my lord!" Umbree blurted out. Orin turned back at the sudden outburst, glaring down at Umbree.

"Th-the Council will be on edge," Umbree clarified. "No doubt Arden has relayed to them my interest in the stone or mentioned me giving it to you. It will take time for them to relax, for an opening to present itself, to find its whereabouts, my lord."

Orin flashed his most egregious smile in response, his cold expression shining out from behind his crimson eyes.

"Worry not, my dear friend," Orin assured Umbree. "You will find I am nothing if not patient."

CHAPTER 5
The Call of the Council

Saiyah sat at a small table in the library as the afternoon sun streamed in through the window. The rays were illuminating her dark brown hair, casting the colors of the gems populating her charm bracelet to paint the page of the tome she was reading. Across from her sat Kestiana, a high-born goblin and her occasional study companion. Saiyah's violet eyes darted from line to line on the page as she quietly sipped her huckleberry root tea. The library was currently filled with acolytes, all congregating during the daylight hours, exchanging hushed knowledge in groups. Saiyah had to admit, she often preferred the library at night. Not nearly as many people or distractions. As she turned the page, one such distraction approached and stopped directly next to the table at which she sat. Both Saiyah and Kes slowly looked up to the elf who stood beside them. It was Thaiden, Maister Valor's acolyte—a point which he loved to remind people of every chance he got. Thaiden placed a hand on his chest and gave a respectful bow to Saiyah.

"Lady Saiyah," he greeted. Saiyah returned the gesture

with a slight nod of her head but did not return the honorific title.

"Thaiden," she merely replied, noting that Thaiden had not even bothered to acknowledge Kes's presence.

"I am happy to run into you today," Thaiden continued. "I was actually hoping that if you had some time to spare, you wouldn't mind joining me this afternoon for a game of Trepidation in the parlor. Maister Valor has recently taught me how to play, and I have heard that you are excellent at puzzles. I believe you would be a most engaging opponent."

Saiyah instantly turned her attention back to her book. "A kind offer," she replied. "But I fear I am too busy with my studies at the moment to spare the time. Perhaps on another occasion."

Thaiden didn't seem to take the hint, adding, "Well, I am most gifted in my studies; perhaps I could tutor you?"

Kes tried her best to hide a small grin, and Saiyah didn't even try to hide an eye roll.

"Again, a most generous offer," Saiyah added with a tenser tone. "But as you can see, I already have Kes as a study partner. A role she has proven most adept at."

Kes flashed a rather condescending smile in response as Thaiden coughed slightly. He shifted for a few moments before he added with some uncertainty, "Well, yes, perhaps another time then. Good day to you, Lady Saiyah."

Thaiden bowed again and started to walk away as Saiyah turned her full attention back to her book. Once Thaiden was well out of earshot, Kes leaned in on the table and whispered to her, "I do believe he fancies you."

"Then it is assuredly a one-sided attraction," Saiyah noted dully.

"There you are!"

Saiyah looked up to see Riley walking swiftly toward her.

His yellow, cat-like eyes narrowed in on Saiyah's location across the library with pinpoint accuracy. Saiyah gave him a smile in response. She had come to Caelum Vallis as an acolyte to hone her magic skills and add to her family's prestige. She had not really been interested in making friends. Riley, however, had changed that. From the time they first met, he quickly became like family to her. He had clearly felt the same, endearingly referring to her as "little sister," even though her elven years far surpassed his shif ones. Riley was the only son of a shifter clan chief on Daiga. Saiyah knew only a bit about his past. He had lost his mate about thirty years ago, and he had clashed with his father constantly growing up. It was clear from his hesitation in talking about his family and his past that they weren't exactly happy memories. Saiyah had asked once if he ever thought of going back to Daiga, and Riley had simply responded, "I can't go back." It had something to do with a fight with his father, but Riley had never elaborated. He seemed completely unbothered that there were no other shifters at Caelum Vallis. Actually, he appeared rather pleased by that fact.

Riley immediately grabbed a chair from another table and sat down next to Saiyah and Kes. He ran a hand through his medium-length blond hair as he gave an exaggerated sigh of exhaustion.

"I have been looking all over for you," Riley added to Saiyah. "What have you been doing all day?"

"Studying," Saiyah stated plainly. "You should try it sometime."

Riley flashed a playful smile in response. "There is no need to study when you are as naturally talented as I am."

Kes snorted to his comment, making her distaste apparent. Kestiana had always had a problem with Riley, seeming to provoke him at every opportunity. And as far as Saiyah could tell, her indignation seemed to be solely based on the fact that he was a shifter. Granted, shifs were not common amongst mages. Mainly because shifters believed their magic to be "natural" and all other magic to be a perversion of the natural order. Riley, however, did not hold to this doctrine one bit.

"Hmph, a talented shif?" Kes added mockingly. "Now that's a contradiction if I ever heard one."

Riley grinned at her. "Now, now, Kes, no need to deny it." He added with a glint in his eyes, "You are positively green with envy."

Saiyah could see the anger flush in Kes's sage-hued cheeks.

"How would you like a muzzle, mongrel?" she hissed.

"Mongrel?" Riley inquired. "Is that your way of comparing me to a dog? That's rather rich...coming from a bitch."

Kes shot to her feet, prepared to strike Riley with the most heinous spell she could think of. But Saiyah clicked her teeth loudly in frustration, gaining the attention of both her friends.

"I believe I already stated," Saiyah began sternly, "that I am trying to study. And will not be cast from the library due to you both brawling."

Kes pulled her chin up, puffed up her lips, and sat back down in her seat begrudgingly, still staring at Riley with malice. Riley was not bothered by her attitude at all. In fact, he seemed to delight in the fact he had successfully goaded her. Saiyah sighed.

"Riley, I am assuming you came here for a purpose other than starting an argument?" she questioned.

Riley turned back to Saiyah as a wave of recollection washed over him. "Oh, that's right!" he continued. "I have heard the most SCANDALOUS gossip, and I simply had to tell you."

"What is it this time?" Saiyah smiled. "Did some highborn mage wear the wrong color to a banquet or something?"

"Oooh—better than that," Riley added with a wide grin.

"Much better. Word around Caelum Vallis is that Maister Arden has finally gotten himself an acolyte."

Saiyah shook her head and muttered, "About time…"

"What a wonder, the drunken degenerate finally found a flunkey," Kes noted dully. "The Council must be delighted."

"Not quite," Riley replied with a sly smile, "cause word is that his brand-new acolyte…is human."

Saiyah and Kes gaped back at Riley. Open-mouthed, eyes wide.

"You must be joking," Saiyah replied.

Riley shook his head. "Not even I could come up with a punchline that good."

"Has Maister Arden completely lost his senses?" Saiyah inquired.

"Assuming he had any to begin with," Kes noted.

"I imagine the Council is asking themselves that very same question." Riley shrugged.

"Well, he won't stay," Kes stated obviously. "The Council will never allow it."

"Maister Arden is saying it is his right to choose the acolyte he deems fit," said Riley.

"Within reason!" Saiyah argued. "A human hardly qualifies!"

Riley shrugged, clearly in agreement but unable to offer an excuse for the behavior.

"I actually pity the poor, frail thing," Kestiana added. "First spell it tries to cast will see its body parts strewn across Caelum Vallis in spectacular fashion. Human lives are short enough as is for it to hasten its end so."

Kes smiled slightly before adding, "The human will not last a week."

While Saiyah agreed with Kes, she hoped that Lord Arden would have more sense than to let this human try spells willy-nilly till it blew itself to kingdom come. Still, he had lacked sense in allowing a human to be his acolyte in the first place, so she supposed anything was possible.

Kye stirred to the morning light seeping through his eyelids. That meant it was already past sunrise. Umbree would be raising holy hell about the location of his breakfast and would come storming in any second to drag Kye from his slumber. But for some reason, it was particularly difficult for him to wake. He was sleeping comfortably, which almost never happened, and having the most bizarre dream he wasn't yet ready to wake from. About travels to Isalia, seeing the Silver City of the elves, becoming a mage himself. The dream was far preferable to reality; as such, he was procrastinating the return to his habitual existence. But he also knew, one could only defy reality for so long. Kye begrudgingly pushed himself up off his pallet, only to be surprised that the ground felt soft beneath him. As he slowly opened his eyes, he quickly sat up to the realization he wasn't in his woodshed. Kye was lying on top of a feather bed and pillow. A couple of bluebirds were on the tree limb outside, singing their early morning song. Kye noticed that several books were strewn about on the bed where he lay. He slowly remembered falling asleep reading some of the volumes on the history of Isalia that had been on the bookshelf in his room. It hadn't been a dream.

Kye immediately shot up with renewed vigor. He swiftly washed up in the bath before dressing in the blue robes in his wardrobe. He put on his gold amulet and leather belt before adding the gold bracers Arden had told him about. Apparently, they helped focus energy and were an important training tool for acolytes when first trying to harness their power. Lastly, he threw on a pair of hardened leather moccasins before heading toward the door. Before he could grab the handle, Kye caught a glimpse of his reflection in a mirror on the wall, causing him to pause for a moment. It almost looked like another person staring back at him. And the reflection certainly looked the part of a mage, even if the person casting it felt far from it. Kye closed his eyes and took a deep breath. He was a mage now, so he had better start acting like it. Without another glance, he turned back and opened his door to the common area.

A warm breeze wafted into the room from the open glass doors on the veranda. Arden sat at the small table by the bar, sipping a cup of tea and casually reading a book. His attention momentarily diverted when Kye entered.

"Ah, Kye. *Sulara anor.*"

Kye's face contorted in confusion. "*S-Sulara-*"

"*Sulara anor,*" Ardern repeated. "It's an elvish greeting. Means 'blessed day.' Celeste brought up breakfast a bit ago. There is tea on the bar if you'd like some."

Arden then returned his attention to his book as Kye headed over and grabbed a cup of tea from the teapot. He wasn't sure what kind of tea it was, but it smelled of cardamom and cinnamon. And with just one sip, it instantly chased away any remnants of sleep. Kye brought the cup over to the table that had several dishes hidden beneath silver dome serving plate covers. He sat down, catching wondrous whiffs of delicious food. He suddenly realized how hungry he was. He had fallen asleep last night before even getting to try the stew Celeste had mentioned. But Kye also knew that manners dictated he shouldn't eat till Arden did. He had never sat at a table for a meal, let alone with an elven maister. And the last thing he wanted to do was to offend Arden. Kye sat staring at his tea cup and out the window for a long while, desperately trying to keep his mind off food.

"Are you not hungry?" Arden asked after some time, still focused on the book he was reading.

"Well...yes," Kye stated. "That is...I could eat."

"Is there something preventing you from doing that?" Arden questioned, raising his eyes momentarily from the book.

"No, I just thought... Aren't you going to eat as well?"

"I already have," Arden clarified, turning back to his book while grabbing his tea. "That is yours."

Kye gawked at the five dishes spread out on the small table. Lifting up one of the serving domes, Kye saw that just one of the plates was filled with a collection of sliced meats, eggs and cut potatoes on the side. Another platter had fruit, bread, and butter. Another had pancakes with syrup. The remaining two contained what Kye could only describe as a cheese and meat casserole, stuffed with bacon and bits of sausage.

"This is all for me?" Kye questioned in disbelief.

"Celeste has never made food for a human before. I'm guessing she didn't know what to make, so she just made a bit of everything."

Kye looked back at the feast that lay before him, appreciative of Celeste's efforts and not wishing any of it to go to waste. But he was also certain ten people would have trouble getting through the banquet she had prepared, let alone just him. Arden seemed to pick up on Kye's train of thought, adding, "Just eat whatever you like. I'll remind her later she is making food for a single person, not a small village."

Kye nodded and dug into the meat and potatoes first, each bite more delicious than the last. It was the first time he could remember that food was still warm by the time he got to it. Kye made it through as much of the buffet as he could and several cups of tea before he was so full he couldn't take another bite. He couldn't help but feel a twinge of guilt looking down at the three plates still remaining, virtually untouched. Glancing up from his food, he noticed that Arden was still engrossed in his book.

"What are you reading?" Kye inquired.

"It is a grimoire on elemental magic. I was hoping there would be some mention of the stones in it."

"Have you had any luck learning more about them?"

Arden shook his head. "Though I don't expect it to be an easy search. The stones are so old, it's possible they predate our current written word. Nonetheless, I am optimistic some mention of them will be buried in the library."

Arden closed the grimoire and placed it on the table. "But today, we will be focusing on a different kind of elemental magic."

Seeing Kye had finished eating, Arden stood up. "*Evanora*," he muttered with a wave of his hand. The dishes on the dining table instantly disappeared as Kye looked on in wonder. He silently questioned if Umbree had known that spell but decided not to broach the topic. No doubt even if Umbree did know it, he wouldn't have wasted an iota of energy to cast it. Not when he had Kye to do the cleanup. Arden walked from the dining table to the buffet in the corner and picked up a single candle within a silver candlestick. He walked back to the table and placed the candle in front of Kye.

"Repeat after me," Arden stated. "*Pyraela*."

"*Pyraela*," Kye recited with perfect accuracy.

"Very good. It means flame in Ancient. Your first task is learning to unleash your magic, and for that, we are going to start with something simple."

Arden pointed to the candle in front of Kye. "Light the wick of the candle, preferably without setting the dining table ablaze. Focus on the word and call forth fire from deep within."

Kye took a deep breath and straightened up in his seat. He held a hand out over the wick, closed his eyes, and recited the word clearly.

"*Pyraela*."

After a few moments, Kye opened his eyes to an unlit candle in the center of the table.

Kye looked to Arden in response, his face contorted in confusion. "Was my pronunciation off?"

"No, kid," Arden replied with a smile. "It takes time to learn to harness the powers of magic. This is an exercise to help you with that. It's like learning to use a muscle you never have before. Over time, you will strengthen it, and it will get easier. Try again."

Kye repeated the same actions from before, only this time focusing harder on the word.

"*Pyraela*," he repeated again. And yet again, nothing happened.

Kye squinted slightly as he looked to Arden. "You're sure that I—"

"You possess the skill," Arden replied before Kye could even finish the statement. "I'd say the only one you are lacking right now is patience. Now, try again."

Several hours later, Kye was staring at the candle in front of him as though it were his nemesis. No matter how he pronounced the spell, no matter how he focused, the wick wouldn't ignite. It didn't even flicker.

"Don't let it discourage you," Arden responded, standing at the bar pouring another cup of tea. "Magic takes time to learn and a lifetime to master."

Kye nodded in acknowledgment. He wasn't about to give up; he was far too stubborn for that.

"How long does it normally take for a mage to master this exercise?" Kye asked.

"There is no normally," Arden replied. "Every acolyte is different. There are some that can light a candle instantly when placed in front of them. There are some who take years to achieve the same task."

Kye felt his eyes widen in response. "Years?" he clarified.

"Like I said," Arden continued, "magic takes time. You can't rush it. The only thing you'll achieve by that is to—"

Arden suddenly froze mid-sentence, as his eyes closed in concentration. Kye was worried for a moment he might be ill. He then noticed the amulet that Arden wore was glowing brightly. He had remembered Arden mentioning the other day that the amulet could be used to communicate by focusing your thoughts. He wasn't sure who Arden might be communicating with, but Kye was certain he should not interrupt. Kye sat frozen, waiting for some movement from Arden. Eventually, the amulet dimmed, and Arden opened his eyes, his brow creased in disapproval.

"Is everything alright?" Kye asked once Arden set his tea cup back down.

"I'm afraid we will have to cut today's lesson short. We have been summoned by the Council."

Kye quickly stood up from the dining table, feeling a sudden surge of anxiety.

"Both of us?" he inquired.

Arden nodded. "The Council, it seems, would like some information on what exactly happened on Helia... Among other things."

Kye followed Arden to the great white building where the Council Hall was located. Walking through the gardens towards the formidable structure, Kye's stomach twisted into knots. He immediately regretted his large breakfast. Arden had stated that they were to give testimony on what happened with Umbree, but Kye was more focused on the greeting he would receive in the High Council chamber. He knew the council was not pleased about his station as Ardens's acolyte. The whispers and glares he received just walking the halls told him as much. Kye had anticipated this day would come eventually, although it didn't make facing it any easier. The first human mage would not be easily tolerated or accepted. Magi code or not, if the council outright revoked Kye's apprenticeship, he knew he would be shipped back to Helia without so much as a second thought. And he already knew what fate would await him there. In the back of his mind, Kye was turning over possible solutions if he was sent back to Helia. Maybe he could hide in Camris from Umbree and Helian law. The settlers would probably take him in, keep his presence there a secret. That is, of course, if he wasn't sent back in chains, straight to his execution.

Kye snuck a sideways glance at Arden, who seemed completely calm. He walked with no more haste than that of an afternoon stroll, as though they were headed to see some sight, instead of certain doom.

"It wasn't your last meal," Arden remarked suddenly, causing Kye to snap his head around.

"What?"

"Breakfast," Arden added with a comforting smile. "You look like you are walking to the gallows."

Kye shook his head defiantly. "I'm fine," he asserted, quickly trying to change his demeanor to reflect as much. Arden gave a suspicious look in response.

"Right..." he answered, unconvinced. "Just remember, kid, you're not facing the headsman alone."

Kye smiled slightly and nodded to Arden in appreciation. It was somewhat of a comfort that at least Arden stood beside him. Though he imagined there were limits to even what he could do, facing a room full of angry mages. If they truly wished Kye gone, they would make it so, arguments from Arden or not.

"They will try to intimidate you," Arden warned as they continued along the path, the High Council hall coming into view. "But no matter how much they goad you, no matter how much they push, don't give them the satisfaction of a reaction. Answer questions directly but otherwise remain silent. Got it?"

"Got it." Kye nodded in understanding.

As Arden and Kye reached the base of the Council Hall, they started their ascent up the marble steps, approaching a pair of double doors the size of full-grown oak trees. A star was drawn on the front, each point tipped in gold. Kye had learned from books in his room on the history of Isalia that each of the points of the star represented one of the Six Realms, with the center representing Isalia. There were words in Ancient cast at the top of the door. "*Omnia Magira qui intrara hara aequala sunt.*" Kye couldn't help but smile sardonically as Arden explained the meaning of the phrase. "All mages who enter here are equal." Something told him they never planned on one of them being a human.

Arden held out a hand toward the great double doors and stated, *"Aperira."* The doors swung open in response to his words. As Arden and Kye entered, they were greeted by a long hallway with multiple doors leading off on both sides. Kye assumed them to be the guest quarters Arden had told him about. At the end of the hallway was a second set of double doors, much smaller than the ones they had just passed through. Kye felt his heartbeat quicken a little bit more with each step forward. When they finally stopped in front of a grand double doorway, he felt as though it might beat right out of his chest. Arden turned to Kye.

"Ready?" he asked.

Kye took one last deep breath and nodded.

As Arden held up his hand, the doors instantly swung open. Kye looked to a center platform illuminated by the light falling in from the glass ceiling above. It stood in the middle of a large circular auditorium, with lines of tables stretching up three stories high. Seated at each table was a mage. About two hundred filled the hall. All had been speaking in hushed voices until the double doors opened—then deafening silence fell over the room as Arden and Kye entered. Kye looked around to the eyes staring down at him, all wearing the same look of disapproval. As Arden approached the center platform, Kye followed. He made sure to keep his eyes off the floor and toward his destination, trying to give the illusion of calm he certainly wasn't feeling. A dark-haired, dark-skinned elf decked out in gold robes was the first to stand. Kye noticed that he was the only member in attendance wearing a golden circlet with a deep blue stone in the center of it.

"This council offers its thanks to you, Maister Arden, for your swift attendance."

"Yeah, well, your invitation didn't exactly sound optional, Valor," Arden noted.

Kye looked at the elf more closely. So this was Valor, Umbree's protege. If his previous master's demeanor was any indication, Kye knew a conversation with him was going to be about as pleasant as a butcher's knife to an extremity. Valor cleared his throat loudly. "Yes, well, there are a few matters that require immediate attention. As such, perhaps it might be best for your human to wait outside for a moment."

Kye looked to Arden but did not budge. Arden simply smiled in response.

"I fail to see why that would be necessary, Valor. He was present at the incident on Helia, and I was led to believe this council was interested in his testimony as well."

Valor shifted slightly. "Well...before we address the incident on Helia, I feel it important to address the status of your new...guest."

"Not my guest," Arden corrected. "He is my acolyte."

A blonde female elf with brown eyes and pursed lips,

squinted down in disdain. "That remains to be seen," she hissed.

"Well, as he stands before you quite clearly, Luell, this gives me cause to question your eyesight," Arden replied.

"I mean it has not been decided that he is your apprentice," Luell bit back.

"Between the two people that matter, it has been."

"This council does not agree!"

"To which I am not surprised," Arden noted. "This council and I tend to disagree on a fairly frequent basis. The only difference in this particular instance is that the council's opinions are of no consequence."

An aging orc slammed his hand on his desk as he stood, causing Kye to snap his head to attention. He had coal-black eyes, grayish skin, and legs the size of tree trucks. Kye was fairly certain the orc could snap any part of him he wished, and with minimal effort at that.

"You dare insult us by inviting a lowly, unfit, pathetic human into our ranks!" the orc barked in anger.

"The choosing of my apprentice is not an affront to any member here," Arden replied, "despite arguments to the contrary."

His gaze then fell on the orc. "And Maister Firen, you will choose your words carefully when addressing my acolyte, or I will return such hostilities—*in kind*," Arden growled. Kye was surprised Arden had offered such a reaction on his behalf. The standing orc clearly was too and seemed to calm almost instantly, averting his eyes from Arden before sitting back down. One thing was certain: Arden commanded attention from every mage present. A short, stout dwarf with a long red beard was the next to comment.

"Ah, I say give the lad a chance if he wishes it," the dwarf stated nonchalantly. "'Tis his own funeral if he fails."

"Which he undoubtedly will," another elder goblin

decked out in gray robes and jewels added. "Humans cannot be mages. Their minds cannot process the ancient tongue or hope to cast with it. As such, they are far too weak to handle the strains of magic and would only injure themselves trying."

Kye could feel a flame of anger spark and cast a glare toward the goblin maister. Though it was not an unusual occurrence, he had never become accustomed to being spoken down to by other races. Let alone so nonchalantly, in his presence. As though his feeble human brain couldn't comprehend an insult when he heard one. Arden turned his attention toward the posh goblin.

"Need I recite to this council the number of orcs, goblins, elves, and dwarves that have met a swift end in the pursuit of the craft?" Arden responded. "Should we take the time to address their shortcomings as well?"

Kye smiled slightly as the elder goblin grumbled in response. Valor once again stepped forward.

"Be that as it may," he began, "members here have—questions—about your choice that need to be addressed."

Arden raised both eyebrows quizzically. "Questions, huh? Very well then, let's see if we can get some answers."

Valor nodded, pleased that Arden easily agreed to the inquisition. As he opened his mouth to speak—

"How is Thaiden?" Arden interrupted. Valor did a bit of a double take, knocked off guard by the sudden inquiry.

"What?" he asked.

"Your acolyte," Arden clarified. "How is he doing? Is he excelling in his studies?"

The other council members exchanged confused looks. No one more so than Valor. "I fail to see how that relates—"

"He certainly seems like a competent mage," Arden continued. "I must say, I was surprised you chose him as your acolyte, though. I remember you had another candidate, a dwarf by the name Gaeric, was it? That seemed like the natural choice. He was gifted in the arts, intelligent, and seemed determined in his pursuit of the craft. There must have been some factor that made you choose Thaiden instead?"

Valor was now getting visibly frustrated that he kept getting interrupted. "I don't see how that—"

"Could it be his upbringing?" Arden added. "His personal connections? His demeanor? His manner of speech? Or could it possibly be the large donation his family made right before he was selected?"

The High Council chamber exploded in a myriad of hushed whispers. Valor glared down at Arden as though he was about to rain hellfire. Arden stared back, unfazed, almost welcoming the flame.

Valor's voice was shaking slightly as he asked, "You DARE insinuate!"

"It was just a question, Valor," Arden replied. "To be fair, I've had quite a few questions about the acolytes chosen by this council over the years. And while, at times, I did not agree with the decisions made by members here, I have kept my opinions to myself because it was not my choice or my place to cast doubt upon any acolyte selected by a maister. But if those rules have changed, if this council now states it has the right to contest my choices, well, then...I certainly have some 'questions' about yours."

In an instant, the whispers in the chamber stopped, and silence fell. The members were caught in a standoff. Kye could feel the tension in the air. Valor was silently fuming, while Arden looked as calm as a raindrop on a pond. Kye silently wondered if an all-out brawl was about to begin. Valor's jaw was clenched as though it was the only thing holding back a slew of curses.

"Many would argue," he hissed, "that selecting a human as your protege would grant you a second before your end of service to this council. Human lives are short. It is almost a guarantee he will not live to see your renunciation as maister."

Kye was caught off guard. He had not thought of that. It was true—elven lifespans far outstripped human ones. It was an indisputable fact that Kye would be long dead before Arden even started to feel the effects of time. But Arden merely chuckled in response.

"Is that your worry?" he inquired. "Very well, then, you have my word. I swear on my life—and death for that matter—Kye will be my only acolyte chosen."

Kye was left speechless by Arden's declaration. Sixty years, if he was lucky, that was all he had left. A blink of an eye in the life of an elf. And for that, Arden was willingly forfeiting any chance of having a protege take over for him as maister, all for the opportunity of taking Kye as his acolyte now. Kye was grateful for Arden's willingness to help him, but he felt guilty at the same time. He knew that serving as Arden's acolyte was sparing him a one-way trip back to Helia. As such, he worried Arden might be giving up too much, just to keep it from happening.

Valor took a deep breath, his mind churning. It was clear he wasn't happy with Arden's choice. But he had run out of arguments. The rest of the council members seemed too intimidated to raise any further objections. They looked at each other and other parts of the chamber, anything to avoid making eye contact with Arden.

"If you are willing to agree to such terms," Valor stated finally, "then the council has no choice but to accept this *human* as your protégé."

"Wonderful," Arden noted dryly. "I am thrilled this council is content with my choice. Now, was there another matter you wished to discuss? The betrayal of your former master, for example?"

Arden's emphasis on "your" was a particular sticking point with Valor, who glared back at Arden with contempt.

"Yes, by all means," Valor replied. "This council would be MOST interested in how a simple request to retrieve an important artifact crumbled into the situation before us. Please, enlighten us as to the events on Helia, Lord Arden."

Arden shared his account, relaying the facts of Umbree's betrayal. He did so without passion or prejudice, merely following the events that had transpired. From Umbree's hesitance to hand over the stone, to Kye approaching him with what he had heard of Orin, to Umbree's appearance in the study, to the rush to escape the burning manor and Umbree. Kye noticed gratefully that Arden seemed to gloss over the part where Kye stabbed Umbree. The council listened in silence, only breaking the sound of Arden's voice with the occasional gasp or sigh. Kye listened intently, too, for he had never heard how it was Arden had managed to get out of the manor. The rush to the passage behind the gryphon statue, the maze below the manor, a wall of water coming toward him. Considering Umbree had been right on his trail, it was even more surprising Arden had taken the time to make sure Kye got out as well. Kye had been prepared to die in that fire. Valor stood still as a statue the entire time, staring down at Arden with an unreadable expression. When Arden finally finished with his tale, the council cast glances around to each other, uncertain of how to respond. Valor was the first to speak, directing his attention from Arden to Kye. He looked Kye up and down as though he were a strange creature that had crawled into the room, and he was uncertain of what to do with him now.

"I thank you for your testimony, Lord Arden," Valor began. "Since you have shared with us your side of events, I now have a few questions for your acolyte, if I may?"

Kye stepped forward and gave a bow to Lord Valor.

"I am at your service, my lord," Kye stated before rising. Valor was surprised by Kye's direct response, and Kye realized it was the first time he had actually spoken since entering the council chamber.

"Is that so?" Valor replied. "Well, perhaps you can enlighten me on a few parts. You are the one who overheard Umbree mention that he was waiting for Orin, correct?"

"Yes, my lord," Kye stated. "I overheard Umbree mention the name Orin to Belthier and Torha while they were in the parlor."

"And you had never before heard of the name Orin before that night?"

"No, my lord," Kye replied. "I have come to learn from Lord Arden that he is a dangerous mage."

"Indeed." Valor nodded. "But you had never met him in person? I find it strange that your master would be on friendly terms with such a dangerous mage without you at least being aware before that night."

"There was a great deal Umbree did not feel the need to make me aware of, my lord. We were far from confidants."

Out of the corner of his eye, Kye could see Arden crack a small, amused smile as Valor's nose crinkled in annoyance. "Indeed," he grumbled. "It is somewhat puzzling that a slave who holds no significance to his master would be the only one to hear of Umbree's connection to Orin."

"Not the only one, my lord," Kye replied. "Torha and Belthier are also aware of Umbree's connection."

"So you say. But they are not standing before this council to affirm that fact, now are they?"

"No, my lord," stated Kye, thinking that he couldn't really blame them on that front. He didn't want to be standing before this council either.

"So upon hearing of this supposed impending danger," Valor started, "you immediately thought of informing Lord

Arden of Umbree's plans. What made you certain he would believe you?"

"I was not certain, my lord," Kye replied. "But I at least had to try."

"Are you aware of the punishment for a slave betraying his master?" Valor inquired. Kye thought this a pointed question. Of course, slaves were aware of the punishment for betrayal; they were reminded of it too often to forget.

"Yes, my lord."

"And that the punishment is often SEVERE?"

Kye could feel his tone sharpen a bit as he replied, "Yes, my lord."

"And yet you risked a lot for a mage you had just met. Why, I wonder?"

Kye was silent for a moment before replying, "Because... my silence would have meant sacrificing a life, simply for the sake of sparing my own, my lord."

Valor held his chin up and stared down at Kye in distrust. "Well, how noble. How very fortunate for Lord Arden that he happened to come across a slave who put so little value on his own existence."

Arden scowled back at Valor in response.

"You were the one to reclaim the stone from Umbree?" Valor continued, unfazed.

"Yes, my lord," Kye answered.

"A human took the stone from a mage. However did you manage that?"

"I lifted the stone from Umbree's pocket when he was... distracted."

Kye's hesitation caused Valor to narrow in on his words with the focus of a hawk on a mouse.

"Distracted?" Valor inquired. "How so exactly? Do you mean by his fight with Maister Arden?"

"Yes, my lord. He was intently focused on the duel."

"And did not notice you coming up behind him?"

"No, my lord."

"And so you simply removed the stone...and then what?"

"I saw Umbree try to strike Lord Arden with an ax, so I attempted to help him."

"And just HOW did you, a human, attempt to help him?"

"By attacking Lord Umbree, my lord."

Kye knew the rest of this conversation was not going to go well by the daggers Valor was shooting at him in response.

"Attack him?" Valor hissed. "Just how did you attack him?"

"Stabbed him, my lord," Kye replied hesitantly. "In the back, with a letter opener."

The familiar sounds of shocked murmurs echoed throughout the hall, all eyes looking at Kye in disapproval. Valor sneered at Kye as Maister Luell raised an eyebrow in surprise.

"Interesting apprentice you have chosen here, Arden," Luell replied. "Might I suggest added precaution be taken with him around knives?"

"Oh, I hardly think that's necessary, Luell," Arden replied, unfazed. "I think he's proven quite proficient with them."

"I do not find a maister being stabbed quite so amusing, Arden!" Valor hissed.

"Nor did I when that maister tried to behead me or butcher my acolyte, Valor," Arden retorted. "You'll forgive my lack of sympathy for his discomfort."

Valor flushed a light shade of red. It was truly difficult to tell by this point, between Kye and Arden, which one pissed off Valor more. Kye guessed he had more than enough disdain to spread equally between the two of them.

"I have heard enough on this matter," Valor proclaimed. "Given the testimony provided, I do not see any imminent danger with the creation stone."

"Really?" Arden inquired. "So do you think Orin wants the stone because he's feeling fucking sentimental?"

"And who said Orin wanted the stone?" Valor replied.

"Umbree did."

"Did you hear him say this? Personally?" Valor inquired. "From your testimony, Umbree stated, 'I have someone coming very soon expecting that stone.' Nowhere did you personally hear him say that Orin was that somebody."

Arden's gaze narrowed. "It was implied."

"Implication cannot be taken as fact, Arden," retorted Valor. "You did not hear Umbree state he was working with Orin."

"Kye did. As he has clearly testified to this council."

"And you trusted the word of a slave over that of a maister?" Luell piped up.

"Well, it became a bit easier to swallow as soon as Umbree attacked me," said Arden.

"You attacked him first," Luell retorted. "Unprovoked, might I add."

Arden froze in utter bewilderment, staring back at Luell as though she had sprouted a second head.

"Unprovoked?" he clarified. "He slammed Kye against a wall and tried to choke the life out of him."

"How he chooses to discipline his servant should be no concern of yours, Arden," she said frostily. Arden glowered in response as Kye focused his attention to the floor. It was not surprising. Of course, the council would rate a maister's life above that of a slave. But it was telling to Kye that Arden so furiously disagreed. Thinking Kye's life was equal to Umbree's was unheard of from a mage till now.

Valor leaned forward in his chair and stared down at Kye, a look he was familiar with, one that Umbree had given him on a daily basis. Repulsion.

"What you have told us today is a good story, Arden,"

Valor started. "But I could think of a good story of my own, one that fits the same narrative. Let's say, this boy was dissatisfied with his service to his master..."

You could say that, Kye thought. *And it would certainly be an understatement.*

"And so he sought to escape..."

Basically every minute of every day.

"But he also knew full well running would get him nowhere. After all, where in Helia could he go?"

Doesn't mean I didn't try.

"So he waited for an opportunity to present itself. And YOU, Arden, were the perfect opportunity."

Wait, what? Kye was casting uncertain glances between Valor and Arden. Arden was stone-faced.

"This boy saw the animosity you and Umbree harbored for each other," elaborated Valor. "So he stoked the fire, so to speak, to be the most advantageous to him. He knew you were there for the stone, so he made up a story about betrayal and certain death in order to instigate your attack on Umbree."

No! Kye could feel his head shaking in disagreement even before a word of objection could be initiated from his lips.

"Once he had you convinced," Valor continued, disregarding Kye's silent protest, "he helped you gain the stone you were looking for in exchange for his freedom and transportation out of the realm. He already knew about the waterway under the manor, and with a maister assisting him, it would be a quick and easy escape. That is, of course, until you ran into Umbree. Umbree, seeing the boy's ruse, attempted to dissuade you from listening to him. After all, you stated Umbree did try to warn you that the boy was a most gifted liar."

"That's not—!" Kye started as he stepped toward Valor, trying to deny the offenses cast against him. Arden threw a stern glance toward Kye, meant to silence him. Kye instantly quieted. Arden was right, after all; there was no point. If the council had already made up their minds about Kye, his arguments to the contrary would merely fall on deaf ears.

Valor smiled slightly, clearly pleased he had instigated a reaction from Kye. "If Umbree believed you were being misled by this human, it would be only right for him to fight to hold onto the stone. To keep it from falling into the wrong hands."

"Well, that is certainly an interesting theory," Arden replied. "If Umbree's intent was so honorable, then I trust he will appear before this council to state his defense?"

Valor fell silent. Arden added, "I didn't think so. So, I suppose we will have to compromise on our own versions of the truth. Now, since this council no longer has need or interest in our testimony, I trust we are done here?"

Valor nodded. "Just one matter remains," he stated. "If you would turn over the stone in your possession to this council."

Arden gave Valor a wide sardonic smile. "Now that's a bit of a problem. Afraid I can't do that."

"Just what is that supposed to mean?" Luell growled.

"Well, I thought the statement rather straightforward, Luell," Arden replied, looking her dead in the eyes. "Or do you require smaller words?"

"Enough, Arden," Valor stated as Luell seethed in response. "You were tasked with getting the elemental stone and returning it to this council."

"Wrong," Arden replied. "I was tasked with returning the stone to the safety of Caelum Vallis, which I have done. You have my word that the stone is safely hidden within these walls. At no point was it specified to return it to the council itself."

"It was implied!" Luell hissed.

"As the council has already stated, implications cannot be taken as fact. One must be clear with the words they speak."

Valor grew very quiet. "I am in no mood for games, Arden."

"Neither am I," Arden rebutted. "In fact, I take this matter quite seriously. Since this council has yet to come to a consensus about the facts surrounding Umbree's manor, I am certain you can agree the stone should be kept in a safe location until that concord can be reached. Seeing as Umbree's betrayal would mean a connection with Orin and danger for us all."

"And we should trust YOU with the stone's safety in the meantime?" Luell barked. Arden turned to her.

"I was trusted by this council to retrieve the stone. Seeing as I have successfully done just that, I'm curious why that trust would have waned. Unless of course, my honor is being called into question here?"

The council chamber erupted in hushed whispers as the mages present exchanged glances and chatter. Valor drummed his fingers on the table in front of him while Luell whispered in his ear. Valor was clearly torn, and Kye could see why. Even if he wasn't leader of the council, Arden obviously held great sway with it. If Valor rebutted Arden and demanded the stone's return, it would be as much as calling Arden untrustworthy in the eyes of the council, which would not go over well. Then again, giving into Arden's demand to keep the stone away from the council could be seen as laxity and weaken Valor's position. Valor was sandwiched firmly between a rock and a hard place. And his mind seemed to be turning over which scenario would be most advantageous to him. After several minutes, Valor held up a hand as the entire council hall fell silent. He looked down at Arden.

"You are quite right, maister," Valor began. "Further investigation of the events at Umbree's manor is required, which I will make sure to address. In the meantime, given your years of service, I see no need to remove the stone from the secure location you have found for it while the investigation commences."

Arden gave a curt nod as Valor added, "However, should the investigation produce that Umbree was not in league with Orin, that this tale was, in fact, invented by an errant slave as I suspect, then you will turn the stone over to this council post haste—"

Valor then turned to Kye. "And your acolyte will be stripped of his title and shipped back to Helia, to face the crimes of attempted murder against a mage. A crime, I have no doubt, he would be found guilty of based on his own testimony."

Kye felt his blood run cold as Valor glared down on him. He had no illusions if that were the case, Valor himself would stand front and center at his trial to testify. And no doubt stick around to watch Kye's head roll afterward. Valor turned back to Arden. "Seeing as you are an honorable mage, Arden, I trust you will agree to these terms?"

Kye looked in Arden's direction but did not meet his gaze. Arden stepped forward and nodded to Valor. "But of course," Arden replied without hesitation. "And I am certain the investigation will find no fault with my acolyte's version of events."

Valor sneered slightly. "Very well then. In that case, till the investigation concludes, mention of the creation stone is to stay between the maisters of this council. The council thanks you for your time, Lord Arden. And we will reconvene on these matters at a later date."

A loud bang echoed through the chamber from an unseen location as Valor declared, "Council is dismissed!"

Arden gave a perfunctory bow and immediately headed toward the doors of the council chamber. Kye repeated the same swift action and quickly followed suit. Leaving the doors of the council chamber and once again stepping outside, Kye was surprised to see the sun hanging so low in the sky. It was late evening, and the air was already starting to cool in preparation for sunset. Arden's face was unreadable as he walked briskly. His demeanor seemed irked, and Kye couldn't tell if his anger was brought on by the several-hour interrogation they had just gone through...or if he might be starting to believe Valor had a point. It didn't bother Kye that the council thought he could be a traitor. It was nothing he hadn't expected. But it bothered him greatly that Arden might have believed the explanation. That Arden could think he had misled him for his own gain. Kye felt compelled to defend himself. To try and convince him that he wasn't lying.

"Arden," Kye started, halting his procession. Arden stopped as well, turning back to look at Kye in confusion.

"What Valor said..." Kye began carefully, "About me, I wanted you to know—"

"Kye!" Arden responded curtly, cutting Kye off. Kye went silent, feeling his assumption of Arden being angry with him was right on the nose. To his surprise, though, Arden took a deep breath, sighed, and shook his head. He seemed to soften his demeanor a bit in response.

"I was there," Arden continued. "Valor can paint any rosy picture he wants, but I witnessed the look in Umbree's eyes. We both did. I saw his intent, whether the council wants to see it or not. It's easier for them to paint you as the villain than admit it is one of their own."

Arden paused for a moment, before adding with genuine sincerity, "It may not be much consolation, but at the very least, you don't have to try to earn my trust. You already have it."

Kye gave a small grin and inclined his head graciously. At that moment, something changed between them. Kye didn't look at Arden with the same tense intimidation he had before. He saw him now as a friend and mentor. If Arden had proved anything today, it was that he trusted Kye. And in return, Kye knew Arden was someone he trusted, too. Arden nodded before continuing his walk toward the castle at a much calmer pace.

"Celeste probably has dinner ready," Arden stated, looking at the sun starting to set on the horizon. "And after a day like today, I could certainly use a drink. How about you?"

Kye smiled slightly in response before adding, "Anything but fire whiskey."

Arden chuckled and clapped a hand on Kye's shoulder. "Alright, kid. We'll work our way up to that."

CHAPTER 6
The Horrible Human Mage

"He hid under the cover of night, cloaked in black, cursed dagger in hand. He lay in wait for the perfect opportunity. The unsuspecting mage could not call upon his skills to save him. No protection spell or defensive magic of any kind. He was too old and feeble to mount a sufficient defense, and the human KNEW that. So when the poor mage turned his back, the human LEAPT from the shadows and plunged the cursed blade repeatedly into the mage's back, coating the floor in blood!"

"*Gasp!*"

"And as the mage lay dying, the human stood over him, smiling the cruelest smile. After the mage drew his LAST breath, he took the mage's head and wore it as a trophy to show to the rest of the mages as a warning."

"How is it that Lord Arden let such a dangerous beast in here!?"

"I heard it was the blade. He used a cursed blade to cast an enchantment upon Lord Arden. It captivated his mind, forcing him to do his bidding. And that is why the council cannot expel him, for he would TURN Lord Arden against them. And there would be a bloodbath."

"So he's a charmer? That can't be true!"

"I heard it from Lady Erdith, who heard it directly from Maister Firen."

Saiyah sighed loudly as she tried to focus on the pages of her book on telepathy. She and Riley were seated at a small table in the library, which was abuzz with whispers of the human acolyte. Word had spread that the High Council had allowed the human to remain Lord Arden's acolyte. Not only that, but his interest seemed to only grow in the last few weeks. The rumors had spread of the dangerous human brute roaming the halls. Few had seen him, feeding the myths. Several invented tales that the reason the human had not been seen was that he only prowled at night, wielding his cursed blade and waiting for an unsuspecting mage to be alone. Saiyah was getting very tired of all the whispers and stories. It was affecting her ability to study. As such, she was developing a defined hatred for the new human. Riley, on the other hand, was completely enthralled. He had become a full-time study partner, though studying was not his main goal. He would lean back in his chair in the library the entire time, munching on nuts and dried fruits and listening to all the wild tales with immense fascination. Today's fable, however, seemed particularly outlandish.

"And here I thought I was sitting in the non-fiction section," Saiyah muttered loud enough for Riley to hear.

"I don't know what you're complaining about," Riley answered with a huge grin. "I'm having a great time. This story is almost as good as the one I heard yesterday, about how the human used to lead an army of bandits with a taste for blood. And here I always thought I hated the library."

"I am certainly glad that you find the fact that we are hosting a renegade brute to be entertaining," Saiyah noted.

"Maister Luell told me he actually did stab his previous master."

Riley raised an eyebrow. "He stabbed a mage and lived to tell about it? Impressive for a human."

"I am sure he would appreciate your admiration," Saiyah bit back. "Just as I would appreciate some PEACE AND QUIET!" she proclaimed, this time loudly enough for the group that had been swapping stories nearby to look over in her direction.

The group at the table looked clearly offended. They quickly gathered their things and moved to a different spot in the library, much to the disappointment of Riley. He seemed thoroughly dejected at their departure.

"Well, now you've done it," he grumbled.

"By showing interest, you are only encouraging this nonsense to continue," Saiyah stated.

"It's going to continue anyway, little sis," Riley argued. "This is the first human mage we are talking about here. Not only that but a particularly BRUTAL one apparently."

Saiyah was about to retort when another group of gaggling acolytes walked by and sat down at the empty table directly across from them.

"...And I heard he has a collection of mage hearts. He draws from them using necromancy and can wield immense power, and THAT is why Arden took him on as acolyte."

Riley immediately smiled and leaned back to listen better as Saiyah huffed and shot up, collecting her books.

"Where are you going?" Riley inquired.

"To find somewhere quiet to study. But by all means, stay, enjoy story time," she added snidely as she turned away and quickly exited the library.

"Shit!"

Kye exclaimed in frustration, unexpectedly breaking the silence in the room as he opened his eyes to an unlit candle in the center of the dining table. The sun had just begun to set, casting an evening glow around the room. Arden was seated in his high-backed chair next to the fireplace, reading from an old-looking tome. His gaze rose slightly from his book with a note of interest as Kye ran his hands through his hair in exasperation. Realizing he had let his annoyance get the better of him, Kye quickly locked eyes with him, muttering a "Sorry..." in response.

"Don't be," Arden replied nonchalantly. "I happen to endorse the occasional cathartic release. That and alcohol," Arden added as he saluted with his current glass of fire whiskey. Kye chuckled slightly in response as he let out a long sigh. For the past few weeks, this scene had been a daily occurrence in the common area of Arden's tower. For hours the pair would sit in silence. Kye would practice his mage studies as Arden delved into volumes on elemental magic, researching the stones. Kye had still been unable to clear the first magical task Arden had given him, but it certainly hadn't been for lack of trying. Kye would focus on the candle every day till his head hurt from concentration. Then he would retire to read as many books as he was able to expand his knowledge of the Ancient language. Which he knew would come in handy if he ever was able to successfully cast anything.

Kye sighed again and leaned back in the dining chair, looking toward the ceiling as though it would grant him some cosmic awareness he was currently missing.

"I'm not thinking this through..." he muttered to himself, working through the puzzle in his mind.

"Overthinking it might be more accurate," Arden noted.

"What do you mean?"

"If it were as simple as reciting a word and waving your

hand, all mages would be maisters. Mages have the ability to manipulate the energy around us, call upon it and bend it to our will. And in order to do that, you need to feel, not just think. You have to create a connection with anything you wish to command."

"So...create a connection...with a candle?" Kye clarified hesitantly.

Arden smiled and nodded. "Yes, kid, even with a candle. Everything is made up of energy, same as you. And until you realize that, all the focus in the world won't help you."

Arden then turned back to his book, adding, "Step outside your head and try to rely more on what you feel."

Kye nodded and looked back to the candle. *Focus less on the words and more on the feeling.* To be fair, the only thing he was feeling at the moment was frustration. Which he imagined wasn't helping with the task. Kye rose from the table to give himself a break. He needed to calm his thoughts before he could try again. He poured himself a cup of tea and sat down on the sofa across from Arden.

"What about you?" he asked as Arden looked up again. "You told me some mages take years to master this exercise," Kye continued. "Were you one of them?"

Arden shook his head. "No, I was one who could light the candle instantly. But that is often the case with a ranger."

Kye eyed Arden, perplexed. "Ranger?"

Arden nodded. "It is a term used for those whose affinity lies with evocation magic."

"What do you mean by affinity?"

"An area of expertise, you could say," Arden explained. "A school of magic a mage specifically connects with. My affinity lies in evocation spells, so I can cast them with a fraction of the effort it would take for a mage who does not possess the talent. While Mireen, on the other hand, is a healer whose affinity lies with remedium magic. Which means she can drag someone from death's door with the same amount of effort that it would take for me to heal a paper cut. Every mage has an affinity. Over time, as you master the craft, you will learn where yours lies."

At the moment, Kye couldn't imagine an area of magic he would excel at. Then again, there had never been a human mage. Maybe he didn't have an affinity as other mages did. Perhaps every spell he learned from here on out would be met with the same hurdle as lighting the end of a candle. Arden did say some mages took years to clear the first task. Perhaps every other spell he learned would take years as well. Kye felt rather disheartened at the prospect.

Later that evening, Kye once again tackled his nemesis. He tried to take Arden's suggestion, reaching out with what he felt. But this, too, proved tricky, since Kye wasn't sure what he was supposed to feel. Would there be some unknown surge of energy he would suddenly be granted by successfully connecting with the world around him? Better yet, how was he to go about creating a connection with an inanimate object? Was a candle supposed to have a different kind of energy than, say, a chair? The whole thing made Kye feel even more frustrated at his inability to understand.

When Arden decided to retreat to his quarters as the moon rose, Kye decided a full night's rest probably wouldn't hurt him as well and abandoned his efforts for the evening.

However, lying in his bed several hours later, Kye realized rest wasn't going to be easily granted. His mind wouldn't quiet, no matter how much he tried to silence it. Kye had his eyes shut tight in the effort to grasp sleep, but he kept trying to sense the energy that was supposedly around him. The energy that he should be able to command as a mage. He opened his eyes when he was unable to detect anything aside from the slight breeze outside his window and the harmonious sounds of crickets. If he had the talent, shouldn't he be able to understand? Inadvertently, a familiar voice popped into his head. *"Humans cannot be mages. Their minds cannot process the ancient tongue or hope to cast with it. As such, they are far too weak to handle the strains of magic and would only injure themselves by trying."*

The council had thought him incapable, and what frustrated Kye more than anything was that somewhere in the back of his mind, he was worried they might be right. Kye sat up and leaned against the headboard, looking out the window. The moon cast a light glow over the utter darkness, only broken by the intermittent twinkle of stars. Everything was calm, at peace. Kye thought that a nighttime stroll might help clear his thoughts. Carefully heading out of his bedroom, he quietly entered the common room, trying his best not to disturb Arden's meditation. Kye slowly and silently exited the tower door. He then quickly proceeded down the winding staircase to the castle below.

Entering the great hall at night, he was greeted by a completely different atmosphere than he was accustomed to. There were no other mages in sight; the place was deserted, and only Kye's footsteps could be heard echoing against the marble floor. As he looked up at the glass ceiling high above him, he could see a cloudless night displaying thousands of shimmering stars. A full moon illuminated the sky in a pale gray glow. Kye took his time exploring the great hall, never really having had the chance before. So far, his days had been spent rushing from one place to the next, trying to avoid the indignant looks of others. He could finally take his time to explore the castle that was now his home. Roaming the halls, Kye poked in and out of rooms, some of whose purpose remained unclear. He wandered into one room which could be best described as an art gallery. Kye noticed there were several beautiful sculptures, as well as flowers in hand-painted vases. In a corner, on the south side of the great hall, Kye noticed one particularly large painting that captivated his attention. It was a mountain top somewhere, covered in wildflowers and shades of green. The wind whipped through the grass, giving the appearance of it swaying even in the still image. The sky was the lightest of blue, without even a trace of a cloud. Coming to a ledge, the scene opened up to a wide, vast ocean. Waves sprayed against the rocks, leaving pillows of white foam in their wake. Birds hovered on the breeze above the water. Kye had never seen the ocean. But the painting was so lifelike, he could easily picture himself standing on the edge of the cliff, looking out at the water below. Feeling the wind and the ocean spray. Not even knowing where it was or if the scene was a portrait of real life, Kye could certainly say it was one place he wished to see. He wasn't certain what the painting was called; the title below seemed to be written in elvish. After several more moments of admiring it, Kye tore his attention away to continue his walk through the great hall.

Exploring the castle, Kye found several other fascinating works of art, along with a multitude of elaborate fountains. He also found some areas he had not previously known existed, such as a game room, ballroom, music room, and conservatory. The castle seemed to be made up of endless rooms, finely decorated walls, and opulence around every corner. During his exploration, Kye realized he had inadvertently wandered to the library. Without a doubt, one of his favorite locations in the castle.

He pushed open the library door and almost instantly felt at ease. The library had a familiar feeling Kye couldn't quite place. He supposed it was due to the fond memories he had reading by candlelight during late hours in Umbree's manor. Some of the only fond memories he had of that place. It had been his peace, his escape, a sensation he felt even now. The library was completely deserted, the silence welcoming him. Kye began leisurely walking through the aisles, looking over the spines of countless books, compendiums of unimaginable knowledge, as he passed. He was still far from fluent in the ancient text. But he had come to find that his understanding had improved greatly. Now he could read the spines of many books. He wasn't exactly sure what he was looking for. Maybe some book titled *Beginners Guide* or *Easy Understanding of Magic,* though he was almost certain such a book did not exist. As Arden had stated, the first task had no shortcuts. It was learning to use a muscle he never had before. And that could only be done the hard way. But amongst the spines, one book did catch his attention. *Serenai Zephyrin,* meaning *The Calming of Winds.* Elemental magic. Arden had said that he was searching for knowledge about the creation stones. While he was here, perhaps Kye could assist in the search. Kye picked up the book and opened it. With just the first page, he could tell his understanding was still seriously lacking. But he was picking up enough words to piece together some of the meaning. Perhaps as he read, his understanding would increase. Kye turned the page and began heading toward the nearest table. As he turned the corner of the bookshelf, he was so engrossed in his reading he did not notice someone standing right in front of him. There was a jarring clatter as a vast selection of books fell to the floor, knocked out of the hands of the female elf Kye had just collided with. As she stumbled back, he instantly dropped to the ground and started helping collect the books. The female elf bent down and began assisting as well.

"Apologies," Kye said as he started handing her the books. "I wasn't looking where I was going."

"Yes, that much is apparent," she added curtly.

Her sharp reply caused Kye to look up. As soon as his eyes met hers, his breath caught in his chest. The elf appeared to be about his age, perhaps only slightly older, and strikingly beautiful. She had a warm olive complexion, and thick, dark brown hair that fell past her shoulders. Her face was a perfect oval, and her eyes were the color of amethysts and seemed to almost glow. Kye felt somewhat immobilized in her presence.

"Well?" she questioned impatiently.

"Well...?" Kye repeated thickly.

The female elf rolled her eyes in response. "My book," she clarified. "Are you planning on returning it to me, or do you intend to hold it hostage?"

Kye looked down to see he still held one of the volumes he had picked up off the floor.

"Oh, sorry," Kye stated, shaking off his befuddlement as he stood up. He started to hand the book back to her, stating, "I'm—"

"I know full well WHO you are, human," the elf shot back as she rose as well, the remainder of her books in hand. "By this point, I doubt there is a soul within Caelum Vallis that is not aware."

Kye was taken off guard by her harsh response. Then again, if he was hoping to exchange pleasantries with another mage in the castle, he best not hold his breath. His presence was tolerated but far from celebrated. Add to the fact he had practically knocked her over moments ago meant any hope of making a good first impression was basically a snowball's chance in hell.

"Yes, I'm sure you do," Kye replied matter of factly. "So I will not waste your time with further introductions."

Kye gave a slight apologetic bow as he presented the book to her. "Your book, my lady."

The elf snatched her book, staring down at Kye as most mages did, as something unfit to be breathing the same air. Kye tried to ignore her glare and bent down and collected his own book from the floor. "I wish you a pleasant evening," he added with a small nod of his head before turning and walking away. This was going to be how he was greeted by the majority of his fellow magi for the foreseeable future, so Kye saw no point in trying to dissuade them otherwise. His attempts would be futile anyway. Many believed a human unworthy and resented his station here. Any arguments to the contrary would only add fuel to the fire. It was a strange sensation, but Kye could swear he could feel her gaze boring into his back, even as he exited the library.

Kye thought it would be best to bring the book back to Arden's tower to study, but at the moment, he still felt too antsy to look over it with the devotion it deserved. He decided to continue his walk around the castle in the hopes it would wear him out and allow his mind to quiet.

He wandered aimlessly around the halls, admiring architecture and artwork as he went. Turning a corner, he suddenly heard someone humming a tune very softly. Following the source of the song, Kye found himself standing in front of another familiar set of double doors with fruit etched in them. Kye carefully opened one of the doors as the wonderful scent of meat and spices hit his nose. Stepping inside, he could hear Celeste humming a tune he was unfamiliar with as she chopped vegetables and sliced meat. As she turned to add the potatoes to the stove, she looked up to see Kye suddenly standing there. Celeste gave a slight jump and squeaked in surprise.

"Oh, Kye!" she replied, clutching her heart. "Ya scared the bewitches outta me."

"I'm sorry," Kye replied earnestly. He seemed to be apologizing a lot this evening. "I just heard you in the kitchen. I didn't mean to startle you. I'll leave you in peace."

Celeste caught him with a stern gaze. "Nonsense. You are welcome here anytime, and don't ya be forgettin' it."

Kye smiled back at her in response. "What are you cooking?" The enticing smells coming from the pot were causing his mouth to water.

"Ollies 'n mash," Celeste replied. "'Tis a dwarf recipe, filled with cream, potatoes broiled in butter, and mixed with basil. It's got to simmer for several hours, so I got an early start on it for breakfast."

Celeste then caught him with a questioning look. "On that note, wha' are you doing about the castle at this hour?" she inquired. "I was under the impression that humans slept."

"We do. I just had a bit of trouble with that this evening. I thought a walk might help."

Celeste snapped her fingers at him in response. "Ah, well, if it's a sleep remedy you be needin', you've come to the right place."

She pulled a kettle out from one of the cabinets and filled it with water before setting it on the stove. She gestured to one of the many empty tables. "Have a seat, I'll fix ya up a cup of me arganot tea. Guaranteed to make even an elf nod off."

Kye nodded appreciatively as he took a seat at the nearest table. Celeste went back to preparing breakfast as the kettle heated.

"It smells fantastic," Kye noted, gesturing to the meal.

Celeste gave a smile and a chuckle. "Thank ya, lad. Ya know, they say that cookin is close to magic...closest I'll ever come at least."

Kye was caught off guard. "You can't cast?"

Celeste shook her head. "Never had the talent for it, no matter how much I wished otherwise," she stated as she stirred the pot. "Arden spent a lot of time on Brooma, he and me cousin were like brothers. When he joined the council, I remember I used to pester him somethin' fierce, wantin' to know each new spell he learned, how to pronounce it, how to stand. I was convinced I would eventually catch on...but sadly, I never did. Then one day, not long after he became a maister, Arden came back to Brooma. He said the castle needed a chef, asked if I'd be interested. I jumped at the chance, of course, but...I don't know how true that was. From some of the whispers I've heard, he had to fight tooth and nail with the council to allow a non-magic wielder in Caelum Vallis. But I think his thinkin' was, if I couldn't cast magic, at least I could be close to it."

Celeste paused for a moment before looking back at Kye with a smile. "He's a softy, that one. Don't let him try to convince ya otherwise."

Kye smiled back as Celeste went back to chopping vegetables. "Speakin of, I hear congratulations are in order," she mentioned, as Kye looked back at her, confused. "I 'erd the council officially welcomed you as Arden's acolyte."

Kye couldn't help but chuckle slightly. "I think 'welcomed' is a bit of an overstatement. I feel 'reluctantly accepted' would be more appropriate."

"Ah, that's to be expected," Celeste added. "A bunch of old codgers, the lot of them. Not good with change, and a good lot of mages thinkin' themselves above certain races, especially humans."

"But Arden doesn't," Kye stated simply. It was a marvel to him, considering the way so many of the council members behaved. Celeste nodded in agreement. "Oh, aye. I suppose that would have a lot to do with his father."

Kye perked up in interest. "His father?" he questioned as Celeste walked over and deposited a cup of tea on the table in front of Kye.

"Aye, Arden's father was a trader," she continued. "But he didn't just sell within Isalia. He peddled fine elven good to all the Six Realms. Didn't matter your station or standin', if you had the coin, he'd do business with ya."

Celeste retreated behind the counter to continue cooking as Kye leaned over and sipped the tea. It tasted flowery but spicy. From just one taste, Kye could tell it had a calming effect.

"He was respected by other races because of it. Treated us all the same, he did," Celeste continued as she chopped meat. "But gained himself a good bit of animosity with the elves, too, thinkin' he was sellin' to races he ought not. He thought the whole 'holier than thou' swish that elves held was a lot of codswallop. Arden took that stance, too. After all, since he traveled with his da so much, spent more time growing up around other races than he did his own. Tends to broaden one's world view a bit. I think that's part of why he became a maister. He saw the bad the races fared when travelin', thought that he could do some good. An' good he has done."

"Considering the animosity the elves harbored for his father, I'm surprised the High Council allowed him to become a member," Kye replied.

After all, the High Council was made up mostly of elves, since magic was far more prominent in elf kind than any other race. Add to the fact the High Council was based in the elves' home realm, if the High Council had that much ire for Arden's father, they could have refused him as an acolyte in a heartbeat. But Celeste just smiled in response.

"Well, it's not exactly like they could argue," she added. "Arden was naturally gifted in the craft. There was not a mage that could stand against him when it came to talent. He is still to this day the strongest mage on the council. In fact, when the previous leader of the council stepped down, the council asked Arden to take the spot."

Kye raised his eyebrows in response. Considering the way Arden clashed with the council, he was surprised to hear they had once wished him as their leader. "I'm guessing his response was no?" Kye replied.

"Aye. I actually think his exact words were, 'I don't give a piss about politics and paperwork.'"

Kye chuckled; that sounded like Arden. "So the council elected Valor instead?"

Celeste nodded. "Oh, aye, with a good bit of resentment too. Valor was offended that the council thought of him second for the job. After all, he came from a high-bred family, had status and prestige, far greater than that of Arden. Thought he should have been the only choice for council leader. And I'd imagine that feelin' is why Arden and Valor butt heads as often as they do."

Celeste then paused for a moment. "Well...that 'n' Arden has a bit of an abrasive personality," she added with a wink. "Still, the council respects him and what he has to say. After all, there has not been a mage with his skill for several generations."

"And...he selected a human as his acolyte," Kye stated in disbelief. The more he heard of Arden, the more he questioned why he had asked Kye to be his apprentice in the first place. Even if Kye did possess the skills of a mage, he was hardly gifted in the craft. Arden could have asked some of the most talented mages in the Six Realms to study under him, an offer it sounded like any would gladly accept. If it was simply for the purpose of keeping Kye alive, Arden could have just offered him asylum in Isalia. Celeste just looked back at Kye with a soft grin. "That surprises you?"

"It doesn't you?" Kye asked.

Celeste shook her head.

"Knowing Arden, not one bit," she stated plainly. Kye must have given her a questioning look, for Celeste merely chuckled and continued.

"A few years back, a mage from an elite elven family reached out to the High Council with the specific interest of becoming an acolyte. Studying under Lord Arden, to be exact. The boy was talented in the craft, and as such, wanted to tutor under the best. He even offered a demonstration of his abilities to the entire council, to prove his skill. I witnessed the demonstration firsthand—much of Caelum Vallis did, in fact—and I have to say, the boy was impressive. Seemed the lad knew it too, the way he spoke. Well, it was obvious he had a bit of a head about him. Throughout the entire affair, Arden looked completely uninterested. In fact, when it was all said and done, he asked the boy just one question. The boy stuttered, stumbled over his response, and Arden outright refused him. The council exploded in an uproar. Called Arden mad, they did. Insisting he change his mind and take the boy on as his acolyte. But Arden wouldn't budge. Later on, I pulled him aside, and I asked him. 'Why didn't ya take the boy on as yur apprentice?' I said. 'It is obvious the boy is skilled.' But Arden just shook his head. 'I don' t care about skill,' he said, 'I care about heart. That happens to be the one thing ya can't teach.'"

Celeste looked up from her cooking and stared Kye straight in the eye. "You got heart, lad," she stated sincerely. "Mountains of it. Everything else…well, as Arden says, that can be taught."

Kye thought over Celeste's words, staring at his now empty cup of tea. "What was the one question Arden asked the boy?"

Celeste gave Kye a knowing smirk. "Would you trade yer life tae save another's?"

Kye felt at a loss for words. Arden thought him a more worthy student than a talented elf mage from a high-born family. He had faith in him, trusted him. For all who in life had told him he was less, Arden was the first to say he could be more. As such, Kye felt determined not to disappoint him. To prove himself a worthy acolyte. His thoughts instantly drifted to the candle waiting on the kitchen table upstairs. Kye stood up from the table and collected his book.

"I feel as though your remedy may have worked," Kye stated as he placed the empty tea cup back on the counter. "I should head back to Arden's tower to try and get some sleep. But I thank you for the tea and the conversation."

"Bah!" Celeste balked with a wave of her hand. "Hardly be needin' thanks, wasting yur time speaking to an old girl like me."

"It is never a waste," Kye stated sincerely. "And you are certainly not old."

Celeste beamed back at him in response and chuckled.

"See what I mean," she said, pointing a finger at Kye. "All heart, you are."

Kye smiled back before giving her a slight bow. "Goodnight, Celeste."

"Aye, sleep well, Kye," she added with a nod of her own.

Standing once again in Arden's tower, Kye could not tear his eyes away from the candle sitting in the middle of the dining table. Such an ordinary object that he had used a thousand times before would not defeat him. Kye found himself sitting down at the dining table once more. Arden had given him clues on how to unleash his magic—that it was more about feeling than speaking. But that was the trick—what was he supposed to feel? Kye reached out and touched the unlit candle. There was no energy radiating off it that he could detect. So perhaps the connection had to be initiated with him. But there lay the problem. You could create connections with people, even with animals. Creating a connection with an object, though, wasn't possible, was it? Arden had said it was, and clearly it was something he could do. "*You are overthinking this.*" Kye placed his hands on the temples of his head, Arden's words bouncing around in his brain. Okay, less thought, more feeling. So, what feeling did he get looking at this candle? Kye stared hard at the formed wax for a solid minute, unable to shake the sensation that this was rather ridiculous. Nothing. He got no feeling from a candle. I mean, it wasn't like it was a beautiful view or a piece of music or a painting. Kye froze as soon as the thought ran through his head. A painting. The painting in the great hall. That too was an inanimate object. But Kye had got a feeling from it, like he was standing on the edge of that cliff, looking out over the ocean before him. He could feel the sun, the wind, and the spray of the water. For a moment, no matter how brief, he had been connected to that painting. It had felt like he was a part of it, and it was part of him. So maybe that was the key. To connect with something, imagine it was a part of you. Kye studied the candle before him in great detail, looking over every inch of it. Memorizing the height, the silver holder it sat in, the wick, the color of the wax. Kye closed his eyes, creating a perfect replica in his mind. Focusing on the candle within him, Kye imagined it ignite. He could feel the heat from the flames, see the fire dancing clearly. This time, as Kye raised his hand for the spell, he imagined the flame not being produced from some unknown location in the ether. This time, he imagined the flame coming from within him, the same place his envisioned candle was burning.

"*Pyraela*," Kye whispered, imagining the heat flowing from his chest and passing through his fingertips, out toward the candle. As Kye slowly opened his eyes, he quickly shot up, knocking over the dining chair with a loud clatter. Kye stood immobilized for several moments, staring in shock. For there, sitting on the dining table in all its glory, was a single—burning—candle. It was casting small shadows around the common area, the flame dancing almost in celebration. Kye chortled in disbelief, slowly approaching the lit candle as though it was about to attack. He had done it.

Clapping could be heard, and Kye spun around to see Arden standing at the foot of the stairs. The ruckus Kye had made seemed to have drawn the elven maister from his quarters. Arden stood grinning and slowly applauded Kye's achievement.

"Very good, kid," Arden commented as he looked at the lit candle. "Hard part's over. Now the fun begins."

The sun was hanging low in the sky as Saiyah crossed the courtyard in a particularly bitter mood. She had just left the library yet again, being unable to focus because of the chatter and nonsense around her. She had thought of merely studying at night, but the other night when she had tried to, she had actually run into the human that was the cause of all this to begin with. And because of that meeting, Saiyah could safely say the stories were a load of bollocks. The human's demeanor did not scream brutal killer or hunter of mages. In fact, he appeared quite ordinary indeed, from what she had discerned. Still, he did not belong here. And if he wasn't here in the first place, these stories would not be swirling around the castle, and Saiyah would not be having such trouble focusing. She was attempting to master telepathy, which was a particularly tricky art to learn in the first place, and certainly made more so if there was no place of solitude in which to study the craft. Riley was of no help whatsoever. He thought the tales of the human were great fun and wouldn't lift a finger to help her silence the masses. Kes had taken the approach of merely studying in her quarters. Saiyah would take that approach as well if she could; however, Maister Luell tended to be quite chatty when she was trying to focus. She would complain to Saiyah about the council or members of it that caused her particular grief (namely Lord Arden). And while Saiyah appreciated that her master felt at ease enough with her to engage in small talk, it did make actually learning the magical arts rather difficult. As it was, Luell didn't really ever teach Saiyah magic herself. Instead, if Saiyah asked her about a spell, she would tell her to "go to the library. All the answers in the world lie there." The library, however, was quickly becoming a useless endeavor.

As Saiyah looked up, she was pulled from her train of thought by a figure walking by. There, crossing the courtyard a few feet ahead of her, was Maister Arden. He was carrying several books and heading to his tower for the evening. Saiyah immediately straightened herself up. If she wanted this issue addressed, she would take it straight to the source.

"MAISTER ARDEN!" Saiyah shouted to catch his attention as she rushed to catch up with him. Maister Arden stopped and turned to Saiyah, looking slightly bewildered. As soon as Saiyah was close enough, she bowed slightly and stated, "*Sulara anor*, Maister Arden."

"*Sulara anor*, Saiyah," Maister Arden replied as he turned and attempted to continue his walk with Saiyah following him.

"I'm assuming you flagged me down for some reason other than a simple greeting," said Arden as Saiyah matched his pace.

Saiyah nodded in response. "Actually, I was hoping to discuss a matter with you."

Maister Arden gave her a confused sideways glance. "If you have questions, Saiyah, might I suggest you take them to your maister? I think Luell's head may actually explode if she hears you sought counsel from me."

Saiyah thought that to be a fair assessment. Maister Luell often had a great many things to say about Maister Arden. None of them could be considered kind. To be fair, from Lord Arden's reaction, the distaste seemed to be shared.

"Unfortunately, this is a matter that only you can address," Saiyah stated insistently. Arden stopped and turned toward her, looking intrigued.

"Very well. What matter did you wish to discuss?"

"It's about your acolyte."

"Ah," Arden responded rather nonchalantly, "most things seem to be, nowadays. So tell me, what grievances do you have with him?"

"I merely wish to know why. Why did you ask a human to be your acolyte?"

Arden shrugged. "Why not? You believe him unworthy?"

"Yes."

Arden seemed amused by Saiyah's direct response. Saiyah had come to learn that Maister Arden appreciated brutal honesty. Which was good because she wasn't in the mood to sugarcoat the situation.

"Really?" he inquired. "And why is that?"

Saiyah felt the answer was obvious. Could he really not see why allowing the human here was a horrible idea?

"Because he is human." Saiyah clarified, "They are weak and frail in comparison to us."

"I have known many an elven maister that has been cut down well before their time. Our healing strengths aside," Arden replied.

Saiyah was slightly frustrated. That wasn't the point.

"His life is short," Saiyah retorted.

"We are mages of the High Council, Saiyah. We could very well die tomorrow. In which case, our long lifespan wouldn't matter one bit."

Saiyah was getting frustrated that every argument she made was immediately countered by Arden. He seemed adamant to shoot down her assertions, no matter what she had to say.

"You do him a disservice by inviting him here," Saiyah shot back. Arden seemed surprised by that.

"Is that so?" he inquired.

"Yes," Saiyah retorted. "He is the first human acolyte. He is not accepted. He is treated as an outcast."

"And yet he was treated so very well as a slave."

Saiyah was momentarily at a loss from his counter, her mind trying to put together her rebuttal so that Lord Arden could understand. So he could see the problem with a human being a mage. Mages were the protectors of all Six Realms, and a human could never be that. But as she silently formulated her argument, Arden merely shook his head.

"You know, I have often considered Luell to be an arrogant, entitled adult child, not possessing enough sense to pound salt," he stated. "But I did applaud her choice of you as her acolyte. You have always struck me as someone with high intelligence, with your head on straight. Clearly, I was far too generous."

Saiyah was momentarily stunned by Arden's insult. As the meaning of his words sunk in, Saiyah's anger flared.

"Excuse me?" she seethed.

"Have you actually spoken to him?" Arden inquired, unconcerned. "My acolyte?"

Saiyah hesitated. She doubted the small, hostile interaction she had had with him in the library could really count as a conversation in Arden's eyes. "N-No, not exactly," she reluctantly replied.

"Then you are merely relaying the opinions of others, without forming any of your own. If you think he is so unqualified, then talk to him. Tell me in your own words why he's unfit. Perhaps then I will take your concerns more seriously. But don't come back to speak with me on this matter until you have."

Saiyah just stood there silently, unable to contest Lord Arden's argument. It was true—her basis for believing this human was unfit to be a mage was not based on personal observation. But she had been around humans enough to know they did not possess the ability to fight. Why, without other races looking after them, they would easily die out. They were injured far too easily to even think of participating in battle. Throwing those breakable creatures into a fight was a recipe for disaster. Saiyah understood this, even if Lord Arden didn't. After a few moments of silence, Arden added, "I trust that concludes our conversation. *Anor norin*, Saiyah." He then turned and walked away without another word, leaving a seething acolyte in his wake.

CHAPTER 7
Comprehension of the Craft

A cool autumn breeze wafted past Kye's face as he followed Arden into the forest behind his tower. The leaves from the trees had started changing colors, from brilliant green to shades of yellow, orange, and brown. Kye had thought that Isalia was beautiful during the summer, but it was stunning during fall. The splash of colors made the landscape almost glow. The crunch of discarded leaves echoed under his feet with each step he took. Kye shivered as he wrapped his scarf a bit tighter around his neck and put his hands in the pockets of his robe. He had spent the entirety of his life till now in a much warmer climate. The changing seasons of Isalia would take some getting used to. Arden, on the other hand, seemed completely unfazed by the colder temperature, braving the cold without a scarf or cloak. They had been walking for some time now, not that Kye was complaining. He was greatly enjoying the chance for fresh air and to observe the landscape around him. He had spent most of his time cooped up in Arden's tower, practicing his spells with renewed excitement. After he had learned to tap into the magic around him, casting became much easier. He had moved on from simply lighting a candle to summoning elements within his palm and moving objects around at will. In fact, Kye had come to find that while summoning elements drained him, it was much less intensive to move existing objects around to his advantage. As such, commanding a fallen tree branch to levitate and smack an opponent upside the head was much simpler than trying to fry them with a lightning bolt. However, Kye could definitely tell evocation was NOT his affinity. Any attack spell he cast left him feeling drained and exhausted afterward. Arden had assured him that even if it wasn't his affinity, in time it would get easier.

Kye had also been branching out and reading up on other areas of magic. Arden had given him lessons on alchemy, teaching Kye how to brew potions. Kye thought since he had spent so much time cooking, maybe alchemy was his affinity. But the poison antidote he tried to brew had actually come out brown and slightly burnt, which had been a wonder to even Arden. Kye had also tried his hand at summoning spirits. But this had very minor success as well, as the spirit that appeared before him had left almost instantly, without answering a single one of Kye's questions. Divination proved equally difficult. Kye stood over a bowl of water with herbs mixed into it. He swirled the water with his finger over and over while muttering "*aspisia*." Seers could see pictures in the water, supposedly of what was to come. It took several hours, and exhausted him, and Kye only got a flash of two images: falling snow and blue flame. This, too, clearly wasn't his area of expertise. He had asked Arden what the images meant, and Arden told him even the most talented seers often have trouble interpreting the pictures. But those with the affinity could see more than those without it.

This morning, however, when Kye had been engrossed in a cup of tea, a plate of eggs, and a book on transmutation, Arden had proclaimed that today Kye would be focusing on dueling magic. Which is how they came to be walking into the woods behind the castle.

Arden finally stopped when the path they had been following opened up to a small clearing. Kye could no longer see the castle from this point, and they were well covered by shrubbery. He wondered why the secrecy around the lesson.

"Is there a reason we came out here instead of practicing in the tower?" Kye asked.

Arden nodded. "Several. For starters, me shooting evocation spells at you in an enclosed space is guaranteed to reduce it to rubble. There are dueling grounds in which most other mages practice sparring with each other. But I don't really want the other mages to be aware of any strengths or weaknesses you may have in your magic, at least till we find your affinity."

Kye nodded, figuring that was Arden's way of saying if others knew his weakness now, they would no doubt try to exploit it. Thus, the enclosed clearing, far away from prying eyes. Kye had done his best to avoid other mages since his arrival at the castle, trying to quickly learn the spells needed to hold his own. He knew he would never be accepted unless he could prove that, while he may be human, he was still a mage. Able to stand with them or against them, as their equal. So almost every waking moment he had spent devoted to that end.

"Plus, it will take some practice before your defensive magic is strong enough to fight toe to toe with another mage. Since you are human, we will need to focus more time on your defensive spells than most other acolytes do," Arden added.

"Why is that?" Kye inquired.

"Because other races have some form of natural defensive capabilities." Arden clarified, "Goblins, for example, have skin no thicker than humans and can easily be damaged. Their bone structure, however, is harder than steel, and they have an interlocking rib cage to protect vital organs. Same goes for dwarfs; their skeletal structure is similar. A shif's skin is tougher, and their bones are flexible in their natural state. Plus they can change their shape into animals at will, swapping from easy prey to a fearsome opponent in an instant. Orcs, of course, are not only massive but have skin as thick as a dragon hide. Many mages have tried to take down an orc and succeeded in nothing more than pissing them off.

"As with elves," Arden stated, as he pulled an athame out of a sheath on his belt. Kye flinched slightly as Arden suddenly sliced the blade across the palm of his left hand, silver blood now staining the steel. "Our skin and skeletons are not as strong as other races. However, we do possess a powerful innate healing ability. Which means unless we suffer a fatal blow to the head or the heart, we are extremely difficult to kill." Arden held out his hand for Kye to see. Kye watched in amazement as the cut on Arden's hand stopped bleeding and mended itself in an instant. Arden cleaned the dagger before sheathing it.

"Then there are humans. You don't have any of the natural defenses the other races possess. You are also slow to heal injuries, and damage you sustain can be extensive. In comparison, you are like a...squishy blood bag supported by a brittle bone structure."

Kye scrunched his face up as he muttered, "That's a charming analogy."

"But a truthful one. You must first admit your weaknesses in order to realize your strengths."

"Do I have any?" Kye inquired. "Strengths, that is. 'Cause as a human, my area of expertise seems to reside in bleeding lots and breaking easily."

"I think you got a few more strengths than that, kid." Arden chuckled. "You might not have the same physical strengths as other races, but intellectual strengths can be just as important. You think quickly on your feet and are good at problem solving, which is essential for strategy. You are rational in difficult scenarios but still feel empathy for others. And you are brave when you need to be, but you also don't disregard your fear."

"You're saying fear is a strength?" Kye inquired.

"Of course it is. It heightens senses, warns of danger, and is the basis for instinct. Don't disregard fear, it can be a sword or a crutch, depending on how it's wielded. The trick is to allow it to sharpen you without allowing it to cripple you."

Kye silently pondered this. He hadn't ever considered emotional or intellectual strengths in a comparison with physical attributes. Also, he wasn't sure how being level-headed or quick-witted would help with a rampaging orc coming at him.

"For any physical traits you may be lacking, that is what defensive magic does. It levels the playing field when facing off against a stronger opponent. Speaking of..."

Arden waved his hand and muttered. Kye watched as a large barrier formed around the two of them, creating a large enclosing sphere.

"Just in case any stray fire gets away from us," Arden explained. He pointed at a spot about twenty feet in front of him. "Kye, you stand there," he instructed. Kye immediately took his position as Arden cleared brush out of the line of sight between him and Kye with a wave of his hand.

"Now, this is going to require a lot of focus," Arden began. "We are going to teach you to create a barrier, much like the one that surrounds us now. Even though it may not look like it, my focus is constant in order to maintain it. As you progress with your magic, you will learn how to maintain a barrier such as this while also casting other spells. But for right now, we just need to get to the point where the barrier you create lasts long enough and is strong enough to ward off any offensive magic coming toward you. Now clear your mind, focus, and repeat after me, *Aegira*."

"*Aegira*," Kye stated, clearing his mind and drawing from the magic within. Sure enough, a small barrier appeared around him for a moment and then dissipated. Kye could add defensive magic to the growing list of areas his affinity did not lie in. Even with that small effort, he felt like he'd just run up and down the stairs to Arden's tower ten times.

"That's okay," Arden stated as Kye leaned over and caught his breath. "Creating and maintaining a barrier takes immense energy. You'll get used to it."

Considering how draining creating one for one moment was, Kye was absolutely stunned that Arden was maintaining a barrier this size without seeming the least bit winded. The clear difference in power between an acolyte and a maister.

"You up to trying again?" Arden inquired. Kye nodded without hesitation, took a deep breath, and shouted in a determined tone. "*Aegira!*"

Several hours later, a small fireball hit Kye with the force of a falling tree. He had improved to the point that his shield held, but the force of the attack knocked him flat on his back. Kye sprawled out on the cold earth, trying to catch his breath. It was strange to remember that the air had felt chilly to him walking out here. Now it was a welcome respite to combat the sweat on his brow.

"Good," Arden remarked as he walked over to where Kye lay. "You were able to hold the shield long enough to fend off the attack, but we still need to work on your stance. Attack spells can hit like a ton of bricks. If you aren't prepared, they'll take you to the ground. Then your opponent will have you."

Arden leaned over where Kye lay, looking down at him. "Ready to try again?"

Kye simply nodded, unable to speak much as he gasped for air. He started to push himself back up off the ground, and his arms shook from the weight. In truth, he was exhausted, but he wouldn't quit. Kye forced himself into a quivering stance and took a defensive position once again. Arden observed the effort it took for Kye to get up, seeming to just now realize how tired he was. Arden cast his attention toward the horizon.

"On second thought, it's starting to get late," he stated. "How about we call it quits for today?"

Kye shook his head, determined to prove he was capable. "No, I can try again," Kye insisted in between breaths. Arden turned back to the rock he had been standing near and pulled a container and a cup out of his satchel.

"Enough, kid," he stated, walking back over to Kye. "Perfection cannot be achieved in a day."

He handed Kye a cup filled with the warm liquid from the container before returning to his rock to sit and pour himself a cup. As Arden waved his hand to dispel the barrier he had been maintaining, it was clear that he was not inclined to continue their lesson. Kye leaned against the nearest oak tree and slid down to seat himself at its base. Settled on the roots, he began to sip on the warm liquid between small gasps of breath. The drink tasted like honey—some kind of mead, was Kye's guess. It certainly helped warm his tired muscles. Arden was sipping from his own cup, looking no worse for wear from the long sparring session. As he observed his master, Celeste's comment popped into Kye's head.

"Is it true that you are the most powerful mage on the council?" he inquired. Arden appeared taken off guard by the question.

"Now, where did you hear that?"

"Celeste. She also said that the majority of the council sees you that way as well."

Arden shrugged. "There are some who believe that. Rangers are often mistaken as more powerful simply because we specialize in attack magic. I personally believe there are mages with far more dangerous talents out there."

Kye tilted his head in interest. "Like who?"

"Blighters, for one," Arden replied as he poured himself another cup. When he looked back at Kye's confused expression, he clarified, "It is the nickname we call those whose affinity lies in necromancy. They are able to manipulate the souls of the departed, bind them to this world to do their bidding. The spirits become corrupted and angry, turning those who were once people into monsters. It's the reason necromancy is a forbidden art."

Kye had heard that necromancy was forbidden before, but hearing the explanation for it made complete sense. It sounded horrific.

"Charmers are another particularly dangerous breed," Arden continued. "Those whose affinity lies in enchantment magic. Rangers may hit like a hammer, but facing off against one, you will fight with all you have. With a charmer, however, you won't fight. You won't want to. They will get inside your head and show you the most beautiful things. Places you've longed to see, loved ones long since lost. They will paint you a wonderful world, an inviting world, and you will want to let your guard down, want to let them in. But you can't let them in because if you do, they will fracture your mind like a mirror, and you will never be able to put the pieces back together. Those with an affinity for mind manipulation usually also take immense enjoyment in breaking them. It's why Umbree was so dangerous."

Kye choked a bit on the liquid he was sipping. "Umbree is a charmer!?" Arden nodded.

"Count your blessings if he never saw fit to use his talents on you, kid," he continued. "He had a skill for breaking minds. It's the main reason he was considered so powerful on the council."

Kye felt a slight chill run up his spine at the thought of what Umbree had been capable of. Umbree had always seemed powerful to him. But hearing Arden talk, he could have shattered him in an instant and left nothing but a shell standing. Knowing that, Kye felt compelled to learn how to defend himself against it. He was determined that Umbree would never hold power over him again.

"So...how do you fight back?" Kye inquired. "Is there a spell or something?"

Arden shook his head. "The illusion is created in your own head. There is no spell to protect you from your own thoughts."

"Then...how?"

"It takes a strong mind to fight back against a charmer. You have to destroy the dream, dispel the source of the illusion. No matter how much it hurts, no matter how much you don't want to, you have to. It's the only way to show the truth."

Kye nodded, still a little confused as to what Arden meant. But he understood that any fighting against a charmer would have to be done within the illusion itself. Mind against mind.

Arden got up from his rock and packed his satchel.

"Well, I think that's enough practice for today. Ready to pack it in?"

Kye nodded, standing up as well. He was already starting to feel the ache in his muscles from the long sparring session. As they headed back to the tower, Kye couldn't help but think how he usually had trouble getting his mind to quiet at night. But after today's lesson, he could already tell he was going to have no trouble sleeping. And tomorrow was going to be rough.

It was well past midnight when Saiyah entered the library. There was not a sound to be heard throughout the castle, a welcome change to the buzzing commotion of the day. Saiyah had finally conceded to studying at night. The constant chatter of her colleagues during daylight hours was driving her mad. That the favorite topic of discussion was still the human acolyte didn't help. Granted, the gossip had died down a bit in the last few months, mainly because so few had even laid eyes on him. Her fellow acolytes were beginning to think he didn't exist. But Saiyah knew he existed, much to her distaste. Trying to talk to Lord Arden about the ruckus he had caused allowing a human to study the arcane arts had been a non-starter. He seemed convinced that the human was fit to be an acolyte, a conclusion Saiyah was having trouble understanding.

Saiyah opened the doors to the library, carrying four books on astral projection. Maister Luell had told her it took a particularly strong mind to master it and that it was very advanced magic. If anything, though, that just spurred Saiyah's determination to prove that she could. Saiyah combed the shelves of old, worn spell books, looking for any book on magic of the mind that she hadn't consumed yet. She was looking over a rather heavy volume covering the magic of telepathy when a rustle caught her attention. Whilst the silence of the library and the lateness of the hour had made her assume that she was alone, there, seated to her right at a table by the window, sat the living, breathing cause of her frustration. The human was leaning over a book, with several more sprawled out on the table in front of him. He was so completely involved in his studies, he hadn't noticed Saiyah in the library with him. Saiyah ducked behind the shelf she had been perusing so as not to have to interact with him. She cursed and instantly thought of cutting her losses and heading straight for the door. Just as she was bee-lining toward the exit, Master Arden's voice popped into her head:

"You are merely relaying to me the opinions of others, without forming any of your own. If you think he is so unqualified, then talk to him. Tell me in your own words why he is unfit."

Saiyah stopped less than two feet from the door. She didn't want to speak with the human, but Arden had basically called her mindless, following the opinions of others as though she couldn't think for herself. Saiyah knew that humans were not worthy of studying magic, and if Lord Arden thought a conversation with the human would help to prove that, then so be it. Saiyah marched over to where the human sat. He still hadn't noticed her presence till Saiyah blurted out, "Why are you here!?"

The human jumped slightly from the sudden voice behind him and turned to see Saiyah standing there, chin held high in the proud stance most elves fell into naturally.

"I'm sorry?" he questioned, confused by her outburst.

"Why are you here?" Saiyah repeated, her patience already spent.

"In the library?"

"At this castle," Saiyah bit back. "Why are you somewhere you clearly don't belong?"

"Force of habit, I suppose," he replied. "Humans have become rather used to hearing we don't belong. I don't see how this is any different."

"Then you are a fool as well!" Saiyah hissed. The human gave a long sigh before closing the book he had been reading to grant Saiyah his full attention, muttering under his breath, "I see we are skipping straight past pleasantries."

"No human has ever been a mage, and for good reason," Saiyah continued on her rant. "Your kind is weak, fragile, irrational, and short-lived. As such, your attendance here is considered an insult. Do you know what the other mages think of you?"

"Very little, I'd imagine," the human replied. "I doubt they would enslave a race they held in high regard."

"Clearly, you think no better of mages," Saiyah retorted. "I'm curious why you would wish to become one?"

"You mean why would a weak, fragile, short-lived human want to learn to defend himself?"

Saiyah scoffed. "I believe we both know your interest in the craft goes beyond mere defense," she snapped.

The human's eyes narrowed in response. "Meaning?" he inquired carefully.

Saiyah held her head up, adding in disdain, "I heard what you did, how you viciously attacked your former master. Betraying the trust of the one who took care of you."

"Took care of me!?" the human clarified incredulously.

"Yes! A most underhanded, brutal act befitting a savage!" Saiyah made no attempt whatsoever to hide her disdain.

The human's face contorted in anger. "Right... Just so I am clear, I am an irrational, fragile, underhanded, savage, fool," he clarified. "Any other insults to my character I might be missing?"

"You believe my assessment unjust?" Saiyah replied. "Do you deny attacking your former master?"

"Not at all."

"And do you have any justification for your actions?"

"Many, throughout the years. But at that particular moment, it was because he was trying to kill Arden!"

Saiyah froze. She had not expected that response.

"You...attacked your master because you were trying to save Lord Arden?" Saiyah asked in confusion.

"If you can believe it," the human retorted. "Though I can understand your skepticism, my lady. I guess that would be pretty out of character for a savage human, after all."

"That...is not what I..." Saiyah felt her voice shrink as her sentence trailed off. In all the stories she had heard about the human, there had not been one mention of him coming to the defense of another. The human shook his head as he stood and collected his books.

"Of course, I doubt any reason I could offer would justify my actions. Not to the council, not to you," the human added with ire, staring straight into Saiyah's eyes. "After all, you and the other highborns have already decided, right? I just don't belong."

The human stepped around Saiyah and headed toward the exit, not sparing even a parting glance as he marched out of the library.

Saiyah trudged back to her quarters, deep in thought. Once inside the room, she began slowly pacing, replaying the conversation in her head. He had to be lying, right? There had not been any mention of the human coming to the aid of another. Especially not another mage. Not even Lady Luell had mentioned the human trying to save Lord Arden's life. No, he had been painted as a villain, a beast. All the stories she had heard couldn't be wrong. After all, humans were quite capable of lashing out in anger. Their emotions tended to get the better of them. That human was no different—he couldn't be. That human was just trying to cover up his offense. That human was just trying to dissuade her. That had to be it.

Saiyah stopped pacing for a moment as a wave of awareness washed over her. That human... She had chastised him, called him unworthy, then berated him and made snap judgments about his character. She had bashed his abilities, his demeanor, his race, all based on the stories of humans she had heard swirling around the castle and ones her own family had relayed to her. Now, she was hit with one blunt fact she couldn't deny, causing her to come face to face with her own hypocrisy. That human... She believed she already knew all there was to know about him, when in truth she had only just realized... She didn't even know his name.

Umbree was drumming his fingers on a crudely designed table as he sat on a wobbly stool, sipping brandy. He listened to the sound of water drip off stalagmites. His eyes scanned the damp, dark cave he was holed up in. Oh, how the mighty had fallen. He should be decked out in jewels and silks, sitting on pillows instead of crammed into this hovel. But it would be more than worth it if his master could bestow on him his greatest desire. He and his cohorts had been teleported back to Isalia, under the council's radar, using Orin's power. They were now hiding in a cave just outside the Silver City. Umbree was keeping close tabs on the castle, waiting for his opportunity to sneak in and take hold of the creation stone. Luckily, he still had those loyal to him and Orin within the castle walls. Torha had gone off to meet up with one of their allies, while Belthier went to procure more supplies and weapons for their cause. Umbree had been forced to keep a low profile inside this damp cave, since he was currently under suspicion from the council. It was a necessary evil but still didn't help with his cabin fever. One of the sigils Umbree had placed at the mouth of the cave alerted him that a presence was coming. Umbree quickly stood up and readied an ice ball within his palm for attack. As the shadowy figure came closer, Umbree sighed and dismissed the spell, seeing it was only Torha. Torha stepped into the candlelight and pulled back his hood. He gave a nod to Umbree, noticing the brandy on the table.

"Glad to see you are starting to relax," Torha noted, to which Umbree snorted.

"Do I seem relaxed to you?" Umbree grumbled.

"Well, you have stopped pacing at least," Torha replied.

"I detest being trapped in this rathole," Umbree hissed. Torha pulled out some food from his pack and placed it on the table in front of Umbree.

"It is only temporary, my friend."

Umbree snatched at the loaf of bread and quickly changed the subject.

"Were you able to meet with our ally?" he asked as he tore into the bread.

"Yes, but it is not exactly great news. I heard that the stone was not turned over to the High Council. It is under Arden's protection, somewhere on the castle grounds."

Umbree slammed a fist on the table and swore. He had been dreading this scenario. If the stone had been turned over to the council, he would have been able to use his connections to sneak in and reclaim it. But the stone under Arden's personal protection complicated things exponentially.

"He will be all but impossible to break," Umbree hissed. "Even with the barrier last time, he was formidable to fight."

"He has probably hidden the stone in his tower," Torha suggested. "If we can pull him away, we should be able to search for it."

Umbree tightened his fist. "A long shot at best."

"There is another option," Torha added. "His acolyte might know where he hid it."

"Arden has no acolyte," Umbree replied as he took a sip of brandy.

"He does now," Torha added with a slight smile. "It's Kye."

Umbree froze mid-drink, his eyes wide. "The boy?" Umbree clarified. Torha nodded.

"He survived his injuries, it seems, and Arden took him on as his acolyte. No doubt to spare him from the noose that awaits him in Helia."

Umbree's mind couldn't comprehend what Torha was saying. "You are telling me one of the most powerful mages of our age took on a pathetic, worthless human as his protégé?"

Torha poured himself a glass of brandy and grabbed himself a slice of bread as well. "Apparently," he noted with a shrug. A silence fell over the cavern. Then, slowly, Umbree began chuckling.

"My my, it seems as though the apple doesn't fall far from the tree," Umbree stated, grinning. "Arden's father had a soft spot for inferior beings. It seems his son is afflicted with the same weakness, and I fully intend on using that weakness to my advantage. If we cannot find the stone ourselves, then we will use the boy. Trade his life in exchange for the stone. And when Arden agrees to the terms—which he undoubtedly will —and delivers the stone to us...we will kill them both."

Umbree leaned over to the table and refilled his brandy glass and Torha's in the process. He then held his glass up to Torha in a salute. In response, Torha grinned and held his glass up as well.

"A toast, my friend!" Umbree exclaimed. "To killing two birds...with one stone."

CHAPTER 8
An Aggressive Altercation

The sun had just risen on a cold, clear fall morning when Kye entered the common room of Arden's tower to an unusual sight. Arden was standing over a large map spread out over the dining table. He had his eyes closed in concentration, and he held an intricate silver spinner top flat in the palm of his right hand.

"*Sulara anor*," Kye stated in slight confusion at the scene before him.

"*Sulara anor*," Arden replied without opening his eyes. "There is breakfast on the bar."

Kye walked over and grabbed a pastry and some tea before sinking into the armchair by the fire to observe.

"What are you doing?" Kye asked.

"Scrying," Arden replied. "Got an idea from one of the grimoires I read for a possible way to scry for the creation stones." Kye remembered reading about this in one of his books. Scrying was a way that a mage could locate objects and people using magic.

"Have you had any luck?" Kye inquired. Arden's answer

was to whisper to the silver spinner in his palm. The spinner began twirling quickly of its own volition. Arden set his palm down, letting the spinner go on the map. Kye watched in fascination as the top danced around the parchment. It never came to rest on any specific area though and finally halted in the middle of the map before tipping motionless on its side. Arden let out a long sigh. "Apparently not," he replied. "Hell, it was a long shot, anyway."

As Arden muttered about what could have gone wrong, Kye was lost in thought. He kept replaying the interaction he had had with the female elf several nights prior and the reactions he had received from other mages since his arrival. Granted, it was not anything he hadn't expected and certainly was not going to deter him from becoming a mage. Still, to be so at odds with those who were supposed to be allies. It rather reaffirmed the point that no matter how talented he might become in the craft, Kye would never be accepted as a mage by others. It seemed this path he walked was going to be straight uphill.

"I'll take that as a no," Arden proclaimed. Kye instantly snapped out of his train of thought, realizing the statement was directed at him.

"Sorry?" he asked his master. Arden held up the spinner.

"I said, would you like to try scrying?" he repeated. Arden studied Kye's face a bit more closely, adding with a slight scowl. "You okay, kid?" Kye shook his head slightly, trying to rid his mind of doubt in the process.

"Fine!" Kye added rather robustly as he quickly rose from his seat and walked over to where Arden stood. Arden handed Kye the spinner, noting, "The trick is to focus completely on what it is you wish to find. Course, you will also need a piece of what it is you are looking for. For that, we will start with something simple."

Arden pulled an herb from a vase by the window. Thanks to Arden's apothecary lessons, Kye instantly recognized it as thistle. Arden placed the herb in Kye's left hand while instructing him on how to hold his palm flat with the spinner in his right.

"Now, I picked that herb from the forest surrounding the castle," Arden stated. "Your job is to tell me from where. Focus on what you want to find and speak the word *Invenia*."

Kye nodded, closing his eyes and concentrating. He focused on the herb, pouring as much energy into the spinner as he was able, willing it to point the way. Kye whispered the word and could feel the spinner warm in his hand, slowly beginning to turn faster and faster. When it was nothing more than a blur, Kye lowered his hand to the map. The spinner coasted along the map with purpose, coming to rest in circles around Caelum Vallis. After several laps surrounding the castle, the spinner froze its position on a small patch in the western woods. Kye looked to Arden, curious if he had located the correct spot. Arden responded with a nod and a smile. "Very good."

Kye smiled back, admittedly proud of himself for accomplishing a magical task on the first try. He was getting better at casting, noticing that while magic tasks still drained him, it was getting more tolerable.

"Scrying is a very useful skill," Arden added. "You will use it often."

"Have you used it to locate people?" Kye inquired.

Arden nodded. "Yes, though that is a bit tougher. To locate a person, you require an object with a strong emotional attachment to them or a bit of their blood. And those objects, as you might guess, aren't that easy to come by if the person is already missing."

Kye thought the bit of blood part would be especially difficult. And you would have to know the missing person well to know of an object that held a strong emotional attachment for them.

"But maisters have been able to help locate people that have been abducted or missing using scrying. In truth, it is the most common request the council sees," Arden stated.

"Can you hide from someone scrying for you using magic?"

"You can. It can be tricky, but you can cast a glamour or a cloaking spell in order to hide from a mage scrying for you. However, if the mage has any of your blood, they can cast a tracking spell. Then it is practically impossible to hide."

Kye had read about glamours and cloaking spells in the library. A glamour consisted of changing your appearance so completely as to convince onlookers that you were, in fact, another person. Cloaking spells consisted of carving magic symbols in the ground to hide a large area from detection. Arden's amulet glowed for just a moment as he communicated in silence with someone. He collected the spinner from the table and folded the map back into the bookshelf beside the potion table. Arden placed the grimoire on the dining table before looking to Kye.

"Could you do me a favor and return that to the library, kid?" Arden motioned toward the book. "Maister Bammel has asked for my assistance with a curse."

Kye inwardly cringed. He had to admit the library was not somewhere he wished to visit again so soon. Then again, he wasn't going to refuse to help Arden. So Kye plastered on a fake grin and replied, "Sure."

Arden nodded as he headed out of the tower. "Thanks. See you at dinner."

Kye was crossing the courtyard later that evening to return the tome. He was thumbing through it as he went, hoping that if he understood more of what Arden was looking at, maybe he could assist in the search. As he rounded the southeast corner of the castle, Kye saw three young elven men talking to each other in a circle, one with sleek red hair and blue eyes, with a pointed chin and high cheekbones. One with short brown hair and green eyes, and a turned up nose, and one with mid-length blond wavy hair and brown eyes and a protruding brow. All three snapped their attention to Kye as he passed them. Kye gave a respectful nod of his head, but the elves merely sneered in response. In a quick fluid movement, the red-headed elf rushed out and stopped directly in Kye's path.

"Well, if it isn't the infamous human. Hadn't seen it yet around the castle, was beginning to think it was a myth," he said to his cohorts.

"Clearly, it has been hiding," added the blonde-haired elf, circling where Kye stood. "And with good reason, I should think."

"It doesn't look like much," the brown-haired one answered. "To be able to stab a mage? I bet I could break its neck one-handed. Heard that humans bleed red, would be interesting to see."

Kye tried again to step around. The red-haired elf once again blocked his path, and the other two fell into place behind him. Kye's pulse quickened. He knew this was headed for a fight, one he was certain he would not fare well in.

"What is your rush, human?" the redhead hissed. "Don't you know it's rude not to address those speaking to you?"

"Yes, clearly offensive," the blond one chided. The red-haired elf stepped closer, getting directly in Kye's face. Kye clenched his fists. He knew he was no match for three elven acolytes. He also knew if he showed fear or weakness, if he tried to run or tried to reason, they wouldn't hesitate to tear him apart. His survival as a mage was dependent on showing them, and all in Caelum Vallis, that he was not afraid and could not be intimidated.

"I think someone should teach him a lesson in manners," the red-haired one hissed.

"Well since you're clearly untutored in the subject, I guess that counts you out," Kye snapped back.

The three elves actually seemed taken aback. That a mere human would dare to speak to them like that was something they were clearly not accustomed to. Obviously, they had been expecting him to cower. Kye used their momentary surprise to step around the red-haired elf and continue on his way. But he had not taken more than ten steps before he heard a shout from behind him, "*Fulmira!*"

Kye's body reacted purely on adrenaline and instinct, whipping around in an instant, dropping the book and shouting "*Aegira!*" just in the nick of time.

The shield spell did the trick, warding off the lightning spell before it struck Kye but also pushing him back a good six feet. Kye fought to keep his stance and managed to remain standing. This elf's attack was weak in comparison to Arden's. Kye quickly dismissed the barrier spell and readied his defensive stance should the elf throw another attack spell his way. The other two spread out in formation around the third elf, preparing to attack Kye from all sides. Kye quickly started running through scenarios in his head, trying to figure out how he was going to defend himself. Just as the red-haired elf readied another spell, a voice cut through the tension.

"What is going on here?"

Kye turned to see Maister Valor standing behind him, looking on like some bored spectator. The three elves quickly abandoned their attack stances and bowed to the High Council leader. Kye followed suit, grateful for the distraction.

"You all know the rules," Valor continued. "Sparring is to

take place on the dueling ground. Would you mind explaining to me why you are exchanging spells out here?"

The red-haired elf stepped forward. "Apologies, Maister. We did not mean to break the rules. We were merely reacting."

Valor's eyes squinted. "Reacting? Reacting to what?"

"The human, my lord," replied the red-haired one. "We were all simply minding our business when the human walked by and suddenly attacked us."

Kye's head snapped up from his stopped stance and glared at the red elf in disbelief. *Lying bastard!* Valor raised an eyebrow. "Really?" He then turned to Kye. "Is this true? Did you attack them, human?"

Kye bowed his head back down respectfully before replying, "No, my lord."

"Ahh, so you are calling my acolyte a liar?"

His acolyte? So the red-haired elf that struck first was Valor's protege. That certainly explained his winning personality.

"I am saying he is mistaken, my lord," Kye responded, figuring this was the most tactful way to tell Valor that he was spewing nonsense.

"Is that so?" Valor replied. He then turned back to the red-haired elf. "Are you mistaken about the events, Thaiden?"

Thaiden merely smiled back smugly. "No, my lord, I am not."

"Ah, well there you have it," Valor replied. "He says he isn't mistaken. So either you attacked my acolyte, or you are calling him a liar. Which is it?"

He is lying. But what good would declaring it do? Kye thought. Everyone here already knew he was lying, but Kye's word wasn't worth the earth elves tread upon, and they damn well knew it. He was already known as the unhinged human that stabbed an honored goblin maister. Arden had told him that Valor had been tireless in investigating the ruins of the manor—looking for any witnesses to prove that Kye was an untrustworthy brute who had attacked Umbree and misled Arden. In his mind, clearly, attacking an acolyte out of the blue wasn't outside his abilities. Either way, Kye was guilty, truth be damned. Valor stepped closer to Kye, a small grin spreading from his mouth.

"I'm waiting, human. Are you calling my acolyte a liar?"

Kye lifted his gaze to meet Valor's. If this was how it was going to be with the rest of the council, if they were going to find any way to condemn him, he was done paying homage while they did it. Kye opened his mouth to respond, when someone suddenly shouted, "Well, if he isn't, then I certainly am!"

A voice called behind the group causing all present to turn around. Kye noticed the familiar sight briskly walking toward them was the pretty female elf from the library. She was moving toward the group with purpose, her violet eyes fixed in a stern, disapproving expression. As soon as she reached the scene, she stepped between Kye and Valor, giving the maister a respectful bow.

"Pardon my intrusion, my lord, but I witnessed the entire event," she replied. "Contrary to Thaiden's version, I witnessed him attack the human first—while his back was turned, moreover."

She then shot a scathing look at Thaiden, adding, "A most cowardly act indeed!"

Thaiden looked dumbfounded, and he wasn't the only one. It seemed to be an emotion shared by all men present. His cohorts were standing with their mouths open, frozen in a state of shock. The female elf focused her attention on Valor.

"Seeing as you are his maister, I knew you would want to be made aware of his tactics so he might be properly instructed in the ways of dueling."

Valor sneered. "Take care, my dear," he growled. "One

might think you were dictating to a maister on the training of his acolyte."

The female elf gave another respectful bow. "Banish the thought, my lord."

Valor held his head up to look down at the elf before hissing at Thaiden and his cohorts to come along. The group grumpily departed, leaving the female elf and Kye alone. Kye was still shell-shocked, staring at her as though she had lost her mind. The female elf finally noticed his gaze.

"What!?" she inquired.

"T-Thank you," Kye replied, unsure of what else to say. He was grateful, albeit flabbergasted, for her assistance. The cause of which he could only assume was some form of temporary insanity. The female elf stood taller, shifting her posture.

"Your thanks is completely unnecessary," she replied. "I simply spoke the truth. I would have been just as forthright had you been the guilty party."

Kye nodded. Even if she had just told the truth, it had been more than anyone else present had been willing to do on his behalf.

The elf turned her attention back to her surroundings before adding, "Still…I was…impressed you were able to successfully fend off Thaiden's attack."

"Oh, yeah," Kye responded. "Arden thought it was important I learn defensive spells. I can see he was right."

There was an uncomfortable silence that fell over the two of them, neither knowing what to say to the other. Kye was taken off guard by the shift in her demeanor. She had been cursing him when last they met, defending him now. He wasn't sure what had sparked the change in her, and he was cautious of saying the wrong thing that might shift the winds yet again. Kye bent down and picked up the book he had been carrying from the ground.

"Well...I believe my master is currently expecting me," he began, thankful to escape the crushing silence.

Kye gave a deep bow to the elf before adding, "Thank you again for your assistance, my lady," before turning to take his leave.

"Saiyah."

Kye stopped and looked back.

"My name," the elf said, clarifying his confusion. "We are both acolytes, after all. Hearing you address me in such an honorific way is...odd. You may call me Saiyah."

Kye paused for a moment before replying. "I see. Then please call me Kye."

Saiyah nodded in agreement.

"Well, I must be going but thank you for your help... Saiyah."

"Think nothing of it, Kye." Saiyah turned and started heading back to the castle as Kye continued on his trek. As he walked on, he felt a little more hopeful. He might still be public enemy number one with the masses. But it seemed as though some headway was being made with at least one of his fellow acolytes. It was a very small victory, but he'd take it.

Umbree was nervously standing in front of a pool of water in the cave. The water was tinted green with his blood. A summoning pool was an outdated form of communication, but without an amulet, his options were limited. After weeks of discussion, he, Torha, and Belthier had finally formed a solid plan for retrieving the stone. The question is, would Orin be on board with it? Not only that, would he be willing to lend Umbree assistance? If Umbree was asking too much, it could very well spell his end. The water started to ripple as Umbree snapped his attention toward it.

"*Umbree?*" Orin's eerie voice filled the cavern.

"Y-Yes, my lord," Umbree stuttered. "Thank you so much for responding to me. I do apologize for the form of communication. If I had any other way of reaching out, I—"

"*What do you require?*" Orin interrupted, his tone stressing that Umbree get to the point.

"Y-Yes, my lord," Umbree continued. "I believe we have come up with a way to get inside Caelum Vallis. We have a contact on the inside who can get us inside the castle to secure the stone, bypassing the magical defenses."

"*That is wonderful news, my friend,*" Orin stated. Clearly he was bored that Umbree was reaching out for any other reason than to report success.

"Yes, it is..." Umbree continued nervously. "The only thing is...the stone is not in the location we believed it to be. We can search for it...but that would involve pulling the mages away from the castle."

"*And how do you intend to do that?*"

"Well..." Umbree continued, "it would require a distraction."

"*What kind of distraction?*"

Umbree shifted uncomfortably, not really wanting to continue his thought but having no choices left. Taking a deep breath, Umbree stated, "A large one, my lord. I would require your assistance."

Orin was silent for a long while. "*I seem to be offering a lot while getting little in return, Umbree,*" he finally replied.

Umbree cringed. Orin's irritation was noticeable. Umbree knew he had to offer something to placate him. He had been holding onto some information in the hopes he could use it as a bargaining chip to gain more power from Orin after he fulfilled Umbree's wish. But Orin's patience was thin. If he didn't offer something of value, he would receive nothing in return.

"If you are willing to assist, my lord, the mages being pulled away would not only help me find the wind stone but also help you gain a second prize."

"And what would that be?"

"A creation stone, my lord. I know the location of another..."

CHAPTER 9
A Talented Traveler

As Saiyah entered the library in the early afternoon, she was greeted with glares and hushed whispers. All eyes seemed to be on her, and she was getting a distinct chill from the onlookers. Saiyah was baffled as to what could warrant such a greeting but tried her best to ignore it, seating herself at the nearest empty table by the windows. She had barely opened one of her books before Kes rushed up to her.

"Can we talk in private?" she started without even issuing a greeting. Saiyah was taken off guard but nodded as she followed her to a secluded area amongst the shelves. Kes kept looking back to make sure they were out of earshot. As soon as she was certain they could not be overheard, she spun around and confronted Saiyah.

"Tell me it isn't true!" Kes stated, with her hands on her hips accusingly.

"Well, in order to do that, I would first have to know what you are referring to," Saiyah noted.

Kes gave an exacerbated sigh.

"I heard that you sided with the human after it attacked

Thaiden. You called him a coward and insulted Maister Valor on his teaching methods."

Saiyah rolled her eyes and sighed. Of course that was what all this was about. Thaiden probably painted himself as the poor martyr in the matter.

"For starters, Thaiden attacked the human first, without justification or cause," Saiyah started, "for which I did, indeed, call him a coward. And I did not insult Maister Valor, merely pointed out the truth of the matter to him."

"You still sided with a human over one of your own kind," Kes argued in disbelief.

"Yes, because one of my own kind was in the wrong," Saiyah reiterated. "Did you miss the part where Thaiden attacked him?"

Kes waved her hand dismissively. "It was a duel. You had no right to interfere!" she spat.

"Duel implies an honorable and fair fight between two mages," Saiyah argued. "Thaiden shot at him from behind."

"The human had it coming!" Kes bit back.

"For simply walking by?" Saiyah questioned. "Had he not reacted so fast, Thaiden's attack could have killed Kye."

"Kye?" Kes repeated in confusion. Saiyah threw up a hand in exasperation. "The human!" she practically shouted back, catching the attention of several library attendees in the process. Kes contorted her face in disgust.

"Well, you really have gotten buddy-buddy with it if you know its name."

Saiyah glared back. "Displaying an iota of common decency is not something I would equate to being buddy-buddy. But I guess that is more effort than you can muster."

Kes glowered at Saiyah in response. "You know, Saiyah, you are not who I thought you were."

"On that fact, Kes, I believe we finally agree!" Saiyah hissed before turning on her heel and stalking away. Saiyah returned to her table and quickly collected her books in a huff. She shot daggers at every eye that met hers as she bolted toward the exit.

Saiyah continued out of the library onto the castle grounds. When she turned a corner toward the courtyard fountain, she almost collided with the prime source of her anger. Thaiden and his lackeys were hanging around outside, without a care in the world. He gave a smug smile as soon as he saw Saiyah.

"Good day, Lady Saiyah," Thaiden greeted mockingly. "You seem troubled today."

Saiyah glared back at him. "I'm always troubled by your presence, Thaiden."

Thaiden dropped the false niceties in an instant.

"You only have yourself to blame for this," he growled, "siding with that human, calling me a coward."

"You ARE a coward! As is any mage willing to attack while their opponent's back is turned. Are you so weak in your abilities that you cannot even face a fight head-on?!"

Thaiden's face flashed in anger as he stepped closer to Saiyah menacingly. His approach was halted by the weight of a sharp-clawed hand on his shoulder. He turned to see Riley standing behind him. He was partially transformed, his fingers ending in knife-like points, his eyes glowing yellow, his mouth displaying fangs. His whole appearance was radiating anger. With a sharp tug, he yanked Thaiden back a few feet while positioning himself in front of Saiyah as a fearsome barrier.

"Step back, silver blood," Riley growled. "Or I'm going to put that healing ability of yours to the test!"

Thaiden was visibly unnerved, stepping several feet back from Riley. He then turned back to Saiyah. "I'll just leave you in the company of your pet then," he hissed before turning away and stalking off with his entourage.

"What an asshole..." Riley muttered, shifting back to his fully human form. Saiyah felt her blood boil as she resumed her heated pace, feeling the need to walk off the anger she felt building.

"Hey, little sis, wait up!" Riley shouted as he followed her. As Saiyah continued through the castle, she noted the occasional disapproving glance and hushed whisper.

"Unbelievable," Saiyah seethed. "Thaiden attacks a fellow acolyte, and I am the enemy for calling him out on it."

"Well...yeah," Riley commented. "Cause he didn't just attack an acolyte, he attacked a human."

Saiyah stopped dead in her tracks and spun round to face Riley.

"And that should matter!?" she exclaimed.

Riley shook his head. "It shouldn't," he responded. "But I think we both know it does."

Saiyah fell silent. Kye had done nothing to warrant attack, but according to everyone's reaction, he was not even expected to defend himself. Because he was a human, because they said he didn't belong, he was deserving of whatever hatred that was thrown at him. And curse anyone who stood to his defense. Saiyah thought back to her first reaction when she had learned Kye was an acolyte and suddenly felt deeply ashamed of herself.

"We are acolytes," Saiyah muttered. "We are supposed to be better than this."

"Well, if it's any consolation, little sis, you've proven that some of us are," Riley replied. Saiyah met his gaze as he offered a reassuring smile.

"Hey, let's you and I go get some lunch, maybe a drink or two," Riley offered. "We can toast being social pariahs together," he added with a grin.

Saiyah chuckled. It was at that moment she knew she had at least one true friend in the world. Her kind, her fellow mages, may have turned their backs. But Riley stood with her, shoulder to shoulder. Saiyah nodded back and smiled.

"Sounds like a fantastic idea."

A slight drizzle of rain fell as Kye followed Arden out of the castle to the lake in the southwest corner of Caelum Vallis. Arden had said that Kye had improved in his magic enough to try something more advanced. Kye was anxious to improve his abilities and followed Arden without question. As they approached the lake, Kye saw the cool mist rising off the water as the sun just began to streak across the horizon. The wind was rustling the grass ever so slightly, and birds were singing their early morning song. When Arden set his cloak over the nearest tree branch, Kye watched as he summoned a bright red painted "X" on the opposite shore. Kye quietly wondered if they would be practicing evocation spells again. If they were, he was absolutely certain he couldn't shoot a fire spell that far.

"Today, we will be focusing on teleportation magic," Arden stipulated. Kye was immediately intrigued. He had seen Arden and other mages around Caelum Vallis suddenly disappear at whim and had always wondered how they did it.

"Teleportation magic is the fastest means of travel for a mage and the basis for the portal orbs that we use to travel between realms," Arden continued. "The magic itself is tricky and can be downright dangerous if you're not careful. Thus, the reason we have waited till now to attempt it. Now, there are rules when attempting teleportation. First, never try to teleport to a location you have not visited before. The magic involves forming a clear picture within your mind of where you have been and where you wish to go. The best way to ensure that is to conjure an image from memory. Second, NEVER try to form a portal between realms. The orbs we use to travel between realms took the lives of many talented mages and many years to create. It is not something to be attempted lightly. Third, keep in mind that every step traveled draws on your energy the same as if you had walked it. Don't think you are able to walk across Isalia yourself? Then I don't recommend teleporting that far. Pushing past your strength and physical boundaries is the easiest way to get yourself killed. Last but not least, DO NOT break your concentration. Think clearly where you wish to go and let nothing else invade your thoughts. One stray thought or daydream is the easiest way to teleport yourself inside a wall or leave pieces behind."

Kye raised both eyebrows. "Pieces?"

"Just maintain focus, and you'll be fine. Ready to give it a try?"

Kye would be lying if he didn't admit he was wary. But pushing down his fears, he merely nodded.

"Since it is your first time, you won't be traveling far." Arden pointed to the other side of the lake he had marked with the symbol. "You see that clearing by the oak tree? That is your destination."

Kye memorized every detail of the spot he was to appear. He committed every leaf and weed to memory. Once he had a clear picture, he turned to Arden.

"You ready?"

Kye nodded and closed his eyes as Arden instructed, "Now focus clearly on where you wish to go."

Kye's mind instinctively began perfectly recreating the location Arden had indicated. It was almost second nature to him; after all, he had plenty of experience building places within his mind from all the books he had read. It had been his escape from the world he was bound to, to travel to worlds his mind created. He could see the oak tree as clearly as if his eyes were still open.

"Once you have the picture clear in your mind, then speak the word *Dimmora*," Arden stated.

Kye took a deep breath, imagining the leaves rustling in the oak tree, and spoke:

"*Dim—*" The vision of the soft earth he would soon be standing on became clear.

"*—mo—*" The image of the wind whipping through the branches.

"*—ra—*" With the water and the way the grass danced and swayed, it sort of reminded him of the painting in the great hall.

In the moment when he recited the spell, a flash of the painting entered his thoughts. The image had been momentary, but he knew it had been enough to break his concentration. And as Kye felt his body fading in preparation to teleport, one word ran through his mind as he disappeared.

"*Shit.*"

The sudden feeling of floating and then hard earth beneath his feet caused Kye to stumble a bit as he landed. Even though the spell had completed, Kye had not yet opened his eyes. He was trying to catch his breath and calm the panicked heartbeat pounding in his ears. As the cacophony started to fade, it was replaced by the roaring sound of water crashing against rocks. The harsh breeze that hit Kye's face stung of salt. As Kye slowly opened his eyes, he could see he now stood on a cliff... the same cliff as the painting in the great hall. And stretching out before him was the endless sea. Water as far as the eye could see eclipsed Kye's vision. Birds hovered in the air above the crashing tides, and the sound of the colliding waves was almost deafening. He was mesmerized for a few moments, looking out at the shimmering water. It was a place he never thought he would actually get to see. Realizing he had teleported further than intended, Kye quickly ran his hands over his extremities, taking note to make sure nothing was damaged or missing. To his complete and utter shock, everything seemed to be accounted for. Once he confirmed he was still very much in one piece, Kye set his mind to returning to the lake. No doubt Arden would be wondering why he had yet to appear. Kye once again shut his eyes, focusing clearly on where he wished to be. This time, not allowing any other thoughts to enter his mind, he burned the image of the lake into his memory. Once he had a clear picture, Kye took a deep breath and uttered the word *"Dimmora."*

Kye was once again enveloped by a floating sensation. And when it abated, he was standing on solid earth next to his intended destination.

"KYE!"

Kye's eyes shot open to a worried and angry Arden charging toward him.

"You know, I thought I had explained the dangers of this particular exercise quite clearly!" Arden snapped as soon as he was in earshot.

"You did," Kye replied quickly, trying to quell his master's anger. "I'm sorry, I only lost focus for a moment. An image of the painting in the great hall flashed in my head, and the next thing I knew, I was standing there."

Arden paused. "You were standing where? The great hall?"

Kye shook his head. "No, on the cliffs overlooking the ocean. Just like in the painting."

Arden was noticeably taken aback. "The Isle of Isolde? You were at the Isle of Isolde?"

Kye had not known the name of the place he had been, but assuming Arden meant the place in the picture, he nodded.

"So...you just teleported halfway across the continent, based solely on the image you saw in a painting?" Arden clarified.

"Apparently..." Kye replied carefully. He had not been aware he had gone that far. Arden, too, appeared surprised and slightly impressed.

"Well, how do you feel?" he asked. "Are you tired? Is everything accounted for?"

Kye shook his head. "Nothing missing, and I feel fine actually..." Which, now that he was thinking it over, was strange in and of itself. Kye had not performed a single spell so far that had not sucked the energy out of him like a leech to an open vein. Until now. Arden's demeanor instantly softened.

"Well...I'll be damned," he chuckled. "I'd say we just found your affinity."

Kye looked back at him in stunned silence, slowly comprehending he had just stumbled upon his proficiency. Something he had honestly started to believe he did not possess at all. A smile spread over Arden's face as he stated, "You, Kye, are a traveler."

Saiyah entered the library, greeted by the silence of the night. While she had often sought out the quiet of night to study, it was a different feeling knowing that this was to be the norm. She had been all but ostracized from the library during daylight hours, thanks to Thaiden. The whispers and glares of those mages she had thought to be allies followed her constantly. Even Maister Luell had chastised her when she had heard that she had confronted Thaiden and Valor, all for the sake of a human. But Saiyah still did not believe she was wrong. And the fact that Riley agreed with her gave her comfort that she had at least one ally. Saiyah picked up a few volumes on remedium magic before heading to the center of the library to find a table. As soon as she stepped into the open area of the library, her eyes rested on a familiar sight.

There, seated at the longest table in the library in front of the fireplace, was Kye. He was engrossed in his reading, but this time, he seemed to notice Saiyah's entrance. He looked up from his book and gave her a slight smile and a respectful nod of his head. Saiyah returned the gesture before he returned to his reading. It was a small greeting but leaps and bounds above their last library encounter. The likes of which, Saiyah had to admit, she still felt ashamed of. As she was about to seat herself at a table in the corner, Saiyah froze, looking over to where Kye was reading. Batting down her nerves, Saiyah took a deep breath, collected her books, and walked over to him. Upon her approach, Kye looked up from his book hesitatingly. Saiyah motioned to one of the empty seats at the table.

"May I?" she asked. Kye quickly stood up and brandished his hand toward the seat, replying, "Please."

As they both sat down, Saiyah opened her books as Kye cast her a slightly confused glance.

"There are just the two of us here, after all," Saiyah explained. "Seems like such a waste of space to spread out so. Especially when this table is quite big enough for both of us."

Kye smiled, nodding his head and adding, "I completely agree."

The pair both turned back to their books, remaining silent for quite some time. Saiyah felt the tension that still remained between them, the cause of which was completely her fault. And would not be mended by her silence.

"Kye," Saiyah started carefully. Kye looked up, giving her his full attention. Saiyah let out a nervous sigh before continuing.

"I fear I owe you a rather large apology," she began. "The way I acted last time we were here was abhorrent. I'm afraid that I was basing assumptions on my own prejudice...and was far too stubborn to admit it."

"Well, you were hardly alone in that," Kye conceded. "I, too, jumped to conclusions about you. For that, I'm sorry."

Saiyah shook her head. She had instigated the animosity between them, and she knew it. "Your apology is appreciated but entirely unnecessary. I was foolish in my assumptions. I fear that the outlandish stories swirling around you have twisted facts in your case."

Kye tilted his head in curiosity. "There are stories about me?"

"Indeed." Saiyah nodded. "Far-fetched fables, more based on fiction than fact."

"Like what?" Kye asked, intrigued.

Saiyah fidgeted, more than slightly embarrassed to admit the horrendous stories being told.

"Well...for example, there is a rumor that you are a dangerous, unhinged human who has killed a hundred mages."

"Ah." Kye nodded in understanding. "Well...that one happens to be true."

Saiyah froze for a moment, staring at Kye in disbelief. "It's...true?" she asked cautiously.

Kye nodded. "Absolutely," he agreed, his tone never wavering.

"You have killed a hundred mages?" Saiyah repeated skeptically.

"Single-handedly," Kye insisted.

"And I suppose it is also true that you beheaded them?"

"Got them mounted on my wall at home," Kye agreed without hesitation.

"That you command an army of bloodthirsty humans?"

"Ready to follow me into hell at a moment's notice."

"And that you collect the hearts of your enemies?"

"Well, what goes better with a wall full of heads?"

Saiyah suddenly burst out laughing as Kye smiled at her. Honestly, apart from Riley, Saiyah couldn't remember anyone possessing the talent to make her laugh. Hearing them now, the tales were so ridiculous, it was absurd anyone could believe them. As Saiyah's laughter died down, she smiled back at Kye.

" I do believe I have misjudged you," Saiyah stated.

"Now there is something else we have in common," Kye replied with a small grin. The remainder of the night seemed to rush past, no longer shadowed with the sounds of silence. The library may have been mostly empty, but it no longer felt that way. It was now filled with conversation, laughter, and the beginning of an unforeseen friendship.

It was the dead of night, the cool desert air cutting through Umbree. He had always hated this time of year on Helia. And he was completely confused as to why his master had summoned him here. He had mentioned in his last communication to Orin that he would require his help to distract the mages in Caelum Vallis to allow Umbree access inside. Orin had responded by asking Umbree to meet him on Helia. As Umbree approached the coordinates, he could see in the dark his master and Amon standing on the edge of a cliff looking down. As Umbree approached the edge, he saw they were observing a human village below. Umbree approached carefully, not wishing to disturb them. Orin sensed his presence, though, breaking the silence by stating, "Good evening, Umbree."

Umbree jumped slightly before responding, "Good evening, m-my lord."

"I must say, I was quite happy to hear you knew of a second stone," Orin replied. "You are certain of the location?"

"Yes, my lord. But if you attempt to take it now, the maisters would undoubtedly respond," Umbree replied. "It would require their attention to be pulled away."

"Naturally," Orin added in agreement. "And I believe we can create a suitable distraction to accommodate that and your infiltration of the castle."

Orin pulled a few more pieces of dried meat from his satchel and offered one to Amon. His side-kick took the dried meat and gave a small bow in response. The three were just standing in silence, looking at the village below. It seemed as though the inhabitants were heading off to bed. They were putting out candles and closing up the doors to their shacks in preparation for night. Umbree could not understand what was so fascinating about this human village, or why they were standing here at all.

"With all due respect, my lord..." Umbree began carefully, "why are we here?"

"Do you know what a shade is, Umbree?" Orin replied.

"Yes, my lord. They are vengeful spirits, often naturally occurring from a violent death. The spirit cannot let go and does not cross over as it should. It is trapped by the pain it has endured, warping the soul into an uncontrollable monster that lashes out at the living."

"Very good," Orin replied. "Except for one point. They are not necessarily 'naturally occurring.' They can be made as well. If one dies violently and the soul is then forcibly restrained from crossing over, the same outcome occurs. And if you can bind a shade to you, then you have a fearsome ally."

Umbree felt his eyes widen as he slowly came to understand the purpose of their meeting.

"The reason we are here is simple, Umbree," Orin continued. "You are in need of a distraction, and I intend to make you one."

Below them, the final light was extinguished as the last human headed inside his shack. Orin crinkled the finished bag of dried meat before holding out his hand. He muttered the word "*Saleibra*." In an instant, a barrier appeared around the human village, enclosing the buildings in a perfect sphere. Once the spell was complete, Orin turned to his right hand.

"Amon, if you would be so kind," Orin stated. "Go and greet our new recruits."

The shifter next to them growled as his skin erupted in pitch-black scales. His face began to lengthen as his body grew. Membrane-like wings sprang from his back, and before Umbree knew it, he was in the presence of a formidable black dragon. Amon growled again and took flight, diving down upon the village. It took only moments for Umbree to hear the first scream, but many more were soon echoing in his ears. A few humans tried to fight the beast attacking them but were easily dispatched by the crunch of fangs and the swipe of claws. Villagers quickly awoke to the commotion, rushing out of their huts to the horror before them. They tried to run but were stopped by the barrier Orin had summoned. They pounded against the magical wall in vain, desperate to escape their fate—only to be swiftly disposed of by the monster within. Umbree retreated a bit, casting his gaze downward, finding it difficult to watch the gruesome scene. He had no love for humans; still, the cries of the victims caused him to cringe and a small twinge of guilt to settle in his stomach. Orin, however, stood on the cliff looking down at the massacre below them without emotion or remorse, as the screams filled the night.

CHAPTER 10
An Atrocious Act

The month after learning he was a traveler, Kye spent every chance he got practicing his affinity and using all of Isalia as his playground. All he had to do was form a clear picture of where he wanted to go, whisper the word, and BAM! He was there. And the longer he was traveling, the easier it got. Kye could zip between continents just as easily as if he were stepping through a doorway. He returned to the Isle of Isolde often to watch the waves crashing against the shore. He toured the luminescent forest of Moora, seeing the plants practically glow in the dead of night. He stood on the cliffs of Novar, looking out and watching the sunrise that painted the eastern continent of Isalia in colors and light. It was a wonderful feeling, a freedom the likes of which he had never known. Arden generally encouraged Kye's travels; however, he did impose some rules as well. He warned Kye of places to avoid, even within Isalia, that would not be kind to humans. And he made Kye promise to NEVER try to portal between realms himself. Kye did finally slow down his excursions, though, when one day he appeared in the tower unexpectedly and collided with Arden as he had just fixed himself a drink. The whiskey tumbled to the floor and shattered as Arden let out a long sigh. He waved his hand and cleaned up the glass as he went back to fix another drink.

"While I'm glad you're having fun with your affinity, kid," he noted, "I feel the need to remind you stairs were invented for a reason."

Kye nodded and muttered, "Sorry" in response. He made a mental note to himself from then on to show more caution when suddenly appearing in the tower.

"Are there other travelers at Caelum Vallis?" Kye asked. He knew that each mage connected to an area of magic, and he was interested to know if there were mages that connected to the same school of study as him. Arden paused for a moment. "There are some. Maister Iston and Maister Bari are travelers. I think I heard of a few acolytes that possess the ability as well. All in all, I think there are about ten in the castle with the affinity."

"That's it?" Kye asked, surprised. There were slightly over two hundred maisters on the High Council. Acolytes accounted for almost two hundred more. It was shocking to him to hear that of that number, there were only ten whose affinity lay in teleportation magic, himself included. Arden nodded. "It is not a terribly common affinity, mainly because it involves being able to paint a detailed image in your mind and requires a great amount of focus. And far as I know, none of them can teleport based on pictures, only memories."

Arden looked up from his glass and gave Kye an impressed smile. "You certainly have a gift, no doubt about that."

Kye was stunned. Something so second nature to him was so difficult for others. Perhaps it was because he spent so much time growing up envisioning other places? Or maybe it was because humans were the only race that dreamed? Maybe that had something to do with it. Creating worlds inside your mind while you slept made it easier to picture places while you woke. Either way, Kye felt fortunate to be a traveler and honored to be gifted in any area of study related to magic. For the first time since he had arrived, he started to believe he might actually belong.

"So...it's like being charmed?" Saiyah asked.

"Sort of," Kye replied, "but it's your own mind charming you."

"Does it take great focus?" Saiyah inquired.

"No, it just sort of happens."

"And this happens every night?" Saiyah questioned.

"Well...not necessarily."

As the clock ticked past midnight, Kye and Saiyah sat at their usual table in the library. What had initially been a relationship fueled by animosity had now blossomed into friendship. Each night, they would meet to study, discuss spells, share stories, and learn more about each other.

Kye had come to realize that Saiyah was not the snobby high-born mage he had first thought her to be. In fact, she was brilliant, compassionate, and honorable. He had also learned that even though she looked to be in her early twenties, she was actually about 125 years old (though elves did not tend to keep track of their age). He had come to find out she was a speaker whose affinity lay in summoning, preferred huckleberry root tea, and was born in the winter.

In return, Saiyah had discovered much about Kye as well. She now knew he was eighteen years old, born in the fall, had a deep love for books, and that he was a traveler. The more she talked to him, the more she saw how mistaken the whole castle had been about him. He was not some brute, unhinged or otherwise—he was, in fact, kind-hearted, rational, and intelligent.

Saiyah also came to know the truth about Umbree, who had been painted to be a noble maister by much of the council. Kye did not speak about his life with Umbree much, but the few stories that Saiyah had been able to get him to tell her taught Saiyah one definite truth: Umbree had not been kind. Honestly, from hearing Kye's side, she couldn't say for certain she wouldn't have stabbed the wretch as well. What she had learned about Kye showed an entirely different side of humanity than what Saiyah had been led to believe. As such, she found herself asking more questions about him and humans in general.

As they sat in the quiet library this particular night, the rain was hammering down on the window as they both sat in the glow of the fire, sipping cups of tea amongst volumes of books spread out on the table. Kye was trying his best (and failing honestly) to describe dreaming—an experience unique to humans.

"And you find dreaming enjoyable?" Saiyah inquired.

"Generally," Kye responded. "I mean, unless it's a nightmare."

"What is a 'nightmare?'"

"Uh...essentially, your inner fears manifest to torment you in your dreams," Kye described. Saiyah stared back in disbelief.

"That sounds horrific."

Kye shrugged. "It's not really pleasant, no."

"Why would anyone choose to have a nightmare?" she asked.

"Well...you don't really have a choice."

"You have no control at all?" Saiyah asked in shock.

"No, I mean, if you realize it's a dream, you have control. But you don't always know that..."

"Why do you not know that?'

"Because you think it's real," Kye explained.

"I thought it wasn't real?" Saiyah asked.

"No, it's not...but it can seem that way..."

Kye paused at Saiyah's puzzled expression before letting out a long sigh. "I'm not describing this well, am I?" He smiled.

Saiyah chuckled in response. "It seems as though it is something one must experience to fully comprehend."

"Or at least find a human better at the explanation."

"What sort of things do you usually dream about?" Saiyah inquired.

"Mostly places I want to see and sometimes Helia," Kye replied.

"Do you miss your home?" she inquired.

"I miss parts of it. The sun, for sure. It's a bit colder here, to be honest."

"And what about your family?" Saiyah inquired. "I'm certain you miss them as well."

Kye stopped for a moment, seemingly caught off guard by the question. "I don't really have any left there," he finally replied.

"None at all?" Saiyah pressed. "What about your parents?"

Kye shifted slightly in his chair. "My father died when I was two. My mother passed when I was thirteen."

"I'm so sorry," Saiyah replied. "How did it happen?"

Kye ran a hand through his hair and cleared his throat a bit. "My father was a quarryman, killed in a rockslide. And my mother...she passed from an illness. At least, that's what I was told."

"You were told? But you weren't there?" Saiyah asked.

"Uh...no," Kye admitted, focusing on the book in front of him. "I was sold to Umbree when I was eight. I hadn't seen her in five years."

Saiyah sat in a state of shock. She had no idea humans were treated so deplorably. Then again, she had never tried to find out. She had just taken all the stories told to be true.

Humans were useless, little better than animals, whose only purpose was servitude. At least that was what all the mages she had spoken to had conveyed. But it was all lies. Kye had been taken from his family when he was still a child, to serve a cruel mage and literally never see his mother again. He had risked his life to save another, an act worthy of the High Council. And for the price of such a courageous deed, he awaited little better than a death sentence should he ever try to return home, and animosity from his fellow mages should he remain. Saiyah felt a surge of anger on his behalf. He didn't deserve this...no human did.

"What about your family?" Kye inquired, swiftly changing the subject from himself. It was clear Saiyah had broached a topic he didn't discuss often.

"Oh...well, my parents are both silversmiths. Our shop has been in our family for generations. Also we have had one mage in our family serving on the council for several generations. As it turns out I was the only one amongst my siblings that displayed the gift. So, naturally, I was selected to join."

"Did you want to join the council?" Kye asked. Saiyah sat quietly for a moment, turning over the question in her mind. In truth, no one had ever asked her that. Not even her own family. Her joining the council had always been a given since she displayed the gift. Her wants hadn't factored into it. It was all to carry on the family honor. That was why she studied so hard, why she was so determined in her craft. But that wasn't the only reason, was it? It made her think long and hard about her response. Kye tilted his head slightly, waiting for her reply.

"Well..." Saiyah began, "I have always had a fascination with magic. And I do enjoy helping others, so yes, I did want to join the council."

Kye smiled back at her. "Are your siblings disappointed they didn't possess the gift?"

"Oh, I doubt it. They are far too wrapped up in their own lives to concern themselves with magic."

"How many siblings do you have?" asked Kye as he reached for his tea.

"Twelve."

Kye froze mid-sip as his eyes widened. "You have twelve siblings?"

"Seven brothers, five sisters," Saiyah replied. "I am the youngest."

"Wow," said Kye, "that sounds...crowded."

Saiyah laughed. "Yes. It is remarkable how I feel I have more space trapped in a castle with four hundred mages."

Kye laughed back as Saiyah smiled and reached for her own tea. Out of the corner of her eye, something caught her attention. Kye noticed Saiyah's face fall as she looked at something disapprovingly. As Kye followed her gaze, he saw that a red-headed female goblin had entered the library. At first, she stared at them in shock but quickly turned her nose up in disgust and stalked out of the library. Kye was confused. The note of disgust directed at him would have been nothing out of the ordinary. But the goblin's disdain seemed to have been directly pointed at Saiyah. Saiyah went quiet after she departed.

"Was she a friend of yours?" Kye inquired.

"There was a time I may have thought so," Saiyah replied. "But I can now say with absolute certainty...no."

The way Saiyah answered the question made Kye curious about something he felt compelled to ask.

"Saiyah...did something happen between you and the other acolytes?"

Saiyah seemed to tense a bit at the question. "What makes you say that?"

"You weren't in the library every night until a little over a month ago," Kye replied. "And she seemed angry at you. I was just wondering if you—"

Just then, an event shot forward in Kye's memory. He let out a deflated sigh. He knew what this was about.

"Because of me," Kye clarified, now understanding. "Because you stood up to Thaiden and Valor for me?"

Saiyah remained silent, simply turning a page of her own book. Kye felt guilty. Even though the altercation was not his fault, he felt responsible that Saiyah was now being ostracized because of it. He knew all too well how that felt.

"Saiyah..." Kye started. "I'm sorry if—"

"Why?" Saiyah shot back at him immediately. "Why should you apologize when you have done absolutely nothing for which to apologize for."

Kye gave a small smile in response as Saiyah turned back to her book. Her eyes narrowed in a contentious glare as she added, "Thaiden, however, would need a lifetime for atonement. I refuse to associate with those who have no honor or ethics. I just hadn't realized how many members of Caelum Vallis were lacking those qualities until now, for which I am grateful." Saiyah sat a little taller in her seat as she stated, "Besides, the library is much too crowded and noisy during the day. I prefer the ambiance at night much more, and the company is certainly better," Saiyah declared matter of factly.

Kye smiled back at her. "Couldn't agree more."

∽

It was a calm afternoon in Arden's tower. Kye was lying on the sofa near the fire, reading a non-spell book for once. It was an elven literary author Saiyah had recommended, though honestly, Kye wasn't getting the full story. He had gained a basic understanding of elvish from Arden, but it was clearly lacking. Arden was seated in his high-backed chair. He had just pulled out his pipe, filling the end with his favorite herb, in preparation to light it.

"For fuck's sake..."

Kye looked over to him just in time to see Arden's amulet stop glowing and his eyes open in a very perturbed expression.

"Is it the council?" Kye inquired.

Arden nodded. "Valor has called an emergency session."

"What for?"

"His desperate need to feel important," Arden growled as Kye chuckled.

"I'll be back in a while," Arden added as he grabbed his cloak and disappeared from the tower.

When Arden returned to the tower later that evening, Kye was enjoying the last remnants of a pot roast Celeste had sent up, along with a cup of tea.

"How was the council meeting?" Kye inquired as he set his cup down. "You and Valor come to blows?" he added with a sarcastic grin as he turned to face Arden. But one look at his master's face caused all humor to subside instantly. Arden looked ragged, solemn, and defeated. It was the first time Kye had seen him so downtrodden. Arden walked over to the bar and instantly poured himself a drink. He took a seat in the armchair by the fire, rubbing his temples and staring out the large veranda doors as he sipped the whiskey and let out a stressed, heavy sigh. He seemed to be avoiding Kye's gaze as though he was uncertain how to begin the conversation.

"What happened?" Kye inquired, causing Arden to finally meet his eyes. Arden gestured at the couch in front of him.

"Have a seat." Kye complied, feeling anxiety swelling up within him at his master's serious tone.

"The council got word. There was an attack on Helia."

Kye felt his stomach drop as Arden continued.

"It is believed that it was Orin's doing. He seemed to focus the attack on a place called Camris. Do you know of it?"

Kye nodded somewhat numbly. "It's a slave town, made up of freed slaves and elderly. They have no arms and are no threat. Why would Orin attack them?"

Arden shook his head. "I don't know. That is why I volunteered to go investigate."

Kye became fixated on the floor, his mind slowly comprehending what Arden was saying. His thoughts immediately shot to Jitar. Kye hoped he and his family got out alright.

"Do you know how many survivors?" Kye asked. His question met with silence. Kye snapped his head back up as Arden began, "We have only gotten secondhand reports. Until I actually investigate, there is no way to be—"

"Arden," Kye interrupted in a more serious tone, "how many survivors?" He desperately wanted Arden to give a positive response.

The truth hit Kye like an avalanche as Arden simply responded, "As far as we know...none."

Kye's mind couldn't seem to comprehend. Camris had been a large town, the largest slave town on Helia. For every citizen to be killed did not seem possible.

"How many dead?" Kye asked, not really wanting to know the number but feeling compelled to understand.

"We don't have an exact count, but from what the council heard...a little over eight hundred."

Arden's words seemed to be far off, even though he was seated right in front of him. The number of people dead seemed incalculable to Kye. A number too large to process. Humans had never been treated well by mages, so a death here and there was not unheard of. But mass genocide on such a scale? No mage had ever displayed such brutality against humankind before. As such, one question kept repeating in Kye's mind over and over again. Why?

He turned back to Arden, desperate for an answer. "Did

the attack have to do with the stone? Was this a form of retaliation?"

Arden shook his head. "I don't know, but believe me, I intend to find out."

"I'll come with you," Kye declared as he stood up. Arden let out a long sigh.

"Kye—" he started to argue.

"I can help!" Kye retorted. "I grew up on Helia. Not to mention you're an elf and a mage. If there are survivors, they'll be wary of talking to you. I'm human. They'll trust me—"

Arden held up a hand to stop the argument before giving Kye a sympathetic look.

"I get it, kid, I do," Arden began. "You're hurt, and you're pissed, and you have every right to be. But Helia isn't safe for you under normal circumstances. And certainly not if Orin is targeting humans."

Kye looked away, wanting to argue but knowing that Arden was right. Forget the fact that there was undoubtedly a bounty on Kye's head for attacking Umbree; he was still new to the craft. If they did happen to run into Orin while on Helia, Kye would be no help against him. And in all likelihood, he could get Arden killed in his defense. Arden stood up and placed a hand on Kye's shoulder. He gave a comforting look as he said, "What I know, you will know. I'll keep you informed, I promise."

Kye closed his eyes and nodded back reluctantly. Satisfied with their agreement, Arden collected a satchel from his room upstairs as he began moving throughout the tower, filling it with vials of potions and magic tomes.

"I'll be gone a few days," Arden stated to Kye. "Don't go traveling throughout Isalia while I'm away. Stay within the bounds of the castle."

"I will," Kye promised.

AN ATROCIOUS ACT

The last thing Arden grabbed was the scrying spinner before tying up the satchel and grabbing for his cloak.

"I'll give you an update soon," Arden promised as he opened the tower door. "Until then, try to focus on your studies and try not to dwell."

Kye thought that was easier said than done, but he nodded, nonetheless. With that, Arden left as Kye stood alone in the middle of the common area for a long time. He was lost in thought, thinking of nothing but Camris. He thought of Jitar, his family, and all the people living there, trying to make a life of their own. Having been indebted to mages their whole lives before finally finding some measure of freedom for themselves, hurting no one. And then for a mage to come along and slaughter them, without mercy, without cause. Kye's fingers felt numb until he looked down and realized his hands had been clenched into tight fists. For the first time in his life, Kye felt his rage outweigh all reason. Orin had attacked his kin because he believed he had no reason to fear humans. But Kye swore, no matter what, he would give him one. Kye's breathing was coarse, and the tower common room suddenly felt very small. Arden was right—he needed to focus on something else other than his fury. And he needed some air.

After wandering the grounds of the castle for a few hours, Kye found himself walking by the lake. The sky was cloudless, showing off the glimmering stars above him as a bright harvest moon cast a light glow. He desperately wanted to travel, get some distance from the castle, but he had promised Arden he wouldn't. Instead, he was turning over the events in his head, pacing in the frigid night air. He kept envisioning the village, the people, their lives, and their final moments. How scared they must have been, trying to fight back against an enemy they had no chance of defeating. Kye finally took a seat on a tree stump by the water. He felt a hard knot form in his chest. Humans didn't deserve this.

"*Kye?*"

A sudden voice in his head caused Kye to jump up in surprise. He looked around; he was alone by the lake. But someone just said his name. Hadn't they?

"*Kye?*" The voice stated again, only this time Kye recognized it. He looked down to see his amulet was glowing. Someone was communicating with him. Kye closed his eyes and focused.

"*Saiyah?*" he asked the voice in his mind.

"*Yes,*" Saiyah replied. "*I was looking for you. Where are you?*"

"*By the lake,*" Kye responded before opening his eyes again. Within moments, Saiyah appeared a few feet from him.

"There you are," Saiyah stated as she approached Kye. "I thought you might be in the library. I was surprised to find you weren't."

Kye nodded as he turned his attention toward the sky above him. "I just needed some air."

Saiyah gazed at the frost-covered grass around them and the wisps of steam that escaped Kye's lips with each breath.

"Do humans not feel the cold?" she asked curiously.

"No, we do," Kye replied. "I'm just...ignoring it."

Saiyah doubted that mind over matter would be enough to keep him from catching his death. She held out her palm towards the ground and whispered a spell under her breath. A small fire ignited in front of them, casting a warm glow and radiating heat.

Kye's tense posture immediately relaxed as he leaned closer to the fire, savoring its warmth. He gave a small smile to Saiyah in response.

"Thanks," he murmured gratefully.

Saiyah returned his smile and settled herself on a rock near the water opposite him. In the flickering light of the flame, she could now clearly see the sorrow and pain etched on Kye's face.

"I heard from Maister Luell about Helia," she began cautiously. Kye's expression darkened at the mention of his home realm. "Kye, I'm so sorry."

Kye nodded silently, his gaze still fixated on the stars above.

"I also heard it was Orin. Does Arden or the council know why?" Saiyah pressed gently.

Kye's tone turned bitter as he replied, "I'm sure he had many reasons why, the simplest one being that he could."

As Kye fell silent again, Saiyah turned her attention to a nearby patch of earth. She didn't know what to say. She wasn't sure if Kye wanted to talk or be left alone. If he trusted her enough to consider her a confidant or still saw her as a stranger. But she also knew she couldn't just leave him by himself when he was clearly upset. To her surprise, Kye was the first to break the silence.

"It's strange..." he began. "Before Arden, I always hated mages. But more than that...I feared them. The wrath Umbree would often unleash no matter how hard I stood my ground or tried to fight back—I was powerless against it. I hated that feeling more than anything."

He paused for a moment before continuing.

"When Arden offered me a chance to be a mage, I thought that I could finally gain the strength to fight back. That I could use that power to help other humans. But despite all that I have learned, how far I've come, it's not enough. Even by mage standards, I'm still weak in comparison. Incapable of helping my own kind. Incapable of even helping Arden."

Saiyah furrowed her brows. "Is that how you see yourself? As weak?"

Kye did not respond to her question, which told Saiyah the answer was yes. Saiyah huffed loudly in response.

"Well, then, you truly are a fool!" she snapped. Kye raised his eyebrows and turned toward her, taken aback by her rather loud proclamation.

"You have made remarkable progress in such a short time," Saiyah continued. "You have shown a determination that a hundred mages could not match. You fought on equal footing with an eleven acolyte, proven yourself a remarkable traveler, and changed the minds of some of the most stubborn mages in the process, myself included."

Kye gave her a small smile.

"You are not weak, Kye, but you are also not all-powerful. Even the greatest mage in the world cannot save all who suffer and would go mad trying. We are not gods."

Kye nodded. "Arden said the same thing to me when we first met."

"Sound advice you should take to heart."

Kye looked back to the sky. "I was not able to save them," he said, "but at least I can avenge them. They weren't able to fight, but I can and will. I will see Orin pay for what he's done."

"To take on one of the most powerful mages of our age will not be an easy endeavor," Saiyah stated.

"Never meant to be a cobbled road..." Kye muttered. Saiyah tilted her head slightly, unsure of the meaning behind the saying. She assumed it was a human motto she was unfamiliar with.

Saiyah took a deep breath in response and proclaimed, "Well, in that case, allow me to assist you in your endeavor. I should like to take a shot at that black-hearted beast myself."

"I could think of no better ally," Kye stated sincerely.

"Then it's settled," Saiyah replied with a nod. "But it is no small task we undertake, and for it we will need to be well prepared. And well rested."

"Is that your subtle way of telling me I should sleep?" Kye asked with a grin.

"Oh dear," Saiyah replied, "was I being subtle?"

Kye chuckled. "Point taken. I'll head in shortly."

Saiyah nodded. "Then I shall meet you in the library tomorrow. We can begin our research and form a battle plan for how to stop Orin. Till then, I will leave you to your thoughts."

Saiyah rose from the rocks and started heading back toward the castle.

"Saiyah?"

She turned as Kye smiled at her. "Thank you."

"Of course," she replied as she smiled back at him. "What are friends for?"

Kye appeared in Arden's tower some time later. He immediately placed himself in front of the fire. Noting the chain of his amulet felt like ice, he put it on the armoire as he warned himself. He was partially frozen and still angry, but he felt better after talking with Saiyah. He now had a new focus, a purpose. Both Orin and Umbree had caused so much pain, and Kye would help return it in kind. On the dining table, Kye noticed a cup of tea and some biscuits. He smiled. Celeste must have brought it up for him. Considering how cold he was, the tea seemed the perfect remedy. Kye sat down at the table to drink it. As he sipped the warm liquid, he was turning over the events in his mind. The attack on Helia had to be linked to the creation stone, but how? Other than sparking fury, what did attacking a town of humans get Orin? Kye was trying his hardest to put the pieces together, but honestly, he was too tired to think right now. He hoped Arden would find out more during his investigation. For now, it was time to sleep. Kye stood up from the kitchen table to head to his room and instantly felt the whole room shift. The sensation was so halting, he had to grab the edge of the table to steady himself. As he tried to focus on the room around him, his eyesight blurred. His legs were unsteady, and his fingertips felt numb. Kye immediately sat back down to keep from falling. Was it exhaustion? He had felt tired, but not to this extent. It was as though he had downed an entire bottle of fire whiskey instead of just a cup of tea. Kye felt his pulse quicken as he slowly focused on the empty tea cup lying on its side on the table. The tea. The realization dawned on him too late that the tea might not have come from Celeste. Kye saw his amulet still lying on the armoire, just twenty feet in front of him. He once again tried to stand up. He had to call Mireen. Whatever this was, she would know what to do. But his mind was too muddled to travel. Every step was a fight, his vision was blurring, and his legs had gone completely numb. When his right leg finally gave out, Kye hit the floor. The common room was dimming, his consciousness fading. The last thought crossing his mind before darkness welcomed him was that Saiyah had been right. He was a fool—and a careless one at that.

CHAPTER 11
A Ruthless Rival

K ye could hear the whistling of the wind long before his eyes opened. As a soft light blurred slowly into view around him, he saw stone walls surrounding him on all sides, with an opening above. His gaze lifted, and Thaiden's face came into view, looking down at him with a smug smile. His two toadies were there right beside him, looking just as pleased.

"Ah, so you are finally awake," Thaiden sneered. "Sure took you long enough."

Kye wanted to ask where he was, but he couldn't. It was then that he realized he couldn't open his mouth, couldn't move a muscle. The only part of him that still had any autonomy were his eyes, which widened and darted around in panic, realizing his situation.

"By the look of you, you are consumed with three pressing questions: How? Where? And why? Am I right?" Thaiden asked.

Kye glared back at him silently.

"Well, the how is a potion, *vigilantes mortuis*. The waking death. A brew that renders the recipient completely immobile.

Can't move, can't speak, can't even twitch a finger. Now, there is a remedy, which I don't have. And a counterspell for such a state, though I will not tell it to you, of course. Besides, it's not really as though you could speak it even if you knew, right? Kind of a conundrum, if you ask me."

Kye's eyes widened as he saw the cruel smile spread across Thaiden's face.

"Now, as for where, you are currently lying in a tomb, my friend. This stone coffin in which you reside used to belong to the great mage Soren. Oh, but don't worry, we have removed his body to give you a bit more room. Otherwise, it would be rather cramped in there. There are sigils carved within that help contain a mage's magic after they depart."

Thaiden pointed to a new sigil, seemingly written in blood on the lid of the coffin.

"This seal in particular I added myself. It is meant to mask a mage's lifeform. So I'm guessing you can imagine that it's rather hard to detect you in here because of it. Even if, say, someone were to scry for you, it would be practically impossible for them to find you, with wards such as these in place."

Kye could feel the frustration welling up within him. He knew where this was headed and could do nothing to stop it. The feeling of being powerless, all over again. Thaiden leaned closer to Kye so that they were practically nose to nose.

"Now, lastly, I imagine you are wondering why? Well, the answer to that should be simple to you, human. It is because you did not know your place. Because you dared to believe you were on the same level as us, when in fact you are not. You are small, insignificant, and so far below us, you are nothing more than a speck. And since you do not understand this, we have decided to give you some time to reflect upon it. Alone. In the cold, and the dark, and the silence."

Thaiden was grinning from ear to ear as Kye's eyes narrowed with hatred. Thaiden leaned back, grabbed the large stone lid, and began to pull it toward him. The scraping of stone echoed in Kye's ears as he watched the light in front of him slowly disappear. The last glimpse of it illuminated Thaiden's face as he gave Kye a final look.

"Remember, little speck," he smirked, "you have no one to blame but yourself." The coffin lid slid completely closed, snuffing out all light, all movement, all sound. To everyone else, the tomb held nothing but silence. In Kye's mind, however, he was screaming.

It was a fight. Every muscle in Kye's body was fighting to move. He was funneling all his energy into moving anything. A finger, a toe. His breath was billowing in and out in his struggle. Though he couldn't feel the cold because of the potion, the puffs of steam from his nose and mouth told him the freezing temperature he was exposed to. The harder Kye fought to move, the quicker he realized how pointless it was, for he couldn't move anything. And this realization caused him to panic and fight even harder. His breath came faster and in shorter spurts, and he couldn't seem to get enough air. The stone coffin was sealed tight—not even a trickle of light was showing through. His heart was beating so fast he could hear the uneven rhythm resonating in his ears. His head was spinning, and his mind was racing; he could feel himself sinking and fighting to stay conscious. Which was yet another fight he was losing. As sleep enveloped him, he realized the truth of his situation: *"I'm going to die here."*

Kye's eyes fluttered open. He wasn't certain how long he had been asleep or where he was. At first, he thought that he'd gone blind, for he was surrounded by dark everywhere. But trying to sit up reminded him of his situation as he once again tried to make his limbs move. He was focusing all his energy on his hand, just to get a single finger to twitch, when suddenly: *STOP!* he commanded himself. *Stop struggling, stop fighting. You will never break free this way, and you know it. All you are wasting is energy and air, and you don't have an abundance of either. Just stop, and breathe, and think."*

Kye slowly took in a deep, calming breath, allowing it to fill his lungs before exhaling. He closed his eyes tight, envisioning himself sitting in the forest behind Arden's tower, listening to the birds, instead of trapped in the shadow-filled terror he was currently in. Focusing his mind, calming his thoughts. Panicking would solve nothing, only hasten his demise. Fear could be a sword or a crutch depending on how it was wielded. Right now, it was crippling him. He had to regain control, or this would be the end. Kye thought back to what Thaiden had said—*the waking death*. He didn't know the counterspell, not that he could recite it even if he did. Waiting for someone to come to his aid wasn't an option either. He fully believed Thaiden that the wards on the coffin would mask his presence, even if someone tried to scry for him. So if he didn't have the ability to break the incantation himself and couldn't wait for someone else to find him, what option did that leave? Running scenarios through his head, Kye tried focusing his mind. Perhaps thinking of a spell, if he concentrated hard enough, would be enough to free him. Arden had mentioned to him that when maisters are advanced enough in their magic, there are some spells they can cast without needing to speak. In fact, on several occasions, Arden had lit candles or summoned fire in his palm without uttering a word. So maybe if he focused hard enough, Kye could do the same. Kye tried to think of a spell strong enough to break his hold. He knew a few basic healing spells, but none of them were terribly powerful. Still, he had nothing to lose. Kye closed his eyes to focus on the spell "*Invertira Venen*," a simple spell used to slow or reverse poisons mages were exposed to in the field. Granted, this wasn't a poison per se, but maybe he could reverse the effects enough to gain some movement back. If he could speak, he'd have more options. Kye concentrated on the spell with every fiber he possessed. He was practically shouting the words in his mind, but after a long time, his current condition remained unchanged. He ran through other healing spells. He recited some evocation spells, and he even tried to travel, but all efforts were met with the same end—nothing. As the hours passed, and with each failed spell, his hope of escape diminished. Dwindling down till only one cold, hard truth remained. Acceptance.

Some time later, Kye felt sleepy again. Whether it was the cold or the lack of air it really didn't matter. Either—or both —would kill him quickly enough. He wondered if anyone would notice he was gone. Arden, for sure. Would he think Kye just ran off? Abandoned his position as his acolyte? He hoped not. He hoped Arden understood how much of a privilege it was to apprentice under him. To meet the first honorable mage in his life and to consider him a friend. He also hoped, at some point, Arden would find his body. Lay him to rest near the castle or maybe on Helia. Of course, he supposed it was fitting. If he was going to die, at least he was already in a tomb. Surrounded by the souls of the departed, he'd have company. It was too bad his affinity wasn't summoning. If he were a speaker like Saiyah, perhaps he would have been able to call upon a spirit to help him

Saiyah...

A knot formed in Kye's chest as her smile flashed in his head. He realized he would never see it, or her, again. As Kye felt himself drifting off once again, he focused his thoughts and recited a summoning call she had taught him in the futile hopes anyone might be listening.

Spirits abound, here my plea

> Soul to soul, I call to thee
> Your untold knowledge, I implore
> to spare this mortal at death's door

The sound of waves crashing and the smell of salt in the air was the next sensation Kye became aware of. As he opened his eyes, he was no longer met with utter darkness. Instead, he was greeted by thousands of shimmering stars against a clear night sky. Kye moved his hands, surprised that he once again had autonomy. Beneath him, warm white sand was streaming through his fingers. Kye sat up and saw he was on a small island, the edge of which he could see in all directions. This island was familiar to him—he was certain he had seen it before. As he stood up, Kye noticed a deep, dark ocean surrounded him on all sides. Off to the distance in the east, there was a deep blue light, almost like a dark cerulean sunset on the horizon. To the west, the rising sun looked gold and orange. As Kye tried to figure out where the hell he was, an orb of light broke off from one of the many glowing trees on the island and fluttered down toward Kye. He noticed it seemed to possess sentience: mimicking Kye's movements as it floated closer, advancing on him as he backed away. Kye readied his stance for an attack, uncertain what the ball of light would do.

"Fear not, young one," a soft voice said. "It means you no harm. It is merely drawn to the light."

Kye turned to see a woman in white walking toward him. All at once he remembered he had seen her and this island before—after Umbree had attacked him. He remembered floating in this water, looking up at those stars, and seeing her walking along the island he now stood upon. The woman held out her hand, and the ball of light hovering in front of Kye immediately flew over to her, drifting around her in slow orbit. Kye noticed the woman was tall, slender, and fair, just like an elf, with long, white hair. Her ears, though, looked human, and her eyes were a dark onyx color, like those of an orc.

"Who are you?" Kye demanded, maintaining his defensive stance. The woman simply smiled at him in return.

"I am not an enemy to you, young one. I can promise you that."

The ball of light floated toward her hand as she turned her attention toward it. It circled her outstretched arms a few times before finally coming to rest within her palms. Realizing that was as good an answer as he was going to get from the woman, Kye tried another question.

"Where am I?"

The woman turned her attention back toward him.

"The between," she stated as though Kye should know where the hell that was.

"The between?" he probed.

"Yes. Between your world and the one beyond."

The crushing weight of reality came tumbling down on Kye as he slowly understood what she meant. Death. This was a waypoint between the land of the living and the realm of the dead. The last sanctuary when crossing over. His mouth went as dry as desert sand as he asked, "Am I...dead?"

The woman smiled and shook her head. "No, young one. The light still shines within you. Though it is dimming. Enough so for you to travel here."

Kye felt relieved that he was still alive but also acutely aware that he wouldn't be for long. He might not be dead, but he was dying, and there was nothing he could do to stop it.

"Then it's only a matter of time," he muttered in defeat.

The woman looked at him quizzically. "I have come to find there is always hope, young one."

"Not much in this case," Kye continued. "I am held by a spell, and it's killing me, and there is nothing I can do about it."

"A spell? But you are a mage, are you not?"

Kye was taken aback that she knew that. He was curious but figured asking her how she knew would be met with a cryptic answer and more silence.

"Yes..." he replied carefully, "but I am unfamiliar with this spell. And therefore, I don't know how to break it."

"Ah." The woman nodded. "*Vincula Ligara*."

"I'm sorry?" Kye replied as the woman turned her attention back to the orb of light now dancing above her head.

"The spell to free you. *Vincula Ligara*."

Kye had just about a million questions as he stood there, flabbergasted. For starters, who exactly this woman was, which she didn't seem inclined to answer. Second, how did she know how to break the spell he was under when he hadn't even told her what it was? It was clear to Kye that she was a spirit of some kind, and Saiyah had warned him about listening to spirits. Communing with the dead was tricky, especially if you were not a speaker, because they no longer had any stake in living. One spirit could offer you the meaning of existence, while the other could feed you lies that could lead you to your doom. It really depended on their mood at the moment. For all Kye knew, this nonsensical spirit could've just told him the spell to stop his heart...but it wasn't like he had a whole lot of options.

"But even knowing the spell doesn't help me if I can't speak it," Kye stated.

"I hear your words quite well, young one."

"No, I mean in the other world," Kye clarified. "Where my body is. I can't move a muscle, let alone recite a spell."

The woman merely smiled at his observation and shook

her head slightly. "For one that draws upon the light, you focus far too much on flesh and blood and bone."

Kye looked confused.

"Body obeys the spirit, young one, not the other way around."

Kye took that to mean that he could break the spell even in his current form. Feeling as though he had nothing to lose, Kye took a deep breath, closed his eyes and recited clearly, "*Vincula Ligara!*"

Nothing. He felt no different and was still standing literally at death's door.

"As I said, young one, the light within you is dimming. You must draw upon the light around you to summon strength."

Kye was thoroughly confused. He had no idea what the "light" was she kept talking about or how to draw from it.

"I don't understand," Kye told her.

"That is because you cannot see," the woman replied. "So I shall lend you my eyes."

She walked toward Kye and held out her hand. Kye took a step back, eyeing her wearily. The woman's expression softened in response. "You have nothing to fear from me, young one. I swear it."

Kye decided to accept she was telling the truth and grasped her hand. He had expected it to feel ice cold, but it was just as warm as his.

"Close your eyes," she said. Kye obeyed. The woman whispered words under her breath that Kye couldn't quite catch. But he felt an energy pass between them.

"Now, open them."

As soon as he did, Kye was mesmerized. Everything around him, from the water to the sand to the trees, was aglow. Everything seemed to possess its own color, its own vibrance, its own radiance. Kye stood stunned, looking at the world around him for the first time. Now, he understood what she meant by the light; it was everywhere. Looking down at himself, he noticed his form had a glow as well. Though, true to the woman's word, it was diminished when compared to everything around him. Looking back to the woman, Kye noticed that her form was entirely different. The light that surrounded her was dark, like a shadow radiating out from all sides. It seemed almost ominous, but Kye didn't sense any animosity from her. The woman looked back at him and asked, "Do you see?"

Kye nodded as the woman continued, "This is the light of your realm. It can be seen even here, at the crossing. This is what you call to with your words, mage. This is what you draw from. You will need the light from around you to break the bonds that bind. For that, you must reach out, spirit to spirit, to add that light to your own. Do you understand?"

Kye nodded once again as the woman released his hand.

"In that case, reach out, young one. Pull energy from all things to set your spirit aglow."

Kye closed his eyes again, this time focusing on the light that was all around him. He imagined the energy from the trees, water, and land flowing into him, like water into a pail. As he did, he felt a warmth within his chest grow till it extended from the top of his head to the very tips of his fingers.

"Now, imagine your physical self. Imagine the spell that binds you as chains. See them clearly within your mind," the woman instructed.

Kye could clearly see himself lying in the tomb as though he was floating above his own body. He was lying still in the dark, his entire form bound by metal that would not break.

"Focus on the words. Imagine them as steel, strong enough to break those bonds that bind. And when you speak, young one, speak not only out loud but from deep within as well."

Kye nodded and imagined the words as though they were a sharpened axe, strong enough to break through steel.

"Very good. Now take a breath, focus with all you have, and command yourself free."

Kye took a deep breath, clenched his fists, and shouted with all that he possessed: *"VINCULA LIGARA!"*

Kye awoke gasping in the dark, his chest heaving against the freezing cold stone. His limbs were finally free but completely numbed by the cold. He clamored at the heavy coffin walls around him. No matter how many breaths Kye took, he could not get enough air. And as his lungs worked harder, he felt light-headed and dizzy. No, he couldn't lose consciousness, for he knew he would not wake again if he did. He was running out of time. Kye struck the lid of the coffin with his fists several times as hard as his strength allowed, but it didn't even budge. He kicked at the hard stone walls with his feet, but they showed no cracks or sign of give. He didn't have the energy to perform an evocation spell, and he didn't have his amulet on him to call out. Kye had but one option left to him, and since he had no way of knowing how far he was from his intended destination, he hoped he had the strength left to complete the journey without it killing him. Kye painted clear within his mind Arden's tower. The wood floor, stone walls, cozy fire. He filled his lungs with what little breath he had left and whispered, "*Dimmora.*"

There was a familiar pulling sensation, followed by a hard landing. Kye's feet barely touched the floor before the rest of him collapsed on all fours upon the familiar wood surface. He rolled into his back, staring up at the carved wood ceiling, hearing the faint crackle of the dying fire and basking in the embers' warmth. He was shivering, his extremities numb from the freezing stone tomb, and his lungs actually ached from trying to draw breath. He almost immediately slipped back into unconsciousness, exhausted and cold, but at the same time relieved. He was alive, and he was home.

"Kye?...Kye!? KYE!?"

Kye awoke with a start, staring up at a familiar pair of violet eyes looking down at him with a worried expression.

"Saiyah?" he asked, his voice raspy, his head still a bit fuzzy and confused from lack of air.

"Yes," Saiyah replied. "Are you alright!? Why are you lying on the floor?"

Kye had completely forgotten that he had passed out almost instantly where he landed and was still sprawled out on the common area in Arden's tower.

"That's a...fair question..." Kye muttered as he slowly sat up. His head instantly began pounding, loudly, protesting any attempts to move. He placed a palm to his head, trying to calm the cacophony.

"Are you ill?" Saiyah inquired. "Should I call for Mireen?"

Kye shook his head, an action he almost immediately regretted. "No, I'm alright," he insisted as he slowly got to his feet.

"You don't particularly look it," Saiyah noted in concern, offering a hand to help him up. "What happened to your hands? And why are you covered in dust and spiderwebs?"

Kye looked down to see that his knuckles were scraped and bleeding from punching the coffin walls. His robes were indeed coated in a thick layer of gray dust, with threaded webbing on his shoulders and in his hair. He quickly tried to think of a response. *Because you often find spiders and dust in a several-hundred-year-old tomb. Because Thaiden thought it amusing to drug me, drop me in a coffin, and leave me there to suffocate.* He couldn't tell Saiyah the truth. She had already suffered the ire of her colleagues for standing up for Kye once. He wasn't about to have her face retribution on his behalf again, and he knew if he told her the truth, she would insist on confronting Thaiden. No, this was Kye's problem, and he would handle it himself.

"I...got lost," Kye replied, quickly formulating an explanation in his mind.

"You got lost?" Saiyah asked skeptically.

"I was traveling around Isalia, just trying to clear my head. I wasn't really paying attention to where I was going, and before I knew it, I found myself lost in an unknown forest. I guess I scraped my hands when I tripped. When I tried to teleport back to Arden's tower, I must have traveled too far and expended more energy than I meant to because I passed out as soon as I appeared."

Kye watched as the skepticism on Saiyah's face slowly faded, replaced once again by a look of concern.

"Then I would say you are quite lucky," Saiyah replied. "Even if traveling is your affinity, there are still limits to your strength, and you must be careful not to push beyond it. Mages have died performing spells outside their capabilities."

"You're right," Kye conceded. "It was stupid of me. And I am grateful you stopped by when you did. But I'm curious what brought you here?" Kye was just now realizing Saiyah had never come to Arden's tower before.

"Orin," Saiyah replied simply. "You were to meet me in the library tonight. We were going to formulate a plan for stopping Orin. When you did not show, and I could not reach you through the amulet, I came to see if you had forgotten."

Kye looked out at the night sky in surprise. This was not

the same evening he had left. A day. He had been trapped in the tomb a full day. He had been unaware of the passage of time, slipping in and out of consciousness.

"Of course," Kye responded. "Unfortunately, I'm not sure if I'd be much use focusing right now. Can we meet tomorrow?"

Saiyah nodded. "Certainly. Just be sure to get some rest."

"I will," Kye agreed. Saiyah started heading toward Arden's door. Stopping just before the threshold, she turned back to Kye.

"Are you sure you are alright?"

In truth, Kye was exhausted, unsteady, and mad as hell. But he plastered on his warmest smile, replying to Saiyah, "I'm fine. Promise."

Saiyah seemed to accept his response. "Well, then, I wish you goodnight, Kye."

"Goodnight, Saiyah."

She smiled back at him as she left the tower. As soon as Saiyah was gone, Kye's anger started to boil as his face tightened in determination. He walked over to the writing desk in the common area and pulled out some ink and a quill. Kye approached the doorway of Arden's tower. On the door frame, Kye wrote the word "Barrin." He rolled back the sleeve on his left wrist and wrote the word there as well. Setting the quill down, he focused the little energy he had left and commanded, "*Sola Arden et Kye intrara hara.*" The word on his wrist and the word on the doorframe glowed as Kye inspected the word on his skin, now ingrained like a tattoo. If anyone tried to enter the tower when Arden or Kye were not here, the word on his wrist would burn like a brand, alerting him to any intruders crossing the threshold. It should stop Thaiden from dropping off any more gifts without Kye's knowledge. Satisfied with the spell, Kye began heading to his room, peeling off his dust-coated clothing as he went. First a bath, then bed. Tonight, he needed rest. Tomorrow, he would deal with Thaiden.

Thaiden strolled through the castle grounds in the early afternoon with his comrades Nerin and Luka in tow. He was feeling rather pleased with himself, having rid the castle of a piece of vermin. It was too bad, of course, that the rest of his fellow acolytes could not know what he had done. Surely, they would thank him and cheer him for it. And he had to admit, it was quite thrilling to watch the fear in the human's eyes as he closed the stone coffin's lid, sealing him away forever in darkness. A death befitting such a worthless creature. He was certain when Lord Arden returned, he would raise a fuss, demanding to know where his acolyte was, trying in vain to scry for him. But Thaiden knew he would never find him. He just had to be careful that Lord Arden didn't discover that he was the cause. His cohorts seemed to be thinking along the same lines.

"Do you think the human is dead already?" Luka whispered to Thaiden.

Thaiden shrugged. "If he isn't now, he will be soon."

"Perhaps we should go and check," Nerin suggested.

"No!" snapped Thaiden, ducking with the pair into a secluded corner of the courtyard, ensuring they were out of earshot of any passersby. "We want to avoid suspicion. Especially when Lord Arden finds out he is missing. You do not want him to believe we are responsible for the death of his acolyte. We will just wait it out. We should just be grateful that the human is gone."

"Well, not quite."

Thaiden spun around, only to see the human standing

directly behind him. Before he even had time to react, the human grabbed his wrist and uttered a single word.

"*Dimmora.*"

Kye released Thaiden's wrist rather abruptly, causing him to stumble and fall on the dueling grounds where they had landed. The grounds were deserted as they were much of the time at the castle. Not many acolytes spent their time actually learning to fight. Thaiden's eyes darted around, trying to get his bearings. He was gawking at Kye as though he had literally risen from the grave.

"What's wrong, Thaiden?" Kye asked without any true sincerity behind the words. "You look like you've seen a ghost. Or were you were hoping to?"

"H-how did you escape!?" he stuttered.

"You don't know?" replied Kye. "Don't tell me there is magic a human knows that an elf does not?"

Thaiden narrowed his gaze and clenched his fists.

"Why have you brought me here!?" he demanded.

"I thought you and I should talk in private," Kye replied.

"There is NOTHING I wish to say to you, human!" Thaiden growled.

"Very well." Kye shrugged. "Then we won't waste time with words."

Kye muttered a spell under his breath. A large circle with a line through the center appeared on the ground. He took his place in the half-circle opposite Thaiden and immediately formed a defensive stance. Thaiden looked down at his own half-circle, recognizing it as the area for a mage duel. He looked back at Kye and chuckled.

"You intend to duel me?" he scoffed.

"That is your goal, isn't it?" Kye inquired. "For us to fight?

Or can you only attack me when I am unprepared or unconscious?"

Thaiden growled back to Kye. "I would murder you, human!"

"Well, your first two attempts have been unsuccessful. What makes you think the third time's the charm?"

"I will not play this game with you!"

"You already started the game. I'm just clarifying the rules. If you wish to fight me, Thaiden, then consider your challenge accepted. I will duel you anytime, mage to mage."

Kye narrowed his gaze. "But if you continue to employ underhanded tactics to come at me, then I will resort to some of my own. I have already proven I can sneak up on you. And as I'm sure you have heard from the stories about me, I am well acquainted with stabbing a mage in the back."

Thaiden's gaze darkened as he stepped toward Kye.

"Do you think I fear you, human?" he hissed.

"No," Kye replied honestly, "but I do think I can change that."

Thaiden's eyes widened slightly as Kye stepped closer in response.

"Your move, Thaiden," he stated. "What will it be?" Kye's manner mimicked one of a cornered animal ready to fight. In truth, he was fairly certain he would lose in a one-on-one match with Thaiden. After all, the elf was much older and had been a mage much longer than himself. But one thing was certain, if Thaiden was hellbent on sending Kye to the boneyard, he would make damn sure he wasn't making the trip alone.

Thaiden seemed to be turning over the options in his head. He looked Kye up and down as if trying to decide if he should attack him or not. Which seemed odd to Kye, considering he hadn't appeared to have any issue with attacking him before. He must have second-guessed himself, for he merely sneered at Kye and hissed, "NEVER touch me again, vermin."

"Likewise," Kye bit back. With one final contemptuous glance, Thaiden turned on his heel and began marching back to the castle. Once he was out of earshot, Kye let out a long sigh, releasing with it the pent-up anger he had been holding in. He muttered a word again, and the duel ground he had created disappeared. His moment of calm was instantly replaced by a surge of adrenaline when he heard a long whistle. He spun around to see a young, blond-haired man with well-defined facial features and sharp yellow eyes step out from behind a large oak. He was a bit taller than Kye, with a muscular and lithe frame. He seemed to be around Kye's age and was grinning from ear to ear.

"So, humans do have fangs," he remarked. "And here I thought your kind had no bite."

Kye kicked himself for not being more careful to make sure he and Thaiden were alone. He hadn't sensed this man at all. But it was fairly obvious by his remarks that he had witnessed the entire exchange.

"You overheard the conversation, I take it?"

The man smiled even wider. "Every—utterly entertaining—word."

Kye sighed. "I suppose you plan to report my actions to Maister Valor?"

To his surprise, the man actually laughed out loud. "Hell, no! I actively try to avoid that uppity asshole whenever possible. And I don't give a shit if his acolyte gets taken down a peg—just surprised that you were the one to do it."

The man grinned as he added, "Looks like the rumors were not complete fables after all. I can see why Saiyah is intrigued."

"You know Saiyah?" Kye questioned.

"We are practically family."

"You're not an elf," Kye noted.

"A fact I'm grateful for every single day," the man replied with a grin. "I'm a shifter. The name's Riley."

Riley stepped forward and held out a hand to Kye. Kye paused only for a moment before accepting it, figuring if he was a friend of Saiyah's, he could be trusted.

"Kye," he responded as Riley gave his hand a hearty shake. Kye had never met a shifter, but he had read about them. Part man, part beast. Kye always figured they would be fearsome beings to encounter, emitting a deadly aura they could easily follow through on. But Riley seemed the exact opposite, appearing agreeable, devil may care almost.

"Well, Kye, you thirsty?" Riley inquired. "Cause anyone that can make Thaiden piss himself deserves a drink."

"Uh...sure," Kye replied uncertainly, still adjusting to the very sudden shift in emotion between squaring off with Thaiden and meeting Riley.

"Excellent!" Riley exclaimed, throwing his arm over Kye's shoulders like they were old friends. "I know this fantastic hole-in-the-wall pub that serves the best ale. And on the way, you can regale me with tales of your life as a renegade bandit."

"My what?" Kye questioned. Riley made a slightly disappointed face as he muttered, "Damn...I was really hoping that one was true."

CHAPTER 12
A Secluded Solstice

The library was completely silent, save for the soft crackling of wood in the fireplace, the intermittent turning of a page, and the impatient tapping of a foot. Kye and Saiyah were focusing during their familiar study time, but this evening, they were joined by a third member. Riley was seated at the table with them, but ever since he sat down, he seemed impatient to leave. He would fidget, tap, roll his fingers, and occasionally exhale loudly. After some time, he let out a long, exacerbated sigh.

"Wow," he mentioned to Saiyah, "you weren't kidding."

Saiyah looked up from her book and gave him a curious glance. "I wasn't kidding about what?"

"When you said you both meet in the library every night to 'study,' I assumed it was code for something."

Kye raised an eyebrow in response as Saiyah leaned forward to scrutinize Riley under an interrogating gaze.

"Code for what, exactly?" she asked pointedly as Riley leaned his chair back to stare at the glass ceiling in boredom

"Something a hell of a lot more interesting than this," he muttered.

"Oh, I'm terribly sorry, Riley," Saiyah tersely replied. "I forgot it was my purpose in life to entertain you."

Riley rolled his eyes and began once again drumming his fingers on the table. "Hey, Kye!" he suddenly exclaimed in excitement. "You're a traveler, aren't you?"

"Yes," Kye replied uncertainly.

"Fantastic!" Riley stated. "Then the night is young, and all of Isalia is open to us."

Kye shook his head in response. "When I talked to Arden he requested I don't leave the grounds of the castle while he's away."

What had started out as a few days' endeavor, had now turned into several weeks. He had communicated to Kye through his amulet, giving him updates on the situation at Helia. The latest information he had was that Arden was tracking down any witnesses who might have seen Orin or knew where he might be headed next.

Riley merely waved his hand dismissively. "He'll never know we left," he argued. "Plus, I heard of this tavern on the eastern continent that serves the best pints. Also, I hear there are these dancers—"

"Riley, stop trying to lead us down a path of drunken debauchery and read your book!" Saiyah snapped.

Riley grumbled as he turned his attention back to the pages in front of him. The familiar sounds of fidgeting fell upon the group again until finally Riley shot up from his seat and proclaimed, "Nope! Can't do it!"

He then immediately turned from the table and started walking away.

"Where are you going!?" Saiyah shouted after him.

"To actually enjoy the remainder of the evening. But do have fun, my boring little bookworms," he replied before shutting the library doors behind him. Saiyah was left with a disapproving glare at his sudden exit.

"So...he's not the studious type, I take it?" Kye remarked.

"Whatever gave you that idea," Saiyah mumbled as Kye chuckled in response. Kye turned back to his studies, reaching across the table to grab another edition about magic stones from the infinite stack he had brought over. Nowadays, he was switching between trying to discover more about the creation stones and trying to find a way to stop a necromancer like Orin. Both equally important subjects. Saiyah looked up and noticed the book he grabbed.

"You have an interest in them, don't you?" she asked as Kye looked at her questioningly. "Magic stones," Saiyah clarified. "I've noticed you read quite a few books on the subject."

Kye halted for a moment, carefully thinking of a response. He trusted Saiyah, but he wasn't sure how much he was supposed to tell her about the creation stone. As far as he was aware, the information had been kept to High Council maisters only, and he wasn't about to be the one responsible for letting it leak." Um...yeah," he replied. "I heard Arden mention some ancient stones that actually held the power of the elements. They sounded interesting to me."

"Ah, the original creation stones," Saiyah remarked. "Yes, it is fascinating what they were able to craft, even when magic was still new. Sadly, they exist now only as rumors. I did hear mention of one discovered about fifty years ago or so. But that, too, must have been just a tale."

Kye focused intently on the pages in front of him, determined not to show even the slightest tell that he knew more than what he was letting on.

"If you are interested in magical stones, though, there are other fascinating examples that exist outside of myth." Saiyah's hand extended forward as she pulled up the sleeve of her robe. On her right wrist was an ornately decorated charm bracelet. Gems of all colors and clarities dangled from the silver chain.

"You see this stone?" she said, pointing to a clear gem that looked like an uncut diamond. "It is an empathy stone. It senses the emotions of those around it. It is said to turn black when you are in the presence of those with evil intentions against you. This one—" She pointed to a green emerald. "—is a spiritual ward. Helps prevent curses. Oh and this one," she noted, pointing to one smooth as river rock, "is a weather stone. It will hum slightly when it is about to rain. Plus, stones such as these have their own unique aura that is unlike any other. Which means that even if you come across a sunstone, for instance, you could not use it to scry for another sunstone because their auras would be completely different, just like with people. It really is fascinating!"

Kye smiled and put back down the book he had just picked up. "Well, I certainly don't need these now that I know I am in the presence of an expert," he remarked. Saiyah blushed slightly while retaining her high-born composure.

"Hardly an expert," she argued. "I simply come from a long line of mages. My great-great-grandmother collected magical stones like these for centuries. In fact, this charm bracelet is given to each new mage of the family. It has been passed down for a few millennia."

That amount of time was incalculable to Kye. The fact that each elf could live up to a thousand years, while humans were lucky to make it to one hundred.

"If you would like, I could show you a fascinating book on other magical stones?" Saiyah inquired.

Kye grinned back at her. "I would appreciate that."

Saiyah beamed at him; this was clearly a subject of great interest to her. She immediately got up from the table and disappeared into the library shelves. She returned a short while later with a large, leather-bound volume. She popped it on the table in front of Kye before dragging a chair over and sitting beside him. Kye caught the faint scent of lilac and lavender. Some sort of perfume, he assumed; he was surprised he hadn't noticed it before. He found the scent rather calming, subtle, and pleasant.

"Now..." Saiyah began thumbing through the pages of the book. "I suggest we start with memory stones. They are quite intriguing."

Kye walked into the tower to see Arden seated in his familiar armchair by the fire. It had only been a few weeks since he had left for Helia, but the expression on his face looked like that of a man who had aged several years.

"You're back," Kye noted as he set down the books from the library on the dining table. Arden nodded in response and let out a long sigh. He looked beaten down, and Kye didn't want to pepper him with questions. But at the same time, he was desperate for information about his home realm.

"Did you find out anything?" Kye questioned.

"Yeah. It turns out the council's intel was correct. Orin was responsible for the attack."

"Were...there any survivors?" Kye asked. He already suspected he knew the answer, but still, he had hope. It was quickly dashed, though, with the silent shake of Arden's head. It had been a long shot; the council had heard there were no survivors even before Arden left. Still, it hit harder to know it was now fact and not mere conjecture. Kye let out a solemn sigh, stung with grief for his fallen kin. And struck with a reignited desire for revenge.

"Were you able to catch up with Orin?" Kye inquired. He really hoped Arden had been able to take a few shots at the cold-blooded bastard. Arden shook his head again.

"I got close," he replied. "But I lost the trail when that fucker left the realm."

"How?" Kye inquired, clearly confused. "How was he able

to portal? I thought the only travel orbs in existence were in the control of the council. Did he make his own? Is he getting help from a traveler?"

Arden shrugged. "I have heard there are other ways between realms, outside of portals. I could not tell you what they are, but clearly, Orin is well-versed in the subject. He has been able to slip in and out of worlds as easily as stepping in and out of a doorway."

Yet another puzzle about Orin. He was a necromancer; traveling should not be his affinity. Therefore, it made sense that if he wished to travel to and from realms, he would need help. The question was, what kind of help and from whom? Arden let out a long, deflated sigh and fell silent, rubbing his temple. He looked tired. And even though elves didn't sleep, Kye thought he probably could use it right now. Arden had been the only one on the council who had gone to investigate the eight hundred human lives lost. He had been the only one who had tried to get justice for the slaves that had been slaughtered. In truth, he seemed to be the only maister on the council who cared.

"Arden...thank you," said Kye.

Arden looked up in surprise. "Thanks for what?"

"For going to Helia, for investigating what happened. For trying to get justice. Thank you."

Arden's face fell a bit. "I didn't catch Orin."

"But you tried," replied Kye, "and that matters...more than you know."

Arden nodded. He knew how humans were treated and was one of the few Kye had met who sought to change that.

"I think I'll head to bed," Kye stated, wishing to give Arden some time alone with his thoughts. He got up from the chair to leave.

"Hey, kid?"

Kye turned back as Arden looked toward him. He pointed toward the door to the tower.

"Do you want to tell me why there is a threshold spell carved in the doorway?"

Shit. Honestly, the spell had completely slipped Kye's mind. Just like with Saiyah, Kye didn't want to tell Arden the truth. Mainly because he didn't want Arden to think he couldn't handle himself against other mages. He had to be able to fight his own battles, and besides, Arden had enough on his mind. Kye's war with Thaiden should be the furthest thing from it.

"Just a precaution," Kye replied.

"Precaution for what?"

"For the creation stone," Kye lied. "In case anyone working for Orin tries to get to it, we can be alerted if anyone tries to enter the tower to obtain it."

Arden raised an eyebrow slightly. Kye was acutely aware his explanation made him sound paranoid. He wasn't able to think up a better story on the spot. Arden finally broke his interrogation-like gaze and simply shrugged. "If it helps you sleep better, then by all means. But even Orin's followers aren't crazy enough to sneak into the castle with so many maisters around. Besides, the stone isn't in the tower."

Kye was surprised by that piece of information. "I just assumed..."

"So would a lot of other mages, which is the main reason I didn't stash it here," Arden stated. "One thing about mages—they are so focused on secrets and hidden truths they often can't spot the forest through the trees. You want to hide something from a mage, you do it in plain sight."

Kye paused for a moment. If Arden wasn't that concerned with followers of Orin breaking into Caelum Vallis, then it sounded like he was concerned some were already here.

"Arden," responded Kye after a few moments of silence,

"do you think other maisters on the council are working with Orin?"

Arden's face grew serious. "I hope not," Arden finally replied. "But let's just say there were a few too many supporters of Umbree for me to take that chance."

Arden's expression seemed to darken for a moment. Kye wondered if he had broached a topic he shouldn't have. There was a tense silence in the tower as Arden stared at the fireplace, his face unreadable. Kye figured Arden was probably just tired. He decided he should leave him in peace.

"Well, I'll head to bed. Good night, Arden."

"Good night, kid," Arden muttered back, never breaking focus with the flames.

Kye awoke one morning several weeks later to a muted sun streaming through his bedroom window and a swift chill wafting over his face. Kye pulled the blankets up toward him and groaned a bit. He assumed the fire in his room had died. As Kye reluctantly shuffled across the cold wood floor to add a few more logs to the fireplace, a flash of white caught his eyes. He turned toward his window and saw something falling from the sky. The closer he got, he realized it looked like small tufts of cotton were raining down. Peering out at the landscape, he saw a blanket of white. Snow. He had heard of it, seen pictures of it, but never witnessed it firsthand. Kye pushed open his window and felt a sharp sting of cold bite his face. He held out a hand to catch a few falling flakes in his palm, watching them melt instantly. He couldn't help but smile. He never thought he would see snow firsthand. It was an incredible sight to behold. Kye finished getting dressed and went out into the common area. A roaring fire was blazing in the fireplace, beating back the chill that was seeping through the glass veranda doors and tall windows. Arden was reading a tome in his favorite chair, sipping on tea as was his morning ritual.

"*Sulara anor*," said Kye.

"*Sulara anor*," Arden responded, barely muttering the acknowledgment.

Since Arden had returned from Helia, his demeanor had completely changed. He no longer taught Kye spells and really spoke to him. He spent all his time head down in a book, as though entirely consumed with finding out what the creation stones were. Kye had tried to give him as much space as possible, figuring his presence was probably more of a hindrance than a help. But Kye was determined to get better at magic, to be useful to Arden and help him in his search. To achieve that goal, Kye spent all of his time nowadays practicing spells with Saiyah and Riley. In doing so, he found each of his friends had their strengths.

Saiyah excelled in form, teaching him the correct way to stand and correct pronunciations. There was an elegance to the way she cast magic that Kye was certain he could never mimic.

Riley, on the other hand, taught Kye how to fight. Riley seemed thrilled to finally know an acolyte who was interested in learning combat, which was squarely his area of expertise. As a shif, he was incredibly fast, hit like a hammer, and could counter on a dime. He didn't really rely on spells to attack, mainly focusing on melee attacks. Kye had found he was learning a lot about hand-to-hand combat. Not only that, but he had noticed his stamina and muscle strength had greatly improved from his bouts with Riley, making it that much easier to maintain spells in dueling. Ever since returning from the between, Kye found he could now teleport without having to speak "*Dimmora*." From what he learned from the woman in white, he now knew how to cast it without having to voice the word. Granted, it only worked with teleportation.

Kye suspected it was because teleporting was his affinity and easier to cast than any other spell he tried. It did make sparring with Riley more interesting, though, as Kye would teleport around the battle area, delivering an attack to Riley, then disappearing before Riley could follow up with a counter. Riley was impressed Kye was able to cast even one spell without speaking, since usually only maisters could achieve that. But as much of a help as Saiyah and Riley were, Kye wished Arden would include him in his investigation. Things between them seemed tense, and Kye was at a loss as to how to fix it.

"I see it snowed," Kye mentioned, grabbing a cup of tea and trying to make conversation. Arden looked toward the veranda doors as the flakes fell and made a malcontented grunt before turning back to his book.

"Not a fan, I take it?" Kye added.

"Of nipping wind, trudging through mounds of shredded ice, then falling on your ass on a frozen puddle? No, not particularly."

"I see," Kye replied, watching the flakes fall onto the veranda through the window. "It's the first time I've ever seen snow."

Arden was quiet for several moments before adding, "Well, I guess it is nice to look at if nothing else."

Kye observed the landscape for several moments before he noticed there were no serving dishes on the dining table.

"Did I sleep through breakfast?" he inquired. Arden shook his head. "Celeste never brought it up. I assumed she was busy preparing for the solstice."

"The solstice?"

"Yeah, the winter solstice," Arden explained, taking another sip of tea as he turned the page. "It is a festivity among elves, celebrating the coming of winter and the ending of the year. Valor throws a big celebration for it every year."

"If it is an elven celebration, does that mean you'll be attending?" Kye asked.

"The only celebration of Valor's I'll be attending will be his funeral," Arden grunted.

"Noted," Kye responded. Arden turned his full attention back to his book. The strained silence fell once again over the tower. Kye figured it was probably time to make himself scarce. "I'm going to head down to the kitchen to get some breakfast. Would you like some?"

Arden shook his head, still engrossed in his book. "No thanks, I'm good."

If Kye had thought Caelum Vallis was covered in silver before, it was draped over every square inch now. The great hall was filled to the brim with people, holding drinks, conversing, and laughing. The noise echoed through the hall as Kye weaved his way in between the groups and headed toward the kitchen. As soon as he entered the dining hall, he saw it was just as busy as the great hall. Celeste was focusing on about four things at once—stirring sauces, chopping vegetables, and issuing orders to the various acolytes enlisted to help set up for the festivities, grabbing drinks and cutlery. Kye slowly approached the counter as Celeste shouted, "No, the bottle in the cellar! Third row on the right from the bottom!" to a dwarf who was carrying an array of wine bottles. She seemed flustered as she turned to see Kye standing there.

"Oh, Kye!" she exclaimed. "You'll be wantin' your breakfast. I'm sorry, lad, I haven't had the time to bring it up."

Kye shook his head. "No, it's fine, I was just—"

"Third from the left?" a voice shouted up from the cellar. Celeste rolled her eyes.

"From the right!" she shouted back.

"I don't see it!"

Celeste huffed as she put the ladle down. "Sorry, lad, just one moment," she added as she headed down into the cellar, muttering the likes of "the daft bastard..." in her wake. Kye glanced over at the pan of sauce she had been stirring and noticed it started to bubble and smoke. Kye quickly snuck behind the counter, grabbed the spoon, and continued stirring. He also grabbed the knife and continued chopping the vegetables Celeste had been cutting in between stirs. After a few minutes, he heard a small shuffle behind him as he turned to see Celeste standing there looking at him in a state of shock.

"Oh," Kye said, pointing to the pan on the stove. "The sauce looked like it might have been burning. Do you need any help? I mean, I'm not a skilled chef, but I'm actually not that bad at cooking."

Kye saw her face tremble as though she might just cry. He was startled by the sudden change; this was not the reaction he was trying to elicit. Did he mess something up? And here he thought he was doing something useful for a change. Kye was just about to apologize, when Celeste walked up and put a comforting hand on his cheek. "Bless you, lad," she added with a large smile. Kye smiled back as he grabbed one of the aprons off the wall and then went back to chopping vegetables. Celeste resumed stirring the sauce and preparing trays of meat. For the next few hours, the pair worked in tandem, prepping dishes and sides and exchanging stories. Kye had to admit it was the most enjoyable cooking had ever been. Of course, he supposed, that had more to do with the company than the food.

The sun had just started to sink on the horizon as Saiyah walked the now-empty halls of Caelum Vallis. Everyone within the castle was currently enjoying the soiree Lord Valor was holding in the High Council auditorium. If it was anything like his previous parties, she guessed the frivolity would continue till the wee hours of the morning.

Saiyah was dressed in her best violet gown, decked out in gems, with her hair perfectly placed. She felt constrained and a bit like a peacock on display. She had attended Lord Valor's party at the suggestion of her maister. Lady Luell thought the party a perfect opportunity for Saiyah to reconnect with her peers. If anything she had spent most of the time sipping a glass of wine in her own little corner. Just as ostracized as she was before. And after watching her self-indulgent peers, she felt completely happy to be so. It was strange how she once considered them her compeers and now felt out of place in their presence. Perspective, she supposed.

Saiyah stopped on her way back to her room. Her final goal was to change out of this get-up, but she decided to pop into the library and grab a book to occupy her for the evening. As she scanned the aisle, she was taken aback to see Kye sitting at his normal table by the fire, engrossed in a tome.

"Kye," she noted with surprise. "I didn't think you would be here this evening. I thought for sure you would be part of some celebration with Lord Arden."

Saiyah awaited an answer, but Kye appeared slightly stunned. He looked at Saiyah as though he had never seen her before.

"Kye?"

Kye blinked a few times, seeming to fall back into the conversation. "Uh, yeah, sorry...I was giving Arden some space. He seems preoccupied after returning from Helia. Plus he isn't much for grand celebrations." Kye gestured toward Saiyah's gown. "You seem to have come from quite the party, though."

Saiyah sighed a bit. "Yes, Lady Luell thought it would be

good for me to socialize at Lord Valor's soiree. I donned this ridiculous attire and made an appearance to placate her and keep the peace. But I could not leave the event fast enough, I assure you."

"Well, you look very pretty–er, elegant," Kye stumbled a bit as he cleared his throat. Saiyah smiled softly back.

"Thank you," she replied as she took a seat at the table across from him. "So, what are you studying today?"

"I was just reading up on a way to deal with curses," Kye replied. "Have you heard of a transference ritual?"

Saiyah sucked her teeth. "Heard of them, yes. Though I don't recommend attempting one. The success rate can be spotty, possibly killing the subject inflicted with the curse. And it is particularly dangerous to the mage attempting it. Nowadays, only skilled maisters deal with the removal of curses."

"Still..." Kye replied. "With Orin spreading mayhem through the realms, it is useful knowledge to have. Anything helps if it can save a life."

Saiyah hesitated. "I cannot argue with that logic, though I do hope you never have to use it. Curses are dangerous, destroying not just the body but also the soul of those inflicted with them. To then take that curse into yourself, even for a mage, could easily kill you. While I am inspired by your determination to save lives, I do hope it does not come at the cost of your own."

Kye looked up from his book to see the worry on Saiyah's face. He was left speechless by her response. He still wasn't quite accustomed to others concerning themselves with his well-being and was caught off guard that Saiyah was one of them. Kye wasn't sure how to respond. They sat in silence, looking at each other for several moments. Kye finally opened his mouth to answer.

The library doors suddenly swung open as Riley entered

in grand fashion, announcing his presence with arms wide as Kye and Saiyah snapped their heads in the direction of the sound.

"Friends!" he proclaimed. "Tonight is the night of the winter solstice. And I cannot, in good conscience, allow you to remain in this dreary place without celebrating the festivities of the evening!"

Saiyah rolled her eyes as Kye chuckled.

"And what, pray tell, did you have in mind for this celebration?" Saiyah asked.

Riley leaned on the table and grinned widely. "I am glad you asked, sweet Saiyah." Riley placed a rather large bottle of liquid on the table and announced, "For tonight, we shall drink and be merry!!"

Kye was on board but looked to Saiyah, questioning her involvement. Riley, as well, jiggled the bottle enticingly with a smile as Saiyah relented.

"Very well," she stated. "But if so, I am going to change first."

Arden was sitting on the veranda on a small wooden chair. He was using a footstool as a table to hold a glass of warm mead and watching the snow fall. His mind was lost in thought and had been since his return from Helia. The weight of what had happened weighed on him heavily. Arden was so engrossed in his thoughts that he didn't hear someone enter the tower.

"Well, this is certainly a change," a familiar voice spoke to him, "as I seem to recall, you've always hated snow."

Arden turned to see Mireen standing at the door of the veranda, smiling at him.

Arden smiled back. "I'm still not a fan, but I'm learning to appreciate it." He rose from his seat and turned to face her.

"To what do I owe this honor?" he asked. "I thought for sure you would be joining Valor's celebration."

Mireen waved her hand dismissively. "I am not about putting on airs, and that seems to be Valor's favorite pastime. Actually, I was wondering if I might join you for a drink?"

Arden raised an eyebrow in surprise. Without so much as another word, he waved his hand, conjuring another seat and glass beside him.

"Please." Arden gestured as Mireen took her seat.

"And just for future reference," Arden added as he poured Mireen a glass of hot mead, "the answer to that question is always yes."

Mireen chuckled as she raised her glass to Arden and took a sip. "Is Kye asleep?"

"That kid hardly ever sleeps," Arden replied as he once again took his seat. "He's taken to waiting till I retire for the night, then sneaking off to study till the wee hours of dawn. He thinks I don't know."

Mireen smiled. "The rebellious acts of youth."

"If he thinks that's rebellious, I still got a lot to teach him, "Arden added.

"Ah yes," Mireen noted, "I seem to recall your youthful antics were somewhat famous."

Arden chuckled. "You should. You were present for most of them."

Mireen straightened her stature, feigning offense. "I was merely tagging along to make sure you did not injure yourself."

Arden cast her a doubtful look and a small smile, uttering "Right."

He turned back to the snow, taking out his pipe and lighting the end before proclaiming, "But I'm guessing you didn't just come here for a walk down memory lane."

Arden's guess appeared correct as Mireen quieted a bit,

staring at her glass intently. "I heard from the council what happened on Helia."

Arden paused for a moment before taking another long pull from his pipe. "I see," he answered, focusing all his attention on the snow coming down.

Mireen looked at him and continued, "You are certain it was Orin?"

"I've been around long enough to know his handiwork by now."

"Does Kye know?"

Arden quieted for several moments before answering. "He knows enough," Arden finally replied. "He knows that the attack was from Orin and that there were no survivors. He knows I laid the victims to rest. But he doesn't know that there were no bodies to bury, just pieces. He doesn't know that they didn't go quick, that Orin had the help of a shifter by the tracks left behind, and that beast tore those people apart. He doesn't know that the earth started out brown but was stained red by the time Orin was finished and probably will be for years to come. He doesn't know 'cause he doesn't need to. Kid has enough trouble sleeping; I'm not adding to that."

Arden took another long drink from his mead and stared off, his face unreadable to anyone but Mireen, who could see the anguish behind the mask.

"Why?" Mireen asked. "Why would Orin extend such brutality on humans? Was it retribution for the stone?"

Arden shrugged. "Could have been. It was quite a coincidence that we took the stone off Helia, and then Helia was attacked. For all I know, he could be sending a message. That he will keep attacking innocent towns till the stone is returned. All the more reason I need to find out why he wants the damn thing."

Mireen nodded. "I see, and you intend to find this information out by yourself, without involving Kye, I take it?"

Arden looked at her incredulously. "Pieces, Mireen," he repeated. "You want me to involve him in that shit?"

"Were you not the one to tell him being a mage was dangerous, that it could very well cost him his life?"

"That doesn't mean I need to help him towards that end," Arden argued.

"You cannot place him in a box either, Arden. Despite your best efforts, Kye is already involved. It was his home that was attacked, his people that were killed. And if Orin truly is targeting humans for some reason, it is far better he is prepared than left in the dark."

Arden sighed and rubbed his temple. Several moments of silence followed Mireen's statement as Arden pondered her words.

"You're right...as usual," he finally replied. "One of your more annoying traits, if I'm being honest."

"Really?" Mireen replied innocently. "Well, I could list off a few of yours, if you would like."

Arden cast her a side-eye as Mireen chuckled in response. "If it's any consolation, I have the utmost faith in Kye," Mireen added. "After all, he has an EXCELLENT teacher."

Mireen smiled brightly at Arden as he returned the smile. She always seemed to have the ability to brighten his mood. Mireen then raised her glass to him. "Blessed winter solstice, Arden."

Arden returned the gesture. "Blessed winter solstice, Mireen."

Kye was fighting off shivers as he followed Saiyah and Riley, trudging through the thick, snow-covered earth. Riley was leading them deep into the forest behind Caelum Vallis. Kye pulled his scarf tighter and placed his hands in his pockets as snowflakes brushed his cheeks. For being absolutely frigid, Kye had to admit snow was quite peaceful. Although, coming from a desert realm, he had serious doubts he would ever get used to the cold.

"Riley, will we be reaching our destination before or after Kye freezes to death?" Saiyah suddenly interjected.

Kye snapped his head in her direction, surprised she had noticed he was cold, considering he had not muttered a single complaint. Saiyah didn't say a word in response, just handed Kye two small stones about the size of his palm. The stones were warm, radiating a small amount of heat, no doubt from some spell Saiyah had cast. Just holding them helped Kye stave off the cold nipping at him. Kye locked eyes with her before returning a smile and a nod of thanks.

"Just a bit further," Riley added. "It's right up here."

After only a few more minutes, the group stepped into a clearing. The trees opened up to a brilliant starry sky, interspersed with clouds dropping soft flakes of snow. Several paper lanterns were strung between the trees, softly lighting the area. Two fallen tree trunks had been lined up around a lively campfire, with an array of crackers, cheese, and meats on a platter placed on a stump. Riley was positively beaming.

"Huh?" Riley gestured, absolutely proud of his celebration. Saiyah chuckled in response.

"Very impressive, Riley." She added, "Quite the event."

"Right?" Riley agreed. "And to the star of the evening, of course." Riley pointed to a keg.

"What is that?" Saiyah asked.

"Three-hundred-year-old elderberry wine," Riley proudly proclaimed.

"Where did you get it?"

"From the storehouse."

"You mean the High Council storehouse?!" Saiyah exclaimed.

Riley sucked his teeth. "See, I don't really like to assign labels to things."

"Riley, you stole it!" Saiyah bit back.

"Not true," Riley argued. "This particular wine was set aside to be enjoyed at the winter solstice. I am merely using it for its intended purpose."

"It wasn't intended to be enjoyed by us!"

"Well, now you're just getting into semantics."

"Riley, they are going to notice a missing keg!"

"It's not missing. I replaced it."

"With what?"

"Orcan Brandy," Riley stated as he waved his hand dismissively. "They'll never know the difference."

"Oh, yes," Saiyah replied, "I myself often mistake the sweet taste of elderberries with that of orcish swill water."

While Saiyah and Riley debated, Kye was preoccupied looking around the clearing. He hadn't noticed it before, but this was the same clearing Arden had sparred with him. The path seemed different now, with the earth cloaked in white.

"Huh, Arden took me here to learn shield spells," Kye noted. Riley and Saiyah stopped their debate and turned their attention to Kye's comment.

"You mean...Lord Arden trained you on spells...personally?" Riley questioned. Kye nodded as Riley and Saiyah exchanged bewildered glances.

"Is that unusual?" Kye questioned.

"Well, yeah, kinda," Riley noted.

Riley took a long drink from his glass of wine before handing one to Kye and Saiyah.

"So...maisters don't train their acolytes?" asked Kye.

"Eh, not really." Riley shrugged.

"Why?" Kye asked. Riley and Saiyah exchanged looks again.

"It is not to say that some maisters don't join the council

for the right reasons," Saiyah began. "Some truly are interested in duty and honor, such as Lord Arden. But for others, it is mainly the title they are after."

Saiyah paused before stating, "My mother, for example, was the last in my family to achieve the title of maister. She served on the council just long enough to train an acolyte to replace her, which was, in fact, Lady Luell. In her case, it wasn't duty she was interested in, but the title ensured a rather prosperous marriage to my father and a fair amount of prestige. I have always been interested in magic, so my studies are my top priority. Whereas Maister Luell might rank them slightly further down on the list after ensuring I make the right connections. Same goes with my family's priorities for me."

Kye was stunned, and grateful to have Arden as his teacher.

"I have been an acolyte to Lord Giveon for about twenty years now. He's a great card player and knows a ton about weapon work, but my magical knowledge isn't exactly his number one concern. Which suits me just fine. I imagine he'll start caring more about my magical know-how when he starts thinking of stepping down from the council," Riley added.

"You've been an acolyte for twenty years!?" Kye asked in surprise. Riley nodded.

"It's fairly common," Saiyah replied. "I have been an acolyte to Maister Luell for thirty years myself. It is said it takes fifty to a hundred years of study to achieve maister status."

Kye chuckled wryly. "Well, that pretty much guarantees I will die a novice."

"I would not be so sure of that," Saiyah replied. "You have shown remarkable progress in just the past year you have been here. Certainly more so than Riley has the last twenty," she noted, casting an accusatory glance toward Riley.

Riley merely shrugged. "Becoming a maister was never really my goal when becoming an acolyte."

"Why did you become an acolyte?" Kye asked Riley. "I've heard shifters don't really subscribe to magic."

"In truth," Riley stated, "to get away from my family. To say I never really 'fit in' with my clan is putting it mildly. Granted, I don't fit in here either, but for the most part, the highborns are too caught up in themselves to give a shit."

Riley then pointed to Kye. "But as for you, Kye, the highborns definitely give a shit about you."

"So I've noticed," Kye mumbled in response.

"The first human mage, after all. I gotta say I don't envy you. And I suspect you won't find friends easily because of it," Riley noted. "Enemies, however, you will find those in abundance."

"I figured as much," Kye replied, "but I didn't expect this to be easy. It was never meant to be a cobbled road."

Saiyah tilted her head. Kye noticed her questioning gaze. "What?"

"Never meant to be a cobbled road," Saiyah replied. "You have said that before, and I am not familiar with the expression. Is it a common phrase amongst humans?"

Kye shrugged. "It's a common phrase amongst this one. It means life is not supposed to be easy. It's from a poem. It was my mother's favorite."

Riley instantly perked up. "A poem, you say? Do you still remember it?"

"Well...yeah."

Riley flourished his hand in response while holding a newly filled glass.

"Well, by all means then, regale us with it. I wish to hear some literary arts from the human realm."

Kye paused tentatively, but Saiyah nodded encouragingly. She seemed just as intrigued as Riley. Kye sighed deeply and relented. He had not recited the full stanza since his mother's passing. Hearing it still caused a twinge of sadness, reminding him of her. But Kye took a long drink from the elderberry wine to help with that:

> "There was never meant to be a cobbled road for me,
> A straight and even path to wander by.
> The path I take, I forged my own
> Through brambles, thickets overgrown,
> On a trek that few would take but I.
> And though I stumble, though I fall, every scrape that I recall,
> Reminds me of this tangled trail I roam.
> There was never meant to be a cobbled road for me
> But this barely beaten path will lead me home."

Saiyah smiled, and Riley clapped, "Bravo!"

"That is beautiful, Kye," she replied earnestly. "I can see why your mother treasured it."

Kye smiled slightly.

"And next up for entertainment, we have Saiyah singing us an elven folksong," Riley proclaimed, presenting a hand to Saiyah.

"No, we don't," Saiyah stated matter-of-factly. "And I can tell you for certain, I have not had NEARLY enough wine to even entertain the idea."

"Oh, I can help with that!" Riley said and shot up to refill her glass, as Kye laughed in response. Even Saiyah chuckled, adding, "Careful, Riley, the beast within you is shining through."

To which Riley replied with a devilish grin.

"Yeah, I was wondering about that," Kye added. "If you're part beast, then what kind of beast are you?"

Riley smiled slyly at the question. "Take a guess, why don't you?" he coaxed. Kye thought long and hard for a moment, the color of Riley's eyes being the only real clue he had to go on.

"Uhh...bear?" Kye asked.

"No, definitely not," Riley replied. "I know bear shifters, a bunch of dense braggarts the lot of them."

"Hawk, then?"

"Ah, to be able to soar amongst the clouds...but no."

"Maybe...wolf?"

"Oh for goodness sake, he is never going to guess it," Saiyah interjected. "Just show him, Riley."

Riley smiled, stood up, and bowed. "If my audience demands it, who am I to argue?" In one swift motion, Riley tossed the robes he was wearing toward Saiyah, who caught them in surprise. To be fair, Kye was a bit surprised as well by a suddenly naked Riley standing in the snow. In an instant, though, Riley's body began to twist, and his face contorted. The way his limbs snapped, the sound of crunching bone, seemed sickeningly painful from Kye's point of view. But Riley didn't seem bothered in the slightest. As he started to grow, his body erupted in white and gold fur and expanded till he was the size of a full-grown gryphon, a creature about fifteen feet tall.

"Whoa..." Kye uttered in disbelief. He stood face to face with a very large, very intimidating, white and gold fox. Unlike the smaller versions, Riley had fangs the size of daggers and claws the size of short swords. Kye had never seen such a creature in his life, nor read about them in any book. It was a marvel to witness.

Riley let out a sigh as he shook his head, the gust of wind strong enough to ruffle Kye's hair and clothing. Kye was fairly certain that if the creature before him wished it, he could easily swallow him in one gulp.

"He is *lira vulin*," Saiyah commented to Kye's bewildered expression. "Fire Fox. They were ancient beasts that once roamed Daiga, much like dragons. And much like dragons, they were hunted to extinction by mages due to their magical qualities. Their white and gold fur is fire-proof. In fact, it is said, they were some of the only beasts that could fight dragons on an equal footing. Unfortunately, they only exist now in the shifters who carry the line. Riley is from a family of Old Bloods. Some of the most honored and powerful shifters in his realm."

"Which is a really fancy way of saying self-centered, entitled old pricks."

Saiyah and Kye turned to see Riley had transformed back to his human form, with only the large paw prints in the snow around them displaying proof he had actually shifted. Riley bowed slightly, extending an arm to Saiyah.

"My clothes, dear Saiyah," Riley stated. "Unless, of course, you prefer the view," he added with a grin. Saiyah scoffed and threw his robes back to him none too gently. Riley laughed as he pulled his robes back on. He then grabbed his drink and drained its contents.

"Now!" he proclaimed once the glass was dry. "Who would like a refill?"

The trio spent the rest of the night huddled around the campfire, laughing and exchanging stories till the stars began dying out. Kye could not remember having so much fun. Of course, he had never really had friends before, either. Close to sunrise, Kye sat on a stump across from Saiyah, leaning in, listening closely and attempting to repeat her words.

"*M-Meerana*," said Kye, trying to mimic her inflection.

"*Mirana*," Saiyah corrected.

"*Abara*," Kye tried as Saiyah chuckled.

"*Ahbirah*," she corrected. Kye chortled in response.

"I fear I lack the subtlety for elvish," Kye stated. Saiyah smiled.

"You are doing fine," she assured him. "It is notoriously difficult to learn a new tongue."

"How long did it take you to learn to speak Common?"

Saiyah shrugged. "A few months at least."

Kye laughed. "Well, now I feel so much better."

Saiyah chuckled and rolled her eyes. "You cannot compare the two," she insisted. "Trust me, you are making good progress."

"Then I yield to your expertise," Kye added with a slight bow as he finished the contents of his glass. Looking up, he saw the pinkish tint on the horizon, meaning sunrise would not be far off.

"Oh, we've been out all night," Kye noted. His head had started to pound from the mixture of sleep deprivation and the sheer volume of wine the trio had consumed. Saiyah looked to the sunrise and shrugged.

"I will bet you Lady Luell has not returned to her room either. Still, I suppose it would probably be best to head inside before our disappearance is questioned. Do you agree, Riley?"

Silence. Kye and Saiyah looked over at Riley to see he was still sitting on the log, but his head was slumped over. Kye and Saiyah walked over to him.

"Riley?" Kye asked as he shook his shoulder. Riley's body tilted and fell off the log, hitting the snow with a muted thud. Kye and Saiyah stood stunned at his perfectly still form laying at their feet.

"Is he dead?" Kye questioned.

"If that is all it took to kill a shif, the species would have never survived," Saiyah replied. No sooner had she said this then Riley twitched a bit and groaned.

"Ah, see, he lives."

"What do we do now?" Kye questioned.

"I suggest we leave him," Saiyah replied, as Kye answered

with an uncertain look. "It is said that a shif can tolerate extreme cold and heat quite well."

"You intend to test that theory?"

"Well, I certainly don't intend to carry him."

Kye chuckled. "I'll make sure he gets back, or indoors at least. Perks of being a traveler."

Saiyah clutched her pocket. She had been carrying something around for a while, and now seemed like as good of a time as any to give it. "Yes...well, on that point...here," Saiyah replied, handing Kye something from her pocket. Kye inspected the soft, stitched, brown leather strap with a single jagged stone wrapped in metal twine on the top of it.

"A bracelet?" Kye questioned.

"It is made from a wayfinding stone," Saiyah replied. "It is one of the many stones from my family collection. Its magical qualities align itself to the earth. It has been used for navigation by travelers for millennia. No matter where you are, no matter what time of day, as long as you wear it, it will improve your sense of direction. I figured you could use it the next time you find yourself lost in the woods."

Kye was speechless. He had never been given a gift and was honored Saiyah had thought of him. But he also felt guilty that the gift was sparked by the lie he had told her when Thaiden abducted him. Kye's face fell.

"Saiyah...such a family heirloom...I couldn't."

Saiyah held up her hand to cut him off. "Before you argue, you should know it is incredibly rude to refuse a gift from an elf. We are very proud creatures and do not hand out gifts often. I feel I should warn you."

Kye smiled. "In that case, I certainly don't want to offend. Thank you, truly."

"Yes, well, it is nothing," Saiyah brushed off. "To my family, these are just stones. They are only of use to mages anyway. Plus, I still carry a shard of the same wayfinding stone as well."

She held up her bracelet so that Kye could see that a much smaller shard of the same stone resided in her charm bracelet. "Though I feel you will get far more use from it than I do."

Kye put the bracelet on his left wrist. Almost instantly, his sense of direction heightened. He immediately knew which way was back to the castle, even though it was completely shrouded by trees.

"Indeed," Kye agreed. "I can already tell it will help me immensely."

Kye beamed at her. Saiyah suddenly felt rather transfixed. In all the time that she had known him, she wondered if she had ever truly taken the time to look at his face. Now that she did, she couldn't help but notice that, for a human, he was rather handsome. Saiyah quickly looked to the ground as soon as the thought ran through her mind, feeling the need to flee.

"I should head back," she stated quickly. "Good night, Kye."

"*Sular norin*, Saiyah."

It took Saiyah by surprise to hear Kye say good night in elvish. She quickly nodded to him as she turned and started heading back to the castle. Behind her, she could hear Kye trying to rouse Riley.

"Riley? Riley! RILEY!! Wake up. It's time to head back. Here, I'll help you."

Saiyah quietly cursed Riley as she quickened her pace slightly. It was all his fault, after all. It was because she partook in that silly wine that she felt this way. Her head was muddled; she wasn't thinking clearly. That was the only reason her heart was beating so fast. And why she was momentarily mesmerized by a warm voice, bright smile, and deep blue eyes.

Water was falling in heavy droplets, hitting Umbree's face as he quietly followed Amon in the dark. Orin had told Umbree to meet him for final preparations. For that, they were heading down, deep into a cave in Isalia. As Umbree continued closer to where his master waited, he could hear whispering in his mind.

"Ugly little goblin, rip him apart."
"Paint the floor green, slice him to bits!"
"Hang him, bleed him dry!"

Umbree could feel the shadows moving all around him, and the voices were getting louder in his head, making it harder to focus. The shadows were getting closer, closing in. Umbree felt the fear rise within him, and he turned in all directions to pinpoint his attackers. Horrible images of his death by dismemberment were being bombarded into his mind along with the voices. He was so engrossed in the shadows, he didn't see Amon stop and almost collided with him. When Umbree stepped around the formidable shifter, he saw the faintest gleam of candlelight in the center of an underground cavern. His master stepped out from the shadows, wielding a long, black staff. Orin held the staff up, and the voices around Umbree instantly silenced. Umbree looked around to see a huge cavern filled with ghostly forms, standing like soldiers around them.

In the low light, Umbree could only make out some features of the shades. In all his time as maister, he had only come across one naturally occurring shade. Looking at the hundreds around him now, Umbree shivered. Their skin was gaunt and whitish, covered in splotches of red blood. Their teeth ended in sharpened points, and their haunting words echoed in the recesses of his mind. They took no stake in Umbree, however, as soon as his master stepped forward. All eyes turned to Orin. The necromancer handed Umbree a dark onyx staff with a crimson orb on its head.

"I know they can be a bit overwhelming, my friend," Orin stated. "You can control them with this."

Umbree bowed on one knee as he reached forward and grasped the staff. An immense dark energy flowed into him. As Umbree slowly acclimated to the power boost, his eyes shone black as coal. He looked up at Orin standing over him.

"Thank you for such a gift, my lord."

Orin held his head up, looking down at Umbree with an expression of displeasure.

"I don't want your thanks, Umbree. I want my stone. Do NOT fail to claim it for me."

Umbree nodded. "I swear it, my lord. If it takes tearing through every soul in Isalia, I will make sure you get what you want."

CHAPTER 13
The Domain of the Dwarves

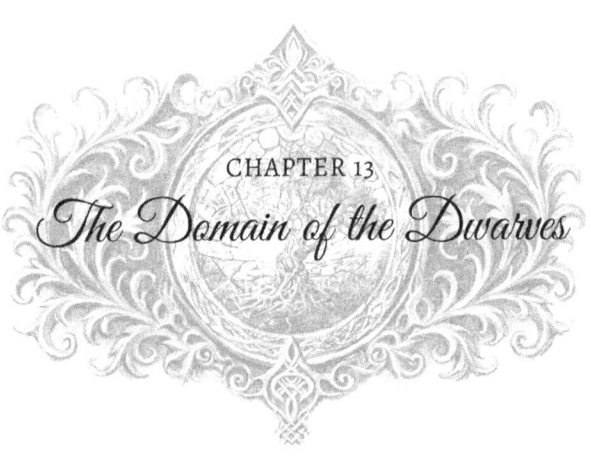

It was almost afternoon when Kye shuffled into the common area, still tired, looking disheveled and feeling a bit like death. The few hours rest he'd nabbed from arriving just after dawn was not nearly enough to sleep off the sizable amount of wine he had consumed. Arden was watching Kye with a fair bit of amusement as he grabbed a cup of tea and sunk his head on the dining table.

"*Sulara anor,*" Arden said wryly. "Fun night, I take it?"

Kye barely grunted in acknowledgment. Arden chuckled as he got up from the breakfast table and walked over to the apothecary table. After a few minutes, he returned with a bubbling concoction and placed it on the table in front of Kye. Kye barely lifted his head to look at the drink. It was a deep brown color and smelled rather strongly like dirt. Kye had to swallow hard to keep down the intense desire to vomit.

"What is that?" Kye asked.

"Hangover cure," Arden replied. Kye must have looked hesitant because Arden added, "Trust me."

Kye picked up the drink and choked down a few gulps, figuring he probably couldn't feel any worse than he already did. Sure enough, within minutes, his headache began to dissipate, and his stomach was calmer. Kye issued a sincere thanks as he went back to chugging the miracle cure.

"What have you got there?" Arden questioned, catching sight of the bracelet underneath Kye's left sleeve.

"Oh, it's a wayfinding stone," Kye replied. Arden was looking at Kye as though he expected him to continue.

"They are magic stones used by travelers. They help you navigate—"

"I know what a wayfinding stone is, kid," Arden replied. "My question is, where did you get it?"

"It was a gift."

"From?"

"Saiyah."

Arden appeared mildly stunned, simply responding with a, "Huh..."

"What?" Kye asked. Arden shook his head.

"Nothing," he stated, hiding a small smile behind his tea.

Arden seemed to be back to his normal self, no longer disregarding Kye's presence in any room he was in. Kye wasn't sure what had sparked the change, but he was certainly appreciative of the switch.

"I haven't been able to find much on the creation stones in the library," Arden began, "so I've decided to take a different approach and investigate where the first stone was discovered."

"So you're going to Brooma?" Kye asked. Arden stated he was. Brooma was the home realm of the dwarves. The dwarf homeland was known for unmatched architecture and formidable weapon work. Kye was fascinated each time he read about it.

"Are you interested in coming along?" Arden inquired. Kye looked up in surprise.

"Really?" he asked, to which Arden nodded.

"Yes, absolutely," Kye replied instantly before Arden could change his mind.

"Good," Arden stated as he went back to his cup of tea. "We'll head out first thing tomorrow."

Kye gazed at the swirling blue portal before him with anticipation. He had, of course, jumped at the chance to see another realm, especially since dwarves were known for being kinder to humans than most other races. Dwarves largely did not believe in keeping slaves, considering it an insult to have another perform labor they could do themselves. The race, on the whole, was big on self-sufficiency, creating impressive works with their hands, rather than relying on the arts. That isn't to say that there weren't talented dwarven mages, but they were the minority amongst the species.

Once the connection had been fully formed, Arden gave a nod to Kye as they both started walking through the portal. It was a strange sensation. This was the first time Kye could remember traveling by portal. The contact on his skin was like dipping into a pool of quicksand, pulling you in. The feeling of floating, however, was familiar to Kye, having felt it each time he traveled. It seemed to only last for a moment. One second, they were heading into a swirling light, the next they were on the other side of it.

Kye and Arden were welcomed by a damp, lush landscape. Rolling hills of green surrounded them on all sides, with tall mountains erupting toward the heavens. Where Isalia was now coated in a thick layer of white, Brooma still seemed to be in the throes of fall, with drizzles of rain and a steel gray sky covering the landscape. Kye noticed the portal had deposited them at the mouth of a ravine, which Kye could see opened up to a flat lea. Kye and Arden started their path through the ravine when Arden froze quite suddenly. Kye was about to ask him what was wrong when a twang cut through the air, and a steel-tipped arrow landed on the ground at their feet. Kye instantly took a defensive stance toward the source of the arrow, muttering *"petra cirana,"* and extending his hand toward the ground. A slew of sharp rocks obediently floated up from the ground and began orbiting around him in a protective form, ready to deflect an arrow or impale an aggressor at the flick of his hand. Arden, however, did not seem fazed at all. In fact, he put a hand on Kye's shoulder, signaling to him it was safe to dismiss the spell. Kye was confused but obliged. The sharp stones instantly halted mid-air and fell back to the ground. Arden then stepped forward in front of Kye, looking directly toward where the arrow had come from. No sooner had he done so than a dozen or so armed dwarves stepped out from behind the trees and bushes, surrounding the top of the ravine. They had their weapons out, with the archers pointing notched arrows toward him and Kye.

"Stay where ya are, elf, lest ya want to greet yur death."

A short, rotund dwarf with a long, brown beard walked forward. He had an elaborate helm fitted with strips of gold, and a battle ax made of what looked like some type of bronze. He stared down at Arden from his perch, unflinching and unafraid.

"It will take far more than a few arrows to accomplish that," Arden replied to the dwarf.

"Aye, which is what me ax here is for," the dwarf said. He approached, quickly sliding down the ravine to the ground, never losing a step. Confident, he sauntered up to Kye and Arden, staring down Arden all the while. Which was an impressive feat, considering he was a good three feet shorter than his quarry.

"Always wanted tae behead me an elf," the dwarf growled.

Arden raised an eyebrow in response. "Then I suggest you fetch a ladder."

Silence fell over the group at Arden's comment. Kye thought antagonizing the dwarves might not be the best approach, seeing as they looked a hair's breadth away from unleashing all hell. To his shock though, the silence was suddenly interrupted by the brown-bearded dwarf chuckling. Which, after a few moments, morphed into full-blown laughter. The other dwarves followed suit, lowering their weapons in response. Kye was bewildered to say the least, as he looked to see Arden grin back at the head dwarf.

"Ah, good to see ya haven't lost your sense of humor, Ard," the brown-bearded dwarf replied. "I was worried living with them high bloods, ya would of picked up their entitlement."

The dwarf then froze, getting a good look at Kye, and began to scowl. "Lookin' like ya have picked up some bad habits, after all," the dwarf sneered. "Didn't know ya was in need of a servant, Ard."

"He isn't my servant. He is my acolyte," Arden replied.

The dwarf was taken aback. "Your acolyte?"

Arden nodded. "Kye, this is the ruler of the west mountains, Delac. Delac, may I introduce: acolyte to the High Council, Kye."

Kye gave a respectful bow to Delac. "Pleasure to meet you, my lord."

Delec nodded back. "Aye, good ta meet ya, lad. Well, let's get out of this weather and get ya boys a proper greetin'."

Delec gave a wave to the procession as the group of dwarves turned and started heading back through the ravine. Delec was in the lead with Arden and Kye.

"Gotta say, I'm surprised," Delec began. "It's been a while since ya visited, Ard. To what do we owe the honor?"

"I can't stop in on an old friend?" Arden replied. Delec smiled.

"Well, ya ain't exactly known for being social," Delec said, "but yur always welcome company here, ya know that. How is that cousin of mine doin'?"

"Celeste is doing just fine. She seems happy in Isalia," Arden stated. Kye was intrigued to hear that Delec was the cousin Celeste had mentioned. Delec grunted and shrugged.

"Never understood what her fascination was with magic, but as long as she is treated well, that is all I could ask for."

"She is treated well," Arden replied. "Honestly, I think others are too afraid of her to treat her otherwise."

Delec chuckled. "That sounds like me cousin, alright."

Kye was taking in the surroundings as the group marched on. The wildlife seemed completely different from Isalia. Kye caught sight of a bird about the size of a small goat whiz by overhead. He quietly wondered what it ate and crossed his fingers he wasn't on the menu. A slight patter of rain began to fall, drumming on the leaves around them.

"Yur first time to Brooma, aye, Kye?" Delac asked, snapping Kye's attention back to the conversation at hand.

"My first time to most of the realms, in fact," Kye responded.

"Well, then, you'll be needin' the grand tour," Delec replied. "Have to get ya a drink too. Probably need one after working for this bastard, aye?" he added as he nudged Arden in the side.

"Actually, Arden has been a great teacher, and I'm lucky to be able to study the craft under him," Kye stated sincerely.

"Is that so?" Delec replied as he turned toward Arden. "Got the kid practically singin' yur praises, Ard. Ya put a spell on him?"

"Course not," Arden answered. "Potions are much more reliable."

Delec laughed and slapped Arden on the back as Kye chuckled. He had to admit, Arden seemed far more at home here than he ever had in the castle.

The lea opened up to a cliff face, the height of which touched the clouds. It seemed to extend for miles in both directions, and Kye was sure they had reached a dead end. Delec pulled a small carved horn off his belt and blew it twice. The sound rumbled the rock face, and Kye watched in wonder as cracks began to show and quickly turned into the shape of two giant stone doors, slowly opening to welcome the group. As Kye looked inside, he was amazed to see a large, bustling city carved inside the mountain. There was a giant atrium, complete with fountains and stone statues. A large walkway split out in all four directions, with three levels stretching up in the cavern. The lower level was crowded with shops and a tavern directly to the right when they walked in. Music and laughter were spilling out of the pub and filling the atrium before them. The upper two levels appeared to be living space, connected by catwalks. Even though they were in a cavern, the inside was perfectly illuminated. Monstrous chandeliers hung from the heavens, and thousands of smaller lanterns illuminated every shadow. Kye didn't even notice his mouth was hanging open until Arden caught his eye and chuckled. Delec led the group through the bustle. Kye noticed other dwarfs stopped their daily routine to give a small bow to Delec and get a better look at his two guests. Once many noticed Arden, they gave shouts of greetings or waves to him. He seemed to be acquainted with the majority of the city. The group approached an impressive building, with spires erupting from the roof that touched the very top of the cavern. It looked almost like a castle carved into the mountain. As they made their way up a long set of steps to the entrance, Dwarven guards decked out in golden helms saluted Delec. The heavy stone doors at the top opened almost on command. Kye noticed the other dwarves stopped at the entrance threshold, speaking in hushed whispers with the guards as Delec, Arden, and Kye continued inside.

The group entered what was clearly a throne room, decorated with warm fires, wood, and stone. For being a place for nobility, Kye thought it gave off a homey, comfortable feel. Much different from the ostentatious decor of Caelum Vallis. It reminded him a lot of Arden's tower, only on a much grander scale. Delec walked over near the wood-carved throne in the center of the room and hung his ax on a wall mount.

"Certainly took yur sweet time scouting, aye," a voice interrupted. Kye turned to see a red-haired female dwarf enter the room. The top of her head was adorned with a golden circlet, signaling her status as some form of nobility. Her green eyes instantly moved from Delec to Arden and Kye. "And I see ya found a familiar face," she said.

The female dwarf smiled as she approached. "Ard, good tah see ya," she added as she opened her arms to greet Arden with a hug. Arden returned the gesture, adding, "Good to see you too, Felicia."

Once they separated, Felicia's eyes fell on Kye. "And a new face as well. Who would this be now?"

"He's Arden's acolyte," Delec responded before anyone else had a chance to. "His name's Kye." Felicia seemed just as surprised by that information as Delec had been.

"Acolyte, ya say?" Felicia replied as Kye placed a hand on his chest and bowed.

"Pleasure to meet you, Lady Felicia," Kye responded.

"Oh, aye," Felicia replied. "You as well, Kye."

"It seems Ard and I got some catching up to do," Delec stated to the group. "Felicia, mah sweet, ya mind giving Kye a tour of our grand city? I'll tell the cooks to get a meal going for our guests."

"Ah wouldn't mind stretching mah legs," Felicia replied. "That is if Kye is wantin' a tour, of course."

Kye looked to Arden, who nodded in agreement.

"I would love one," Kye stated earnestly. Felicia beamed back in response. "Well, then, by all means, follow me, lad."

Delec waited until Felicia and Kye left the room before casting a rather serious look at Arden.

He shook his head with a sigh before stating, "Always knew ye wur one for poking the bear, Ard. But you usually left others out of the line o' fire."

"You're referring to Kye?" Arden asked. Delec nodded.

"Helluva thing, taking on a human as yer acolyte. Guarantee the council wis pissin' nails over that one." Delec continued, "Bit dinnae you think it paints a rather large target on the lad's back?"

"Guess I thought it was preferable to the chain that was around his neck," Arden replied. Delec fell silent before slowly nodding in response. "Aye, cannae argue thare…"

Arden gave a long sigh, sitting in a chair by a small table across from Delec. "Kid saved my life, Delec," Arden explained. "He didn't have to and almost died in the attempt."

"Lad's got heart then?" Delec asked to which Arden nodded.

"That he does. Besides if this was just about pissing off the council, hell, I would have made you my acolyte."

Delec laughed out loud, adding with a gleam in his eye, "Ah that would o' bin a sight."

Delec slid off the throne and walked over to the table, picking up a pitcher and a couple of goblets.

"Sounds like we have a fair bit o' catching up tae do," Delec stated. "Care fur a drink?"

~

Felicia was an excellent tour guide, pointing out impressive dwarven structures and also giving a detailed account of their history. Kye was surrounded by a lively city, with laughter and conversation reverberating off the cavern walls. Everywhere he looked, everyone seemed happy, relaxed. What surprised Kye the most was how Felicia was greeted. If Kye had been addressing Umbree when he was still a slave and had forgotten to put "Lord" in front of his name, he assuredly would have felt the back of Umbree's hand. Felicia, on the other hand, was clearly nobility in this city but was greeted by others as though she was just another member of town. It was refreshing to see a ruler more concerned about her people than her title. Kye also noticed the manner in which he was greeted. In Isalia, he often got looks of disgust or distaste at his presence. Here, the dwarves were curious but welcoming. He was greeted with smiles and handshakes, and in more than one instance, a dwarf tried to hand him a mug of ale for a toast.

Kye followed Felicia into a large town square surrounded by market stalls. Dwarven tradesmen were peddling everything from clothing to meats and fine wine. Kye even saw a weapons vendor, with a vast array of armor to longswords proudly on display. Kye noticed two male dwarves haggling over the price of a rather intimidating spear. Felicia was enumerating the different stalls and what they sold when two pretty female dwarves, who looked to be in their twenties in human years, came up to her.

"Guid forenicht, Felicia," they stated in unison.

"Guid forenicht, May, guid forenicht, Tally," she responded to the pair. May had dark brown hair that was braided far down her back, and deep brown eyes. Tally, on the other hand, had soft blonde curls with bright blue eyes.

"What brings ya here this evenin?" Felicia asked.

May held up a handkerchief, opening it up so the group

could see a broken necklace made of silver, with a sapphire gem hanging from the center of it.

"Oh dear, what happened there?" Felicia inquired.

May waved her hand. "Oh, one of the young'uns got to it. I was hoping the silversmith might be able to give a quick mend, but there is a bit of a line."

"What brings you to the market this evenin'?" Tally inquired, casting a side look in Kye's direction.

"Ah just giving our guest here the grand tour," Felicia replied, motioning to Kye. "Kye, this is May and Tally, my ladies in waiting. May, Tally, this is Kye. He's Arden's acolyte."

Kye bowed to both of the women as he watched their faces contort in surprise.

"Acolyte?" replied Tally as the pair looked Kye over, intrigued. Just then, a ruckus caused the group to turn as the two men who had been haggling over the price of the spear began shouting at each other, announcing to everyone in the square that the discussion had quickly devolved into an argument.

"Ah, excuse me fur a moment," Felicia replied, heading straight over to the fighting men without the slightest hesitation. "Awright, whit's th' kinch ower 'ere!" Kye heard her shout before she was out of earshot.

"So, how long have you been Arden's acolyte?" May asked Kye, drawing his attention back.

"Oh, almost a year now," Kye replied.

"An you can do magic? Like Arden?" Tally inquired.

"Well, not nearly as well as Arden," Kye admitted. "But I do know a few spells. For example..."

Kye held his hand over the handkerchief May had clutched in her grip and muttered, "*Sarcia*."

The handkerchief shook lightly as May unfolded it to find a perfectly mended necklace. Both women were flabbergasted, looking back at Kye as though he had just performed a miracle.

"Why, it looks brand new!" May commented, turning the necklace over in her hand. "Thank you, lad!" She beamed as Kye smiled back in return. He felt happy he was able to finally help someone with his skills, even in such a small way. "Arden indeed chose an excellent apprentice," she mentioned to Tally.

"Oh, aye, and a handsome devil tae boot," Tally added with a smirk and a wink. Kye's smile slowly turned to surprise, as it took him several seconds to realize that she was referring to him.

"Oh...um...thank you," he replied as he nervously ran a hand through his hair and cleared his throat. Both May and Tally chuckled. Kye wasn't quite sure how to respond to the compliment. It was one he had honestly never heard before.

"Oh, leave him alone, Tally, yer makin' th' lad blush. Mah thanks, Kye," May added as she gave Kye a sultry smile of her own. Kye stood slightly stunned in response.

Just then Felica returned from the skirmish. "Well, now that that's sorted. Care to continue the tour, Kye?"

"Yes!" Kye replied rather enthusiastically, happy to remove himself from the two women's teasing. Kye bowed at his departure, adding, "Pleasure meeting both of you," before turning to continue the tour.

Felicia issued a parting greeting as well before taking the lead. As they exited the market, Kye turned back briefly to see that Tally and May were discussing something quietly, giggling to each other. And Kye had a suspicion he knew who that something was when he noticed Tally point to him.

Felicia gave Kye a tour of the dwarven library next. Kye entered a vast structure lined with golden shelves and gears. The floor was chiseled stone, but the staircases leading up were brightly shining metal, as were the catwalks above Kye's head. Kye walked to the shelf nearest him, scanning through the volumes to see what he recognized. The books appeared to be written in dwarven, a dialect he had no familiarity with. But some were written in Ancient, noted by the words on their spine. He picked up one and opened it, seeing the pages were soft, a clear sign of a very old book.

"This is quite the collection," Kye remarked but turned to nothing but silence. Kye noticed that in his excitement he appeared to have lost Lady Felicia. Kye put the book down to walk through the library to search for her. There were only a few dwarves in the library, the silence almost a different world from the bustling city outside the doors. Kye walked through, examining faces, but could not see Felicia's amongst them. As Kye continued, he noticed a door off the main center of the library was ajar. Figuring Felicia broke off to settle another dispute, Kye poked his head inside the room to see if she was there.

It appeared to be a study, with a few desks spread out throughout the room. What caught Kye's attention was the ceiling. Painted to look exactly like the night sky, the image was so detailed even the stars seemed to shimmer. Kye was so absorbed in the ornate painting, he didn't even notice he was not alone in the room. A shuffle of papers caused Kye to snap around to see an elderly dwarf sitting at one of the desks. His hair and beard were a deep white, with wrinkles under his bright green eyes. He wore a golden circlet on top of his head. Kye immediately offered a bow in response.

"Apologies, my lord. I didn't notice this room was occupied."

The elderly dwarf hopped down off the stool and shuffled over to where Kye stood. As Kye slowly raised his head from his bow, he noticed the dwarf standing in front of him was just staring at him. Looking at him, Kye now noticed that the dwarf's eyes seemed to be a bit glazed over as if he was confused by the entire situation. He was perfectly silent, just standing there, staring.

"My lord?" Kye questioned, hoping to elicit some sort of response from the dwarf. Instead of words, the dwarf simply reached a hand up toward Kye, motioning Kye to bend down to his level. Kye acquiesced to the request, kneeling on one knee so he and the dwarf were now eye to eye. The dwarf's hand instantly shot forward, wrapping his fingers around Kye's amulet and pulling the chain so that the symbol was inches away from his eyes. Kye watched as the elderly dwarf traced a finger around the outside, around the star and back again. As though it was a maze he was trapped within.

"It's the sign of the Magi High Council," Kye explained, uncertain if the dwarf was aware of what he was holding or not. "Do you know this symbol?"

The dwarf stopped tracing for a moment. He looked Kye straight in the eye. He opened his mouth several times as though he wished to say something but couldn't. Kye could see the frustration and confusion behind the old dwarf's eyes. Desperate to be understood, but unable to articulate. Kye opened his mouth to ask another question—

"There ya are!"

Kye turned to see a young, black-haired female dwarf enter the reading room, looking flustered. She immediately brushed past Kye and collected the hand of the old dwarf.

"Ya shouldn't be wandering off like that," she replied, looking relieved to have found him. She then began leading the old man out of the reading room. "Come, let's go back, shall we?" She walked past Kye, the old man shuffling behind. Kye stood as the elder dwarf gave him a parting glance. Felicia entered afterward, casting a sad smile as the old man left her sight. She then turned back to Kye.

"I see you have met our King Borak," Felicia stated. Kye startled.

"Your king?" he questioned. "Lord Delec's father?" Felicia nodded.

"Aye, I'm sorry if he unnerved ya a bit, lad," Felicia continued. "He can't really understand like he used to."

"What happened?" Kye asked Felicia. She shrugged.

"Old age is mah guess. He always wis a tad forgetful. Then his mind just...wandered off one day. Bin this wey ever since."

Kye's face fell. "Can nothing be done? I know healers with the High Council. Lady Mireen, I could ask her to come take a look—"

Felicia simply shook her head in response. "Appreciate it, laddie, but there's nothin' to be done. We've tried. No sickness tae heal, no injury tae mend. He's just...lost in th' dark."

Kye fell silent, thinking over what Felicia had said. He had always thought mages were all powerful. Capable of building or destroying at will. But now that he was one, he was finally coming face to face with the limitations of magic and learning the truth firsthand. Kye wanted to help that old man. He seemed so confused, so frustrated, so...scared. But he also knew Felicia was right. If a healer could not mend him, then there was nothing Kye could do to help. Felicia gave Kye a small smile.

"Well, I'm guessin' Ard an mah husband have had a long conversation by now. What do ya say we head back, aye, lad?"

The boisterous sounds of laughter bouncing off the walls of the throne room greeted Kye and Felicia as they returned from their stroll. Kye saw Delec and Arden sitting at a small table in the corner, mugs in hand, laughing themselves breathless. Kye chuckled at the sight. Felicia smiled as well, hand on her hips while she stated, "Well, you lot are making a right bit o noise in here."

Delec shot up upon Felcia's proclamation. "AH, Felicia, mah sweet! Kye! Come, join us. Ard and I were just remembering the time he challenged an orc to an arm-wrestling contest."

Kye shot Arden an amazed look. "You did?"

Arden shrugged. "Well, in my defense, there was a fair amount of whiskey involved in the decision."

"Who won?" Kye asked.

Arden chuckled. "Your faith in me is inspiring, kid, but no. The fat bastard broke my arm in five places."

"Well, ya did insult his lineage," Delec replied. "Might've had something to do with his temper."

Arden took a long drink before adding, "I would argue implying his family tree didn't fork was a legitimate statement."

Delec let loose a hearty laugh, and Kye found himself joining in as well. Delec motioned again to Kye and Felicia. "Come join us!" Kye began walking over. Felcia gave a smile and a small bow.

"Ah, thanks for the invite, mah luv, but I think I shall go check on dinner." Felcia added, "But you lads have fun."

Kye bowed to her respectfully, and Delec pulled out a chair for him to join. Kye took a seat as Delec passed him a mug filled with a dark ale. Kye took a drink and listened to the conversation. He was interested in learning more about his elven master's life. After all, Arden had already lived several lifetimes compared to Kye. From the stories they told, Delec and Arden had known each other for a very long time. In fact, from the sounds of it, Arden was somewhere around four hundred years old, which was incredible from Kye's point of view since Arden didn't look much past thirty. Their fathers apparently had a trade agreement, which meant Arden had spent much of his time on Brooma. It explained why he seemed so at home here. After several hours of swapping stories and laughing, Delec leaned back in his chair and pulled out a pipe.

"Tis good to catch up with ya, Ard," Delec added. "Good of ya to swing by."

"Well, if I'm honest, my visit wasn't solely for the purpose of reminiscing," Arden replied.

Delec shrugged. "Aye, I figured as much. So, what brings ya here?"

"I need to see the cavern where the creation stone was found."

Delec perked up. "Whatcha need to be seeing that for? You lot have the stone, dontcha? Fail to see how the cave it was in is of any importance."

"It is," Arden stated without question. Delec grunted and ran his hands through his beard in response. "That's a helluva walk, Ard, deep to the center of the mountain. And that assumin' no caves-ins have blocked the path, which I can't rightly say for sure."

Arden paused for a moment before asking, "Do you have any drawings or sketches of the cavern where the stone was found?"

Delec looked confused. "I think so. I believe some lads took a few—not every day you find an ancient mage treasure in your home, after all."

"Can we see them?" Arden inquired. Delec grunted and shrugged, getting up from his table and heading toward a door off the throne room. Arden and Kye followed, seeing that the door opened to a study. Bookcases lined all three walls in front of them, with a sturdy wooden desk in the middle. Delec was rifling through paper on the wall on the left bookcase, muttering, "Now, where did aye put 'em?"

Looking around at the haphazard mess made Kye believe locating anything in this study would be an impossibility.

Much to his surprise, though, a few minutes later, Delec proclaimed, "Ah! Here they are!"

Delec pulled out a few pages and handed them to Arden. Arden looked over the sketches carefully before handing them to Kye. Kye noticed that the artist who drew them was talented indeed. Even though there was no color, the shading and texture practically caused the image to come to life. Kye could clearly see the walls of the chamber and the circular pedestal in the center that had housed the creation stone.

"Detailed enough?" Arden asked. Kye nodded.

"Detailed enough for what?" Delec inquired. But Kye didn't waste time answering. He immediately closed his eyes to concentrate. Creating colors and figures, he focused on building the picture in his mind. He could see the walls of the cave. He could hear the cold draft whistle through the hallowed halls. He could smell the stagnant air. He could touch the center pedestal that had held the stone. As soon as the picture was real to him, Kye reached out and placed a hand on Arden's and Delec's shoulders before muttering, "*Dimmora*."

The familiar pulling sensation vanished as Kye opened his eyes to see that they were standing in the inner chamber from the picture. Arden immediately opened his hand and created a fire within his palm, lighting up the pitch-black area. Now that he could see clearly, Kye noticed that Delec was a few shades paler than he was a few moments ago.

"Are you alright?" Kye asked. Delec was noticeably unnerved, and Kye realized he probably should have explained what they were about to do.

"I-I'm not entirely sure," Delec replied, holding a hand to his chest to catch his breath. "What the devil was that?"

"In Ancient, it literally means fading," Arden noted as he inspected a cave wall with sigils. "It's a mage's form of travel."

"I see. Well, we dwarves' form of travels called walkin'," Delec muttered. "So let's not be doing that again, shall we?"

Kye walked over to the wall Arden was inspecting. It had chiseled pictures on it, depicting the dwarves putting the stone in a chest and sealing the chest inside the cavern. But nothing depicting why the stone was sealed away. If it was such an important artifact, wouldn't the dwarves want it displayed? Perhaps they didn't know what it was and thought since it was a magical item it was best left undisturbed. One thing was certain from the images, they had gone through a hell of a lot of effort to seal it. Kye was baffled. The creation stones held no real power. Why go to so much trouble to seal something that couldn't hurt you? Arden seemed to have this same line of thought, running his hand over the images. He then turned his attention toward the box sitting on top of the pedestal. He ran his fingers along it, trying to detect any strong magic from the box itself. It seemed completely ordinary.

"And you found this cavern while you were excavating down here?" Arden inquired to Delec. Delec shook his head.

"Hells, no," he replied. "We don't dig this far down as a rule. Earth is unsteady down here, prefer to keep the mountain in one piece, if ya know what I mean. Would have never found the thing if Umbree hadn't arranged the expedition."

Arden shot him with a questioning gaze. "Umbree knew this was here? Before you found it?"

Delec shrugged. "Seemed to. Else why take the trek? I assumed some magic scroll, crystal ball, or whatever you lot use told him about it."

Arden and Kye exchanged confused looks. The story the council had heard was that Umbree had just stumbled upon the stone. However, he seemed to already know its location.

The question was...how? When even the dwarves didn't seem to be aware.

"Maybe Orin knew? And he told Umbree about it?" Kye theorized. But Arden shook his head.

"Then why involve Umbree at all? He could have just taken the stone without a third party getting involved. It seems like Umbree was the first one to know of a creation stone's location. Which tells me he got the information from someone else. Umbree isn't exactly a historian, after all."

"Then whoever told him might know where the other stones are," Kye answered. Arden nodded.

"It's a start. We'll just have to—" Arden's sentence cut out as the amulet around his neck began to glow, and he closed his eyes to focus. When he opened his eyes, Kye noticed his face looked agitated.

"What?" Kye asked.

"We are heading back, now!"

Kye didn't even attempt to argue as Arden reached forward and grabbed Delec's shoulder. The dwarf started to protest, but Kye and Arden stated in unison, "*Dimmora*."

A familiar pulling sensation, then all three were standing back in the throne room.

"Damn it all, Ard!" Delec shouted as he stumbled away from Arden. "What the blazes did I just finish tellin' ya—"

"Seal the city," Arden commanded. Delec was taken aback.

"What are ya talking about? Are ya daft?"

"I'm serious, Delec," Arden insisted. "Sound the alarm, seal the gates, and don't open up till you hear from me."

Arden's gaze was boring straight into Delec's, unflinching and stern. Delec finally seemed to understand the sense of urgency. "Felicia!" he shouted. A few moments later, Felica entered the room.

"Tell the guards in the tower to sound the alarm n' call our people back. I'll let the gatemasters know. We're sealing the city."

Felicia was clearly alarmed and just as confused as Kye but nodded in response and rushed off. Arden immediately headed out of the throne room, with Kye two steps behind him.

"Arden, what's —?!" Kye's question was interrupted by a monstrous bellow. The sound of a great horn shook the walls and floor, booming straight out into the evening.

The laughter and chatter of the atrium instantly halted, replaced with the eerie silence of hundreds of dwarves. Another horn blast told them they had not misheard. Panicked shouts and cries exploded, with people rushing away from the entrance and further into the city. Arden and Kye were weaving through the crowd with purpose, heading toward the great stone doors to the outside. Kye looked at the scared faces all around him as people called to family and friends to make sure they were present before the city was sealed.

As Arden and Kye walked through the entrance, he caught sight of the last few groups of dwarves rushing into the city. The guards began to close the doors. A deafening creak and a reverberating groan echoed when the heavy stone doors sealed. Kye was hit with the last blast of air from inside the dwarven city. The lines of the doors instantly vanished as Kye looked up to nothing more than a cliff face.

The whole time Kye followed Arden, he never slowed his pace, moving with purpose back to where the travel orb had first deposited them.

"Arden, what's happened?" Kye asked as they rushed along.

"Isalia is under attack," Arden answered. "If they get inside Caelum Vallis, the travel orbs could give them access to all the Six Realms."

Kye's mind had trouble processing the information Arden was relaying.

"Under attack?" Kye questioned. "Under attack from who?"

"Shades," Arden replied. "A fuck ton of them."

CHAPTER 14
A Hellish Horde

As Arden and Kye exited the portal into the grand hall, they were greeted by the same panicked uproar they had witnessed on Brooma. Four hundred acolytes and maisters were all talking at each other and shouting, the fear palpable within the room. Maister Valor finally stood atop a table gaining the attention of everyone around.

"PLEASE, CALM YOURSELVES!!" Valor shouted. The voices quieted down a bit.

"How are we supposed to be calm when there's an army of shades out there!" shouted a dwarven maister. "There must be hundreds!"

"A little over eight hundred would be my guess," Arden interjected. The whole room turned toward him, instantly silent to hear what he had to say. His eyes narrowed before falling on orc Maister Firen. "Looks like a bunch of dead humans are our problem now, wouldn't you say, Firen?"

Firen's eyes drifted toward the ground as Kye turned several shades paler, understanding what Arden meant. The people of Camris. Shades were only created by violent deaths, angering and twisting the soul into an unrecognizable state.

Orin had murdered and tortured his kin...just to make an army for himself.

"Eight hundred...by the gods..." a goblin maister muttered. "We can't possibly fight that many."

"Oh, in that case, we'll just leave it in the hands of the citizens then, shall we?" Arden shot back.

"No one is suggesting that, Arden," Valor replied. "But we also cannot leave Caelum Vallis unprotected. The fate of the Six Realms could fall if we do."

"So then we don't," Arden stated. "Acolytes remain at the castle to protect the travel orbs. Maisters, go out and protect the people. If you are okay with that, of course, Valor?"

Valor seemed to hesitate for a moment, desperately wanting to disagree with Arden. But sensibility seemed to take over as he turned and shouted to the group.

"We shall follow Lord Arden's suggestion," Valor declared. "Acolytes, you are to split up into groups, protecting the north, south, east, and west walls of the castle. Do not let a single shade breach our perimeter. Maisters, we shall divide ourselves into groups of about twelve and spread throughout Isalia to protect the people. Rangers will lead the offensive. Other affinities will focus on defensive and light magic."

"Healers, to me!" shouted Mireen. "At least one healer to a group. The rest will be following me to the most populated areas!"

In an instant, the hall erupted in purpose. Maisters broke off and grabbed weapons before teleporting out of the great hall. Acolytes were lining up, being given orders on which walls were theirs to protect. But Kye didn't follow the other acolytes, instead falling into step behind Arden as he rushed off to issue orders to the maisters within his group.

"Arden!" Kye shouted as Arden turned back toward him. "I can come with you," Kye stated sincerely. "I can help. I can fight."

Arden gave a wry smile. "Of that I have no doubt, kid. But I need you here. If the shades get inside the castle, I need you to get the stone out of Caelum Vallis and as far away from Orin as possible."

Kye froze for a moment. "But, Arden, I don't know where the creation stone is." Kye turned to see several maisters looking at him at the mention of the stone. He quickly quieted his tone in response. If there were maisters working with Orin as Arden feared, alerting them of his knowledge of the stone or its location would not be wise. Arden responded by shaking his head.

"But you do," he replied quietly. "You already have that knowledge, and that knowledge is power."

Kye answered with a confused look. He was about to ask another question, but twelve maisters were now standing around them. Arden turned to his group.

"We are starting on the eastern continent! Remember, shades have the ability to invade your thoughts, whisper in your head. It will make focus and communication with the amulets difficult. Keep your wits about you and have light magic at the ready!"

The twelve maisters he commanded nodded in agreement as they instantly called forth balls of light within their palms. Arden turned back to Kye, tossing something to him. As Kye caught it, he noticed it was Arden's flask.

"Hang on to it for me, would you?" Arden replied. "It's kind of a family heirloom."

Maisters by the dozens began teleporting out of the great hall, heading into battle. The room was clearing in an instant. A panicked thought crossed Kye's mind. What if this was the last time he saw Arden? The concern on his face must have shone through, cause Arden looked back at him with a reassuring smile and said, "See you soon, kid." And with that, his master was gone.

A HELLISH HORDE

Kye was standing in the frigid winter breeze, at his post on the southern wall. The acolytes had divided into groups, each protecting a portion of the rampart. Kye noticed that his posting was solo, though, his fellow acolytes seeing a human in their group as a detriment rather than a help. Kye was scanning the horizon for any signs of the shades. Caelum Vallis had barrier magic around the castle to help prevent trespassers and outside magical attacks from breaching the walls. But it had its limits against an army, especially an army of shades. The acolytes standing guard were the last defense against the enemy gaining access to the Six Realms.

Kye was turning over Arden's flask in his hand, trying to think of what Arden had been trying to tell him about the creation stone. Kye had never heard Arden tell him where the stone was hidden directly, so why did he think Kye already knew? He had to be missing something. Kye saw the sun starting to sink, signaling night was not far off. Shades preferred to come out at night; they thrived in darkness. That being said, even the sun could not stop them. One of the few things that could was a spell, a purifying light. He remembered Arden teaching him the spell as part of his training. Kye practiced his attack as he held open his palm and muttered *"solaris lirael"* as a bright ball burned in his hand for a moment before he dismissed it. Kye took a deep breath. From what he had read, he knew that fighting shades, he would have to keep his fear in check. Shades reveled in fear, and they instilled it in their prey. They would whisper things, show you things. They could drive you mad just as easily as they could kill you.

"Hey, Kye!" Kye turned to see Saiyah and Riley walking toward him. "I see you were assigned to the south wall as well.

It must be where they are sending their strongest fighters," Riley added with a wink.

"Or where they are sending those they deem to be the misfits," Saiyah added earnestly. Riley shrugged. "Either way, I can think of no two people I'd rather die beside."

"That is both incredibly sweet...and horribly morbid, Riley," Saiyah stated honestly. Riley leaned over the side of the ramparts, looking out at the pure white landscape.

"You see any sign of them?" he asked. Kye shook his head.

"It doesn't make sense..." Kye began. "If Orin went through all the trouble of amassing an army, it would seem like he would want to focus his attack on Caelum Vallis itself. It is the stronghold of the council after all. Wouldn't spreading his forces just make them easier targets?"

Riley conceded the point, adding, "True, but spreading the maisters also makes them easier targets. And what better way to take out an enemy. After all, two hundred versus eight hundred is not great odds."

Kye's face fell. Saiyah noticed his concern.

"Despite the odds, maisters are the most powerful beings in the Six Realms," Saiyah added. She smiled at Kye. "I'm sure they will be victorious."

Kye nodded as he twirled the flask again in his hands. Riley caught sight of it as he did.

"Well, I would offer you a drink, but it looks like you brought your own," Riley noted.

"Oh," Kye replied. "It's not mine. Arden asked me to hold onto it for him, said it was a family heirloom."

"Ah, so Lord Arden carries a flask, huh?" Riley inquired with a grin.

"Why am I not surprised?" Saiyah noted dully. Riley reached out a hand to Kye. "Can I see it?"

"Oh, sure," Kye replied, handing it to Riley. Riley popped

the top and took a whiff, immediately pulling back from the pungent alcohol that caught his nose.

"Whoa, what's in there?" Riley inquired.

"Dwarven fire whiskey," Kye replied. "It's Arden's favorite."

Riley let loose a long whistle. "Strong stuff. And aptly named too. I once got drunk on it playing cards with a group of dwarves. Let me tell you, that stuff is lava going down and coming back up."

"Charming mental image, Riley," Saiyah added in disgust as Kye chuckled. Riley turned the flask over to inspect the image on the front and grinned.

"Gotta respect a man that puts the image of Yggdrasil on a flask. Paying homage to the deity of wisdom while you drink yourself stupid."

Riley passed the flask back to Kye, but Kye froze slightly as he took it, slowly looking it over in his hand. The gears turning in his brain.

"Yggdrasil...the deity of knowledge and wisdom..." Kye stated.

"Yeah," Riley replied, slightly confused.

"And...knowledge is power..." Kye continued.

"So I've heard..." Riley said uncertainly.

As the picture became clear, Kye chuckled slightly in disbelief.

"I'll be damned," he muttered, shaking his head. Arden was right. He did know where the stone was; he'd known for a while. He had just been too distracted to notice. Riley and Saiyah exchanged confused glances. Before they could even ask a question, Kye disappeared.

Kye appeared in the library, kicking himself for his own ignorance. A hundred times. He had been in the library over a hundred times since he had come to Caelum Vallis. Now what Arden had been trying to tell him made sense. When Arden had shown Kye the library, he had told him that knowledge was power and explained that Yggdrasil was the deity of knowledge. Then the night he met Saiyah, he sensed a familiar feeling as soon as he entered the library. He had chalked it up to nostalgia, but it wasn't. It was literally an energy he had felt just once before, in Umbree's study. Kye rushed up the staircase to the fourth floor of the library, where the huge stained-glass window of Yggdrasil resided. The sunset on the horizon cast a focused beam through the stained-glass panels. Kye carefully scanned the panes, looking for his quarry. His eye caught what appeared to be a bubble between the two yellow panes, part of the sunset behind the tree. Kye smiled, knowing that someone staring at the window would easily mistake the bubble as a defect in the glass. Kye, however, knew differently.

"If you want to hide something from a mage, you do it in plain sight," he muttered with a smile.

Kye closed his eyes, focusing as he did when he teleported but stopped short of actually jumping to another location. As his body began to fade, Kye reached his arm forward, his translucent hand easily passing through the glass. He grabbed the bubble in the glass as it faded in his hand as well. As he pulled his arm back through, Kye's form became solid again. He looked down at his left hand where he now held the bright yellow creation stone. Kye turned over the stone that had started this whole thing, looking at it up close for the first time. This small stone was the cause of so much mayhem, but he couldn't understand why. Kye didn't get a feeling of powerful magic from it. This artifact wasn't capable of leveling cities or subduing armies. It didn't offer the gift of life or grant a sudden death. It was just a magic stone, one which Kye could feel a small amount of wind magic radiating from. It wasn't immensely strong, so why did Orin want it so badly? As Kye was examining the stone, a sudden sharp pain shot through his left arm, almost causing him to drop it. It felt like he was holding his arm to a piece of hot metal. As Kye rolled up his sleeve, he saw the tattooed words "barrin" burning on his arm. The threshold spell. Someone had entered Arden's tower. Kye suddenly remembered he had rather abruptly ditched Riley and Saiyah at their posts without a word. They had probably come looking for him. In response, Kye once again faded, reaching back through the stained glass and putting the stone back in its hiding place. Now that he knew where it was hidden, Kye would be able to grab it quickly if any trouble arose. As soon as it was safe, Kye immediately teleported, heading back to Arden's tower to greet his friends.

"Hey, sorry I—" Kye started as he appeared in the tower. But his thought was interrupted as he stood in stunned disbelief. The tower was in complete disarray. The buffet was broken, the dining table was in shambles, and the sofa had been gutted, with the cotton fluff strewn all about the floor. Even more surprising was that two elven acolytes Kye had never seen before, cloaked in black, were standing in the tower with him. It was clear that Kye had interrupted them in their task, and both looked at him with the same shock Kye felt. The surprise only lasted for a moment, though, as they immediately raised their hands to attack. They were fast; Kye was faster. He appeared behind them before they could even finish their incantation.

"*Gaiste*!" Kye shouted. The long drapes hanging from the veranda window whipped out as though they were flowing arms. They enveloped the two trespassers quickly, cocooning them and pinning them against the wall. The cloaked figures struggled inside the fabric as Kye glared down at them.

"Who are you?" he demanded, but the elven figures gave no answer. Kye's hand twitched in a sudden fluid movement. The fabric that bound them swung to his command, peeling away from the wall only for a moment before knocking the bound intruders back into it. The two elves groaned slightly as they once again hit the stone wall.

"Allow me to clarify," Kye stated clearly. "You are trespassing in my master's tower. So you will answer my questions, or I will—"

"You will what, boy?"

Kye turned to the familiar sound of a voice, just in time to see a flash coming toward him. Something hard struck him on the back of the head before he even got the chance to teleport. Kye hit the floor, his senses completely dazed. His disorientation had given the other acolytes a chance to escape. They freed themselves from the drapes and began walking toward him. The common room was nothing but a blur as Kye saw a figure in black with a staff standing over him. Despite the high-pitched tone resounding in his ears, Kye raised a hand to try and shoot a spell toward the aggressor. But the figure in black simply held out a palm and stated, "*Somnumia*."

And that was the last thing Kye remembered.

CHAPTER 15
An Execrate Encounter

The first thing Kye was aware of was the sound of dripping water. Then he felt a cold wind rushing over his skin. Slowly forcing himself back to consciousness, he opened his eyes to the dim light of a damp cave illuminated by a few floating candles. Kye was sitting on the frigid cave floor against a stalagmite. As he tried to sit up, he panicked. His arms were bound behind his back around the stalagmite. He immediately tried to pull against his bindings, but the metal shackles that linked his hands behind his back could not be broken. Beneath him, Kye could see a sigil drawn in what appeared to be blood painted on the cave floor. It reminded him of the sigil that had been on the lid of the stone coffin.

"It's called a blood seal."

Kye looked up to see Torha and Belthier nonchalantly standing against the cave wall, observing Kye like he was an insect ensnared in a web. They were both wearing black acolyte robes. The same ones Kye had seen on the elves in Arden's tower. Kye's eyes narrowed. A glamour. These two had been the ones to break into Arden's tower; they had just made themselves look like elves. Torha grinned.

"Blood seals are used to mask any living being. Meaning even if someone scryed for you, they would be unable to find you."

Kye glared back at them. He then closed his eyes and focused. *Dimmora.* But he was hit with a shock when he didn't fade. Belthier and Torha laughed in response.

"Wouldn't be trying to teleport, would you?" Torha asked. "We know about your disappearing act." He pointed to the shackles binding Kye's wrists.

"They are enchanted. You won't be using magic."

Kye looked down to notice his amulet was missing as well. There was no way for him to call out.

"Not as though a human like you could ever wield magic effectively anyway."

Kye snapped his head up to see a third figure approach him from the shadows. He narrowed his gaze in pure, seething hatred.

"Umbree," Kye growled, uttering his name much as you would a curse.

Umbree was dressed in dark robes and seemed, unfortunately, no worse for wear since Kye's last encounter with him. The only difference was that Umbree now wielded a staff. It had a red glowing orb attached to the head, with the shaft carved out of onyx and a sharp, silver point on the end. Kye wasn't sure where he had gotten the new staff, but he could sense a dark energy radiating from it. Umbree sneered at Kye's greeting.

"You DARE address me by an informal name, boy?" he hissed.

"Well, I doubt you would prefer the other names I have for you."

Kye's head forcibly snapped to the left as the handle of

Umbree's staff struck the right side of his face. His vision was dazed, and his right cheek felt like fire. He wasn't sure if Umbree's strike had broken his jaw, but he tasted blood in his mouth.

"I suggest you watch your tongue, human," Umbree hissed. "Or I will remove it."

Kye spit out a small amount of blood at Umbree's feet before replying, "That would make this conversation rather short-lived."

Umbree glared at him. "Where is it, boy?"

"Where is what?"

This time, it was the heel of the staff. Umbree lifted it like a spear and drove the hard, sharp metal end into Kye's left shoulder. Kye cried out as the point pierced through flesh. The wave of pain that washed over him caused the world to spin. Kye had to swallow hard to suppress the bile rising in his throat. Warm blood from the wound on his shoulder trickled down his tunic.

"I have VERY little patience, boy."

"I wasn't aware you possessed any at all," Kye hissed through gritted teeth. Umbree responded by twisting the staff as Kye bit back a scream.

"I will ask you again," Umbree growled. "And before you respond with another smartass remark, allow me to remind you. I will beat you to death without batting an eye."

Umbree ripped the staff point from his shoulder with a final shout from Kye and grabbed him by the back of his hair. He forced Kye's gaze up as he bent down to his level. His eyes mere inches away, his foul breath invading his nostrils.

"Where-is-the-stone?" Umbree seethed.

"I-don't-know," Kye bit back. Umbree shoved his head down as he released Kye's hair, scoffing as he did so. "You expect me to believe that?" Umbree replied.

"What makes you think differently?" asked Kye. "Arden hid it. I have no idea where."

Umbree looked unconvinced. "The fool seems to trust you. I find it unlikely he would also not make the mistake of sharing the stone's location with you."

Kye could feel a swell of anger rising within him. It did not sit well with him to hear Umbree badmouth Arden. Umbree was the fool here, not him. Kye smiled sarcastically at Umbree.

"You believe yourself above Lord Arden," he stated. "I am curious then why he doesn't sit here instead of me. One surefire way to find the stone is to ask him these very same questions. But I'm guessing there is a reason you won't face him, and I think we both know what that reason is."

Kye leaned forward and inspected Umbree's face with great interest before adding with a smirk, "Could that be fear I see in your eyes?"

That had done it. Umbree spun around and pointed a hand at Kye, shouting, "*Fulgor Tela!*"

A blue bolt of lightning hit Kye, and he felt a thousand searing daggers stabbing him. The pain robbed him of his thought, his breath. Every muscle protested in agony as his body convulsed, and his eyes rolled back in his head. He would have screamed if he had the ability. The torment seemed to go on for what felt like eternity. Finally, Umbree suspended the spell. Kye's form slumped forward. His ragged breaths echoed inside the cave.

"You don't learn, do you, boy?" Belthier noted dully.

"I think he has lost his mind," Torha added with a sickening smile.

On the contrary, Kye was thinking quite clearly and following the only option available to him. He didn't want to die, but that choice was out of his hands. He didn't know if Arden even knew he was missing, or if he would be able to find him even if he did. The only choice that remained was to ensure Umbree did not get what he was looking for. Kye would not betray Arden or give Umbree the stone, even if it cost him his last breath. But he feared, given enough time, Umbree would break him. And that was a risk he couldn't take. The simplest way to avoid that was to incite Umbree, causing him to lose focus, to let his anger consume him. All it took was finding the right buttons. And after nine years with the intolerable bastard, Kye knew exactly what buttons to press.

Once he found his breath, Kye laughed weakly at Umbree.

"Have I...struck a nerve?" he asked.

Umbree clasped the staff in both hands and shoved the shaft against Kye's throat, cutting off his air supply. His face was scarlet, and his hands shook in fury. Kye was slipping into unconsciousness, a welcome reprieve.

"YOU WILL TELL ME WHERE THAT STONE IS, BOY!!!" Umbree boomed, removing the staff from Kye's throat at the last second before darkness overtook him. Kye coughed and gasped, trying to speak.

"Or...what?" Kye sputtered. "You will...kill me?"

Umbree's demeanor shifted quite suddenly. The fury seemed to quell as he crouched to Kye's level, staring back with sincerity.

"Oh, no. No, you will die," Umbree insisted. "That much is assured. I have dreamt of nothing else since you DARED to betray me. You have no control over your death. The only thing you have control over is how prolonged and painful it might be. If you tell me what I wish to know, I will show you mercy and put a quick end to your misery. But continue to defy me, and I swear, you will pray for death LONG before I tire of your screams."

Kye knew Umbree meant every word, and he had no illusions about survival. His entire life he had feared Umbree's retribution. But now, the once towering giant was just a small, cruel old man.

"Well, what is your choice?" Umbree sneered.

Kye didn't hesitate, leaning in closer to Umbree and disdainfully replying, "Go to hell!"

Umbree merely chuckled in response. "I am a maister, boy. Hell is a realm of MY making."

Umbree held his hand out toward Kye's forehead. "Allow me to demonstrate. *Menis incantari*."

Like a sudden punch to the side of his head, Kye felt something invade his mind, rattling him. He tried desperately to block it, but it swiftly bypassed his defenses as the cave around him went dark.

When Kye opened his eyes, he was lying on a straw mat on soft earth, with a handwoven blanket over him. As he slowly sat up, he realized he was in a very familiar place. He lay in a wood-covered shack. There was a small fireplace made out of clay situated in the corner. The heat from the daylight desert air blasted through the cracks. He was back on Helia. Kye stood up, looking around the shack. Hand-carved furniture made from fallen trees was scattered around the domicile, each piece adorned with carefully stitched pillows. Memorabilia he recognized but had long since forgotten hung from the walls as he inspected every corner of the room from the depths of his memory. The door of the shack swung open, and a petite woman in her early thirties, with long, black hair and deep brown eyes, came bustling in carrying a bundle of twigs. As soon as her eyes fell on Kye, he felt his heart actually stop for a moment.

"Ah, you are up!" she exclaimed, depositing the bundle of

twigs in the corner. "I feared you would sleep the day away, little cub."

Kye was frozen. Unable to take in air, unable to comprehend what he was seeing.

"Mother?" he asked in breathless disbelief. His mother turned to him and laughed.

"Son?" she asked in return, as though his question was meant to be a game. "Come on, if you are awake, there are chores to be done. I collected kindling, but I could use help with chopping firewood."

But Kye didn't move. He couldn't. She was here. She was standing right here. In the shack that was his home, before... everything. This was a dream, but it felt so real. How could it be? His mother turned to him again, her face contorted in confusion.

"Are you alright?" she asked in concern. "You look pale."

He wasn't alright; this felt wrong. But the longer he stood in this room, the more the nagging doubt at the back of his mind quieted. The more he felt like he was home. No, it was just a dream. He had to remember—it was just a dream.

" You...died..." Kye stated, trying to remind himself of the truth. His mother stared back at him, confused.

"So you had a nightmare?" she asked. Kye shook his head.

"No, you died...five years ago," Kye replied, trying to remember the truth. But it was slipping away the harder he tried to hold onto it. Like sand through a sieve. "And you look the same. How do you look the same?"

His mother approached him and gave him a compassionate smile.

"It was just a dream, little cub," she replied. "Don't let it bother you."

Kye looked around the shack carefully. Had it just been a dream? He was having trouble remembering. Where was he before here?

"Come on," his mother replied, "help me with the firewood, and I'll get lunch started. You will feel better after you eat."

Kye nodded numbly. He felt foggy. His thoughts were clouded, but...this seemed real. As Kye collected the wood ax from the wall, he dutifully stepped outside to begin chopping wood.

Kye felt as though he was in a daze as he stood there, rhythmically chopping one wooden log after another. It was a task he recalled performing a thousand times before, but now it felt...out of place. But why? He was a human; mundane tasks were common in his life. But Kye felt as though he should be doing more. After some time, his mother stepped outside with him. She was hanging wash on a clothesline behind him when Kye heard her gasp.

"Oh my gosh, look at this!"

Kye turned to see she held an amazingly clear yellow gem. It was about the size of a fist and glowed slightly. Kye instantly felt a connection to the stone. It was important somehow. His mother pointed to the ground.

"I found it here, beneath the clothesline," his mother explained. "Do you know what it is?"

Kye felt drawn to the stone, reaching his hand out for it. A warning was practically shouting in the back of Kye's mind, telling him this gem was dangerous. Kye retracted his hand and backed away.

"I think you should leave it," he stated. He didn't know why, but he instinctively pulled away from it. His mother looked confused.

"But we should return it to where it came from," his mother insisted. "Do you know how it got here?"

Don't tell her! His thoughts were practically shouting at him, but Kye didn't know why. Why was this gem important? He didn't know anything about it...did he? Somehow, he felt it was not only important to him...but someone he knew...

Suddenly, the memory of a voice echoed through his thoughts. It was the voice of a man. Although he couldn't recall the name, the voice sounded so familiar to Kye. *"Some say that a ranger is the strongest of magi,"* the voice stated. *"But they are wrong. A ranger may hit like a hammer, but facing off against one, you will fight with all you have. With a charmer, however, you won't fight; you won't want to.*

"Kye?" his mother asked as Kye stood frozen. Shutting his eyes tight, desperately trying to hold onto the memory of the voice.

"They will get inside your head and show you the most beautiful things. Places you've longed to see, loved ones long since lost. They will paint you a wonderful world, an inviting world, and you will want to let your guard down, want to let them in. But you can't let them in. Cause if you do, they will shatter your mind like a mirror, and you will never be able to put the pieces back together."

"Kye, look at me," his mother requested. But Kye didn't open his eyes. Instead he sought help from the voice inside his head. *What do I do?*

"Destroy the dream, kid, dispel the source of the illusion. No matter how much it hurts, no matter how much you don't want to, you have to. It's the only way to show the truth."

"Kye?" Kye jumped slightly as he felt a hand touch his cheek. As he looked down at his mother, she smiled brightly back at him.

"It's alright," she consoled him. "I'm right here."

Kye felt a sharp stab in his chest. Warm tears spilled from his eyes and rolled down his cheek as he placed a hand over hers. He understood now what the voice meant.

"But...you're not..." Kye stated, his voice breaking. "No matter how much I wish you were...no matter how much I want you to be... You're not here. And you haven't been for a long time..." Kye slowly pulled her hand from his face and stepped away from her. He knew what he had to do.

"This is the dream," Kye replied. "And I have to wake up."

His mother searched his face, her brown eyes squinted in confusion. Kye was shaking like a leaf as he looked back at her. Her gaze felt like a dagger piercing him.

"Kye?"

"I'm sorry," he whispered as his hand tightly gripped the wood ax he was holding. It happened in an instant. Kye shut his eyes and swung the ax. There was a scream, there was blood, and then just silence. When Kye opened his eyes, he expected the dream to be gone. But he was still there, standing in a blood-soaked nightmare.

Wake up! he commanded himself, begging the picture to fade.

Wake up!! he repeated. His head was spinning now. He couldn't seem to wake. Kye stumbled back and slowly slid down the outside wall of the shack. It was a dream, it was just a dream. It had to be.

WAKE UP!! Kye was shaking uncontrollably, unable to breathe as he looked at the ax he still held in his hand. The blade glistened in the sun, inviting sweet relief from this living hell. Kye held the sharp point to his throat, pressing down in preparation to drag it across his neck. He was going to end this nightmare, one way or another.

"Well," a voice stated. Kye's eyes snapped up to see Umbree standing outside the shack with him. All of a sudden, his memories came rushing back as he realized he was in Umbree's illusion.

"I see you murdered your own mother," Umbree noted in frustration. The illusion around him began to fade. "I must say, you are a far more brutal bastard than I gave you credit for."

Kye bellowed and rushed toward the goblin maister. In that moment, it didn't matter they were inside his head, and it didn't matter how long it took. Kye knew without a doubt, he was going to kill Umbree.

Orin and Amon stood atop the Taleera mountain ridge, overlooking the town of Liena. The shades had descended on the Isalia townsfolk, but the mages had been successful so far in keeping the shades at bay and civilian casualties to a minimum. Orin did take comfort in the fact that it had come at a cost to their ranks to do so, though not as much as Orin would have hoped. Orin sighed.

"What on earth could be taking Umbree so long?" he noted to Amon. "He relayed that he simply had to get the stone's location from a human. I would not have thought it to be such a lengthy task to accomplish."

Amon furrowed his brow. "I told you the old goblin was not up to the task. If you allow me, Master, I will drag the information from the human and put a quick end to this."

Orin shook his head. "No, my friend, it is best we keep to the shadows this time. We are not yet ready for a fight with the magi. Best keep a low profile till we are."

Orin looked back to the shades that were descending on the mages in madness, their fury unleashing devastating, bloody attacks on every soul that they crossed. Orin couldn't help but smile at the savagery of shades; they were delightfully terrifying creatures to behold.

"We simply must have faith in Umbree to complete the task we have set out for him," Orin replied. "We have set the stage. Nothing left to do but sit back and enjoy the show."

"Kye?"

Kye awoke on the small sofa in the common area of Arden's tower. The snow was falling outside, and a roaring fire was warming the room. Arden was standing by the veranda doors, looking at Kye as though expecting an answer.

"Did you hear me?" Arden inquired. Kye shook his head; he felt fuzzy, like he was still half asleep.

"I'm sorry, what?" Kye asked. Arden sighed.

"I said, have you had any luck with the research on the creation stones?"

Kye looked down to see he had a book clasped in his hands. He slowly remembered he had been reading it, but he must have dozed off.

"Oh, uh, sorry," Kye replied as he collected the book once more and started pouring over it. As Kye began to inspect the pages, he found that it was difficult for him to concentrate on even a single word. His eyes were tired; his thoughts were muddled. His mind felt drained, like a sponge wrung dry. He couldn't seem to focus on anything. Maybe he was just tired. Kye stared at the page for the longest time, unable to take in any information.

"I'm wondering if we chose a safe enough location to hide the wind stone," Arden stated after a prolonged silence as he sat in his high-backed chair. "What do you think?"

Kye looked back at Arden and blinked. The location of the wind stone... Where did Arden put it? He knew the answer to that question...didn't he? But it had to stay safe. Kye had to help keep it safe. How did he do that? Kye placed his head in his hands. He couldn't think clearly; his thoughts were a mess.

"I'm sorry...I think I'm just too tired to focus right now," Kye replied. "I think I'll turn in for the evening."

Arden sighed. His disappointment was palpable. This seemed off. Arden didn't usually care if he took a break or not.

"Very well, we will continue when you are rested," Arden stated.

Kye nodded and began heading toward his bedroom.

"Goodnight, Arden."

"Goodnight, boy."

Kye froze mid-step, still as a statue. *Boy*? Arden didn't call him that; Arden never called him that. It was Kye, kid, occasionally smartass, but never *boy*. There was only one who referred to him as such. The one he hated more than anything. Kye's fists clenched into tight balls as he turned to face the thing called Arden. Arden cocked his head in confusion at Kye's stern gaze.

"Something wrong, kid?"

"Yes," Kye stated simply. "You."

"*Volara*!" Kye shouted as he pointed to a fire poker resting by the hearth. In an instant, the tool flew up, zipping through the air like a spear and impaling the thing that was Arden through the head. The surprised look on Arden's face froze as silver blood ran down his head and his lifeless body hit the floor. Kye was unfazed, standing over the corpse completely unmoved. He knew this wasn't real. "Bit of advice, Umbree," he stated loudly and clearly. "Do not attempt to mimic Arden. You're a poor shadow at best."

Instantly, the illusion around him began to fade, dissipating like smoke rising up from a burning log. Arden's body was replaced by a very angry Umbree, standing there fuming. Kye glared back at him. How many of these illusions had he been in now? Dozens by this point. He was having trouble keeping track. Each one designed to try and break him. And in each one, it became harder and harder to tell what was real and what wasn't.

"Think you're clever, do you, boy?" Umbree hissed.

"More so than you, it would appear."

Umbree's reply was a cold smile. "Took you longer this

time to notice my illusion. In fact, it's been taking longer and longer each time."

Kye just glowered, remaining silent. But Umbree could see the unease creeping over his face. He began to slowly circle around where Kye stood like a vulture circling its prey.

"Those walls of yours are cracking, boy, no matter how hard you try to keep them standing. They just keep falling down, one by one. Soon enough, there will no longer be a barrier to protect you from me."

Kye tried to hide his distress, but he knew that Umbree was right. His focus was already breaking; reality was blurring. It was just a matter of time before Umbree had the information he was looking for. Kye was fighting back with all he had…but it was a fight he was losing. Instead of showing fear, though, Kye turned to Umbree with determination.

"Are you trying to convince me or yourself?" he asked. Umbree seemed slightly surprised at the question.

"It must be quite frustrating for you, a pathetic human putting up this much of a fight. I'm not the only one who's slipping, Umbree, and your mistakes are getting easier to spot." Kye stepped right up to Umbree, inches away from his face, as he seethed, "We'll see who breaks first!"

Umbree glared back as he opened his mouth to respond. Suddenly the whole room shook, almost knocking both Kye and Umbree off of their feet. Kye could hear shouting from somewhere as Umbree turned toward the sound.

"What the devil..." he hissed.

In an instant, the tower around Kye disappeared, and he found himself once again sitting on a cold cave floor. Black smoke enveloped everything around him, invading his nostrils, clogging his throat. His mind was having trouble focusing on the cacophony around him. Even in the dim light and clouds of smoke in the cave, he could see the flash of spells being exchanged and people shouting. A scream sounded like it came from Torha. Suddenly, a huge creature's silhouette lunged through the smoke. A second scream sounded like Belthier. Umbree immediately ran into the smoke after the shout, issuing a spell as he went. Kye leaned forward, coughing, trying desperately to catch his breath as the smoke invaded his lungs. An unknown hand suddenly touched his wrist, where the metal cuffs had him bound. He felt something hard clang against the metal, cutting through the links. The shackles broke. A strong grip grabbed hold of Kye's other arm, pulling him to his feet.

"*Dimmora.*"

Kye was hit by the floating sensation of teleporting before he found himself standing in another cave. The cavern was completely black till the form standing on his right whispered, "*Liraela.*"

Saiyah's face was instantly illuminated as the ball of light she conjured filled the cavern. She rushed forward to the cave wall and began tracing a symbol in the rock. Kye turned to see Riley helping to hold him upright. Kye noticed small bits of blood around his mouth, as though he had bit into something...or someone.

"Wow, he looked pissed," Riley noted to Saiyah. "Like, exceptionally pissed."

"I'd say that's a fair assessment," Saiyah replied as she continued tracing symbols.

"Sooo...you might want to hurry up with that cloaking spell there, little sis."

"Yes, thank you, Riley!" Saiyah tersely replied. "Your talent for stating the obvious never ceases to amaze."

Kye couldn't understand what was happening. His head was pounding, making understanding anything difficult. How were they here? Why? They should be at Caelum Vallis preparing for the attack. How did they know what had happened to him? And why did they come for him? No one should have been able to locate him, not with the blood seal Umbree had cast. Then a sickening thought spread through Kye's mind. He hadn't been rescued at all. This was a trick by Umbree, to coax him into letting his guard down so that he could invade his mind and gain control of the stone. This was still part of his game...

And Kye was done playing.

Saiyah finished the last symbol, standing up to observe her handiwork.

"There, that should cover our tracks...for a while, at least."

"How long is a while?" Riley asked.

"Shorter than indefinite," Saiyah replied.

In a surge of adrenaline, Kye ripped himself from Riley's grasp and jumped to the back of the cavern.

"*Shalira!*" Kye shouted. The stalactites hanging from the ceiling instantly broke into hundreds of tiny, sharp pieces. With a wave of his hand, Kye sent the shards hurtling toward the imposters standing in the room. Riley quickly jumped out of the way, landing near Saiyah as the sharpened rocks hovered inches from his and Saiyah's skin. Both of them were wearing shocked, betrayed expressions. It wasn't real, though; it was just a ruse. Still, the look on their faces caused Kye to hesitate to inflict a lethal attack.

"Whoa, Kye?! What the hell!" Riley demanded as he tried to approach. Kye responded by sending a shard toward his throat, stopping just before it impaled his jugular. Kye was just waiting until he saw the slip up, the proof of the illusion. Umbree would make a mistake soon and show his tell. Riley instantly stopped moving and went white as he saw the sharp point of stone hovering mere millimeters from his neck and Kye's cold stare boring down on him.

"Kye?" Riley asked carefully. "What are you doing?"

"Not real," Kye muttered to himself, reaffirming the truth.

"W-What?"

"YOU'RE- NOT- REAL!" Kye shouted back. He had been fooled by Umbree enough; he could recognize the trick by now. He wouldn't be misled this time. Riley's face was contorted in confusion.

"He has been charmed," Saiyah stated to Riley, suddenly understanding the situation. "His mind has been tampered with. He believes we are illusions, nothing more."

Kye glared back at the manifestation of Saiyah. It wasn't a belief; it was a fact. And she wasn't going to convince him otherwise.

"Listen, man," Riley started, "I don't know what happened, but this isn't in your head. This is real. WE are real."

Kye responded with a twitch of his hand as several more rock shards surrounded Riley. Riley held his hands up in surrender, adding, "And I would prefer not to have to bleed to prove that point."

This time Saiyah took a step toward Kye. In response, a portion of the rock shards that had been floating around Riley shot toward her, hovering menacingly around her skin. Unlike Riley, though, the shards did not intimidate Saiyah into stopping. She continued to approach Kye in small steps.

"Stay back!" Kye hissed in warning.

Saiyah halted her approach, holding her hands to her side in an attempt to show no malice. She caught Kye's gaze, holding it as only she was able to.

"Kye," she started softly, "listen to me. Listen to my voice. Amongst the noise and the doubt, ask yourself if it sounds familiar. If the words you are hearing truly belong to me, or if it is another speaking. You know me well enough to trust that feeling. As I do you."

Kye hesitated for a moment. It sounded like Saiyah. It looked like Saiyah. He wanted to believe it was her. But he couldn't. Too much was at stake if he were wrong.

"How did you find me?" Kye asked. If they were real, how were they able to locate him when he was in Umbree's grasp?

"Riley and I became concerned when you did not return to your post," Saiyah began. "So we went to Arden's tower to see if you were alright. We found the common room in disarray. There were signs of a struggle. We didn't know what to do. We could not call out to you through your amulet. Nor could we reach out to the other maisters because of the Shade's attack. So Riley and I attempted to scry in order to find you."

Kye's vision narrowed. They were lying. They wouldn't have been unable to scry for him. Umbree's blood circle took care of that.

"You couldn't have scryed for me," Kye clarified with a cold smirk, recognizing their slip up.

"I never said we scryed for you," Saiyah replied. "We scryed for that."

Saiyah pointed to the bracelet attached to Kye's left wrist, tucked slightly underneath the sleeve of his robe. The one she had given him. Kye cast a look at the wayfinding stone resting on his arm.

"I told you before, didn't I?" she continued. "Magical stones are unique because each one possesses their own distinct aura, which means they are practically impossible to scry for. Unless, of course, you already know what to look for."

Saiyah held up her own bracelet, which still contained a small shard of the same wayfinding stone she had given to Kye. Her words echoed in his mind as Kye glanced at his bracelet, *"For the next time you find yourself lost in the woods."*

Kye faltered for just a moment. Was what she said true? His head was killing him. It was hard to think...and harder to believe. Saiyah noticed Kye pause and once again began walking forward. Kye snapped back to attention, inching the stone shards closer to her in warning.

"I said STAY BACK!!" he commanded.

"So you have," Saiyah replied, "but I've noticed that despite your threats, you have not harmed us. If you truly believe us to be a trick, why stop at only words? Why not strike us down?"

"Uhhh, Saiyah...I don't think he needs encouragement," Riley added nervously. But Saiyah continued, unfazed.

"Only two choices lie ahead for you, Kye," Saiyah said, "for this stalemate will get you nowhere. You must either trust us or kill us. "

Kye was shooting glances between the two of them, trying to decide what to do. This had to be an illusion. It had to be. But Kye couldn't quell the nagging thought in the back of his mind—what if it wasn't? Was that a risk he was willing to take? Kye's hands began to shake as he tried to hold the weapons at his quarry. But try as he might, his determination was fading. After several minutes, he whispered, "*Solvia*."

The shards instantly stopped mid air and fell to the ground with a clatter. Kye lowered his arm slowly as the fight all but left him in an instant. He was fairly certain this was a trick, a hallucination created by Umbree. But if there was even a chance that it wasn't, the possibility that he was wrong, Kye couldn't strike. He couldn't hurt his friends. He knew that Umbree would take full advantage to assume control of his mind. He would be lost now; it was all but certain. The room tilted as Kye felt pain and exhaustion firmly take hold, replacing the fight of adrenaline that had flooded him. He swayed in place, trying to regain his balance as his eyesight blurred. Despite his efforts to remain standing, his footing gave way as he watched the floor coming toward him. To his complete shock, Riley caught his arm before he hit the ground.

"Easy," he replied as he helped Kye sit down. Saiyah shot forward, uttering, "*sylven tela,*" while holding her hand over the injury on Kye's shoulder. Kye could feel the pain start to subside as he caught the slight scent of lavender and lilac. It grounded him. He slowly began to understand. This wasn't a hallucination. It wasn't a trick. This was real. They were real.

"Forgive me," Kye stated softly, tormented with the thought he could have hurt them.

"Nothing to forgive," Riley replied. "If I had someone fucking around in my head, I'd be second-guessing reality too."

Saiyah nodded in agreement as she gave Kye a smile of reassurance.

"But now that we're all on the same page about our tangible existence," Riley began. "You want to tell us who the hell that bastard was?"

Kye took a deep breath. It was a long story, one he wasn't certain they had time for. Saiyah caught his eyes.

"It was Umbree, wasn't it?" she asked. She was already two steps ahead, as usual. Kye simply nodded in response.

"Umbree?" Riley questioned. "Like your former master Umbree? Like...the guy you stabbed?"

Kye nodded again.

"Well...that certainly explains the hostility," Riley added. But Saiyah shook her head.

"He took a great risk attacking you on High Council ground," she stated. "Not to mention he knew precisely when to time the strike. This goes far beyond retribution against a slave that betrayed him."

Kye hesitated to give her the answers she was looking for. He didn't want to get them involved any more than they already were. Umbree wouldn't hesitate to string them up as well if he got the chance. But Saiyah's gaze was telling him she wasn't about to let this go.

"Kye...why is he after you?" Saiyah pressed.

Kye sighed. "He wants the creation stone."

Saiyah and Riley were taken aback.

"And why does Umbree think you would have that?" Riley asked.

"Because I assisted in its removal from his manor," Kye explained. "It was how I met Arden. He was at Umbree's manor to reclaim the stone at the request of the council. But things went wrong. Umbree was willing to kill Arden to hold onto the stone. I helped Arden escape from the manor with the stone in response."

Saiyah and Riley were silent for some time, taking in the information.

"So, I hate to point out the obvious here," Riley started, "but why don't we just give Umbree the damn thing? If this is all about some valuable trinket, I personally don't give two shits if he hocks it."

"Because it is not just Umbree that wants the stone. Orin wants it, too. They are working together," Kye stated.

"What does Orin want the stone for!?" Saiyah asked, clearly alarmed.

"Nothing good. At least that's what Arden suspects, and I believe him," Kye replied. "Arden hid the stone to keep it away from Umbree or anyone else who may be working with Orin."

"Annnd, I'm guessing you know where he hid it?" Riley inquired.

Kye nodded again. Riley let out a long sigh as he ran his hand through his hair.

"Okay," he began. "So we just have to keep Umbree away from the stone and you, right? Shouldn't be too hard."

"I fear that task may be more complicated than you believe," Saiyah replied, her tone tinted with unease as she stared at something. Riley and Kye followed her gaze to the symbols she had placed on the walls. As Kye observed them, he saw tiny cracks starting to appear. Almost like paper tearing, very slowly.

"Someone is attempting to break my cloak...my guess would be Umbree," Saiyah clarified. Riley's mouth fell open.

"How the hell did he find us so fast!?"

Kye's eyes drifted to his wounded shoulder. Umbree had stabbed him with his staff, the same one he still had on him.

"He has my blood," Kye clarified. Knowing all too well if Umbree had that, hiding was not an option. "He'll be able to track me wherever I go."

Riley let loose a slew of curses as he began to pace back and forth in the cavern.

"I'm really hoping you got a plan B here, little sis," Riley inquired, looking to Saiyah for answers. "I'm thinking, Riley," Saiyah replied, deep in thought, trying to run scenarios through in her head. "We could attempt to fight."

"Against a maister!?" Riley asked incredulously.

"We could try to enlist the aid of the other acolytes."

"I see that conversation going well," Riley replied. "Hey, comrades, come! Risk your life for a human you don't like and a stone you don't care about."

"We can try to reach out to the other maisters again," Saiyah replied.

"We already tried that, and they're a bit preoccupied at the moment!"

Kye knew if Umbree caught him again, he would have the location of the stone. He had been close to breaking him as it was. Not only that, but he would kill Saiyah and Riley to make it happen. He had to get the stone and his friends somewhere far away from Umbree. And he had a plan for doing just that. But he doubted either one of them was going to like it. Kye reached into the pocket of his robes, pulling out Arden's flask.

"I have an idea," Kye stated as he slowly stood up. He threw the flask to Riley, who caught it in surprise. "You both head back to Caelum Vallis. In the library, in the stained-glass mural of Yggdrasil, you will find a yellow stone in the sunset. Take the stone to Arden. You can use the flask to scry for him. Tell him what's happened and how to find me."

Riley and Saiyah looked back at him incredulously.

"And what? We simply leave you to your fate?" Saiyah asked, clearly angered by the suggestion.

"Yeah, no offense, man, but I doubt you can stand your ground against Umbree," Riley replied. "You barely look like you can stand upright."

"I have no intention of standing my ground against him, Riley. I don't have a death wish. Umbree is stronger than me, but I'm faster than him. I can lead him on a chase around Isalia, buying you both the time you need to get to Arden."

"And what makes you think he will follow?" inquired Saiyah.

"Cause I'm the only card he has left to play," Kye stated. "If he can't get to the stone himself, he will try to use me as a bargaining chip to get Arden to turn it over."

"You are certain of this?" asked Saiyah

"It worked for him once before," Kye replied.

Riley shook his head. "That's assuming you can stay ahead of him. If he catches you..."

"Then I'm as good as dead," Kye stated matter-of-factly, "but that will happen if I try to hide or try to fight. At least this way, I have a chance."

Riley looked clearly hesitant about the idea. "Well then, screw it, one of us will get the stone, and the other will come with you," Riley argued.

"We are neither travelers nor maisters," stated Saiyah. "We

could never hope to keep up." Kye nodded in agreement, but Riley still looked unconvinced. "Am I the only one that thinks this is a really bad idea?"

"No," Saiyah replied, "but neither can I think of a better one."

Saiyah closed her eyes for a moment as she walked toward Kye. Once she was standing face to face with him, she opened her eyes and whispered something. She reached up and touched Kye on the side of his face. Instantly, Kye felt a warmth spread through him. His shoulder was less painful, and he felt energized, stronger.

"What was that?" Kye asked as Saiyah pulled her hand away.

"A healing art," Saiyah clarified. "A spell to lessen the pain and give strength, nothing more, and it will not last forever. So do NOT push yourself," Saiyah added sternly.

Kye smiled back at her. "I won't."

Riley sighed. He reached into the back of his belt and pulled out a dagger that he extended toward Kye.

"A dagger?" Kye inquired.

"A blade made of dragon bone," Riley added. "The preferred weapon of the shifter people. It can cut through almost anything."

Kye grinned slightly. "I appreciate the sentiment, Riley, but I don't stand much of a chance against Umbree using magic. If my survival comes down to hand-to-hand combat, something has gone horribly wrong."

"Then take it in case something goes horribly wrong," Riley replied.

Kye nodded to his friend and graciously took the blade. Kye slid the weapon into the side of his belt. Riley walked over beside Saiyah, grabbing her hand in preparation to teleport. The look in Saiyah's eyes clearly told Kye she was afraid for him. Kye tried to offer her a smile of reassurance.

"We will see you soon," Saiyah stated. "Until then...stay safe."

"Yeah," Kye replied. "You too."

With one last look, Saiyah closed her eyes and whispered, "*Dimmora*."

Kye was now alone in the cave, turning toward the sigils on the wall. They were actively crumbling, alerting Kye to the fact that Umbree was closing in. Kye took a deep breath, preparing himself for the fight ahead.

"Okay, Umbree..." he muttered in determination. "Just you and me now..."

As the last sigil fell away, Kye tensed and whispered, "Catch me if you can."

CHAPTER 16
The Shadows of Shades

Saiyah and Riley appeared in the middle of a small town, standing in the glow of the full moon above them. They had returned to the castle and successfully reclaimed the creation stone. Scrying with the flask, they had found that Lord Arden was several miles outside the town of Amira, in the woods of Redethe. Both doubled over as soon as they landed in the village, attempting to catch their breath from having to teleport so much.

Riley immediately sprawled out in the snow, breathing heavily. "Damn," he gasped. "How the hell...does Kye...make that look...easy?"

"Because he is...a traveler," Saiyah replied, "and we...are not."

As she caught her breath, Saiyah slowly stood up to observe her surroundings. The village looked much different from the last time she had visited. The villagers had clearly evacuated from the attack of the shades. The darkness and quiet seemed to invade every building, almost like a sickness. The only sounds heard were the snow falling and the soft patter of ice hitting the fountain in the center of town. Saiyah looked at the forest to the west. Not even the moon's glow could penetrate the thick, interwoven trees. It made it a prime location for shades. As Riley stood up, Saiyah pointed to the forest.

"That is our destination," Saiyah stated as Riley nodded. Thankfully, their eyes were well-adjusted to seeing in the dark. Which was good, since Saiyah desperately wanted to avoid attracting any attention by summoning a light. Shades were still scattered in droves throughout Isalia, and Saiyah wished to avoid a confrontation with them at all costs.

Saiyah and Riley slowly made their way into the forest, keeping their eyes peeled. Riley's animal instincts were in full swing as his focus narrowed on every sound and slight movement. A soft crunching could be heard as the pair trekked through the freshly fallen snow. Saiyah wasn't sure how deep Lord Arden was within the forest. She desperately hoped that he had not already teleported to another location by this point. Riley suddenly stopped, issuing a low growl.

"Saiyah," he warned. Saiyah followed his line of sight to see a person standing in their path. They stood a bit away, so Saiyah could not make out any facial features—save for their eyes, reflecting light, like a night bound predator. Saiyah already knew this was not a villager; this was not a person at all anymore. This was a shade. Saiyah heard a chilling voice echo inside her mind.

"Pretty little elf...cut her open...watch her bleed."

"You know how to fight these things?" Riley inquired as his fangs began to grow, and his fingers sprouted claws.

"I have read about them," Saiyah admitted as she took a defensive stance. Riley chuckled slightly.

"Nothing like practical application," he muttered. Riley didn't even waste time removing his robes, instantly shifting into his fearsome fox counterpart. Riley bared his fangs toward the creature and growled. The shade responded by tilting their head and letting loose a bone-chilling scream. Saiyah cringed, the sound rattling around inside her skull. Moments after the horrible sound ended, Saiyah saw the shadows around them begin to move, slowly forming into shapes, becoming one shade after another. Dozens of voices now bounced around inside her mind, bombarding her with images of her and Riley's death, dismemberment, and nightmarish end. Saiyah steeled her thoughts to block out the horrific images, focusing on the shades around her.

"Skin the fox."
"Take their eyes."
"Make them scream."
"Watch them die."

Saiyah turned in a circle, and her pulse quickened. They were now completely surrounded. The original shade held up its hand as its fingers grew to knife-like points. The other shades immediately followed suit and began closing in.

"*Well...fuck,*" Riley uttered in his animal form.

In an instant, the shades shrieked and rushed toward them. They were as fast as lightning, moving through shadow like a fish through water. Saiyah responded by summoning a ball of light. The shades retreated from the light and simply kept to the shadows of the trees to continue their advance. Riley lunged forward, clasping one in his teeth and biting down. The shade issued a horrifying scream and continued to slash at Riley's face even as he was killing it. Two other shades rushed behind him as Riley swiped at them with his claws. Saiyah tried to shoot a light spell toward him to help, but a shade rushed up toward her and slashed at her from behind. Deep claws tore at her back as Saiyah was knocked to the ground. She quickly rolled over in the snow to shoot an evocation spell at her attacker.

"*Soinneáin!*"

A ball of light shot the shade square in the chest, knocking it back about twenty feet. It lay on the ground, shrieking from Saiyah's attack, as she felt the wounds on her back already starting to heal. Saiyah spun around to a yelp. Riley had about five of them on him, slashing at him from all sides, black blood staining his fur. Saiyah began to summon another ball of light when sharp claws tore open the side of her face. Saiyah was knocked back down into the snow as three shades descended on her at once. They were ripping furiously at her, wounds being created as soon as they healed. Saiyah tried to utter a spell as one tore at her neck. She choked as silver blood filled her throat. She attempted to roll away from her attackers to protect her head and heart. As she pulled her arms up, the shades continued to swipe at her, not even offering the smallest opening for her to fight back. Suddenly, a booming voice echoed through the trees.

"*SOLARIS LIRAEL!*" it shouted. A wave of light stampeded through the forest, bending trees in its wake. It was daylight in the dead of night. Every shadow was illuminated, leaving nowhere to hide. As soon as the light hit the shades, they let out a horrendous scream and began twisting on the ground in agony, dying. Two of the shades attacking Riley broke off, outrunning the light by rushing out further into the darkness. Saiyah lifted her head up in time to see Maister Gaylic and Maister Varen race out into the night after them. The light spell slowly faded away. Saiyah looked at Riley as she carefully stood up. He had shifted back to his human form and had a hand over some fairly deep claw marks on his left side.

"Acolytes were told to remain at the castle and protect the travel orbs," a familiar voice stated. Saiyah and Riley turned to see Maister Arden step forward from the shadows. Unlike Saiyah and Riley, he did not carry even a scratch from his prolonged battle with the shades. Considering the light magic he had just summoned to save them, Saiyah seriously doubted the shades could even get close enough to lay a finger on him. After witnessing it first-hand, she could not deny he was truly a powerful mage indeed. Arden looked back and forth between Saiyah and Riley.

"So," he began, "you both want to tell me what the hell you're doing out here?"

"We were looking for you actually," Riley replied. He had collected the torn bits of his robe off the ground and was trying to use them as bandages over his wounds. Arden raised an eyebrow in response.

"Me?" he inquired as Saiyah stepped toward him.

"Kye asked us to come. To give you this." Saiyah pulled the creation stone from her pocket and handed it to Arden. As soon as the stone touched his hand, Arden's eyes narrowed in confusion, looking between Riley and Saiyah.

"And why did my acolyte entrust this to the two of you instead of delivering it himself?" Arden asked, puzzled. "Where is Kye?"

Saiyah's face fell. "In trouble, my lord," she stated softly. "In very serious trouble."

Kye suddenly appeared in an underground forest temple, one of the hidden areas he had found while exploring Isalia. It had clearly been an impressive structure during its time. But it had now fallen into disarray, nature almost completely overtaking the stone.

Kye leaned against one of the nearest stone pillars, desperately trying to catch his breath before he jumped again. For the last few hours, he had been leading Umbree on a chase around Isalia. Now his stamina was about at its end, the cold sapping the strength from him as much as traveling was. The healing spell that Saiyah had cast had long since worn off, and the wound on his shoulder was still not completely healed. After hours of running, exhaustion and pain were starting to overtake him. Kye knew he had to keep going, though; he couldn't let Umbree catch up. He only had a few moments to rest before Umbree would locate him.

"*Phasma Lira*!" Kye heard a voice shout. He looked down to see something like a rope of light shoot up from the temple floor and wrap itself around his left leg. Shit! He had waited too long. Kye didn't waste time trying to figure out what the light rope was. He immediately tried to jump again to escape its clutches.

"*Dimmo—*" Kye screamed before he could even finish the incantation. He was forcefully ripped back to his current location mid-jump as his body hit the stone floor, writhing in agony. As he had tried to teleport, Kye could feel the rest of his body start to disappear in preparation to jump. His leg, however, did not. The rope that bound his left leg seemed to prevent it from jumping with the rest of him. Kye had felt the flesh and bone tearing away from the rest of his body as he tried. Kye looked down at his left leg. There was a clear cut in his robes around the newly formed injury as blood seeped into the surrounding cloth. A deep gash was now visible in a full circle around his thigh, just above where the light rope ended. Kye was shocked his leg was still attached to the rest of him, for it had felt as though it had been torn clean off.

"Spectral snare," Umbree clarified as he approached. "One of the few things that can trap a traveler. By all means, feel free to jump again, boy. That leg of course, will not be going with you if you do. Should make running a bit more difficult."

Kye rolled over and held a hand toward the ceiling.

"*Intrica*!" he shouted as the vines stretching across the ceiling immediately extended down and wrapped themselves around Umbree. He took advantage of Umbree's momentary distraction to pull the dagger from his belt that Riley had given him and began slashing at the light snare around his leg. No matter how hard he cut it, the rope wouldn't break. Umbree burned the vines trying to ensnare him, hissing, "*Percura,*" as he pointed at the weapon Kye held.

The dagger was knocked from Kye's hand and flew into the opposite wall, inserting itself deep within the stone. Kye spun in response and shouted, "*Lapis sicca!*" as a stone shard from the floor hurdled itself furiously at Umbree. Umbree easily waved the attack away and responded by pointing his hand at Kye. "*Fulgor tela!*"

Kye tried to bring up a barrier, but Umbree's spell easily shot through it. Once again, the bolt of lightning tore through Kye, bombarding him with anguish and robbing him of the last ounces of energy he had to fight. When Umbree silenced the spell, Kye was still. Unable to move as air filled his lungs in uneven spurts. He turned toward Umbree, his eyes glaring, telling him he would fight to his last breath.

"Still stubbornly denying your fate, huh, boy?" Umbree growled. "I must admit, you are certainly more surprising than I thought possible for a human. Had you not betrayed me, I might have considered keeping you as my vassal."

Kye began to laugh weakly, reveling in the absurdity of Umbree's statement. Umbree, however, was unamused. "What is so funny?" he hissed.

"You, speaking to me of betrayal," Kye replied. "You sold out your brethren, betrayed your oath, and cost countless lives. For what? A few pieces of silver and gold?"

"You think this is about money?" Umbree inquired.

"Isn't everything with you?" Kye shot back.

Umbree walked up to Kye and knelt beside him on the floor. Kye tensed, preparing for another assault. The goblin master, however, seemed to take a moment from torturing him to make him understand.

"If I had sold that stone to a collector," Umbree began, "I

would have been wealthy beyond my wildest dreams. I could have bought a magnificent mansion, silks, gems of the rarest variety. I could have had women, admirers, power. But do you know the one thing I couldn't buy, boy?"

"A conscience?" Kye spit back.

"Time," Umbree clarified. "That is what Orin offered me."

"I don't understand."

"I am old," Umbree stated. "I will die far sooner than I would like. Orin offered me freedom from death. He offered me immortality."

Kye's eyes widened in dismay. The longest-living creature in the Six Realms were elves. And even they got a thousand years, no more. Nothing was immortal; nothing could be. All life, eventually, came to an end.

"That's...impossible."

"For many mages, yes," said Umbree. "But my master has already lived beyond the span of an ordinary elf's life, far beyond. He has the power to bestow it and will do so to those that serve him. And what of you?"

"Me?"

"You are human," replied Umbree. "Your life is short. Growing shorter by the minute. Would you not like to live longer? To see more? Orin can grant it."

Kye's vision narrowed. Humans had the shortest life of any being. To offer the chance for a longer life—what human wouldn't wish for it? But some prices were too high to pay, and Kye understood that, even if Umbree didn't.

"And all it would cost me is my soul?" Kye clarified. "If those are my options...I choose death."

Umbree snarled. "So be it."

Umbree held a hand up to Kye's head. "*Mentibus oculus!*"

Kye instantly tried to raise his barriers as Umbree attempted to invade his mind once again.

"No worries, boy," he heard Umbree state as the temple around Kye began to dim. "I shall grant you the death you seek. But first, I will shatter your mind to turn you into an obedient puppet and arm you with that dagger of yours. Then, when Arden arrives with the stone to collect you...you will be the one to run him through."

"*NO!*" Kye shouted internally as the room around him once again went dark. In an act of desperation, Kye's hand shot up and grabbed hold of the staff in Umbree's hand. Umbree's face contorted in a look of surprise as he temporarily stopped the spell and tried to rip the staff back from Kye's grasp. But Kye held fast.

"*Dimmora!*" Kye shouted as his body and the staff started to phase in preparation to jump. Kye could feel his leg being torn from him, but he fought through the pain and grabbed the onyx staff with both hands. The staff faded along with Kye, slipping from Umbree's hold. Once the staff was ethereal along with the rest of him, Kye shoved the staff forward like a spear, driving it through Umbree's chest. He then instantly suspended the spell, bringing the staff and himself back to corporeal form. Umbree shot up and stumbled back, looking down at the fully solid onyx staff now impaling him. He looked back at Kye in shock as Kye stared back at him, frozen in disbelief. Umbree tilted and began coughing up green blood as he stumbled forward. His upright position only lasted for a few moments before he dropped to his knees, continuing to throw up green blood on the cold stone temple floor. He tried to speak, but the only sound that came out was a wet, gurgling noise. He gave Kye one last look of shock as he reached for him, almost as though he was seeking help. Umbree's body then fell forward and shuddered slightly before remaining still.

Kye's breathing was heavy. He sat for a long time, staring at Umbree's immobile form. He slowly looked down to see his hands coated in the green blood that belonged to his former master. His breath came in short bursts, and the world around him seemed quiet, save for the tumultuous sounds of his heartbeat. He kept waiting for Umbree to rise, to attack, to lash out. But he just lay there, silent and still. Kye looked on in dismay. His whole body was shaking uncontrollably. He wasn't sure if it was from shock or blood loss. It took a while for the truth to sink in... He had killed him. He had killed Umbree. Kye felt as though he were sinking. Why should he care? Shouldn't he be glad that Umbree was dead? Shouldn't he be glad that he killed him? The mere mention of the word caused Kye's stomach to turn as he shut his eyes to try and calm himself. Kye turned his attention away from the corpse, looking down at his leg. The light rope that held him was now gone, but his leg was twisted at an odd angle, as though it was no longer a part of his body. A pool of red blood was forming underneath him, and Kye felt cold. He didn't have the strength to even attempt a healing spell. He tore off strips from the hem of his robes. He wrapped the cloth around his wound as tight as he could stand. He had to slow the bleeding, at least until Arden could find him. As Kye worked on bandaging his wound, he thought he caught a movement out of the corner of his eye. Kye looked up at Umbree. He was lying perfectly still, but Kye couldn't shake an eerie feeling.

"Umbree?" Kye whispered. He somehow knew he would not receive a response, but he could not stop himself from asking the question. Had the movement he thought he saw been just a figment of his imagination? Kye looked once again at Umbree's still body, focusing on it intently, just to be sure.

"Umbree?"

A hand shot forward and grabbed Kye's throat. Kye tried to jump back, but the grip on his neck was unbreakable. Umbree's immobile form began to contort in an unnatural fashion as his head snapped upward. He was smiling, and his grin stretched far past the normal confines of his mouth. But

Kye could only see his eyes. His pupils were black as coal, revealing an unending emptiness. This was not Umbree. Kye thrashed at the arm that held him with both hands, trying to lessen the hold. Trying to breathe, trying to cast, trying to escape. The unknown entity responded to Kye's attempts to break free by slamming him hard against the stone ground. The thing now towered over Kye, that ever-expanding smile looming over him. His eyes were drilling right into Kye's, and Kye felt the darkness consuming him as he fought for breath.

"You think you can kill me, human?" a voice asked Kye. It sounded so far away, even though it was right in front of him. The words caused ice to spread through Kye as he struggled harder to free himself.

"I am death itself," the voice replied. *"I am immortal. And you, spawn of Aine, are not."*

Kye wasn't able to get free, even though he fought with all the strength he had left against the hand that held him. He could feel himself floating, those black eyes boring into him. And that unnatural smile welcoming his death. Kye's grip on the hand that held him was loosening. His eyes began to roll back, and he slowly started falling into darkness.

"MANUS LETIO!!!"

A voice boomed as the hand that held Kye's throat was ripped from him. Kye filled his lungs with a raspy breath, lying on the stone temple floor. As he forced his eyes open, he slowly focused his gaze. He could see Umbree pinned to the ceiling above him. As Kye turned his head, he saw Arden standing in the middle of the temple, his right hand pointed toward Umbree, and his face contorted in rage. Kye had never seen him so angry. All things in the room seemed to bend to his command. The thing that was Umbree flailed and fought against the ceiling fruitlessly.

"*Inferna Pyraena*!" Arden hissed as the entire ceiling erupted into a bright blue fire that spread from Umbree and to every corner of the room. Kye could feel the heat from the ceiling blasting against his skin, even from the floor. It seemed to beat back the ice that was creeping over him. Umbree's body quickly burned from flesh to bones to ash. Arden didn't hesitate, didn't falter, staring at Umbree's burning form without compassion or remorse. It was at that moment, Kye understood why Arden was said to be the strongest mage on the council. Why it was that Umbree had feared him, and he'd had cause to. Arden was a terrifying force, different from the blunt, sarcastic master that Kye had come to know. This mage controlled hellfire and would burn all those deserving of the flame.

Once the thing that had been Umbree was gone, the magic staff disintegrated in the fire. Ash rained down like snow upon the floor. As soon as he suspended the flames, Arden immediately turned his attention to Kye, rushing over to where he lay. He seemed to be moving in slow motion, along with the ash and snow falling down around them. Kye was trying to keep his eyes open, but his eyelids felt like they were lead, and he found them drifting closed despite his best efforts. He just needed to rest; he would just close his eyes for a moment. Kye was vaguely aware of Arden kneeling next to him. He sounded like he was casting a spell. He thought Arden was talking to him, something about staying awake, but he could barely hear him. Almost like he was speaking through water. His words were garbled, and the quiet was slowly drowning it out.

Amongst the silence drifting over him, Kye thought he caught Arden shout, *"Kye, stay with me, kid!"*

Kye was confused as the darkness overtook him. What did he mean? Arden sounded concerned, but Kye didn't know why. He wasn't going anywhere. He was just tired... That was all.

He just...needed...to...sleep...

The sun was breaking over the horizon. Orin stood on the hill, watching a group of shades chased by an orc mage into a cave. He was disappointed that all his efforts to gain his prize had gone to waste. The fact that Umbree had failed was disappointing, to say the least. The fact he had met his end at the hands of a human was even more so.

"So Umbree was useless..." Amon growled, equally frustrated that Umbree had proved so utterly disappointing.

Orin sighed. "Yes, but we know who has the stone. So we can gain it at another time. And if his information was correct, the council should be sufficiently distracted so we can collect a consolation prize."

Orin then turned to Amon. "Go and fetch it for me, would you, my friend?"

Amon bowed. "Yes, master." In an instant, Amon vanished. Orin pondered the events of the evening. He would have strangled that annoying human mage had Arden not arrived. He was proving to be a nuisance. One he would have to take care of soon enough. For now, the magi had won this battle. However, Orin would win the war. With a final look toward the horizon, Orin vanished from sight and from Isalia.

CHAPTER 17
A Daemon of Death

The sprawling manor was completely silent. A full moon hung in the skies of Proxa. Two reptilian eyes stalked its quarry, unbeknownst to the human he was tracking. A young servant in his late twenties named William rubbed his eyes wearily as he tried to finish his task before heading off to bed. He was sitting at a wooden desk, illuminated by the light of a small candle, poring over an order form for the pantry. It seemed as though they had been double-ordering some essentials, which meant last month some of the bread and potatoes had rotted before they could be eaten. He was taking detailed inventory of the manor's staples before they placed the order for next month. He was fairly certain he had pared down the list and was now just going over a few last checks before he called it a night and headed off to bed. When he was satisfied with the final result, William rolled up the order form and placed it in the letterbox by the servant's entrance. He would be sure to go over the contents with the head housekeeper, Viktor, tomorrow. He could look over the details and tell him if there was anything he was missing.

William grabbed the candle and began heading back to the servant's quarters. He was fairly certain he would be asleep by the time his head hit the pillow. Upon entering his dark room, though, he was met with a surprise. His window was open. William slowly approached the open window in confusion. That was strange; he was sure he had shut it this morning. He poked his head out and observed the outside of the manor walls. He couldn't see anything suspicious. William shrugged slightly. It was possible he had left the window open. It had been a warmer day today, after all. As he closed the pane, he looked up to see a reflection in the glass that was not his own. He spun around just in time to see a form fly toward him and grab him by his neck. The hulking man standing over him was clearly a shifter by the way his eyes reflected the light. William stared back at him, frozen by fear. He immediately thought of trying to rip the hand from his throat and screaming to awaken the rest of the manor. But the shifter's gaze narrowed, and his hold on his throat seemed to tighten the instant the idea ran through his head.

"I know what you are thinking," the shifter growled. "I have seen that look on prey before. You think that if you scream, if you run, that will save you. I can assure you, it will not. If you try to scream, I will crush your throat. If you try to run, I will rip your spine out. Your only hope for survival is to do exactly what I say. Do you understand me, human?"

William was shaking like a leaf, staring back at the fierce gaze boring into him. He nodded slightly.

"Good," the shifter replied. "Now, take me to your master's vault."

The shifter's claws dug into his left shoulder as William slowly guided him down a long, dark staircase underneath the manor.

His mind was racing—how to escape, how to fight back. The vault contained his master's most prized magical artifacts, many of them dangerous. He wasn't sure what this shifter could be looking for, but if he was able to gain hold of some of the more powerful objects, there was no telling the damage he could do. When the pair finally reached the bottom, they stood before a two-foot-thick steel door with intricate locks and gears. He was confident that even if the shifter charged the door full speed, he would be unable to force his way inside. To his utter shock, though, the shifter turned toward William and commanded, "Open it."

"I-I can't," he stuttered. In response, the shifter scowled, digging his claws deeper into Willliam's shoulder, causing him to flinch.

"Why do you feel the need to lie to me, William?" the shifter replied. William snapped his head up. How did he know his name?

"I am better versed on the situation than you think I am," the shifter stated. "For instance, I know this door is protected by magic—blood magic, to be precise. And that only a select few are able to open it. And I happen to know you are, in fact, one of those few."

William stared back in shock. How did he know so much?

"I also know that to unlock it requires a drop of blood from a living host with access," the shifter continued. "But if you don't intend to help me, then I don't see any point in you living any longer."

William started to tremble under the shifter's threat as he reluctantly unclasped the gold circle pin he always wore, symbolizing the sigil of the house he served. He poked his pointer finger with the end of the pin. A small drop of blood appeared. He placed his finger on a plate with a magic circle on it to the right of the door. The symbol glowed as the gears and locks of the door began to click open. The giant door slowly swung free, granting the pair access to the treasures inside. Instantly, dozens of chandeliers ignited, illuminating the steel room they stepped into. Multiple display cases lit up, proudly displaying the artifacts they held. The shifter carefully made his way into the room, still holding onto William's shoulder. Willian assumed the shifter would start grabbing items indiscriminately, but he was calmly scanning the room. Almost as though he was looking for something in particular. As they continued through the room, William looked over to see that at the seating area in the center of the room, left on the table to the side, was a drink tray. It contained a half-finished bottle of brandy along with a wine opener. As they walked past the sofa, he carefully and swiftly clasped the corkscrew tool, hiding it in his right hand without alerting his captor. The shifter was too focused to notice as he seemed to have finally located his quarry—a golden scepter beneath the farthest display case. It had once belonged to the goblin monarchy and was, by far, the most prized piece of his master's collection. As the shifter headed toward it, William clasped the wine opener firmly and drove the sharp point into the shifter's hand. The shifter immediately released his hold, and William turned and bolted for the exit. He was rushing up the stairs as he began to shout, "INTRUDE—"

But he never got to finish his thought. His breath swiftly left him, and a sharp pain shot through his chest. He looked down to see the shifter's claws protruding through his middle. William slowly turned to see the shifter glaring back at him.

"Foolish, chiftele," the shifter hissed. "Very foolish."

The shifter ripped his hand from William's chest as his legs gave out and his body hit the stairs. He couldn't breathe. His lungs desperately tried to take in air and instead filled with blood. He could feel the warmth leaving him and his vision going dark as he looked back at the shifter. The last thing he ever saw was the shifter lifting the display case lid and grabbing his master's golden scepter from its rightful place.

The orcish tavern of Belak was abuzz with the sounds of drinks clattering and laughter. The tavern was nestled high in the mountains, remote in its location in the orc realm of Savena, but still well known amongst the town folk of Imar at the base of the mountain. The air was full of the sounds of fiddles and conversation emanating from the pub. The people inside were so preoccupied with their jubilation, they paid no attention to the cloaked figure approaching in the dark. The tavern door swung open as a blast of wind and snow pummeled through the tavern attendants. A fair-skinned elf with white hair stepped inside.

Removing the hood of his cloak, he displayed deep red eyes as he looked carefully upon the scene before him. Every eye in the building turned to him. The noise and voices instantly died down. The patrons were casting disapproving looks in the elf's direction as he calmly strode to a table, unfazed by the glares. The elf sat down and casually began scanning the menu propped against the wall.

A tower of an orc stood up from his seat and strolled over to the table where the elf sat.

"You lost?" he questioned with a deep growl. The elf turned to him and smiled.

"Oh, not anymore," he responded. "Though I must admit getting turned around more than once coming here. But I do thank you for your concern."

The orc slammed his fist on the elf's table, spilling some of the large stein of beer he was holding.

"I say you are still lost," the orc reiterated. "Elves aren't welcome here."

The elf seemed generally surprised by this. "Oh, I see. My deepest apologies. I wasn't aware. But tell me..." The elf leaned toward the orc and asked in a soft tone, "Would it help if I told you I'm not really an elf?"

The entire room erupted in laughter as the orc standing in front of him chuckled and leaned forward, feigning interest. "Ya don't say?" he inquired. "Well, then, what are you?"

"A god," the elf stated simply. "Or at least by your standards, I am. Though I have been out of practice for quite some time and am a tad bit rusty."

"You are quite the arrogant prick," the orc replied.

"What you mistake for arrogance is simply fact, my friend."

The orc leaned closer menacingly. "Well, the fact is, you're not welcome here. And I have killed elves for less. So I suggest you leave before you become one of them."

The elf began to smile. Though despite his tone, there was nothing kind about this creature. Anyone with the slightest instinct could tell, he was emanating an aura of malice that would make even a dragon run for cover.

"You think I fear death?" the elf inquired. "On the contrary, my friend, it happens to be my specialty. Would you care for a demonstration?"

The orc reached forward to grab the elf when a loud coughing suddenly erupted behind him. The orc turned to see the barkeep clutch his throat and gasp for breath. As he looked up, the other orcs could see his eyes were black as coal. One female orc tried to help but immediately began choking as soon as she stood up. Next was the fiddle player, then the waitress. One by one, each of the twenty-five orcs within the pub began dropping to the floor, suffocating slowly. The original orc turned back to the elf in surprise, noticing that his eyes were now practically glowing. Looking down, the orc saw a black fluid in his veins, running up his arm and finally resting at his throat. The orc grabbed at his neck, dropping his drink on the table and collapsing to the floor. The elf calmly grabbed ahold of the stein the orc had been drinking and began sipping out of it.

"I do thank you for the greeting and the drink, my friend," the elf stated to the orc dying on the floor. The rest of the tavern was silent, save for the feeble sounds of a few orcs still clinging to life. The elf gave one last glance to the orc as he added with a cruel smile. "Oh, and should you cross paths with a woman cloaked in white...please, give her my best."

CHAPTER 18

Last Light Before the Night

Hundreds of voices began to grow slowly, cutting through the quiet and the dark. Kye wasn't sure who the voices belonged to, but they seemed to all be talking at once. He instantly focused on two voices he recognized as Arden and Mireen's words cut through the noise.

"You think you can mend the wound?"

"I have stopped the bleeding, but for mending it completely, I am not sure. It is too soon to tell."

Kye opened his eyes, now staring up at the glass ceiling of the great hall. The sun had risen, and a cloudy sky rained soft snowflakes that hit the glass, coating it in a blanket of white. He became aware he was lying on a bedroll, with people and voices all around him. Turning, he saw that the great hall had been made into a makeshift infirmary, with hundreds of people tending to wounded lying on bedrolls spread throughout the room. Sick beds were laid out all over for the injured, with healers rushing from one to another.

Acolytes were tending to their masters and reinforcing defenses around the castle. Kye could hear crying and shouts of pain. He could smell blood and herbs in the air. He saw a goblin mage sitting directly across from him on the opposite wall, shaking, both his eyes gouged out. A healer was bandaging his head. Kye was in a daze, looking at the horrific scene around him. Arden's face faded into his view as he realized Kye was awake.

"Hey, kid," Arden said to him. Kye slowly began to lift himself up off the bedroll into a sitting position. He noticed the wound to his shoulder was fully healed but that his left leg was completely wrapped in bandages, and two strips of wood were secured on either side of it, bracing it.

"It's important not to move your leg as the blood flow returns," Mireen stated as Kye observed the injury. "It will take time and several more treatments to find out if the damage is permanent."

Permanent? The statement gnawed at Kye, as did the very real fear that he could lose his leg. Of course, considering how bad the wound had been, he guessed he really shouldn't be surprised.

No sooner had Mireen finished tending to Kye's injury, then another acolyte rushed over and whispered, "Lady Mireen, you are needed." Mireen nodded. She gave Kye a slight smile. "I will be back to check on you," she assured him before rushing off. Kye didn't get a chance to thank her for her help. Once Mireen was gone, Kye turned back to Arden.

"The stone?" Kye asked.

"Your cohorts were able to get it to me and told me how to get to you." Arden reached into his pocket and pulled out Saiyah's bracelet, handing it to Kye. He turned over the bracelet in his hands, inspecting the gems and the shard of the wayfinding stone. Such a gift had saved his life more than once. He owed Saiyah the world.

"The shades?" Kye asked.

"The maisters had the majority of them on the retreat

when I left," Arden replied. "It seemed they were meant to serve as nothing more than a distraction."

"Were there casualties?" Kye asked. Arden nodded quietly. Kye fell silent. All of this destruction, all this death, just to get to the stone. It didn't matter why he wanted it. If Orin was willing to go to such extremes to get it, they had to keep it from him at all costs.

"It can't be for nothing..." Kye muttered. "Orin can't get the stone. No matter what."

"He won't get the stone," Arden stated before looking Kye straight in the eye and adding, "WE will make sure of it."

Kye noted he was included. He nodded at his master in determination. Moments later, two more acolytes approached Arden, giving him a deep bow.

"Apologies, Lord Arden, but Lord Firen has chased several shades into a cave in the northwest province. He is asking for assistance in clearing them."

Arden paused for a moment in hesitation before turning to Kye.

Kye looked back and said, "Promise I won't go far." Arden grinned.

"You know, I somehow believe that this time," he said. He put a hand on Kye's shoulder and added, "Rest up. I'll be back in a bit."

Kye nodded as Arden rushed off with the acolytes. Kye let out a deep sigh and ran his hand over his face, thinking over the events of the night. He looked at his hands. Umbree's blood no longer stained his palms, but he felt as though there were still traces of it on his skin. Like a curse mark he couldn't get rid of. Kye shut his eyes tight and forced the thought from his mind. He felt numb and drained. He was about to lie back on his bedroll when a familiar voice caught his ears, causing him to immediately sit up.

"What? No, I'm not drinking that. It smells like shit. Ugh, gods, it tastes like shit too."

"It's not meant to be a cocktail, Riley."

Kye instantly began searching the crowd. There, on the north wall of the atrium, were Saiyah and Riley. Riley was seated on a bedroll, with bandages on his right side. Saiyah stood beside him as an acolyte attempted to hand him what Kye supposed was a healing potion. One which he seemed adamantly against taking. Kye smiled widely. He felt a rush of relief that they were both alright. As he was looking on at them fondly, Saiyah turned and caught sight of him across the great hall.

She froze in surprise as their eyes met. She silently mouthed his name. It happened in an instant. Saiyah bolted the distance of the great hall toward him and dropped to her knees on Kye's right side, wrapping her arms around his neck, pulling him to her. Kye's breath caught for a moment in surprise. Mainly because he honestly couldn't remember the last time someone had hugged him. It was a forgotten experience, but one he could get lost in. Kye returned the embrace, wrapping his arms around Saiyah's waist and pulling her close. Already, he could hear the whispers around the great hall, the scandal of a human hugging an elf. But Kye closed his eyes and tuned them out, taking a moment to revel in the warmth of lilac and lavender.

"You're alright," Saiyah whispered. Kye nodded as they slowly broke their contact. He felt the loss of her warmth instantly.

"I am, thanks to you," Kye replied. He reached in his pocket and pulled out Saiyah's charm bracelet. He wrapped the bracelet around her right wrist and secured the clasp, returning the precious heirloom back to its proper place. Saiyah looked down at the bracelet and back at Kye. Their eyes connected in silence for several moments as the great hall around them almost seemed to grow quiet. Kye and Saiyah's gaze were so focused on each other, they didn't notice Riley approach.

"Hey, look who's still in one piece...well, sort of," Riley remarked. He took a seat against the wall on Kye's left side. Their connection instantly broke as Kye turned his attention toward Riley, and Saiyah took a seat against the wall on Kye's right side.

"You're looking a little worse for wear yourself," Kye replied. Riley waved his hand nonchalantly.

"This? They're just scratches," Riley said. "Those shades definitely got the worst of it."

Riley looked down at Kye's leg before asking, "Umbree?"

Kye shook his head. "Dead," he stated plainly.

"Good," Riley growled. "Be sure to show me where he's buried so I can piss on the fucker's grave."

Kye fell silent. Wishing Umbree dead was one thing... being responsible for causing it was another. He had never killed anyone before, and honestly, he didn't know how to feel about it. Thankfully, Riley changed the topic. "So how's the leg?"

"Attached," Kye replied. "So that's an improvement."

Riley cringed a bit at Kye's injury. Saiyah cast a look of concern as well. The pair seemed uncertain what to say.

"You know...on the bright side, with shif kind, it's a sign of respect," Riley added after several minutes. Kye turned toward him.

"Really?" he inquired.

Riley nodded. "Oh yeah, it's the sign of a warrior," he continued. "In fact, in the shifter clan, the more injuries and scars you have, the greater your social standing."

"Huh," Kye replied slowly. "Then I would probably be nobility by this point."

Saiyah chuckled as Riley playfully nudged him in the side.

"Now you're getting it!" He grinned. "All hail Kye, king of the humans!"

Kye smiled back at his friends, appreciative of their attempts to cheer him up. He leaned back against the wall as Riley and Saiyah began to relay their epic fight with the shades. As he listened, Kye was hit with a realization that had taken him far too long to grasp. Arden, Saiyah, Riley, even Celeste and Mireen. He had friends, people who cared about him as much as he cared about them. In the cave with Umbree, he had been certain he was on his own as he had been for most of his life. But he now knew without a doubt…he wasn't alone anymore.

Amon approached the snow-covered orc tavern. His master had elected this meeting place specifically because it was out of the way and deep in the mountains of orc territory. For the most part, mages and other races tried their best not to mess with orcs, and for good reason. They were short-tempered, irrational, and prone to fits of anger. Not to mention, they were massive and difficult to kill. All in all, Amon considered them worse than animals, with no redeeming qualities. As he approached, Amon noticed the unnatural silence emanating from the building. Which was unusual, considering orcs were known for being boorish and loud. The reason for the lack of sound became apparent as Amon reached for the tavern door and was hit with the smell of death. He slowly opened the door to the gruesome scene before him. Twenty-five orcs lay dead, spread over various tables and on the floor. It had been a few days since they died, by the stench of decay that met Amon's nose. This was not fresh meat. Fluids had started to leak from the corpses out onto the tavern floor, adding offense to the aroma. Amongst the decay, Amon noticed only one living person. His master had stationed himself at a table in the back, calmly sipping beer from a stein and watching the snowfall outside. He was unbothered by the death and decay around him. Existing without remorse, only purpose. Amon had never known one of his shifter kind to exhibit even a fraction of such a killer instinct. A true hunter, worthy of respect. As Amon approached the table, Orin seemed to finally grant him his attention.

"Ah, Amon. Good to see you, my friend. Would you care for a drink?"

Amon raised an eyebrow, feeling there were probably better places to enjoy a drink.

"What the hell happened here?" Amon asked, to which Orin waved his hand dismissively.

"A minor skirmish."

"Minor?" Amon questioned. It was fairly clear to see whatever had happened had not been minor. Orin merely sighed.

"I know what you are thinking, Amon, but I am not the one who started this escapade. Merely the one to resolve it."

"You call this a resolution?" Amon asked, in which Orin nodded.

"Indeed, a swift one."

Now, it was Amon's turn to sigh. "Master, I am sure you had cause," Amon began. "But you were the one to stipulate we are not ready for a direct confrontation with the mages. We are supposed to be keeping a low profile."

Orin smiled and nodded. "I understand, and your concerns are quite valid. Do not worry, I intend to clean up after myself."

Orin gestured to the other seat at his table as Amon sat down.

"Now, tell me. Was Umbree's information about another creation stone correct?"

Amon reached into a pack attached to his back and pulled out an item wrapped in cloth.

"Turns out he was actually useful for something," Amon stated as he handed the cloth to his master. Orin's eyes were bright as he unwrapped it, producing a short, ostentatious scepter. It was glistening gold, jewels lining every inch of it. But Orin's focus was on the jewel at the top. A bright red ruby, about the size of a fist, glowing slightly.

"Oh yes," Orin grinned brightly. "His last act was bestowing on me such a wonderful gift."

Orin held the scepter up against the tavern wall. In a flash, a fire sparked along it. Moving like water, it coated the walls and the floor and ignited the corpses on the floor. The smell of burning meat and hair invaded the senses. It was mere moments before Orin and Amon were sitting in an inferno, unmoved and unafraid.

"After all," Orin stated, admiring the scepter in his hand, a cruel smile spreading on his face. "I've always LOVED to play with fire."

In the weeks that followed, spring had finally begun to melt the last of the winter snow surrounding the castle of Caelum Vallis. Kye sat out on the veranda in Arden's tower, reading a tome on the first warm day in a while. It was close to sunset, with the light slowly dimming on the horizon. The one thing he had learned about Isalia was that he better enjoy the warm weather when it came, for it was guaranteed it would not last for long. The trees had just started sprouting leaves, signaling the beginning of longer days. Kye found it hard to believe it was almost this time a year ago he became Arden's acolyte. From a slave on Helia to a mage of the High Council. He had never imagined his life would take such a turn. Kye shifted in his chair as an unexpected pain shot through his left leg. The warm weather seemed to help with his injury, but he knew this was something he would have to get used to. In the time that followed Umbree's attack, the serious wound to his leg had miraculously healed. It was all thanks to Mireen's skills—she had been able to save his leg. But the damage had been so extensive she had told Kye there were limits to her ability to mend it. He would probably walk with a limp for the rest of his days. Kye was simply grateful to be able to keep his leg, consequences be damned. Arden had been surprised about Kye's recovery as well. When he heard from Mireen that he would make close to a complete recovery, he told Kye he was, quote, "one lucky son of a bitch."

While he had been stuck in the infirmary, it wasn't just Arden who had checked in on him. Celeste would often appear with soups and desserts which she insisted would help with a speedy recuperation. Saiyah and Riley had come to visit every day, bringing him books and chatting with him. Kye was definitely appreciative of the company, especially as cabin fever began to set in close to the end of his several-week stay. Now that he was released, Kye immediately dove back into his studies. If his fight with Umbree had taught him anything, it was that he still had a long way to go as a mage. And now, with the injury to his leg, he felt as though he needed to compensate for his already lacking abilities.

"Here you are," Arden stated to Kye as he walked out onto the veranda. "I thought you might be in the library."

Kye turned toward him and shrugged. "Normally, I would be. But I figured I'd take advantage of the weather."

Arden nodded in agreement as he pulled up a chair. He had just returned from a High Council meeting to give an update on the creation stone. Since the attack, Arden had hidden the stone far outside the castle, where no one but him could find it. Kye wasn't even sure it was still in Isalia and didn't think it was safe for him to ask, either. Considering how close Umbree had come to getting the information, he felt his knowing the hiding place was more of a liability than a help. It was still unknown how Umbree had been able to sneak inside the castle when the maisters were gone, but both Arden and Kye suspected he had help from within the council itself. Which meant they had to be careful who they trusted.

"How was the council meeting?" Kye inquired.

Following Orin's attack, the council had been in disarray. Twenty-eight maisters had lost their lives to the shades Orin had unleashed upon Isalia. Not to mention several hundred citizens. It had shone a glaring light on the deficiencies of the High Council and their need to prepare for battle. Simply—gone were the days of galas. Now was a time of war.

"Well, you will be happy to know the council has OFFICIALLY cleared you of all suspicion in the events on Helia and of the charge of attacking Umbree," Arden replied.

"I feel so relieved," Kye answered, not even attempting to hide his sarcasm.

"Yeah, even Valor himself added that he may have been mistaken about Umbree."

Kye leaned forward in his chair. "MAY have been mistaken?" he cried incredulously.

"Make note of it, kid," Arden replied. "Cause it's the closest Valor will ever get to a fucking apology."

Kye shook his head in disbelief as Arden pulled out his pipe and lit the end.

"Honestly, I think the council is just relieved that Umbree is dead. A bit of an embarrassment for them to have a morally corrupt murderer as a former colleague."

Kye turned away and nodded. He had not really talked about Umbree since he died. Mainly because of how he felt about the fact he had been the one to kill him. Arden took note of Kye's sudden silence.

"You okay?" he asked.

"Yeah, I'm fine..." Kye replied, but Arden caught him under a focused gaze.

"But?" he prodded. Kye froze for a moment, running a hand through his hair and trying to think of how best to explain.

"I don't know...I just," Kye began. "Umbree was an evil, heartless bastard. He tried to kill you, he almost killed me, and who knows how many deaths he is responsible for. He DESERVED to die. But..."

"But you feel guilty about killing him?" Arden finished. Kye turned away in response. How pathetic was he?

To his complete and utter surprise though, Arden simply responded, "Good."

Kye stared back in confusion. "Good?"

"It's not supposed to be easy to kill, Kye," Arden replied. "The fact you feel guilty about it is just proof you have a conscience, and that's not something to be ashamed of."

Kye fell silent. Umbree had caused so much destruction, all out of his desperation to stay alive. And it was that desperation that had ended up being the death of him. Just for the hope of immortality.

"Is it possible to gain immortality through magic?" Kye suddenly asked.

Arden gave Kye a serious glare in response. "It's what Umbree said that Orin promised him," Kye clarified. "He said Orin was immortal, that he had lived far beyond the lifespan of a normal elf and that he could grant that immortality to him."

Arden shrugged. "Well, then it sounds like Orin is full of shit, but I guess that depends on your definition of immortal."

Kye turned to Arden, surprised. He had thought immortality in any form was impossible. Arden took a long pull from his pipe before he began. "A long time ago, there was a goblin mage named Fraylic who sought to live forever. After spending most of his life searching for a way, he finally found a solution. He crafted a golem in his image, was able to separate his soul from his living body and attached it to the stone golem. Well, it worked. His thoughts were still intact, and he was technically immortal. He lived for several centuries like that until one day, out of the blue, he just hurled himself into a volcano. He left behind a piece of paper with just a single sentence written on it: 'I now only wish it to end.' Cause you see, what he didn't realize is that while a stone statue doesn't get sick, or old, or injured…it also doesn't feel anything, doesn't need anything, doesn't want anything. An immortal life, trapped within an unfeeling shell."

Arden leaned back in his chair before looking back at Kye. "So technically, you could live forever using magic. But I tell you what. It's a living hell I wouldn't wish on my worst enemies."

Kye looked back out to the landscape as the sunset painted reds and gold on the horizon. Orin wasn't a soul attached to stone golem; he was flesh and blood. So why was it that Umbree thought he was immortal? It seemed to Kye that Orin was as capable of dying as any other elf. Even if he wasn't afraid of it. Suddenly, Orin's words from the temple popped into his head.

"Arden," Kye began, "who is Aine?"

Arden blew out a puff of smoke. "Aine?"

"In the temple, when Orin possessed Umbree, he called me the spawn of Aine."

"Ah," Arden replied. "He must have been talking about the old gods."

"Old gods?" Kye asked, to which Arden nodded as he took another pull from his pipe.

"Long ago, the realms worshiped gods," Arden stated. "Course, this was before mages started thinking we were ones.

The races even built temples in the gods' honor. If I remember correctly, Aine was the goddess of life and light. Story goes, she split her physical body into six pieces, which became the Six Realms of all life."

Kye had never heard any stories of gods or such beings. It would make sense that Arden knew of them, though, since the elves' history was much longer than that of any race. But something about Arden's story bothered him.

"But if Aine literally made the realms," Kye clarified, "then wouldn't that mean all life in the Six Realms are spawns of Aine?"

Arden nodded and shrugged. "If you believe in the mythos, that is."

Kye fell silent, looking out at the sinking sun. He watched the light flash its last gasp before disappearing fully behind the horizon. The darkness followed closely behind. The way that Orin had spoken gave Kye the distinct impression that he did not consider himself a spawn of Aine. But if that was the case, then he wouldn't have come from the Six Realms either. So the question that remained—just who or what was Orin? And where the hell did he come from?

*****Continued in Book 2, *Beyond the Cobbled Road: Darkness Falls*****

Thank you so much for reading! If you wish to support this work and the others in the series, please leave a review. I look forward to sharing book 2 with all of you, for updates feel free to check out www.beyondthecobbledroad.com. *Sulara anor.*

Acknowledgments

I want to take the time to thank the team of talented individuals who made this book possible.

Cover and illustrations: George Miroshnichenko

Descriptive editor: Margaret Diehl

Copy editors: Margaret Diehl and Allison Smith

Beta readers: Allison Smith, Dominic Crescente, and Alyssa Thomsen

Marketing advisor: Ben Galley

Website design: Darren Bowden

Audiobook narrator: Finian Schwarz

And of course, thank you so much to my readers.

Made in the USA
Coppell, TX
18 January 2026

69500303R00204